Encircling

BOOK ONE OF THE
ENCIRCLING TRILOGY

Sort Of
BOOKS

ENCIRCLING by CARL FRODE TILLER

This English translation first published in 2015 by

Sort Of Books
PO Box 18678, London NW3 2FL
www.sortof.co.uk

Distributed in all territories excluding the United States and Canada by

Profile Books
3 Holford Yard, Bevin Way
London WC1X 9HD

First published in Norway as *Innsirkling* (2007) by H. Aschehough & Co.
(W. Nyggaard), Oslo.

Translation © Barbara J. Haveland/Sort Of Books, 2015

Typeset in Trump Mediaeval and SansSemiLight to a design by Henry Iles.

Printed in Italy by Legoprint.

10 9 8 7 6 5 4 3 2

336pp

A catalogue record for this book is available from the British Library.

ISBN 978-1-908745-29-3

ASSISTANCE

This book has been selected to receive financial assistance from English PEN's
"PEN Translates!" programme, supported by Arts Council England. English
PEN exists to promote literature and our understanding of it, to uphold
writers' freedoms around the world, to campaign against the persecution and
imprisonment of writers for stating their views, and to promote the friendly
co- operation of writers and the free exchange of ideas. *www.englishpen.org*

Barbara J. Haveland's translation has been published with the financial
support of NORLA (Norwegian Literature Abroad).

THANKS

Carl Frode Tiller thanks Marita, Oline, Othilie and Cornelia.

Sort Of Books thanks Andrine Pollen of NORLA, Even Råkil,
Peter Dyer, Henry Iles and Nikky Twyman.

Encircling

Carl Frode Tiller

Translated from the Norwegian by
Barbara J. Haveland

Jon

Jon

We drive slowly into the town centre – if you can call it a centre, that is: a mini-roundabout and a scattering of houses. I lean forward in my seat, scanning the street, not a soul to be seen, the place is totally dead, deserted, scarcely a shop even, nothing but a closed café and a grocer's with darkened windows. We're playing here? Fuck's sake, doesn't look as if anybody even lives here, can't think who'd want to live here, who'd do that to themselves. I sit back in my seat, roll down the window, rest my elbow on the sill. A cool, fresh breeze wafts over my face, nice breeze. I lay my head back and shut my eyes, breathe in through my nose and sniff the air, so many scents after a shower of rain, that scent of damp earth, the scent of lilac. I open my eyes, lean forward again. Christ, the place is deserted, totally dead, not a bloody soul to be seen, and hardly a sound to be heard, nothing but the drone of our engine and the swish of wheels on rain-wet tarmac. Can't think who the hell would choose to live in a place like this.

"If there'd been time before the concert I'd have tried a spot of fishing," Anders says. "There's supposed to be a good salmon river here!"

I turn to him and grin. But he looks like he's serious, sits there in the back seat looking at me, nods off to the right. I put my head out to see what he's nodding at. There's a cardboard sign in a window on the other side of the street: "Fishing permits sold here" it says in black felt tip, the handwriting sloping down to the right. I turn to look through the windscreen again.

"Yep," I say. "Apart from inbreeding I don't suppose there's much else to do around here except hunting and fishing and stuff."

I look back at Anders, grin again. But he has turned to the side and I don't think he caught it. I face front again, stare through the windscreen.

"And sport, of course," I add. "Skiing and all that! No team sports, though," I say. "I doubt there are enough folk here to make up a team."

Brief pause.

Lars turns off to the right and we drive down a gentle slope leading to the harbour. I glimpse the glittering blue sea way down there, some gulls circling a green skip. But not a single person. Christ, the whole place is dead, it's the middle of the day, and yet it's utterly deserted. I lean forward slightly, glance from side to side, grin and shake my head.

"Fuck!" I say, wait a beat, shake my head again. "Looks like the Centre Party have got their work cut out for them if they're to reach their goal of a dynamic small-town Norway," I say. Another beat, then I turn to Lars, nod at him. "If you hear swift-licking banjo music, put your fucking foot down!" I say with a quick laugh. But he doesn't laugh back, he just sits there with both hands on the wheel, eyes fixed on the road ahead. I'm not sure if he's ever seen *Deliverance*: music is all that matters to Lars. He's not the slightest bit interested in films, or not that sort of film at any rate. I turn and stare out of the windscreen again.

"For fuck's sake," I mutter. "I'm glad I don't live here."

Brief pause.

"Here as well?" Lars asks, saying it under his breath and without looking at me.

"Well, there's not a fucking soul to be seen," I say.

"No," he says shortly.

I look at him again, don't say anything, wait a beat. What the hell's the matter with him? He sounds so serious. Looks serious, too. His face seems so tight, still. He stares straight ahead. I wait a second or two, never taking my eyes off him.

"What's up with you?" I ask. He doesn't answer, just sits there with his arms stiff and his hands locked on the wheel, staring straight ahead. There's total silence in the car; nobody says a word. What's going on? This isn't like Lars, he's almost always in a good mood, hardly ever anything but positive, optimistic.

"What's up with you?" I ask again.

"With me?" He raises his voice and juts his head forward a fraction as he says it.

Total silence.

I stare at him in amazement.

"I'm getting fucking fed up of you being so negative," he says.

"Negative?" I murmur.

"Yeah, negative," he says, keeping his eyes fixed front, then he pauses, swallows. "Doesn't matter where we go it's always a dump," he says. "The food's always crap, everybody we meet is a moron!"

I just sit here staring at him, speechless. What's he talking about? Me, negative? I wait a beat, face front for a moment, then turn to Lars again, don't know what to say, he's never said a word about this before, but now, sudddenly, I'm negative. Am I? Negative? Two beats, then I turn around. Look at Anders in the back. He's gazing out of the window, his brow pressed against the glass, pretending not to see me, acting as though he hasn't heard anything. I eye him for a second or two and suddenly I realize that they've talked about this before, that they've discussed this and they both think I'm negative. And now I feel my heart start to beat faster than normal, feel my pulse start to race. I stare at Anders and feel my jaw instinctively drop. Sit here open-mouthed, gawping. Then I shut my mouth, swallow once, then again. Turn back to face Lars, look at him.

"You're such a pain in the ass to be with," he says. "A real fucking pain in the ass! This whole fucking tour has been one big pain in the ass!"

He still doesn't look at me, just sits there staring rigidly through the windscreen, his face is tight and white and he swallows every now and again. I don't take my eyes off him. Don't say anything, don't know what to say. Because this is so sudden, I hadn't seen this coming, that they think I'm negative, no fun to be on the road with.

"It started off badly and it's just got worse and worse," Lars says. He clears his throat, still not looking at me. "I don't think you've any idea how much effort it takes just to keep you in a reasonably good mood," he says. "You go around bad-mouthing everything and everybody, you criticize everything under the sun. It makes you a real pain to be with, don't you see that?"

I hear what he's saying and I realize he's been rehearsing this, I can tell by the way he says it. I can tell that he genuinely means it, too. It feels as though it has come out of nowhere, but I can tell by his voice that he really means it. I stare at him. Wait a beat. Don't know what to say. But I can't just blurt out the first thing that comes into my head, I have to watch what I say. Because I have to be able to take this, have to be grown-up enough to take such criticism, I mustn't be unprofessional and just blow up in his face. But it's so sudden, I wasn't expecting it, I mean they've always laughed at me being such a pessimist, they've joked about my gloomy view of things and my wry comments. In fact I've often acted more gloomy and cynical than I actually was, been sour and sarcastic just to make them laugh. I always thought everything was fine, that they enjoyed my company as much as I enjoyed theirs, that they liked me as much as I liked them. Because I do, I like them a lot, don't think I've ever fitted so well into a band before, musically or personally. Even though I'm so much older than them I've felt this.

Brief pause. I turn my face slowly to the right, rest my head on my right hand and gaze out of the open window, raise my other hand and scratch my nose with my finger. And then all of a sudden I start to cry. It just comes, as if cracks have appeared in a dam inside me that I didn't know was there, my eyes crack and the tears start to fall, streaming cold down my cheeks. I turn my face a little further to the right. Wipe away the tears, swallow. But what the hell is all this, sitting here blubbing, what the hell's the matter with me, I haven't cried in I don't know how long and now here I am, blubbing, bursting into tears over a little thing like this, because they say I'm negative, what the fuck's the matter with me, it's so stupid it's laughable. Two beats, and then I burst out laughing, it just happens. I let out a hoot, a great roar of laughter. This is so ridiculous, such a silly little thing, and I try to somehow laugh off the tears, but it's no use. They just keep pouring down, and now I'm laughing and crying by turns, like a hysterical female, it sounds totally crazy, sounds as if I'm losing my mind, and the other two don't say a word, they're probably wondering what's got into me, because this isn't me, this couldn't be less like me. No, this won't do, I need to pull myself together. I draw a finger across my upper lip, sniff. Clench my teeth and stop laughing. Give a little cough, clear my throat. I'm no longer laughing, but I can't stop crying, cry softly, my lips are wet with tears and the salt tingles on my tongue.

Total silence.

Then: "So where's this arts centre?" Anders asks. "Wasn't it supposed to be outside the town centre?" he says. Trying to talk about something else, to act as if nothing's wrong, giving me the time and the chance to dry my eyes and pull myself together, to save me making a bigger fool of myself than I already have. "Well, I say town centre, but there's no way of telling where the centre is in this place." He's trying to side with me a little now, agreeing that this town is a dump, as if that will make things better.

Silence again.

I just sit here crying. And Anders and Lars say not a word, they probably understand as little of this as I do. Because this could not be less like me. I feel empty, feel flat, all the strength seems to have drained out of me. Just more and more of a pain in the ass to be with, Lars said, sour and negative. But why didn't they say something earlier? I mean, they've always joked about me being so pessimistic, they've always laughed at my sarcastic comments. How can I change my ways if they never say anything, if they simply go along with it? They might at least have given me the odd hint, I always assumed that they liked me as much as I liked them, and all the time they thought I was a pain in the ass to be with, negative. I turn my head another notch to the right, press my lips together and swallow.

"Stop the car!" The words burst out of me. I hear how angry I sound, angry and determined. I put my hand to the seat-belt clip, press the red plastic button and undo the belt, keeping my eyes front as I do it.

"Aw, Jon, come on," Lars pleads.

"Stop the car!" I say.

"Hey," Lars says.

I turn to him, stare at him.

"Stop the car, for Christ's sake!" I shout.

Total silence. A moment, then Lars puts on the brakes. Gently. Pulls into the kerb and stops.

"Jon, come on!" Anders says.

But I open the door, climb out.

"Hey!" Anders pleads.

"Jon!" Lars says.

But I slam the door and walk off, striding out, straight ahead, don't look back, don't know where I'm going, just have to get out of here, away.

Dear David,

I was on the bus, on the way to the cottage, when I read that you'd lost your memory, and once I'd got over the shock and began to wonder what I could do to help you, there was one memory that kept coming back, although I'd no idea why, so I've decided to start this letter with it. In my mind I saw the two of us on one of our countless long walks around Namsos town centre. I didn't even know I had it, this memory, until suddenly, sitting there on that bus, it came flooding back and I felt again what it was like to be seventeen and roaming the streets, just you and me, walking side by side, going nowhere in particular. I seem to remember we had some notion that we went on these walks because we were bored and had nothing else to do in the evening, but when I think back on the conversations we had, on how much we had to talk about, how caught up and how intense we could become and how quick we were to dodge down a side street if we spotted anybody we would have had to stop and speak to, I can only guess that we must have regarded those walks as being meaningful in themselves as well. Or, even if we didn't think of them as meaningful, we must still have sensed that they were.

And maybe it was thanks to this unconscious sense of meaning that the first and brightest memory to pop up when I saw your ad was such an undramatic, everyday one. I don't know, but an awful lot of the things I mention in this letter – opinions you held, for example, or descriptions of things that happened when I wasn't there or of people you knew but that I never met – is drawn from these conversations.

In our earlier years at school I didn't know much about you except that you had a stepfather who was a vicar, that you played football, and that you could throw the rounders ball further than anybody else at the school sports day. I don't quite know why these last two stuck in my mind, maybe because I was hopeless both at throwing the rounders ball and at football. When it was my turn to throw the ball I threw it girl-fashion, underarm, and I was known for being the first and, so far, the only kid at Namsos Lower Secondary to make such a mess of a penalty kick that it ended up as a throw-in for the other side, something I actually claimed to be proud of once I got to know you.

We became friends in our first year at senior secondary. An anti-drug rally was being held in the gym, and I remember that I'd decided to skip it. I was cultivating a punky, anarchist image at that time and doing my best to hide my teenage insecurity behind a mask of apathy and bravado. So I slung my rucksack over my shoulders and sauntered as nonchalantly as I could towards the door, trying to convince everyone – including myself – that this was me striking a blow for what the alternative press called "consciousness-expanding substances". That wasn't it at all, though. My dad was in prison on a drugs charge and it was out of misplaced loyalty to him that I meant to boycott this rally, so when the headmaster called out my name and told me to come back and sit down at once, and when everybody turned and stared at me, I was suddenly overcome by all the emotions that I'd managed to keep more or less in check up to that point and I dissolved into tears in front of the whole school. Most of the other kids probably knew that my dad was inside and what he'd done, but at that moment you were the only one to grasp the connection between that and this totally unexpected breakdown. After a few seconds of utter silence, during which the teachers and what must have been over three hundred pupils stared at me in amazement, I heard you ask the headmaster in a loud, clear voice: "How would you like to take part in a demonstration against your own father?"

Later, after I'd fallen in love with you and my love had refined my memory, I pictured you as a kind of James Dean figure when you said this. The way I remember it, you were sitting on one of the benches, leaning back against the wall bars with your elbows stuck through them, and you smiled as you looked straight at the headmaster with sure, steady eyes. That image has faded now, of course. All I know for sure is that you were wearing a white T-shirt and that you said what you said.

At first I felt that you had somehow shown me up, and I was furious with you for that, but the more distance I was able to put between myself and this incident, the more grateful I felt and it wasn't long before I began to feel quite touched that you had defended me the way you did. I admired you for the courage and sense of fair play you'd shown and from then on until we became friends and started hanging out together all the time, I would go out of my way to turn up, accidentally on purpose, in places where I knew you'd be. If I heard that you were going to some party I'd do everything I could to get an invitation to that same party; if I heard that you were going to the cinema I'd drop whatever I was doing and head for the cinema too, and on my way to school or down to the town centre I almost always took the route that led past the house where you lived with Arvid and Berit, just in case I might bump into you or simply see you. That this took a few minutes longer didn't matter.

I did also try, though, to maintain a certain dignity. I kept my distance and never intruded. I would smile and say "Hi" when we met, but I never dared to strike up a conversation, and since you were the sort of strong, silent type who rarely said more than was absolutely necessary it's a wonder to me that we ever got round to speaking to one another at all. But we must have done so, because by the end of the year we were inseparable.

I don't have an internet connection at the cottage, so to send a mail to your psychologist, to ask how to go about helping you, I had to pop over to one of my neighbours. He let me in and allowed me to use his computer, but he was gruff and unfriendly and he clearly couldn't wait to get rid of me again, so unfortunately I didn't have time to ask all the questions I would have liked to ask. But as far as I could tell from the only email your psychologist got round to sending me, you were being kept in isolation, so I couldn't visit you, as I really wanted to do. Any contact, I was told, would have to be by letter. And when I wrote these letters I wasn't merely to try to revive your memory, I gathered. Even if nobody who wrote to you managed to bring back your memory, it was vital for you to learn as much as possible about the person you used to be, what sort of life you'd led, who your friends were, who your family were, where you came from and so on, so your psychologist urged me to include absolutely everything I knew about you, not just the things we had seen and done together. So before I go on to tell you about us, you and me, I'll try to write down the little I know and remember of your background and of the life you led before we met.

In the hall in your house hung an aerial photograph of a white wooden house sitting right down on the shingle on the island of Otterøya. Before Berit married Arvid and moved into his home in Namsos, you had lived in this house along with her and her father, your grandfather, Erik – a man I know of only from an old black-and-white photo of him when he was young: a big, burly road-worker with a shock of thick hair, a broad, hunched back and a bushy black moustache that stuck out like pigtails on either side of his face.

Berit had kept house for your grandfather ever since the death of your grandmother in the early Sixties. When she was about seventeen or eighteen she left home and moved into a bedsit in Namsos, where she started her training as an auxiliary nurse at the same time as my own mum. But within the year she was pregnant with you and had to move back to Otterøya. No one was ever told who your father was: for some reason Berit refused to say and she kept it a secret as long as she lived, even from you.

Mum used to tell me stories about your mother and what she was like back then: such a pale slip of a thing, she said, with red hair, freckles and a little turned-up nose. To begin with Berit had seemed shy and a little unsure of herself, but she had turned out to be anything but. Like lots of people who've had a tough upbringing and survived, she'd been hardened and according to Mum she seemed not the slightest bit shy or afraid, as folk from small towns often were when they came to the city to study. She had a sharp tongue, talked nineteen to the dozen and always said exactly what she thought, no matter who she was talking to. She could be ruthlessly spiteful to anyone who crossed her and would go to almost any lengths to hurt and humiliate them. Physical defects, speech impediments, a dodgy past, it was all fair game to her and her jibes were so spot-on and so witty that no one listening could help but laugh, no matter how hard they tried. And if her victim gave as good as they got and commented, for instance, on her bad front teeth, she would just grin, baring those same teeth. Self-pity and sentimentality were luxuries she'd never been able to afford and she never let anything get to her. "If anyone had told me back then that one day she'd nab herself a vicar, I'd have died laughing!" Mum used to say.

Your grandfather found it hard to get used to the idea of his daughter marrying a vicar. According to you he was an atheist and a communist, red as they come, till the day he died. He shook his head and scoffed at a lot of what Arvid believed in and stood for and he never seemed to tire of asking for concrete descriptions of, or rational explanations for, various miracles and wonders mentioned in the Bible. "Could you not explain that business of the virgin birth in a way that a simple man from Otterøya can understand it?" he would say, and if Arvid chose to ignore the ironic undertone he detected in Erik's voice and gave him a serious answer, your grandfather would listen with a gleeful look on his face, and when Arvid was finished he would chortle and shake his head indulgently. "Aye, those were the days!" he'd say. "You'd never see that happening now, that's for sure!"

He thought these conversations were great fun, you told me, and the same went for teasing Berit by reminding her of the sort of family and the sort of background she came from. His talk was broader and coarser than usual when he was with her and it was like he just always happened to remember the juiciest incidents from the old days, the one thing common to all these stories being that they didn't go down at all well in the Christian circles which Berit was trying so hard to fit into and become part of. "Then there was that New Year's Eve when you drank all the menfolk under the table," he would say, roaring with laughter. And if your mother didn't laugh along with him he would act surprised and puzzled. "Oh, don't tell me you don't remember that?" he'd say, then sit back, gloating, and wait for an answer while Berit turned white with rage.

You used to laugh when you told me all this, but at the time it had left you feeling uncomfortable and insecure. Arvid, on the other hand, did his best to pretend that it didn't bother him. According to you, he might have been annoyed, angry even, but he wanted to convince you and your mother that it was beneath his dignity to be shocked by that sort of thing, so he would merely sit there smiling and showing endless patience and tolerance. This fits, as it happens, with my own impression of him as a person after we got to know one another and I began to spend a lot of time at your house. My memories of those days may be coloured by my hearing later that Arvid had had a mental breakdown after your mother died; still, though, I seem to remember thinking that he was the sort of man who hides inner turmoil behind a calm, solid exterior and who, without knowing it himself, overcompensates and ends up seeming intimidating. He had a smile so warm and gentle that it was hard to credit the love it was supposed to reflect, and he spoke so slowly and softly and with such sincerity that I for one felt uneasy in his company and not calm and relaxed as I was probably meant to feel.

A lot of people misinterpreted his manner and took it as proof that the stereotype of the rather smug, pompous man of the cloth was actually true. As my mum said, "It's easy to be gentle and kind and tolerant of people when you're sure that you're going to heaven and everyone else is going to hell!" But none of us who knew Arvid saw him as smug or pompous. Quite the opposite. He honestly seemed to see himself as a perfectly ordinary man who just happened to be a vicar, and wanted to be seen that way, as a man of the people. He couldn't quite pull it off, though. When this rather straitlaced man wrapped his blue-and-white Namsos FC scarf round his neck and took his place on the terraces to cheer on the home team a lot of people laughed and eyed him with the contempt normally reserved for politicians indulging in the same sort of antics. To them this was all an act, an attempt to woo the man in the street. Not only that, but Arvid, like so many other clergymen, had an irritating habit of eventually bringing every conversation round to the subject of Christianity, something that tended to alienate people and make them feel uncomfortable. If, for example, we were sitting out on the steps at your place on a winter's night, gazing up at the stars, I knew that at some point he'd be bound to mention the Star of Bethlehem – just by the bye, as it were – and if there was a natural history programme on TV that showed how well some species of animal was adapted to its surroundings, I'd be sitting there just waiting for him to express his amazement that there could actually be people who seriously believed something so wonderful could have come about purely by accident.

You said yourself that you hated this side of him. When you were younger you had often noticed how the atmosphere changed when he walked into a room. A loud, lively conversation could fizzle out completely the minute he appeared and and the mood in the room became unsettled and edgy. There were always one or two people who made a show of talking and acting quite normally, but they were very much on their own and stood out so much from the rest that their efforts always seemed more strained and awkward than heroic, and in the end they either gave up and shut up or they did the same as everyone else and switched, instead, to talking about things they felt it was safe to talk about when the vicar was there. They gabbled on about nothing in particular, voiced opinions that no one in their right mind would disagree with. And while you burned with embarrassment, Arvid seemed quite oblivious to what was going on, or so you said. Thinking about it now, though, I'm not sure you were right about this. I remember Arvid as being both intelligent and observant, and I can imagine that such situations must have been every bit as painful and embarrassing for him as they were for you.

The unsettled, faintly edgy mood that was generated when Arvid walked into a room was something I actually sensed in your home, too. There was a slight stiffness and artificiality about the way he spoke and behaved. It was as if the apparent air of calm that Arvid radiated represented a standard of behaviour and an ideal that all the family should aim to achieve, and not only the family, but friends of the family too. Most of the members of the Christian community seemed to do their utmost to appear as gentle and kind and full of brotherly love as possible, as if dead set on reminding themselves of how much they cared about one another. At your house I had the feeling that while it was all right to disagree with something, you should never argue; it was even all right to get annoyed or angry, but it really wasn't done to raise your voice. All fluctuations in mood and tone had somehow to be played down and smoothed out, not only the troughs, but the crests as well. It was great to be happy, but you didn't need to make a song and dance about it, so to speak, a smile was sufficient. And if, even so, someone did get carried away, the others would fall ostentatiously quiet for a few seconds, or they would smile pleasantly, then change the subject completely.

But despite, or maybe because of, this unspoken insistence on constant self-control, violent emotional outbursts did occasionally occur and once, when I was at your house, I witnessed one such outburst. Your mother had just finished washing the floor when Arvid came in and walked right across it in boots caked with clay. Then I caught a glimpse of the Berit that Mum had told me about. Mind you, it was no small thing for her to have somebody walk into the house in mucky boots right after she'd finished cleaning it. For housewives like your mother and mine it was a point of honour to keep an immaculate house, and they expected their husbands, neighbours and anyone else to appreciate all their hard work. My own mum even went so far as to leave the mop and bucket standing in the hall for a whole day after she'd done the cleaning, so that everybody who came in would be sure to see them and comment on how fresh and spotless she kept the place. Seen in that light, to go tramping across Berit's newly washed floor in muddy boots was to treat her like dirt.

All the same, the fury that Berit unleashed on Arvid when he walked in wearing mucky boots was completely out of proportion to the crime he'd committed. "You dirty fucking pig!" she screamed at him, and just hearing someone use that voice and those words in your home made me jump and then sit there open-mouthed. I was even more astonished when she swept everything off the kitchen counter. Her forearm swished like a scythe across the worktop; cups, bowls, glasses and cutlery fell to the floor with a deafening crash and when a terrified Arvid gathered his wits enough to ask what on earth had got into her, she flung out her arms, grinned manically and, said: "I'm only doing the same as you, making sure I've plenty to do this evening." Then she burst into tears.

I never heard of you giving way to similar outbursts and I can't imagine you doing so. Like I say, at school or when you were with friends you were more the strong, silent type, and you had taken this even further at home, adopting a cold, almost stony manner, particularly towards Arvid. It wasn't that you were directly hostile, more as if you'd taken the insistence on self-control to the extreme, as if you'd decided not to show any emotion at all, and your manner was often formal, bordering on mechanical. If, for example, Arvid asked you to do him a favour, you would do as he asked without a murmur, you didn't answer him, didn't even look at him, you simply got up and did as he asked, then went back to what you'd been doing. You behaved as if he was your boss and not your stepfather. And when he spoke to you and tried to start a conversation, you would often reply in words of one syllable and in a flat, indifferent voice. "Fine," you would say, if he asked how one of our trips to the cottage had gone. "No!" you would answer if he asked if we'd caught any fish.

In such situations I often felt sorry for him. He would smile and act as if it didn't bother him, but I saw how it hurt him, you being so offhand with him. When I confronted you with this on one of our walks, you got surprisingly het up about it, I remember. You couldn't stand it, you said, his friendliness towards you, his endless patience. You didn't believe in the love that all of this was supposed to be proof of and you didn't know how to defend yourself against it. You could also feel sorry for him, you could be overwhelmed with guilt when he showered you with kindness. You said you often felt pressured into being nice in return, but you didn't want to – not because you were still jealous of him for marrying your mother, but because being pleasant to him made you feel as though you were losing sight of yourself and becoming the person he wanted you to be. He had always tried to mould you, to form your character, you said. His methods were just a bit more subtle now. When you were younger he had read and told you stories from the Bible, he had subscribed to *The Blue Anemone*, a Christian children's magazine, for you, took you to church and Sunday school and scared the wits out of you with tales of the Devil and eternal damnation when you said your prayers together in the evening. He had done all he could to lead you onto what he believed was the right path, but none of it had done any good, so now, instead, he was deliberately using the power of example and trying to ingratiate himself with you. He was kind and affectionate because he saw this as the only way to win you over, you said, and it wasn't just him: the whole of the Christian community to which your family belonged was involved in this conversion project, they prayed for you, they tried to talk Berit into making a bigger effort to get you to join the church youth groups (especially the choir, since you weren't a bad singer) and were nigh on shameless in their idealization of the Christian way of life.

Although I thought you were being unfair to Arvid by cold-shouldering him the way you did, I was impressed by the strength of your resistance to him and the rest of the

Christian community. Your mother they had managed to "tame", as my mum put it. She was a secret smoker, though (I remember the half-disintegrated butts floating in the toilet and the smoker's breath she tried to camouflage with the aid of chewing gum, usually Orbit, but sometimes Trident), and you suspected that she let her old self off the leash a bit on those rare occasions when she visited her old girlfriends on Otterøya, but that she had changed her ways and truly accepted Jesus, of that everyone was certain. For a while she had even attended meetings at the home of one of Arvid's aunts, but that had proved too much of a good thing. She couldn't bear to sit for hours, embroidering some prize for the raffle at the next church bazaar, while drinking coffee, eating waffles with brown goat's cheese and listening to women twenty and thirty years older than herself who laughed themselves silly and thought they were being really naughty if they dared to say the word "fart", as she put it.

But no matter how hard Arvid and the others tried, they couldn't "tame" you. Quite the reverse, in fact: the harder they tried, the farther they drove you away from them and when they were at their most zealous you used to refer to Arvid and his cronies in almost hateful terms. You tried to assume a wry and slightly indifferent tone, but behind the grin and the laughter lay rage, frustration and sadness and you spent many a long evening at our house, delaying going home until you were sure that Arvid would be in bed. Neither of us ever mentioned that this was why it could be eleven, twelve or half-past twelve before you started yawning and saying that, well, it was a school day tomorrow, but I knew this was the reason and you knew that I knew, and I could tell just by looking at you that you appreciated that I was there for you and never asked questions. As far as I was concerned that went without saying, and I knew you would do exactly the same for me if the day ever came when I needed someone to be there for me.

Namsos, July 5th 2006. Home to Mum

I place my hand on the doorhandle and press it down, try to pull the door to me, but nothing happens. It's locked, but she never used to lock the door, so this is something new she's started doing. So many darkies, she says, roaming the streets since those asylum flats were built, she doesn't dare not lock the door. I put a finger to the doorbell and press it, once, then again. Stick my hands in my trouser pockets and try to look casual. Take them out again, place them on the banister, ease myself up onto it and sit there, gaze at the yellow frosted glass in the front door, wait a moment, but she doesn't open up, so I hop down again. I'll have to fetch the key and let myself in, the spare key will be hanging where it's always hung, I suppose. I walk round to the shed, flip up the latch and open the door, which emits a long, plaintive creak. Sounds like I'll have to oil the hinges while I'm here.

"Well, hello," I suddenly hear Mum say. "It's you, is it?"

I turn and look at her. She's standing in the doorway, looking a little tired. Strange how old she's got lately. She stands there smiling faintly at me.

"So you are home" I say.

"Of course I'm home."

"You took so long to come to the door, I thought you must be out gallivanting," I say, closing the shed door behind me.

And she laughs that mournful laugh of hers.

"Oh, and where would I go?" she says, smiling sadly at me, as if to let me know how seldom she gets out of the house now, let me know how lonely she is. I've only just got here and she's started already.

"Ah, now how would I know that? You could be having a high old time of it for all I know," I say, trying to make a joke of it.

"Oh, you think so, do you?" she asks, laughing her mournful laugh again. "No, I think my gallivanting days are pretty much over."

I look at her, say nothing. She always has to start with this, I've only been here half a minute and here she goes, it's so bloody tiring, but I keep smiling, walk up to her with a smile on my face, I'll just have to ignore her moaning, there's no point in saying anything. I lay a hand on her shoulder, give her a hug. Tobacco fumes waft across my face and I feel her hard cheekbone bump lightly against mine. She places a hand lightly on my upper arm, barely touching me, then takes it away again almost immediately, positions herself by the door and gives a flourish of her hand, as if ushering me in.

"Do please come in!" she says.

"Thank you," I say, stepping into the sweltering hall. A fly buzzes on the windowsill, butting gently against the glass of the little hall window every now and again.

"Well, this is a pleasant surprise, I must say."

"Yes, isn't it?" I say, looking at her and smiling, then I bend down and take off my shoes.

"I've got coffee out on the veranda," she says, pointing to the veranda with one hand and closing the hall door with the other. "Go on out and have a seat, I'll fetch you a cup!"

"Oh, that sounds good, I'm dying for a coffee," I say, trying to sound cheery, upbeat, trying somehow to lift her spirits.

I wander into the living room, casually, with my hands in my pockets. Sunlight slants through the window and a grey, shimmering veil of tobacco smoke ripples over the coffee table. I stroll out onto the veranda, sit down on one of the patio chairs and run an eye over the garden. The flowerbed is a little overgrown and the grass is long. I might cut the grass later, give her a bit of a hand. Then Mum comes out onto the veranda, a floorboard creaking under her foot as she steps on it.

"Ah, well," she says, in a voice that's self-consciously bright, the sort of voice designed to gloss over something, then she glances anxiously at me and gives a quick smile. "At least you gave it a go, eh!" she says, setting a coffee cup in front of me.

I look at her, not immediately sure what she's getting at.

"And we all have to make some mistakes in life!" she says in that false, supposedly cheery voice. And then I see what she's getting at, she's acting as if she thinks I've given up on my music and that's why I'm here and not on tour, she's trying to give me the idea that she thinks I've thrown in the towel, and she's pretending to be relieved, pretending to be pleased, so that I'll feel guilty when I tell her I haven't given up after all. I'm no longer in the band with Lars and Anders, that's true, but she doesn't know anything about that, it's all an act on her side, all this, and anyway, I haven't given up, I'm going to go on trying.

"That's that, then," she says.

"Mum!" I say, trying to smile, to humour her.

She acts as if she hasn't heard me.

"Ah, well, that's how it goes, eh!" is all she says, avoiding my eye, smiling faintly.

"Mum!" I say again, a little louder. "A couple of gigs were cancelled and we had a few days off, so I thought I'd come and see you," I say, and leave it at that, can't bring myself to tell her that I've left the band. That would only make her even more convinced that it was a mistake to give it a try.

One beat.

"You'd better help yourself!" she says, just ignoring me, not even looking at me, she simply bends down, picks up the coffee-pot and places it on the table in front of me, gives the glimmer of a smile. "I'm liable to spill it," she says with an attempt at a little laugh. "I've changed my medicine and these new pills make my hands awfully shaky."

I lower my eyes, stifle a little sigh, glance up, am about to tell her again that I haven't stopped playing, but I stop myself, there's no point. I brace myself and look up at her.

"Have you told the doctor?" I ask, pick up the coffee-pot and pour for both of us: strong, black boiled coffee. I look up at her, see that mournful face with the affectedly plucky smile, feel annoyance growing inside me.

"Nah!" she says, and now she sounds almost indignant, curling her lip slightly and waggling her head, so that she looks indignant, too.

"Well, you should!" I say.

"Nah! Why would I do that? There's always some side effect, no matter what pills I take," she says.

There's silence for a moment. And then she seems to realize that she's gone too far, takes a deep breath as she leans across the table.

"No, you're right," she says hastily, anxiously, as though trying to retrieve the situation, trying to smile. "I suppose I should talk to the doctor."

"Of course you should, you can't go on like this." I swallow my irritation and meet her halfway, try to give her a little of the sympathy she's angling for, cheer her up by playing along with her a bit, discussing her illness with her.

"Yes, well, we'll see," she says, looking down at the table.

"Surely you've got enough problems already without having to cope with this as well," I say, knowing this is the sort of thing she likes to hear. I look at her, see how her face lights up a little, she waggles her head, smiles her plucky smile again.

"Well, I'm still here," she says.

"Yep – fortunately," I say and give a little laugh.

She looks at me and smiles quickly, a little more sincerely this time; she liked hearing me say that. So now I just have to carry on in the same vein, have to say something I know she likes to hear, doesn't matter what, just say something to cheer her up, I won't let her drag me down into the dumps, I can't, not right now at any rate. I am just about to ask her if she's been in a lot of pain lately when the phone rings. She looks at me and smiles, places her hands on the arms of the chair and gets slowly to her feet. A little wince passes across her face when she is half out of the chair and her hand flies to her back, she stands with her eyes shut for a second, then she starts to walk, stiffly and slowly to begin with, then more easily, more loosely, you might say. I watch her go, regard the narrow shoulders and the twisted, slightly stooped back. I feel the guilt welling up: here she is, living all alone in this big house, racked with pain, day in, day out, no wonder she feels the need to moan a little, no wonder she feels the need to unburden herself when somebody finally shows up, I can live with that, surely. She's sacrificed more for me over the years than anyone could ask for, the least I can do is to lend an ear to a little self-pity without getting fed up or annoyed. I pick up my coffee cup, take a little sip, put it down again. Look out at the garden, it's totally overgrown, must be ages since the flowerbed was weeded and the hedge is running rampant, it's huge and straggly, it's even made inroads into the lawn, nasty little shoots sticking up here and there. After a few minutes Mum comes back, with her tobacco pouch in one hand and her lighter in the other, she looks at me and smiles. And I smile back.

"That was Eskil," she says, sitting down. "He's coming over!"

I don't say anything for a moment. She sticks her hand into the tobacco pouch, takes out a pinch of tobacco and spreads it along the cigarette paper.

"Okay," I say, picking up my coffee cup and lifting it to my lips. I've no wish to see Eskil, but I try not to let on, sip some coffee, clear my throat. "When?" I ask, trying to smile.

"He's on his way, but he has a few errands to run first, so he'll be here sometime in the afternoon, I suppose," Mum says, smiling as she licks the paper, seals her cigarette and pops it in her mouth.

I look at her and nod, feel my heart sink.

"Just Eskil?" I ask.

"Hmm?"

"Is he coming on his own or is Hilde coming with him?"

Mum looks at me in surprise.

"I don't know," she says, crossing one leg over the other as she lights her cigarette and draws on it. "I didn't ask, but ... oh, if she comes she comes." she says, pauses, then looks at me and grins. "Well, she's so busy, you see. I don't how long it's been since I saw her, but it's a good while, anyway."

"And how long's it been since you last saw Eskil?" I ask, knowing full well I shouldn't. It's a sore point with her that Eskil hardly ever comes to see her, but I can't help it. She looks straight at me, just for a fraction of a second, then gives me a quick, wan smile.

"I know, I know," she says. "But Eskil has his political commitments, as well as his job. And that does make a difference."

"Yeah, but you didn't see that much more of him before he was elected to the district council, did you?" I say. I can't help it, it just comes out.

Mum keeps that faint smile on her face, takes another drag on her cigarette.

"Well, well, let's not say any more about it." She blows smoke through her nose and I hear the faint hiss as she does so.

"No, let's not," I say with the ghost of a grin. All the good humour has drained out of me and suddenly I feel pissed off.

We both pick up our coffee cups at the same time, each take a sip and set them down again with a little chink and then there's silence.

"Oh, by the way," Mum says, "I ran into Wenche the other day."

I look at her, don't say anything for a moment. Christ, now she's going to start harping on about Wenche again, will she never quit? I'm so sick of this.

"Oh yes?" is all I say, can't be bothered asking how she was and all that, can't be bothered discussing Wenche with her, so all I say is, "Oh yes?"

Brief pause.

"She was in great form," she says, puffs on her cigarette.

"Oh," I say with a little intake of breath.

Pause.

"I think we must have stood there chatting for a good half-hour at least!" Mum goes on, glancing up at me and flashing me a quick smile. "It was so nice," she says, pauses, then: "Oh, and she was asking for you?"

I look up at her, feel annoyance growing inside me. I open my mouth, all set to snap at her, but I think better of it, look at the table, give it a moment. Look up at her again.

"You can go on all you want, Mum," I say, trying to speak as calmly as I can, forcing a smile of sorts. "But Wenche and I are never going to get back together."

"Oh, but ... I've never said so much as a word about that, Jon," she says in a surprised and rather hurt voice, playing the innocent now. I know she's trying to make me feel guilty because I left Wenche, gave up my job and staked everything on the band, but she's all innocence, gazing at me all sad-eyed.

"All right," I snap. "Fine."

She lowers her eyes, sighs and gives a faint shake of her head, sits there with one leg over the other and the smoking roll-up in one hand, looking sad.

"No matter what I say it's always the wrong thing," she says. "No matter what I do!"

Silence. I look at her, know she's only saying this so I'll say it's not true, but I say nothing.

"I just wanted ..." she says, then stops, sighs and looks at the table, shaking her head slightly. "I don't know, I really don't," she mutters, taking another drag on her cigarette.

Silence.

I look at her, the narrow shoulders, the gnarled, skinny body pulled out of shape by years of hard work and illness. She's not that old, but she looks old, worn out. Two beats, then I feel the guilt welling up again, don't want to feel guilty, but here it comes nonetheless. I glance to the side. Take a breath and let it out again, silently, sigh inaudibly, then I turn to face Mum again. Have to try to rise above her self-pity now, swallow my irritation and give her the comfort she's asking for, have to be big enough to do that. One beat. I open my mouth, am all set to apologize, but I don't, can't bring myself to do it, can't allow her to carry on like this much longer. It's not fucking right, I've told myself so many times and now I have to get a fucking grip and not give in.

Silence.

"I thought I might mow the lawn for you." It just slips out.

She doesn't say anything, merely nods, looking like a wounded animal.

"Do you have any petrol for the lawnmower?" I ask.

"The can's in the shed," she says, not even looking at me.

I look at her, feel the guilt growing. I'm filled with annoyance and guilt, don't know what to say.

Silence.

"Right, then," I say, planting my hands on the arms of the chair. "Might as well get on with it, I suppose," I say, "get it out of the way."

"Yes," she says, stubbing out her cigarette in the ashtray.

My back's running with sweat after mowing the lawn. It itches, so I wriggle around a bit, rubbing it against the blanket, then shut my eyes and lie perfectly still, feel the sun blazing down on me, smell the sweet scent of new-mown grass. One beat, then I hear the sound of car wheels crunching over the gravel. I sit up, stay perfectly still, listening. It's Eskil, he wasn't due to get here till later in the afternoon, but it's him, I can tell by the rumble of the engine, it's that big four-wheel drive of his. One beat, then a wave of resentment washes over me again. I'm overcome by a kind of panic and I get to my feet, bend down and pick up the blanket, do this quite automatically, there's something inside me that can't cope with seeing Eskil, so I walk over to the soft fruit bushes, quickly, before he rounds the corner and sees me. I spread the blanket out on the patch of grass behind the biggest blackcurrant bush and then I lie down behind the bushes, it's so stupid really, lying here hiding, it's bordering on crazy, but there's no help for it, I just can't take him, want to put off seeing him for as long as I can. After a moment or two I hear the little creaks and clunks made by an engine that's just been turned off, hear the sound of a car door opening, that little click. Then the sound of another car door. "Well, at least Hilde's with him," I mutter to myself, "that's always something, he tends to tone it down a bit when she's there."

Silence.

"Yes, well we're here now!" I suddenly hear Eskil say in a brusque, but low voice.

No reply.

"Okay?" he says.

Still no reply.

"Christ al-fucking-mighty!" he says.

I lie very still, hear shoes crunching over the gravel. And then a car door is slammed shut.

"Get a grip on yourself!" Eskil growls softly.

I feel my lips curling in a little grin, can't help gloating a tiny bit that everything's not as rosy and idyllic as Eskil likes to make out. I feel a ripple of malicious glee run through me. Roll carefully onto my side, reach out a hand and make a little parting in the blackcurrant bush, peer through it. They come walking round the corner of the garage, Eskil in front, Hilde right behind him, both of them tight-faced. Then Eskil whirls round and wags his finger at her. He says something to her, but I don't catch it, hear only that he's angry, speaking in that low growl, and Hilde simply stands there, looking him straight in the eye, saying nothing, but she looks angry, too, definitely.

Then the front door opens and Mum comes out onto the front step.

"Well, well, look who's here," she says, wiping her hands on her blue-and-white checked apron, then holding them out and walking down the steps, up to Eskil. And Eskil takes off his sunglasses, holds out his hands, too, stands there smiling with his hands outstretched. They put their arms around each other, sway from side to side, stay locked like this for ages. Christ, it looks so sick, anybody would think they hadn't seen one another for a whole year, I know Eskil doesn't come to see her very often, but there are limits, it's fucking ridiculous. Then Mum places her hands on his arms, pushes him away from her slightly and sort of stands there, eyeing him up and down.

"Have you lost weight?" she asks, sounding anxious, though she's obviously pleased.

"Oh, Mum," Eskil says and laughs.

"No, but you have, you have lost weight," Mum says.

"Not at all," Eskil laughs.

"You are taking the time to eat properly, aren't you?"

"Oh, Mum!" Eskil laughs again.

"But you are, aren't you?" Mum says.

"Yes, of course!" Eskil laughs.

I peer at them from my hiding place, try to smile at this, but can't quite manage it, it comes out as a strained and rather bitter grin. I glance at Hilde, she's standing back, trying to smile and look unfazed, but I can tell by her face that she thinks they're behaving ridiculously, that she finds their little show embarrassing. After a moment or two Mum goes over to Hilde, lays a hand on her arm and gives her a hug.

"How lovely that you could come too!" she says.

"I know," says Hilde, forcing a smile.

Mum turns round, wanders back across to Eskil all kind of casual like, slips her arm through his, smiles as she says something I can't hear, and Eskil smiles and raises his eyebrows, pretending to be pleased and surprised. I don't quite catch what he says, but it's something about how he's looking forward to something, and then they start to walk arm in arm into the house with Hilde right behind them. I roll over onto my back again, feel everything turning sour inside me, going mouldy, I should never have come here, how was I to know Eskil would be coming, but still, why the hell didn't I go somewhere else, no matter where, just anywhere but here. I close my eyes, take a deep breath and let it out again in a long sigh, try to calm down a bit. One way or another I'll get through this as well, I suppose, and I don't need to stay any longer than necessary anyway, I can just stay for dinner, have coffee and then take myself off somewhere else, make up a story about having to meet somebody and get out of here, I don't need to stay the night. I swallow, feel myself growing calmer at the thought, becoming a little more relaxed. I put my hands behind my head and close my eyes. All's quiet, not a sound to be heard.

Then: "So this is where you're hiding?"

I open my eyes and find myself looking straight up at Eskil. He's standing over me, grinning, with a pair of fake Ray-Bans pushed up onto his brow. His face is tanned and his white teeth look even whiter than usual, they gleam at me. I don't say anything for a moment, just try to act surprised.

"You're here already?" I say.

He doesn't answer right away, looks me in the eye, making no secret of the fact that he knows I've only been trying to avoid them, that's Eskil, tactful as always. I feel a surge of annoyance, but don't let it show, try to smile.

"You didn't hear the car, then?" he asks, grinning.

"I nodded off for a minute," I say.

"Right!"

I try to keep a smile on my face, but it's no good, the best I can manage is a sheepish grin, I know how it must look and I could kick myself, I ought to cut the crap and admit that I was trying to escape, but I don't, I can't. Instead I feign a big yawn, trying to make it look as though I really had nodded off.

"Well, do you want to come in and join the rest of us?" he asks. "Or were you planning on having another forty winks?"

Annoyance grows inside me, I feel my whole body being filled with a fierce resentment, but I don't let it show, pretend not to notice the wry note in his voice, the sarcasm.

"Be right with you," I say, rubbing my eye, as if rubbing the sleep out of it, then I get up. He nods and grins, then turns on his heel and walks off. I wait a couple of seconds, then I bend down, pick up the blanket and shake off the fresh grass cuttings, bundle it up, tuck it under my arm and follow him, taking care to walk a little more slowly than him, I just can't face talking to him on the way in. I walk a few yards, then stop and make a show of having stepped on something, lift one of my feet and make a face, stand on one foot and feel under my heel, stay like this until Eskil has disappeared through the veranda door, then I start walking again, force my feet across the lawn and up onto the veranda, my resentment growing and growing, but there's no way round it. I step across the creaking veranda floor and into the living room, stop short just inside. I can hear Mum's laughter in the kitchen, closely followed by Eskil's pompous laugh, a laugh that drowns out everything else. A moment, then Eskil says something, I don't quite catch it, but Mum hoots with laughter and calls him a big idiot. Everything's as it should be: Eskil being entertaining in his usual smug fashion and Mum laughing at everything he says and does. I feel my mood growing more and more sour, I can't face going in there and joining them, can't face having to stand there and act as though I find Eskil as witty and entertaining as he's trying to be.

Then: "Hi, Jon."

I look round. And there's Hilde, with a pack of Marlboro Lights in her hand. She gives me a friendly smile. She's always friendly, Hilde, I don't know how the hell Eskil ever managed to snare her, don't know how she puts up with him either, he certainly doesn't deserve her.

"Hi," I say, and I walk over to her, lay a hand on her bare, tanned arm, just next to her tattoo, she has a tattoo of some Asian symbol on her upper arm. "Long time, no see," I say and give her a hug.

"I know," she says. "Last time I saw you was at Grete's sixtieth birthday party."

"Ugh, don't remind me. It's a long time since I've been that drunk," I say with a little laugh.

She doesn't laugh, looks straight at me and smiles kind of hesitantly, a strange little smile, as though she feels sorry for me, I don't see why she should feel sorry for me, but that's how it looks, as if I'd done something at Mum's sixtieth birthday party, as if I'd made a fool of myself or something, I don't remember making a fool of myself, but it's possible, I suppose, I was so fucking plastered. But don't think about that right now, it can't have been that bad if nobody's mentioned it.

"So, how're you doing?" I say.

"Oh, fine," she says, looking at me and smiling, smiling a perfectly ordinary smile now. "Great!" she says. "And you?"

"Yeah, I'm doing just great!" I say, trying to sound reasonably upbeat, give her a smile.

Two seconds.

Then: "And the band?" I hear Eskil say.

I turn. He saunters over to us, his sunglasses still pushed up onto his brow. He looks at me and grins.

44

"How's it going with the band?" he asks again, blinking lazily, seeming to radiate self-assurance, calm.

"Oh, great!" I say, trying to smile back at him. "We're hard at it!"

He nods, waits a moment.

"You're not getting a bit too old for all that?" he asks.

"Too old?"

"To go around dreaming of becoming a pop star," he says.

"Yeah, well I don't actually dream of becoming a pop star," I say, feeling another surge of annoyance, but I keep smiling.

"Oh, no, that's right," he says. "You're an artist!"

I look at him, feel like firing off an equally sarcastic retort, but I can't bring myself to do it, don't feel like starting anything, no good would come of it anyway. So instead I look at him and chuckle, pretend to take it as a joke, pretend not to hear the sarcasm in his voice. Turn to Hilde, look at her and smile, but she doesn't look at me, just stands there smacking her lips, giving Eskil a look that says: behave yourself. Her eyelids droop pointedly, as if to let him know she's had enough of him.

"Is something wrong?" Eskil asks. He raises his eyebrows, puts on a butter-wouldn't-melt face.

"No, no," Hilde says.

"But you look so tired!"

She doesn't say anything, simply looks him straight in the eye.

"You're sure there's nothing wrong?" Eskil asks again.

"There's never anything wrong," Hilde says.

"Gosh!" Eskil exclaims.

"Yes, I know!" she says.

I bend down and pretend to be picking at a tiny spot on my shorts, rather relishing the fact that they're arguing, although I feel a bit awkward, too, it's kind of embarrassing. One beat, then I act as if I've suddenly thought of something I meant to ask Mum. "Um," I say, scratching my chin as I start to walk off, walk across the living room and into the kitchen. Mum is standing with her back to me, at the cooker, stirring the sauce. She turns and looks at me, smiles, carrying on as though everything from this morning is forgotten, she's like a changed woman now Eskil's here, no longer so down, she's never down when Eskil's around, she's almost cheerful.

"Thanks for mowing the lawn for me, Jon," she says. Turns away again, stirs. I study the gnarled blue veins on her hands, her work-worn hands.

"It's the least I could do," I say.

Two seconds.

"Anything I can do for you here?" I ask. She turns to face me again, smiles.

"No, no!" she says.

"Are you sure?" I ask.

"Quite sure," she says.

Two seconds more.

Then I hear Eskil say: "Oh, go on, let him help!"

I notice the way Mum's face immediately lights up. She stops stirring and glances to the side, smiling.

"What are you babbling on about now, you silly idiot?" she cries gaily.

And Eskil strolls in to join us. He has removed his sunglasses from his brow and nibbles on one leg of them as he flashes that lopsided grin he thinks is so charming. He eyes Mum, removes the sunglasses from his mouth.

"Let the lad help you, I said! You know it's not easy for him!"

46

He slips his free hand into his pocket and leans against the door jamb, stands there looking smug. And Mum looks at him and laughs.

"Silly idiot!" she says.

Eskil grins, enjoying this whole situation. He's just like all other ordinary, average individuals, he loves being called an idiot. I stare at him, feel annoyance growing inside me, there's something bitter building up in there, a vicious resentment.

"This brother of yours is so silly, I'm at my wit's end," Mum says and she turns to me and shakes her head, smiling. "I don't know what I'm going to do with him," she adds.

"Oh, really?" I say.

She gives me a slightly puzzled look. And this bitterness grows inside me, this resentment. I'm so close to telling them that I've got several good suggestions for what to do with him, but I manage to restrain myself, just stand there. There's silence, and Mum and Eskil look at me and now I have to say something, it doesn't matter what, just say something.

"Think I'll nip down to the beach for a swim!" I blurt.

Silence again.

Mum looks at me, frowns.

"Now?" she asks.

I yawn, give a little shrug, try to act casual, but don't quite manage it.

"I've got time before dinner," I say, look at her and force a little smile, turn slightly, look at Eskil, he grins and his eyes bore into mine. I hold his gaze for a split second, then look at the floor, feel my face grow hot, feel myself flushing with anger and embarrassment.

"Yeah, well, you don't need me here, do you?" I say, and I hear how bitter I sound, hear the self-pity in what I say. And I feel myself growing even hotter, even more embarrassed.

"Oh, but Jon," Mum says. "Surely you could put off swimming till later. It's not often that we're together, all three of us."

I look at her.

"All three of us? What about Hilde, doesn't she count?" I say, so loud that Hilde is bound to hear. I look at Mum and force a smile.

Total silence.

I look at Mum, see her mouth slowly drop open, see her eyes change colour, darken. She glares at me and I bleed inside, shame burns inside me and my anger glows red, but I stare straight at her and go on smiling. A moment, then she simply turns away and goes back to the sauce, stirs.

Silence.

I just stand here, flushed and smiling. And Eskil looks at me. He raises his eyebrows a fraction, shakes his head, doesn't say anything. I don't say anything either, keep the smile in place as I walk out of the kitchen, bleeding inside, but trying to look as nonchalant as I can, stroll, back burning, through the living room and out of the veranda door.

Vemundvik, July 10th–13th 2006

.

The longing to get away was one of several things that bound us together. We both had the same urge to leave Namsos and never come back. I can't have been more than eleven or twelve when I hung a poster on my wall of New York by night, and in the evening before I fell asleep I would often lie in bed and imagine what it would be like to live in that particular street, in that particular skyscraper, behind that particular window. Even at that age I had the feeling that the life I was meant to live could never be possible in the small, sleepy sawmill town where I'd grown up, and I became all the more convinced of this after I met you, developing as we did a kind of common disdain for the small-town life that we knew. We loved to put down and sneer at Namsos and the local folk, we worked ourselves up into a kind of mutual ecstasy as we wandered aimlessly around the streets, vying with each other in our dislike of the town and its inhabitants. We longed to be far away from the streets of a town centre that was dead and deserted after four in the afternoon, far away from the wind and the rain that swept in off the fjord and lashed against the grey Fifties housing blocks, away from the hotdog stand where rowdy teenagers with bottles of home-brewed hooch and grape soda in their inside pockets hung out on Saturday nights, and where the cloying smell of deep-frying mingled with the acrid reek of scorched rubber from Taunuses burning down on Havnegata. We liked to think of Namsos folk as insular country bumpkins and ourselves as broad-minded and inquisitive, with our sights set on the great, wide world; we never tired of telling each other how small Namsos was, how cut off and sheltered from the rest of the world. "*Ben Hur* should be coming to Namsos cinema any day now," we'd say when we were discussing films we thought sounded interesting, films that were already showing in the major towns and cities, but which we would have to wait maybe two or three months to see, if they ever reached Namsos at all. "He probably thought I was talking about cigarettes," I said once, when the assistant in one of the town's two record shops told us they didn't have any Prince in stock. We pretended to be dismayed, frustrated and even angered by such incidents, but looking back on it it's easy to see how we relished them and relied on them to make us feel as smart, socially conscious and sophisticated as we wanted to feel. "Set aside a couple of nights a year for a variety show and they'll be all for it," I said when the popular outcry against building an arts centre was at its height. And you, who had just started smoking and were doing your best to look laid-back and worldly-wise with a cigarillo jutting between your fingers, laughed and shook your head at these uncouth peasants who sat cooped up inside their detached bungalows, watching *The Cosby Show* and other inane TV programmes, and who – unlike us – never looked as if they had any idea that art and literature and music were what gave life meaning and the only things worth talking about.

And when talking about art and literature and music, especially if there was anyone else around, we adopted a rather elaborate, long-winded manner of speech. We would often stop in the middle of a sentence, making lengthy pauses for thought, during which we closed our eyes, blew down our noses and acted as if we were giving a lot of thought to something, imagining as we did that this made us look and sound clever and intellectual, as well as giving the impression that whatever we had just said was something we had come up with at that very moment, as indeed it sometimes was. Just as often, though, it was something we'd read and memorized from a newspaper or one of the magazines we sometimes went down to the library to read. As it happens, it was in one of these magazines that we first learned of the Beat Generation and for us this marked the beginning of a new era, since it was the literary heroes of the beats and their free-and-easy attitude to sex that encouraged us to give in to the attraction we had gradually begun to feel for one another.

We had come close to having sex before this, too, though: not nearly as drunk as I made myself out to be and with a nervous laugh intended to underline that this was just a bit of fun, I had asked you to pull down your trousers and let me suck you off, and with a laugh that was every bit as uncertain as my own, you did as I asked. But just as I went down on my knees I glanced up and met your eye, and even though I knew that you really did want me to do it, my courage failed me and the whole thing ended with the two of us bursting into strained, almost hysterical laughter. Both then and in the days that followed we were so eager to show each other that we hadn't meant anything by what had happened that it's hard to believe only six months later we'd be having sex just about every chance we got.

The first time it happened we were in my room. We'd been out in the sun all day, we were hot and sweaty and lying on my bed, one at either end, taking it easy and talking about the hole in the ozone layer and how neither of us could recall our parents ever putting suncream on us when we were kids, despite the fact that, as far as we remembered, we had been out in the sun all day long during the summer. At first you acted as if you weren't aware that I was lying there gazing at your glistening, perspiring body, but after our eyes had met a few times it became hard to act normal and eventually, when the air around us was charged and tremulous with all that had gone unsaid and it was no longer possible for either of us to concentrate on the actual conversation, you came up with a sort of bridge between our words and our thoughts: "I've got a mole on my groin that's looking a bit dark," you said, thus giving me the sign I'd been waiting for. Not daring to look you in the eye I asked you to pull down your shorts so I could have a look and, struggling to look as though this was all about the mole and nothing but the mole, you did as I said. Even when my fingers began to probe under the thick, black pubic hair, prompting your cock to rise slowly to one side and gently brush my trembling hand, we tried to maintain the pretence. But moments later, when I found the mole and, in a thick, husky voice, told you it was nothing to worry about, we had to make a decision. Either we had to do what we both wanted to do, or we had to do as we had done in previous, similar situations, which is to say: continue the pretence and act as if it had all simply been an innocent examination of a mole. And it was at this point that I suddenly happened to think of the Beat poets. While we had tried to regard the average Namsos resident as being hampered by the old idea of not getting above yourself and by an inherited sense of shame, we had done our best to see ourselves as being as bold and experimental as Allen Ginsberg, William Burroughs and Jack Kerouac; and if it hadn't been for my urge to emulate these role models, I wouldn't have dared take you into my mouth the way I did at that moment. If it hadn't been for Ginsberg, Burroughs and Kerouac I'd probably have felt embarrassed afterwards too, but I didn't, and nor did you. Quite the opposite, really. Having sex with one another was proof of a sort that the image of ourselves which we had formed was real, so afterwards we felt quite proud of ourselves. We lay there side by side, naked, running with sweat and sated, blowing smoke rings, listening to Prudence and trying to look as though what we'd just done was as normal for us as eating a sandwich or watching television.

In the spring of 1988 we met Silje Shiive and for the whole of our second and third years in senior secondary we were the best of friends, you, me and her. Her father was dead, she lived with her slightly eccentric artist mother and a grumpy ginger tom called Laurence, after Laurence Olivier.

Silje had an air of charming arrogance about her. Her veiled, lazy eyes and distracted manner, her habit of being forgetful, inattentive and a little on the careless side made it look as though she wasn't particularly interested in what was going on around her, and this apparent lack of interest and involvement appealed to a lot of young and not quite so young men, all of them eager to prove that he was fascinating enough to capture and hold her attention. Silje was well aware of this, of course, it was often a deliberate ploy on her part, and sometimes she would go too far and make a show of not paying attention. She would pretend that she hadn't seen someone or hadn't heard what they said, or she would yawn openly when they were speaking to her. But contrary to what one might think, she seemed no less charming on those rare occasions when she was caught out and accused of playing hard to get and trying to make herself seem interesting. Far from it: if her cover was blown she would simply shrug it off with a rueful laugh, turning the whole situation to her advantage and making herself appear even more attractive.

But her arrogance wasn't always charming. She could be tactless, rude and ruthlessly honest and a lot of people dreaded being in her company because you never knew what she was likely to come out with in the way of awkward questions or hurtful comments. She often asked things that a lot of other people wondered about, but would never have dared to ask, just as she often said things that lots of people agreed with, but either didn't dare or were too polite to say. And almost always she would express herself in a way that made it difficult to challenge her. She would act innocent, make a joke of it so that her victim seemed churlish if he or she protested, or she would confuse the person concerned by making them think that whatever she said it was out of kindness and with the best of intentions: "You're really brave, I'd never dare to get my hair cut that short if the back of my head was so flat," she said once to a girl with whom she had a score to settle, when she walked into the classroom with a new haircut. She was at her most merciless, though, if she thought she detected the slightest whiff of male chauvinism. She was the sort of feminist who could hurt a boy most cruelly on behalf of all the hard-done-by women in history. That there were men who raped and beat up women seemed justification enough for her to pass comment on the size of some poor guy's penis, and that Latin males had a reputation for being womanizers seemed reason enough for her to fool a nice Italian musician friend of mine into believing that she fancied him, only then to give him the brush-off in the most humiliating fashion. "There, that'll give him some idea of what life's like for women in his country," she said afterwards.

I don't remember exactly how we got to know her, but I do remember that we were both very surprised to meet a girl who was genuinely interested in the same things as us. Despite the reckless, almost sinister sides of her character, we hit it off with her right from the start, and there were times when we slept and ate almost more at her house than we did at our own, something which made Oddrun, Silje's mother, very happy. "If you want to stay young," she used to say, "you have to spend time with young people." And when word got around that Oddrun had a voracious sexual appetite and enjoyed the company of young men, she laughed that coarse, husky laugh of hers; it would never have occurred to her to be more discreet or hold herself more aloof. Quite the opposite. Oddrun liked being provocative and shocking people. Once, when you were helping her to change the washer on the tap for the garden hose and she noticed the retired army officer who lived next door watching the two of you through binoculars from his living room window, she suddenly pulled you to her and kissed you full on the lips. Back inside the house she could hardly stop laughing. "That phone of his will be red hot till tomorrow morning, I bet you," she said.

Oddrun didn't seem to give a toss what people thought of her. She would sit on her balcony, knocking back the drink on a Tuesday morning while people walked by down below. She would march straight into the newsagent's and buy *Playgirl* no matter how big a queue there was, and instead of hiding it in her bedroom she'd leave it lying on one of the bookshelves in the living room. But according to my mum she hadn't always been like that. Silje's father had been a Freemason and businessman with a reputation to maintain. He had expected Oddrun to be respectable and presentable at the very least, and it wasn't until the early Eighties, after he had contracted some sort of lung disease and died, that Oddrun "became hellbent on being a Bohemian and doing all the things her husband wouldn't let her do," as Mum put it.

Silje pretended to despair of Oddrun's unconventional habits, the little scandals she caused and the way she occasionally set tongues wagging, but from the way she acted it was clear that she was actually proud of this side of her mother and admired it. "Oh, Mum, for heaven's sake," she would say, rolling her eyes. "Oh, God, I'm so mortified," she would sigh, putting her hands to her face. But unlike you and me, who were still embarrassed by and blushed for our mothers, she never blushed, not at all, she simply laughed at it all and the very next day she would be entertaining friends and acquaintances with the latest antics of her crazy Bohemian mother. Oddrun, for her part, knew that Silje was only pretending to be shocked and dismayed and she responded to this playacting with a little playacting of her own: "What?" she would say, frowning and looking as though she had no idea what was so shocking about what she had just said or done.

And we admired her and looked up to her as much as Silje did. She was well-read, well-informed and intelligent and we found it hard to understand how a woman like her could take the time to talk to us as often and at such length as she did, why she would ask us in for a cup of tea even if Silje wasn't home, why she invited us to her parties and treated us exactly the same as all of her other, adult, guests.

She didn't hold the sort of parties that Mum and the other adults I knew held, though. She held salons. And at her salons she served apéritifs in long-stemmed, wide-bowled glasses with glacé cherries on plastic cocktail sticks propped against the rims, and her guests – often well-known faces from local arts circles and occasionally from the world of commerce – mingled and chatted until it was time go in to dinner, which never consisted of lamb stew or a casserole with lager on the side – the usual fare when grown-ups had a party – but of some French-sounding dish served with mushrooms that Oddrun had picked herself, and always accompanied by a fine wine, more often than not from the same region as the dish itself, which, according to Silje's mother, would go very well with the food.

Incidentally, Oddrun could never open a bottle of wine without sighing and shaking her head at the thought of the Wine Monopoly shop in Namsos. They had hardly a single drinkable wine in that place, she had to order almost everything from the catalogue and the staff knew absolutely nothing about the products they were there to sell, she used to say. When she went to the Wine Monopoly she always ended up telling them about wine and not the other way round, as should have been the case.

Unlike Arvid and Berit, my mum had been known to buy a bottle of wine on the odd occasion when she was having people to dinner, but no matter what sort of food was served the wine was always either Bull's Blood or the Monopoly's own home-bottled red, because they were cheap and perfectly okay as far as Mum was concerned. If I made the mistake of pointing out that not all wines went equally well with all sorts of food, she would respond with some caustic remark to the effect that she was afraid she wasn't as sophisticated as I would like her to be; or she would act hurt and sigh something about how she was doing the best she could and she was sorry if it wasn't good enough. As far as she was concerned, being open to and learning new things was as good as admitting defeat, or so it seemed. All the things she didn't know or couldn't do were regarded by her as a threat and a reminder that she wasn't good enough, and not as the key to a richer, fuller life. This was also reflected in conversations around the dinner table. If, for some reason, anyone brought up a subject that hadn't been discussed a thousand times before, or on which there was a risk that opinions might differ, this would give rise to a sense of unease, rather like the atmosphere generated by Arvid, the local vicar, when he came to call. In such cases, Mum, and everyone else who knew the unwritten rules for appropriate conversation in their circle, would promptly take steps to bring the conversation back onto safe, familiar ground.

At Silje and her mother's dinner table there was absolutely none of this. No topic was too small and or too big and whether an opinion was voiced by an irate or an ecstatic dinner guest did not appear to matter. While Arvid and Berit and the whole Christian community approved of people demonstrating self-control and never letting themselves get carried away, here the exact opposite was the case; if anything was frowned upon it was a lack of enthusiasm and interest in what was being discussed. "The Lord likes you hot or cold. If you're lukewarm he'll spit you out," as Oddrun the atheist was fond of saying.

And we were thrilled to be included. We did our best to seem as worldly-wise and self-assured as we could, but it must have been pretty obvious that we were very pleased with ourselves and almost grovellingly grateful. We admired everyone there for all their knowledge and their skills and for all the things they'd seen and done. Oddrun had her own studio in the attic, where she painted pictures in which condors were a recurring motif;

one lively, talkative character with a Lenin badge in his lapel had taken part in the student revolt in Paris in 1968, and a guy in a suit and bottle-glass specs had been a hippie and driven across America in a rainbow-coloured Volkswagen Dormobile. Our own travels were limited to the odd motoring holiday in Sweden and, strange as it may sound today when foreign travel is so cheap and so common, neither Mum nor Berit nor Arvid had ever been further from home than that either.

We drank in every word these people said, we tucked away every story, every remark and observation, and at school or at a party with chums of our own age we repeated it all, presenting it for the most part as if it were straight out of our own heads.

After dinner, too, the format was, on the whole, pretty different from what we were used to. In our homes it was always the women who cleared the table and retreated to the kitchen, and the talk over the washing-up was usually of family matters. My mum's favourite topic was illness: pain and suffering in general and the poor children in particular, and I've never known this to be anything but a popular talking point with other women, too. Meanwhile, the men sat in the living room, waiting for the women to bring in the coffee, to which they would add a dash of something stronger. They smoked roll-ups, swore, and robustly debated the national budget or talked of a pipe that had sprung a leak in someone's basement, and every now and again they would shout something to the woman, something meant to be a bit daring and close to the bone: "Oy! Get a move on with that coffee, will you! We're bloomin' parched in here!" And Mum and the other women would pop their heads round the kitchen door and pretend to be annoyed. "Oh, shut your mouth, you old rogue, or you'll get nothing!" And they would all laugh.

After dinner at Silje's and her mother's place, on the other hand, it was as natural for the men to clear the table and help with the washing-up as the women, and the conversations in the kitchen were extensions of the conversations that had been conducted during dinner. And I, for one, could detect no male–female divide in these. Oddrun's contributions to discussions on progressive taxation, German literature between the wars and Soviet foreign policy were as impassioned as the men's and, unlike Mum, who might occasionally venture to make a joke, but never anything that went beyond the bounds of what was considered decent for a woman, Oddrun could be every bit as crude and blunt as the male dinner guests. Once she'd had a bit to drink she would often start to joke about the number of lovers she'd had and how easy it was to trick a man into doing this or that: "All you have to do is show a little cleavage and they'll do whatever you ask," I remember her saying late one evening, and neither you, I, nor anyone else thought her improper or immoral on that account.

That said, when people got drunk at Oddrun's they tended to behave in ways that would have been absolutely unheard of at the grown-up parties you and I had been used to up till then. There was, for example, a former actress with the Trøndelag Theatre, a skinny woman with long, white hair and bulging eyes, who stripped naked, stepped out onto the balcony and sat down, and there she stayed, smoking and staring defiantly at everyone who walked past on the street below. No friend of Mum or Berit would have dreamed of doing anything like that, no matter how drunk or far from home they were, and if such a thing had ever happened and had got out it would have been a personal disaster and an eternal source of shame. But the next morning, when we were all up and sitting at the breakfast table, this same white-haired woman emerged from the bedroom and, contrary to what you might think, she had neither forgotten, nor did she pretend to have forgotten, the incident; she didn't look the slightest bit embarrassed, instead she laughed until the tears rolled down her cheeks as she described the looks on the faces of the male passers-by and everyone else at the table laughed just as hard.

But no matter how broad-minded Oddrun and her friends and Silje herself were, we never dared to tell them about what went on between us. Not that any of them would have had anything against it, of course, we knew they wouldn't. But oddly enough that was why we kept it to ourselves. Because if Silje were to find out about it she would think nothing of telling other people. She simply couldn't see what was so shocking about two men sleeping together, and even if we begged her not to say anything, and even if she promised on her honour not to do so, she would do it anyway, and afterwards she would wonder why we were upset. "Oh, for heaven's sake, relax," she'd say. "It's not that big a deal, is it?" She had a confidence in herself that rendered her immune and she acted as though everyone around her was just as self-confident.

Eventually, however, Mum's suspicions were aroused. She never actually said anything, but it was obvious that she was growing less and less keen on you. She would give a little sigh or roll her eyes and look almost annoyed if I said I was popping over to your place, and I discovered, quite by accident, that on several occasions when you had phoned and asked for me she had said I wasn't in, even though she knew I was up in my room, practising or listening to music. At first I put it down to her illness and the fact that she had become so dependent on me at home. She had been plagued for years with chronic pain in her joints and muscles, but during the winter and spring it had been unbearable, and when, on top of everything else, she lost a lot of the grip in her hands she could no longer carry on with her job or do the housework. Although she never said it in so many words, she let me know in no uncertain terms that she didn't think it was too much to ask for me to spend a bit more time at home and do a greater share of the household chores than I'd been doing, and I thought that the dislike of you that she'd suddenly begun to show was just one of many ways she had of telling me this. But when I noticed that she didn't look unhappy if I said I was going to see anyone else it began to dawn on me that it had to have something to do with you, and it was only once I'd realized this that I noticed how her manner towards you had changed. She wasn't directly unfriendly, but she was short with you and not as chatty, and sometimes when both you and Silje were there she would make a big show of being nice to Silje and interested in her, while ignoring you in an ostentatious, almost childish manner.

More and more, though, I also had the feeling that she was trying to check whether or not we were gay. It was remarkable how often, when your name was mentioned, she would bring the conversation round to HIV and AIDS. It's true that the virus had only recently been identified and there was a lot about it in the papers, but that still didn't explain all the times when, out of the blue and apropos of nothing, she would start going on about what a long and painful death it led to, how far medical science was from discovering an effective antidote and how much she agreed that all HIV sufferers should have to wear some sort of badge, so that everyone else could take precautions. "Although it's mostly homosexuals who catch it so we can rest easy on that score," she would say, while keeping a close eye on me to see how I reacted. For a long time I played it cool when she carried on like this, acted as though I didn't know why she was saying all these things. I would yawn and try to look as if it had nothing to do with me, and I hoped and expected that this would eventually persuade her to give up, but it didn't, and one day when you had come over and she had brought the conversation round, by dint of some weird detours, to a male hairdresser whom she was convinced was gay, even though he had a wife and kids, I exploded. "We're not gay, Mum," I yelled.

First she went bright red, then she was angry with me for saying it straight out, thereby breaking the unwritten rules for how she believed such things ought to be discussed, but only a minute later she seemed happier and chirpier than I had seen her in a long time. All of a sudden she could see herself having grandchildren to spoil, after all, as well as a daughter-in-law to train up and a son she could tell her women friends about without having to lie or blush. The second and third of these my brother Eskil could be said to have given her, but to Mum's great sorrow in his teens he had caught mumps and this had left him sterile, so it was up to me to provide grandchildren and pass on the family name, as she had given me to understand on more than one occasion.

I was as unsure then as to whether I was gay, straight, or bisexual as I am now, but it was no less painful to hear her talk and carry on the way she did. You thought she was just a joke and there were times when you had to bite your lip to save laughing out loud when she sat there sounding us out. But even though I agreed with you, and even though a lot of what she said was so stupid that it was hard to believe it could be hurtful, these conversations always left me feeling depressed. At the time I didn't know why, but now I can see that it was the fact that she set conditions for loving me that left me with what I remember as a vague sense of shame.

Unlike Mum, I don't think either Berit or Arvid suspected that we were anything other than friends at that point. But then Arvid thought and acted as if he were living in the heaven that he sometimes believed in, and since there definitely can't have been such a thing as homosexuality in that heaven, I don't think it ever occurred to him that anything of that sort could be going on between us. Berit was much more down-to-earth and under normal circumstances she might have been able to spot what Mum had spotted, but the silent, stiff, almost cold manner you had adopted when you were at home had become more and more marked during '88 and '89 and this made you all but impossible to read or to fathom, not only for Arvid, but also for her. On one occasion, for example, when we popped in to your house to pick up a camera we needed for one of our endless art projects and you needed to eat something to boost your blood sugar levels before we headed out again, I remember you asking Arvid if you might "be allowed" to take a couple of slices of bread. Silje and I thought you were kidding, but when we saw that Arvid wasn't smiling, but reacted by sighing heavily and walking out of the kitchen without replying, we realized that this was pretty much par for the course.

One might have thought that Berit would be worried about you when you acted like this, and maybe she was, but she also seemed to admire this side of you. I think she interpreted your defiance and all your little acts of rebellion as signs of inner strength and courage, and on several occasions I saw her smother a little smile when you behaved in ways that would probably have troubled other mothers.

Namsos, July 5th 2006. Darkie

I pluck a dry white stick off the ground, put it over my knee and imagine that it's Eskil's arm, then I snap the stick in two and toss both halves into the sea. I attempt a triumphant grin, but can't quite pull it off, all I can manage is a grim, bitter sneer. I lean forward, prop my elbows on my knees, sit there gazing at the blue sea sparkling in the bright sunlight. After a few moments I smack my hands down on my knees and get up off the rock. Got to be getting back. There's no way round it. I'd better head off again as soon as I've eaten. Don't know where to, but no matter what, I have to go, just go somewhere. I start to walk, walk through the forest and out onto the dusty, dirt track, yellow dirt track. Stride out smartly to begin with, slowing down as I get closer to the house. It's as if my body doesn't want to go back there, my legs grow heavier and heavier, my feet harder to lift and I have to push them into the garden, force them across the lawn. Then I hear their voices, hear Mum's laughter and Eskil's loud, domineering voice, jolly and animated. Sounds like they're having fun. Mum laughs again and Eskil laughs, gives his booming laugh. And now I hear Hilde laugh too. All three of them are sitting there laughing, and here I am, about to walk in and ruin everything again, about to kill the mood. A moment, and then it hits me, because it's true, not just something I'm saying so I can wallow in self-pity, it's actually true. I stop dead, swallow, stand perfectly still. I'm bleeding inside, the urge to turn around grows and I feel more and more like just doing a runner, getting out of there, but I can't, they might think I'd drowned or something, they might organize a search party and all that, you never know, better take off straight after dinner, drive over to the cottage, or maybe to Wenche's. Don't feel like seeing Wenche either, but it would be better than staying here. I shut my eyes and open them again, force my feet round the corner of the house and up to the veranda. They're all smoking, Mum with her roll-up, Eskil and Hilde with their Marlboros. As soon as they see me they fall silent, the laughter dissolves and dies away, only for a second and then it's as if they realize that this is precisely what has happened and they try to pick up where they left off, chuckle and make a few desultory remarks so it won't be too awkward, try to sort of gloss over it.

"I don't know where you get it all from," Mum says to Eskil, she never tires of saying this, it seems. I look at her, she shakes her head as she leans forward and stubs out her cigarette, ventures another little laugh. She acts like it's no big deal, me coming back like this, but it doesn't quite work, she's uncomfortable, I can tell by her face.

One beat, then everyone turns to look at me, all casual like.

"Ah, you're back," Eskil says.

"Yes," I say. "And just when you were having such a nice time," I add. I feel a pang of remorse as soon as I've said it – I was only saying what they were all thinking – but still,

I shouldn't have said it, it just came out. There's silence. I keep my eyes on the floor as I walk over, aching more and more inside, bleeding. I try to smile, to look as if I don't care, but don't quite manage it, smile this agonized smile, a grim smile. Raise my eyes as I pull up the empty patio chair, see Mum give her wan smile, trying to appear plucky and long-suffering again. A moment, then she gets up.

"Oh, well," she says, groaning softly and putting a hand to her back as she straightens up. "I'd better see if dinner's ready," she says, then she slips past me, not even looking at me.

Silence again.

"Well," Eskil says, blowing cigarette smoke down his nose, then pausing for a moment. "So, how was the water?"

"Not bad," I say, trying to hold his gaze, trying to look confident, but not quite managing it.

"Where did you swim?"

"Off the beach."

He nods, says nothing for a moment. Then: "That's where you pulled the shorts off me," he says.

I look at him, puzzled. What the hell's he on about, it was him that pulled the shorts off me, not the other way round.

"Did I ever tell you about that?" he asks, turning to Hilde and nodding at me. "Packed beach, and this little bugger goes and pulls the shorts off me. Some of the girls from my class were there and all, Christ, I was mortified," he says, turns and looks at me again. One beat. Then suddenly it dawns on me what he's up to, he's trying to lend me some of his own traits now, giving me the starring role in one of his countless stories about himself, hoping to make me feel better. This is his way of boasting about me, his way of saving the situation.

"Do you remember?" he asks.

"No, I don't remember," I say, looking at him, holding his gaze for a second, trying to show him that I know what he's up to, but he doesn't get it, just goes on talking.

"You don't?" he asks, acting amazed. He takes a last puff, stubs out his cigarette in the ashtray. "Well, you may have forgotten it, but I haven't, I can tell you. An experience like that leaves its mark," he says and laughs as he turns to Hilde, nods at me: "He was a bit of a joker that one, you know!"

"Were you, Jon?" Hilde asks, leaning forward and stubbing out her cigarette as well. Sits back in her chair again, regards me, looking slightly surprised, impressed almost.

I don't answer straight away.

"Hmm?" she asks.

And then I feel it starting to work on me. It's so stupid, but I'm flattered in spite of myself. I glance down at my feet, then up again, can't help smiling a little, as good as admitting that I was a bit of a joker, not just withdrawn and shy, and that I could be wild and unruly, too. It's not true, but it feels good to be seen that way.

"I wouldn't have thought that of you," Hilde says.

I look at her. And she looks at me, looks at me with soft, kind eyes, eyes that are a little too soft and kind actually. Her smile is a little too kind, too. And suddenly I realize that she knows this is all just a pack of lies, that she's pretending to believe Eskil's story because she feels sorry for me, that she pities me. A moment, then the hint of pleasure I had felt at the flattery drains away and shame comes flooding back. I mean, how small can you be, how much of a little brother can you be. Eskil lends me his own traits and I sit here like a fool, accepting them. Sit here, giving the impression that I long to be like him. As if I look up to him, a smug, swaggering right-winger, the last thing in the world I'd want to be, for Christ's sake. What the hell's the matter with me? Hilde doesn't take her eyes off me, she knows I'm wise to the whole charade and that I'm ashamed, I can tell by her face that she knows.

"Well, well," Hilde says, trying to change the subject somehow, get me out of this before it becomes too embarrassing. She opens her mouth, about to say something, but before she can do so Mum appears, I hear the floor creak as she steps out onto the veranda, and both Eskil and Hilde turn, look at her.

"Not quite done yet," Mum says. "But it won't be long now."

"Mmm," Eskil says, leans back in his chair, laces his fingers together and makes a horrible cracking sound with his knuckles, as if to show how much he's looking forward to dinner.

"It smells great," Hilde says.

"Delicious," Eskil says.

"Ah, well, I'm not sure it'll taste as good as it smells," Mum says.

"Oh, I'm sure it will!" Eskil says.

"I'm not all that used to baking fish in the oven," Mum says. She's not about to give in, she's bringing herself down so that Eskil and Hilde will feel moved to protest and contradict her, so bloody typical, sitting there craving compliments.

"You made it once before when we were here and it was delicious," Eskil says.

"Was it?"

"Oh, yes. We were still talking about that meal weeks later," he says, looking at Mum and nodding, and Mum smiles gratefully back at him. Un-fucking-believable, he's lying in his teeth and we all know it, we all know he's exaggerating, but it doesn't seem to matter. It's so fucking ridiculous.

"Oh, by the way, let me know if you run out," Eskil goes on. "I'll get someone to nip over with a fresh batch for you."

"Oh, yes, please!" Mum exclaims happily. "But can you do that?"

"Ah, what wouldn't I do for my old Mum," Eskil says.

I look at him, he's got some fucking nerve, he's never there for Mum, he hardly ever comes to see her, and yet he has the gall to talk like this. He looks at Mum and laughs. And Mum laughs too. He's never been there for her, not even when she was at her lowest, and yet she laughs when he talks about doing things for her, as if she's forgotten everything, as if it doesn't matter.

"I'll have a word with one of the lads and get him to run over with a box of fillets and a box of whole fish at the weekend," Eskil says. "That should keep you going for a while."

"Oh, what would I do without you," Mum says.

"Starve to death!" Eskil declares bluntly and laughs that big, booming laugh of his again, opening his mouth wide and glancing around as he laughs. And Mum hoots with laughter.

"You're unbelievable," she says, shaking her head.

Two seconds.

Then Eskil turns to me.

"Oh, by the way, we're looking for another driver," he says, lifting his sunglasses off his brow and pausing for a moment, nodding at me. "You wouldn't be interested, would you?"

I look at him, don't answer straight away. You wouldn't be interested, would you? he asks, asks as if I were looking for work. I've told him again and again that my plan is to concentrate on my music, but it seems to have gone in one ear and out the other, either that or he simply can't imagine that such a thing would ever be possible, it's so arrogant, so fucking patronizing. And I feel my annoyance growing, I turn and look at Mum, and Mum sits there eyeing me expectantly. And then it strikes me: they've been discussing this while I was down at the beach; I picture Mum playing the long-suffering mother, acting all weary and dejected because I'm never going to amount to anything, and Eskil assuming the role of father figure, the big brother who has to sort out the family problems. As if – him, the least responsible of us all, drunk or stoned all through his teens and early twenties and then he does a complete about-turn and suddenly he's oh-so-fucking-responsible, even goes into politics, and starts ranting on about stiffer sentences and law and order, him, after all those years of stealing from Mum to finance his drug habit, and now he sits there, expecting to be regarded as the responsible, trustworthy member of the family, it's un-fucking-believable, the man has no fucking shame.

"The pay's not bad, either," Eskil says.

"How much are we talking about?" Mum asks.

"About two hundred and ninety thou, I think."

"That much?" Mum says.

"Yes, or it might have been more," Eskil says.

I just sit here looking at them. They know I don't want to be a driver, but they pretend not to know. Talk in a way that makes it hard for me to say no, trying to press me to say yes, do they think I don't see that. They turn to me, look at me. One beat, then I force a wry grin, give a faint shake of my head. Another beat, then Mum twists her lips into a rueful smile. She looks at Eskil and sighs, playing the despairing mother again, like she's at her wits' end.

"Ah," Eskil says, smiling at me, "but you may have plans with the band," he says, saying it without a trace of irony, acting all sincere suddenly, wanting to look as if he, at least, respects me, knowing that it makes him stand even taller in Mum's eyes.

"Oh, that ... band!" Mum snorts, making it sound as if she's talking about a venereal disease.

"Well, you can think about it," Eskil says, looking at me – he's acting all innocent, but I know he's enjoying this, he's making me look like an ungrateful sod and himself like the magnanimous, considerate big brother, and he's enjoying every minute of it. I look at him, feel a wave of loathing wash over me.

"There's nothing to think about," I say. "I'm not interested."

Mum gives a little sniff as I say this.

"It's not good enough for you, is that it?" she asks peevishly.

I look at her and a loud bark of laughter escapes me: that she can bring herself to say something so stupid, that she can spout such an unadulterated cliché, in all seriousness. Jesus Christ, it's fucking unbelievable, she's like something out of a bloody film by Ken Loach or Mike Leigh, it's a fucking farce.

"No, driving a fishmonger's van isn't good enough for me," I say. "I believe I'm better than that, you see," I add, sneering at her and seeing how hard my sarcasm hits her, seeing how angry it makes her.

"Now, now," Eskil says quietly, speaking now as if he thinks we should just forget all about it. He's still playing the big man, taking the lead as it were, urging us to rise above this, relishing the fact that Mum and I are arguing, but acting as if he wants us to be friends. He knows it raises him even higher in Mum's eyes.

"Jon only has himself to think about, you know, he's not as dependent on a regular income as so many of us are," he says, as though he's defending me now. He's so bloody calculating, belittling my rejection of his offer, so Mum will disagree with him and say again how stupid she thinks I'm being.

"Yes, but he still needs a roof over his head," Mum sighs, doing exactly what Eskil wants her to do, continuing to criticize me. "He still has to eat," she says, "and there are bills to be paid," she says, "electricity, phone and I don't know what else," she goes on. She eyes Eskil helplessly. It's me she's talking about, but she's acting as if I'm not even there, ignoring me, treating me like a child, that's just what she's damn well doing, it's so fucking patronizing, so fucking arrogant. "He still needs to have an income, even if he doesn't have a family to support," she says. "I mean, you and Hilde, you only have yourselves to think about, too, but you both still have good steady jobs."

"Well, till now we have," Eskil says, looks down, fiddles with his sunglasses, then smiles slyly.

Silence.

Hilde turns to him, flashes him a look that says he has brought up a subject she'd rather he didn't mention. But Eskil doesn't look at her, he looks up at Mum and smiles.

"What do you mean: 'till now?'"

"Hilde and I, only having ourselves to think about," Eskil says and then he turns to Hilde, smiles at her, too. "Oh, come on, Hilde," he says, almost imploringly. "That's why we're here," he adds.

"What are you talking about?" Mum asks.

"We're going to adopt," Eskil says. "We didn't want to say anything until it was all arranged, but now it is. A month and a half from now we'll be going to collect our little boy."

Silence.

Then Mum puts her hands to her face, claps them to her cheeks and opens her mouth, but no words come out, she just sits there gaping. And Eskil starts to laugh, he sees how happy Mum is and he can't help but laugh, only moments ago she was feeling bitter and depressed and now he has sent her into raptures.

"Oh, my God, Eskil!" Mum cries, and she stands up and reaches across the table to hug him. And Eskil laughs and stands up as well and puts his arms around her. They rock from side to side. And then Mum starts to cry, stands there with her eyes shut, weeping. I watch as the tears stream down her cheeks, tears of joy, I ought to be happy too, I suppose, but I'm not, I can't find it in me to feel happy for them, not right now at any rate, not after all that's been said. I try to force a little smile, but it's no use, all I can manage is a grim, tortured grin. And there's Hilde, looking at me with pity in her eyes, as if she can see right through me, I feel a wave of embarrassment wash over me and promptly look away, the smile fixed on my face.

"Oh, my," Mum says, sniffing and wiping away her tears. She turns to Hilde. "Oh, Hilde," she says, reaching out her arms and hugging Hilde, too, resting her chin on her shoulder and squeezing her tight. And Eskil just sits there beaming, observing them, touched by this scene, and suddenly he turns to me, smiles as he places his hands on the arms of his chair. Looks as if he's about to get up and shake my hand or something, probably assumes I'll want to shake his hand and congratulate him. But I don't. I ought to, and I'd like to, but I can't bring myself to do it. I remain seated. And then Eskil realizes that I'm not about to get up. He raises his backside slightly, adjusts the cushion underneath him, tries to make out that he's just getting more comfortable, and I feel a stab of conscience.

"Well, congratulations!" I say, manage to squeeze out the word, but it sounds half-hearted, my tone indifferent, cold almost. It just comes out that way. And the guilt grows inside me, I shouldn't be behaving like this, it's awful, but I can't help it.

"Thanks," Eskil says, pretending not to notice. He turns back to Mum and Hilde, and Mum and Hilde are still hugging. I've never seen our mother be so affectionate towards Hilde before. She has never liked Hilde, never really accepted her, but now it seems she has been accepted. Mum hugs and hugs her and Hilde gazes over her shoulder, straight at me, she smiles, but her eyes are grave, she can tell just by looking at me that I can't feel happy for them.

"Congratulations," I say, trying to smile and look unfazed, but she sees right through me, knows how I feel, I can see it on her.

"Thanks," she says, in a rather sad voice designed somehow to show that in the midst of all this she feels sorry for me.

At last Mum lets go of Hilde.

"Oh my God, I don't know what to say!" she cries, pauses for a moment and just stands there smiling, mouth open, then she claps her hands together. "Well, come on then," she says eagerly, "Let's hear all about it," she says, sitting down. "Where's he from? What country? Have you decided on a name? I want to know everything, everything!" she cries, her voice almost a little too bright, I don't think I've ever seen her quite like this before. Hilde looks at her, she smiles, but doesn't seem to want to get too carried away, shoots a glance at me as she slips her hand into her bag, it's like she's considering my feelings, like she's toning down her own happiness for my sake.

"Ah, here it is," she says, producing some papers, yellow and pink papers stapled together in one corner. "There," she says, detaching a photo held in place by a paper clip.

"Oh, you've got a photo?" Mum exclaims eagerly. She shunts forward in her seat and puts out her hand. "Let me see, let me see," she says, takes the picture and stares at it, wide-eyed, doesn't say a word, just sits there staring. Then all of a sudden she starts crying again. Tears well up in the corners of her eyes. "Oh my God, he's beautiful," she says, then swallows. "Where's he from?"

"Colombia," Eskil says.

"Where's that?"

"South America," Eskil says.

"Oh, my, look at those beautiful eyes," Mum says and then she turns to me, hands me the photo. "Look, Jon!" she says. "Isn't he beautiful?!"

I take the photograph from her with a rather limp, indifferent hand, hating myself even as I do so, I don't want to be like this, but I am, I want to show an interest, but I can't find it in me, I look at the photo, see a small, dark-skinned child with black curly hair, take a quick, perfunctory glance at him and hand the picture back.

"Hmm," is all I say. My stomach wrenches as I say it, I don't want to be like this, but there's nothing to do about it. And the other three look right through me. And I burn with shame, I bleed inside, but I keep smiling, try to act nonchalant, but don't quite manage it, and Mum glares at me, furious, she doesn't say anything, but there's contempt in her eyes, just for a second, and then she looks down at the photo and smiles again, smiles and gives a slight shake of her head, looks up at Eskil and Hilde again. Then come the questions: how old is the child, do they know anything about the parents, what sort of background does he come from, have they decided on a name? She asks eagerly and Eskil replies enthusiastically.

"Oh my God, I can't wait," Mum says. She picks up the coffee jug, fills the cups on the table, all smiles.

"Did you forget to take your pills?" I blurt.

She turns to me and I can almost see the happiness fade from her face, see that sour look return.

"What?" she asks, she has no idea what I'm talking about, she's probably forgotten all about what she told me earlier today: those new pills made her hands shake so badly that she couldn't even pour coffee, she said.

"I mean, your hands are so steady! Did you forget to take your pills?" I say again. Don't want to say it, but I say it anyway, the words spat out as if they were just aching to be said. I try to smile and act as if I'm only joking, but it's no use, all I can muster is a spiteful grin. A moment, then Mum simply turns away, can't even be bothered saying anything, she looks upset now. She glances down at the picture of the little boy again and suddenly she's all smiles once more, seems to melt as soon as her eyes fall on that child. There's silence. Eskil picks up his pack of cigarettes, flips up the lid, raises the pack to his mouth and pulls out a cigarette with his lips.

"Oh my God, he's so beautiful," Mum says again, her eyes fixed on the picture, and I look at her and grin: this woman who has always referred to dark-skinned people as darkies and wogs, she and Eskil both, ultra-right-wingers the pair of them, petty racists, but here they are, gazing adoringly at a dark-skinned toddler, it's so fucking phony it's just not true.

"Even though he's a darkie?" I say. It just comes out, spat from my lips. I try to make it sound funny, but it doesn't sound funny, just nasty, mean. And Eskil turns to me, and Mum and Hilde turn to me. There's total silence and I feel the heat rising, I'm bleeding inside.

"What the hell are you're saying?" Mum snaps, looking at me.

"You and Eskil, anybody dark-skinned has always been a darkie to you two," I say, trying to sound artless, still grinning. They stare at me, there's total silence, and I'm bleeding harder and harder, but I keep the grin in place.

"You know what, Jon," Eskil growls, then he takes the cigarette from his lips unlit, pauses. "You know what ... just fucking stop it."

I don't say anything, just sit there trying to keep that grin on my face, look at Eskil, try to hold his eye, but I can't, I look down at my lap.

"You always have to go too far, don't you?" he says. "Anyone would think you wanted to turn people against you. I don't know why you do it, why you always have to show yourself up. It's as if ... when you sense that something you've said or done has upset people, you never try to make it right, the way other people would, instead you do your level best to make things worse. You're so destructive it's not fucking true," he says.

I glance up at him, try to look as if I don't care, try to grin, but can't quite manage it, it comes out as a pained, uneasy smirk.

"It's society's fault that I'm the way I am, Eskil," I say, trying to sound ironic.

"Please, Jon," he says earnestly. "I mean it."

"We're living in the free-market society that you and your party are so much in favour of," I go on, refusing to back down, trying to take refuge in irony. "The ideals of solidarity and fellowship are dead. These days we're all supposed to be masters of our own fortunes, which in practice means that we all believe we're totally responsible for the lives we have."

I hear Mum sigh.

"Jon!"

"The winners think they can take all the credit for their success, and the losers think it's their own fault that they've failed," I say, simply cutting him off, I won't back down, know that I'm making an even bigger fool of myself, but I go ahead anyway, can't help myself. "And since I'm a loser, I feel I have to be punished," I go on, can't stop, have to somehow see it through.

"Jon," Eskil cries. "I mean it! This is not funny!"

But I won't back down, I whip myself on.

"I want to be humiliated and ridiculed, because society has taught me that as a loser I don't deserve any better,"

I say. "That's why I am the way I am. While you, as a winner, believe you ought to be celebrated and saluted."

"Stop being so fucking flippant, dammit!" Eskil suddenly shouts, roars at me, and I flinch, stare at him with fear in my eyes, only for a second, then I twist my face back into a grin, look at the floor and try to laugh the whole thing off, give a little chuckle, but I look unsure, I know I do, look uneasy.

Two seconds.

"You don't have to take it out on us, just because you're a poof," Eskil cries.

Silence.

What the hell did he just say? Where the hell did that come from? I look up at him, stare at him and feel the grin fade, the grin seems to slide off my face, and his words seem to lodge inside me and swell, lodge and resound inside me.

"Don't pretend you don't remember, Jon," Eskil says, frowning and curling his upper lip, baring his front teeth. He eyes me, gives a little shake of his head.

"Remember what?" I say, look at him, don't know what he's talking about.

"What you said to Hilde at Mum's sixtieth birthday party."

I turn to Hilde, she's sitting there looking straight at me, grave-faced, and I must have said something to her, I can tell.

"How you thought there were so many attractive men there," Eskil says.

My stomach lurches at his words, I can't remember saying that, but I realize I must have done, I can tell from Hilde's face that I must have done. There's total silence,

Mum is confused, her eyes flick back and forth, she looks quite distraught. She picks up the picture of the little boy again, looks at it and puts on a smile, tries to block out what's being said, pretending not to hear what she's hearing, and Hilde regards me with eyes full of pity, a look designed to tell me that she knows how I feel. Both she and Eskil imagine that they know how I think and feel, they think they've found me out. Hilde has heard me pass some remark when I was drunk, they've discussed it at home and come to the conclusion that I'm gay, and now they have the idea that this is what lies behind everything I say or do. They're so fucking naive it's just not true, they've given Mum a grandchild and they think I'm hurt because I'm gay and can't give her the same, that must be why Hilde has been feeling so bloody sorry for me all this time, that must be why she didn't want to say anything about the adoption. Now I get it. Mum told them I was here when they called from the car and Hilde didn't want to say anything about the adoption after all. That's probably why she and Eskil were arguing when they got here, too. I look at them, one beat, I look at them and twist my face into a wrathful grin, make a desperate attempt to show them how ridiculous they are, and then I get up and go, don't know where I'm going, just go.

Vemundvik, July 14th–16th 2006

Once they reach their mid-forties, once their kids are old enough to fend for themselves, it's a well-known fact that many women take advantage of their new-found time and freedom to "go all arty-farty" as Mum so scornfully used to put it. With laughter in your voice and a faintly despairing note that became only moments later as scathing and scornful as Mum's, you told me how Berit had suddenly started taking an interest in art and culture. Out of nowhere this woman who had scarcely ever opened a book before had taken to buying and borrowing books: either what you so contemptuously described as novels about long-suffering, hard-pressed, but strong women in the Norwegian provinces, or volumes of poetry – which is to say, rhyming verse, always with a simple, straightforward message that almost invariably boiled down to the importance of seizing the day. You also told me that she'd started popping into the Arts Centre gallery after doing the shopping on Saturday mornings, and that unfortunately she didn't always confine herself to simply looking. On one occasion she had come home lugging an enormous figurative daub by – to quote you – some local nutter who thought all it took to be an artist was to slap a beret on your head. On another occasion she bought an abstract painting to which the so-called artist had glued a feather and some pencil shavings: a touch which, according to you, fooled Berit into thinking that this monstrosity of a picture was a fine example of cutting-edge modern art. Inspired by a woman friend who, according to you, kept anxiety and depression at bay by redecorating her whole home once a year, she also started subscribing to an interior design magazine, to give her ideas on how to do up the house. You said it was bad enough that she couldn't get her tongue round the foreign words and said "coroco", instead of "rococo" when you had guests – not just once, but again and again, until you had to leave the room, red with embarrassment – even worse was the fact that her dream home appeared to be some sort of layer-cake palace, all pillars and spires, carvings, balconies and glazed roof tiles glittering in the sunlight – a style which she would probably manage to trick Arvid into imitating when they eventually got round to doing up the outside of the house.

I remember being surprised by the aggressive, not to say hateful tone in which you related much of this, and more than once I had to calm you down and remind you that, still, it was good that Berit was trying to broaden her horizons. Never in my wildest dreams could I have imagined my own mum doing anything like that, so intent was she on fleeing from everything that wasn't directly entertaining. She moaned and sighed her way through the news every time she watched it, because it was so boring, and before they were halfway through a television debate she would be wagging her head and saying "blah, blah, blah", or breaking into her eternal "why can't they talk so ordinary folk can understand them!" rant. While Berit had actually started visiting galleries, and while she had attended at least one play staged at the Arts Centre by the National Theatre, my mum spent every single evening glued to *Falcon Crest* and *Wheel of Fortune* and the like, and while Berit actually went to the library and borrowed books, Mum went to the newsagents to buy the women's mags and scandal sheets which were the only things she read, apart from the *Namdal Workers' Weekly*. Although it's true she was always saying, "I don't know why I bother buying these rags, they print nothing but smut," as if to show that she wasn't a complete idiot, but a week later, when I reminded her of what she had said, her eyes would narrow and a sly look would come over her face, a look that seemed to say she knew she was doing something illegal, but she didn't give a shit. "I still have to have them, though, you know," she would say in a quick whisper and then she would laugh that husky smoker's laugh of hers.

All of this I told you, not just once, but lots of times, and because it made you feel that Berit wasn't so bad after all, you were always glad to hear it.

But when your mother started wearing a hat, it didn't matter what I said. A hat was a powerful and highly visible symbol in a small town such as Namsos. Berit might just as well have worn a sign round her neck saying, "I'm better than you lot". You hated that hat. It was round and red with a broad, flat brim that made it look like half of Saturn with one of its rings. You never said a word about it, but if we were having coffee in Hamstad's café on a Saturday morning and she came in wearing that hat you turned scarlet with embarrassment, and if she spotted us and came over to talk to us you were so surly and brusque and offhand with her that it was almost farcical, and then Silje and I would feel sorry for her and try to smooth things over as best we could.

Because, no matter how hard we strove to kid ourselves and everyone else that we didn't care what our mothers said or did, it made no difference. We told ourselves that we had our life and they had theirs, but no one could make us more embarrassed, annoyed, angry or worried on their behalf than our mothers, and there was no one we could less stand to see being slurred or slighted, unless we were the ones doing the slurring and slighting. Before Mum was diagnosed as having fibrositis, for instance, no one took her seriously when she complained that her back hurt and she couldn't work, and I remember the anger, bordering on hate, that I felt towards friends and neighbours who said, "Oh, but you look so well," thereby implying that she was only whingeing and whining.

Our mothers were also there in just about everything we said, thought and did. We didn't always do what they wanted, obviously, but what they wanted was never irrelevant to us, and we craved their praise as much as we dreaded their rejection. We might be embarrassed by how shamelessly eager they were to tell other people how well we were doing at school, and how far we would go in life, but we did nothing to stop them, apart from rolling our eyes while they stood there boasting about us. "Well, it's not that he isn't bright, that's for sure," Berit was always saying about you, before adding: "Although he's not very practical, it has to be said." As if she thought such a slight jocular modification would lend more credibility to her words and make the listener forget that this was a mother talking about her son.

The constant fear of them finding out that we were more than just friends was another instance of the way in which they were always with us. Mum settled down a bit after I told her straight out that we weren't gay, but she was still wary and we became even more careful than we had been before. No more locking my bedroom door, turning up the music and trusting that she wouldn't know what was going on. No more of you sleeping over because it was late and you "couldn't be bothered" going home, this being our usual excuse. If we went away together for a few days, renting a cottage somewhere, we also started booking it under false names, so no one would know who we really were if they found out what we were up to. At night we usually shared a sleeping bag, but we always made a point of unrolling the spare one, laying it on the other bed and rumpling it up a bit to make it look as if we were each sleeping in our own bed, just in case somebody happened to look in. And on the rare occasion when we used a condom we were very careful not to just chuck it in the bin afterwards. We always took out whatever was on the very top, dropped in the condom and made sure it was well covered by other rubbish.

Still, though, so we did get caught once. We had rented a cottage at Namsos Campsite under fake names and spent a great first couple of days drinking white wine, writing songs and having a lot of fun making everyone around us think that we were rich men's sons from the west side of Oslo. We sauntered about with our sweaters tied around our shoulders and our hands in our pockets, calling each other Rikard and Wilhelm Jr. I never really got into the part, though. Either I didn't dare to let myself go completely or I was so determined to let myself go that I wound up overdoing it and sounding and acting like a bad caricature of a drawling upper-class twit. You, on the other hand, simply became Wilhelm Jr. You pretended to have difficulty understanding the Trøndelag dialect of the woman in the campsite kiosk and whenever we passed other campers you would be sure to say things like, "in my father's circles", but you never took the snooty, west-side manner any further than that. You were also affable, gallant and extremely polite. You held the door open for ladies going into the kiosk, you smiled and nodded to the other campers and when we were queuing for the sinks in the campsite shower block you would happily give up your place to someone older or someone with children.

But on the evening of the second day we got caught. We were sitting drinking in the light of a low red sun that hung glowing behind the pines, and we were so busy trying to come up with the right tune for some lyrics that Silje had written for us that we forgot where we were and fell back into the Namsos dialect in between all our humming. I don't know how long we'd been out of character, but suddenly the owner of the campsite was standing right in front of us. He was a tall, skinny, stooped man with a comb-over and dark sweat stains under the arms of his shirt and he glared at us for some time with beady, hostile eyes before spitting out a question as to what we had to hide if we found it necessary to go around pretending to be somebody we weren't. You immediately switched to an Oslo drawl and tried to explain it away by saying that we had just been fooling about and trying to imitate the accent, but he said we could stick our imitations up our arses, because he knew who we were and what we were up to.

I automatically assumed that he really did know who we were and what we were up to and – slightly drunk as I was, and angry and half in panic at being found out – I surprised you and myself by jumping up from my camping chair and snapping at him that it was none of his fucking business what we did in bed. The minute I said it I was filled with a mixture of delight, relief and pride, but then I saw the baffled look on his face and realized that he hadn't the faintest idea of what we got up to in bed. I stood there gaping, humming and hawing and trying to come up with some sort of excuse. I couldn't, but it didn't matter, because he appeared to be every bit as flustered as I was. He asked no more questions, just slunk quietly away.

We reassured ourselves by saying that he probably thought we'd given false names because we were crooks or were planning to leave without paying, and after a while, once we were sure that he wasn't coming back to ask for our real names, we grew positively elated, our spirits higher than ever. Again and again we told each other how we had really put him in his place. We laughed and described the look on his face and the way he had plodded off, feeling more and more like the two liberated, proud, invulnerable young men we so very much wanted to be. In our own eyes we had shown ourselves to be every bit as brave as Ginsberg, Burroughs and Kerouac and it was not the disconcerted and somewhat bemused owner of Namsos Campsite we had defied, but the average Namsos man as we liked to think of him: a bigoted, intolerant, narrow-minded provincial who was out to stop us from living the way we wanted to. I can still remember the deep sense of togetherness I felt as we sat there, going over the whole experience again and again. No, it was more than that – I'd go so far as to say that what I felt was love, and for the rest of that evening and night I remember longing for and dreaming of a chance to show that love.

Mind you, that was something I often dreamed of. Banal though it was, I used to imagine you falling ill or getting hurt or being in some sort of danger and I would be the one who came to your aid when everyone else had failed you and, again banally, I always imagined that this would lead you to declare your great and unconditional love for me, something which was hard to envisage ever happening in real life, actually, because even though I knew you enjoyed being with me, that you relaxed, opened up, and that you were less concerned then with maintaining your cool, tough image than when you were with other people, it bothered you if I behaved towards you the way a lover would normally do. When we had sex you weren't the slightest bit shy, but afterwards, if I snuggled up to you, wanting to lie in the crook of your arm, or if I put my arms round your waist when I was on the back of your moped, or if we were standing next to one another and I brushed you gently with my hand you became edgy, embarrassed, and you would immediately try to find some tactful excuse to pull away. "Shh," you might say, putting your finger to your lips. "I thought I heard someone." And then you would wrench yourself free and go over to the window, as if to check whether there was anyone out there. I knew you didn't want to hurt me, and I didn't want to put you in a situation where you felt pressured into doing so, and this – as well, of course, as the fear of being hurt and rejected – led me to act as if I'd been taken in. "There it was again," I would say, and then I'd prick up my ears and be on my guard as well.

I knew why you shied away from me, or at least I thought I did. Exchanging such physical gestures of affection would make it more difficult to carry on acting as though sleeping with a person of the same sex was no more than an innocent exploration of our bodies and our sexuality. It would take our relationship to a new and more serious level, and you weren't quite ready for that yet. There was so much at stake, you needed time, so I decided to stop coming on to you like that for a while.

But then it happened, what had been bound to happen: our secret got out, the rumour that we were gay began to spread and we were forced into making the decision that we had put off making for so long.

Mum never got what you'd call drunk, certainly not when I was around, but one evening, when she had braved the pain of the fibrositis and the attendant dread of social gatherings and gone to one of those hen parties that she had been to so often in the past, she came home in a taxi at half-past eight, obviously plastered and with a bitter, tortured look on her face. "If only it had been you and not your brother whose balls had been ruined. You don't need yours, anyway," she said as I crouched down to help her off with her shoes, and after a brief fit of hysterical laughter she put her hands to her face and burst into tears. Later, I discovered that the owner of the campsite had got hold of your name by checking the registration number of the moped and that this was where the rumour about us being gay had started. But just at that moment I couldn't figure out where Mum's friends could have heard what they'd heard, and so I sat there listening numbly to an incoherent, tearful account of how the party's hostess, seemingly in all innocence but secretly desperate to humiliate her, had asked Mum ever so sweetly if it was true that I was gay, and that I was going out with the vicar's stepson. According to Mum, the other women at the party had spent the whole evening talking at great length and in glowing terms about their own husbands, children and grandchildren, and in the endless competition to see who was the happiest and most successful, Mum had milked me and my excellent school grades for all I and they were worth, "just to have this thrown in my face", as she put it.

The next day she tried to make out that she'd forgotten the whole thing, but she wasn't fooling anyone. She stayed out of my way as much as she could and if we did find ourselves in the same room she avoided my eye and made a show of being busy with things that weren't important or that certainly didn't need to be done right then. Not only that but she kept saying that she hadn't blacked out like that since her teens. "I don't remember a thing, I really don't. When did I actually get home? In a taxi? Was I very drunk? Oh, I'm so embarrassed! Just as well the neighbours didn't see me!" and so on, and I put on a smile of sorts and tried to look unconcerned.

I remember we were roaming around the east side of the town when I told you all this. You were white with rage. Why the hell did I let myself be treated like that, you asked, and even though I made excuses for Mum by saying that she'd been drunk, and even though I tried to explain how much she had sacrificed for me and what a good, caring mother she could be, it touched me to see you like that. Whether it was because I couldn't bring myself to be angry with her myself and needed you to be angry for me, or whether it was simply good to see and to know that you cared about me and that it upset you to see someone hurt me, I don't know, but I remember telling you that I loved you. I had never said it before and I still remember how it felt, standing there just after the words had left my mouth. I've never had children, and I doubt I ever will, but if I were trying to be poetic, I would say that uttering those particular words was much like a mother letting her child go out into the world and hoping that people will receive him or her well and be good to them.

As you did. "I love you too," you said, and since you didn't like extravagant words and shows of emotion and because I was so happy and felt so moved at that moment that I was afraid to spoil it all by saying something you would consider pompous or pathetic, I said nothing else for some time. We strolled side by side past the wire fence around Van Severen's sawmill and I remember the spray from one of the hoses that kept the timber damp falling right over onto the pavement, leaving a dark, narrow band on the sun-baked tarmac. I don't know whether it's nostalgia for my childhood in the sawmill town of Namsos or an echo of the happiness I felt at that moment that runs through me today when I catch the whiff of wet timber and sawdust, but I am filled, at any rate, with a strange little surge of happiness, a sense of belonging maybe.

Alongside the happiness I felt right then and in the days that followed there was, of course, uncertainty and fear. We were at an age when you tend to be self-centred and quick to make a big drama and a big deal out of the smallest things, but this really was a big deal. It's true that we thought people were more interested in whether we were gay or not than they probably were, nonetheless we were right in thinking that the way in which we chose to deal with our relationship and the rumours of our homosexuality would have major and definitive consequences for our own futures. I'm as convinced of this now as I was back then. In a way it was kind of exhilarating, this feeling that everything really was at stake, and there were times over the next few days when I was pompous enough to tell myself that at least I was leading a more intense and more fascinating life than most people. There were other times, though, when I was seized by a paralysing sense of dread: I could be sitting practising or maybe watching TV and all at once and for no reason that I could see the nausea would rise up in my throat, a cold sweat break out on the back of my neck and my brow turn cold and clammy. At times like that I had a desperate urge to resolve all of the questions that were churning around in my head, and even though I felt sick at the thought of broaching the subject with you, I probably would have done if it hadn't been for Berit's sudden death, after which, for a while, none of this mattered.

I'm not exactly sure what the post-mortem revealed, but I seem to remember that it had to do with some sort of heart defect. In any case, she simply keeled over in a shoe shop, without any warning, and she was dead before the ambulance arrived. I'd never known anyone who had lost someone close to them, so I wasn't sure what to expect when Silje and I were standing on the front step of your and Arvid's house, waiting for you to open the door. I had the idea that the grief you bore would be so great that it would show itself in ways I would never forget, and I remember being surprised at how relaxed you seemed. It knocked me off-balance when, as if it were the most natural thing in the world, you started talking about some lyrics that Silje had just written or a film you were looking forward to seeing, and I didn't quite know how to react when you told a funny story you had heard and then roared with laughter. To begin with I thought this was some sort of defence mechanism, that your apparent air of calm was a sign that your mother's death hadn't sunk in yet, but that couldn't be it because you spoke about Berit and her death as well. Even then, though, it was no heartbroken, devastated young man who spoke, as I had imagined and as I had hoped, since that would have given me the chance to comfort and support you, thereby proving the love that I so longed to show. The only time I saw you betray any kind of pain or sorrow was when you and Silje and I were walking along Havnegata and we passed the artist whose work Berit had liked so much, but whom you had once called a local nutter who thought that all it took to be an artist was to slap a beret on his head. You didn't say anything right away, but you went very quiet and a little later when we were sitting in Silje's living room, listening to Captain Beefheart's *Trout Mask Replica*, you gave vent to a brief but moving emotional outburst in which, in a voice that shook slightly, you admitted to feeling guilty for the way you had treated Berit. You blamed yourself for having been cold and hard and you couldn't forgive yourself for having made fun of her when she told you about a book she had read or showed you a picture she had bought. You also believed that her sudden interest in the arts had actually been an attempt of sorts to get closer to you, which just made the whole thing worse. The novels, the volumes of poetry, the art gallery, the National Theatre productions; the way you saw it, it wasn't because she had woken up one morning feeling like a new woman that she had decided to explore all of this. No, she had simply been trying to get through to you by showing an interest in, and learning more about, things that she knew meant a lot to you. "And even though I knew this right from the start, I pushed her away," you said.

Namsos, July 5th 2006. At Wenche's

It's okay now, everything's cool, just forget what happened back there, don't think about it. It'll be a long, fucking time before I talk to Mum again, though, not to mention Eskil and Hilde, can't think when I'll ever want to see them again. I walk up the steps to the front door. Ring the bell. Hook my thumbs into the loops on my belt and stand there trying to look laid-back. I glance down at the steps and up again. Then I see my name underneath the bell button. If she still hasn't taken my name down, she must still have some faint hope. I could be doing the wrong thing showing up here like this if she's hoping I'll come back, I don't want to give her false hope, either. Maybe I should have gone to the cottage after all, bought food and wine and taken the bus over there, spent some time on my own, read books, gone fishing, taken it easy, but it's too late now. I hear the sound of the hall door opening, I'll have to ask if I can stay here till things sort themselves out. They always do, eventually. I take a step back, lean one elbow on the iron banister behind me, try to look relaxed, laid-back, look as if I just popped by to say hello, just happened to be in the neighbourhood. And then the front door opens, slowly, and there's Wenche. She looks at me, I try to smile, but she doesn't smile back, her face is still, expressionless almost, and she doesn't say anything, just stares at me.

"Hi, Wenche," I say.

"Hi."

Two beats.

"Well, you look thrilled to see me," I say, attempting a little laugh. But she doesn't laugh, she shuts her eyes and breathes a big sigh, opens her eyes again and stands there looking at me. She has these kind of affectedly weary eyes.

"What do you want, Jon?" she asks.

"What do I want?"

"Yes."

I nod at the label under the doorbell.

"Well, it looks like I live here," I say with another attempt at a laugh, but she doesn't laugh back, just blinks her eyes languidly and curls one corner of her mouth.

"Oh, please!" she says.

I look at her, realize this is a bit awkward, embarrassing, and I stop laughing.

"Sorry," I say.

"What are you doing here?" she asks.

I look into her green eyes, eyes like gooseberries.

"Because I've nowhere else to go, simple as that," I say, just telling her the plain truth.

She rolls her eyes.

"Oh, thanks a lot," she says. "You really know how to flatter a girl."

"I didn't mean it like that," I say with a short laugh.

She looks me straight in the eye, holds my gaze for a second, then a small smile spreads across her face, she thaws slightly, shakes her head and steps aside, motions me into the flat.

"Oh, come on in," she says. "You can sleep on the couch."

"Thanks!" I say, smiling, feeling relieved, didn't even have to ask if I could stay the night, it sorted itself out. I kick off my shoes, dump them on the shoe rack, hang my jacket on the slightly lopsided wooden coat stand. The same shoe rack, the same coat stand as when I lived here, it's weird, it feels as though I've hardly been gone at all, and yet everything's totally different. It's like coming home and being a visitor at the same time.

"But where are your things – didn't you bring them?" she asks.

"Nope," I say, being totally straight with her. I know she likes that side of me, my impulsive, spontaneous streak. She used to say that it drove her crazy, but I knew she liked it, liked being the one who straightened things out and looked after me, the one who was in control.

"No bass, no clothes, no toiletries even?" she asks.

"Nope, I just upped and left," I say.

She shuts her eyes and shakes her head despairingly, looks at me and smiles. Just as I thought, she likes it, I can tell.

"I see," she says, putting her hands on her hips, smiling at me. "So what is it this time?"

I shrug, smile back.

"Oh, I had a bit of a set-to with Mum and Eskil," I say.

"With Grete and Eskil? I thought you were on tour."

"No, no! I left the band," I say, come right out with it, I might as well, she'll find out anyway when she talks to Lars and Anders.

"What?" she says, sticking her head an inch or so further forward, staring at me round-eyed. "Oh, for heaven's sake! You know what, you never change. You left – just like that? One minute it's the best thing that ever happened to you, and the next ... why on earth did you leave the band?"

I look at her and smile rather ruefully, indicating to her that I don't feel like talking about it right now. But she's not about to quit. She's still the same, still as persistent.

"Well?" she says.

"Please, Wenche," I say. "Let's talk about this later."

"Why?"

"Hey. Don't start interrogating me straight away," I say a little wearily, but still smiling. "I'm just in the door," I say.

"Interrogating you? I only asked."

I look at her, give a faint sigh.

"It just got to the point where we had to go our separate ways," I say. "I suppose we were less alike than we thought, both musically and personally."

"I see. And the three of you just suddenly discovered this? You couldn't have waited till after the tour?"

"Yeah, well, we probably could have. But it didn't work out that way."

"Oh, no?" she says. "And why not?"

I eye her beseechingly, don't feel like talking about this any more, not right now. But she won't quit, still the same old Wenche, persistent as always, looks me straight in the eye, demanding an answer. I wait a moment, sigh.

"Oh, you know, it was just a case of the proverbial last straw," I say, a mite reluctantly. "They started accusing me of being negative and I was pissed off because they hadn't spoken up sooner, instead they'd actually laughed at my black humour and played along with me, and then we started arguing, and well ... here I am!"

Wenche stares at me, shakes her head despairingly.

"Okay, okay!" she says, raising her hands as if to say, "I give in," as if agreeing that I'm hopeless.

"Oh, Jon, really!" she laughs. It suits her to have me like this, suits her that I'm the sort of person she can take care of. "Go on in and sit down," she says.

I smile, stick my hands in my pockets and stroll into the living room, the sweet smell of incense fills my nostrils and Joni Mitchell's voice comes slinking to meet me, a number from *Blue*, can't remember the title. Halfway into the room I stop, look around me. The ceiling light is gone and there are lighted candles on the windowsills and the dining table, tall candelabra with white candles that cast rippling shadows on the white walls.

"The place looks great," I say, looking at a big Rosina Wachtmeister print in a gold frame. "I really like it."

"Yeah, I'll bet you do!" she says, laughing.

"No, I mean it," I say, trying to sound sincere, smiling at her.

She smiles back.

"Well, thank you," she says, pauses, then: "Would you like a cup of tea?"

"No, thanks," I say.

"A glass of wine, then?"

"Well, only if you're having one! Don't open a bottle for my sake."

"As if I would," she says.

"Cheeky!" I retort.

We look at one another, laugh again, one beat, then she goes out to the kitchen. I walk across to the couch, flick a cushion out of the way and flop down, stretch my arms along the couch back.

"So, how's the course going?" I ask.

"Oh, fine," she says, then she pauses and I hear her pulling the plastic seal off the top of the wine bottle. "Not bad," she goes on. "It's a bit tough, though, obviously, what with me living here and not in Trondheim. But it's going okay."

"Hmm."

"And they've started putting the lectures online now, so it's easier than it was."

"Right," I say and I hear the hollow plop as the cork is pulled out of the wine bottle. A moment later she comes back into the living room.

"Here we are," she says, placing the bottle on the table and crossing to the glass-fronted cabinet in the corner, there's a nice tinkling sound as she pulls the doors open, a bit of chinking and clinking. She takes out two wineglasses I've never seen before, slender, orangey-red ladies' glasses, the sort that cost three hundred kroner each, made by some middle-aged woman wearing only one earring.

"So what happened at home this time?" she asks as she turns and comes back to the table. She doesn't look at me, takes the chair on the other side, picks up the bottle and fills our glasses.

"Oh, it wasn't any one thing," I say. "You know what it's like, we just don't get on all that well," I add, don't feel like talking about it, play the whole thing down, act as though there really isn't anything to talk about, it's just the usual story.

"Have you ever wondered why you don't get on?" she asks, putting down the bottle and looking straight at me with those green eyes, gooseberry eyes.

I don't answer immediately, force a feeble little smile, a plea to her to leave it alone.

"Huh?" she asks.

"Wenche, please!" I sigh.

"Well, have you?"

"Can't we talk about something else?"

"But it's important," she says, looks at me and smiles. "It's your mother and your brother we're talking about."

I look at her, the fire in those green eyes of hers, this intensity that I've never understood, don't know where she gets it from, this intensity. She smiles and tries to appear relaxed but she's so bloody persistent.

"I know, but I can't be bothered talking about it right now," I say and I pick up my glass, try to smile. "Cheers, then," I say.

She picks up her glass and takes a quick sip, doesn't even say cheers, it's like she's in a hurry.

"Why do you think you have such a difficult relationship with your mother and your brother?" she asks, looking straight at me, still smiling, but she's on the attack, I've only been here a few minutes and she's at it already.

I look at her, give it a moment, feel my hackles rising.

"Wenche, please," I say, irritated now, but keeping that pleading note in my voice, a voice that's begging her to stop. "Don't interrogate me," I add.

"I'm not interrogating you," she says.

"Well, it feels that way to me," I say. "It's always felt that way to me."

"Really."

"Yes," I say, managing a smile of sorts. "Being questioned like this, I've always felt like I was being interrogated."

Silence.

"If I've questioned you it was only because I loved you," she says. "Because I cared about you."

"Yeah, I know," I mumble, "but ..." I stop, sit there shaking my head gently, don't really know what to say, simply can't take talking about this right now and she's got no right to question me anyway, analyse me, I don't need to put up with it, it's her flat now, but still.

"But what?" She won't let up, sits there glowing, waiting.

"I don't know," I say, my voice sullen now, resigned.

"It's got nothing to do with interrogation," she says. "It's about closeness, the willingness to get close to another human being, the willingness to let another human being in. That's what it's about," she says.

"Yeah, sure," I mutter irritably. "That'll be right!"

"That'll be right?" she says.

I stare straight at her, don't say anything, let her know I'm not joking, I can't take this and it's time she understood that. But she doesn't get it, and she doesn't care, she's always been the same, she just won't quit.

"See, this is exactly the problem with you, Jon," she says. "Do you know that?"

"This?" I say.

"Yes, this!" she says. "The way you're carrying on right now. The fact that you shy away any time someone tries to get close to you."

"Is that so," I say in that irritable, indifferent voice.

"Yes, I mean just listen to yourself. Listen to the way you're talking right now. 'That'll be right', 'Is that so', 'Yeah, sure', the last thing you want is to talk to me!"

"But we are talking," I say.

"Yes, but not properly," she says.

I pick up my wineglass and take a little sip, put it down again, saying nothing, just getting more and more irritated, feel my heart starting to beat a bit faster, my pulse to pound, why did I come here, why the fuck did I come to her, will I never learn. I should have gone to the cottage after all.

"Have you ever wondered why you're like this?" she says, not letting up.

"All right, that's enough now," I say.

"Yes, but have you?"

"Okay, now stop it," I say, a little louder this time. If this isn't an interrogation I don't know what is.

"Stop hedging," she says, trying to seem less aggressive by smiling. "Couldn't you just try to have a proper conversation? Have you ever given any thought to why you're like this?" she asks again.

I look at her, shake my head.

"Wenche!" I say. "For the last time. I simply can't be bothered discussing myself and my character."

"No!" she says. "You never can, and you never could. And that's exactly what I wonder – whether you've ever given any thought to that? Have you? Have you ever asked yourself why you never want to talk about yourself, why you never let anyone in, not even the woman you live with?"

I look at my feet, give it a moment, it's fucking incredible, beyond belief, that she can go on like this, nagging at a person like this. I feel a surge of annoyance, give a loud snort and look up at her again.

"I thought there was something familiar about this," I say. "Us sitting like this, getting nowhere."

"Yes!" she says earnestly. "That's exactly what I'm saying. What I'm asking is why you think that's how it almost always ends up. Why does it stop there, why won't you talk, why are you so afraid of revealing yourself, showing who you really are and what you think and feel, why won't you let anyone in?"

"Look ... we're different you and I." I fling out a hand, pissed off, fed up. "Can't you just accept that? Maybe it's a gender thing, I don't know. In any case, I don't feel like discussing this right now. I'm exhausted."

"Do you know what I think?" she says.

"Wench!" I say. "Enough!"

"Do you know what I think?" she says again, not letting up. It's like she's not even listening to me, it's like an instinct with her, this, the way she lays into me. "This fear of intimacy and of letting people in," she says. "I think that this and what Lars and Anders call your negative attitude are two sides of the same coin. The same goes for the way you sometimes were with me when we were together. You know ... my friends thought you were gorgeous and since then more than one of them has told me that she envied me when we were together ... but when I told them how you treated me they didn't think you were quite so hot. It was as if I didn't even exist," she says. "There were times when you treated me as if I was invisible."

"Oh, really," I say.

"Well, didn't you? Even the way it ended. Out of the blue, almost as an afterthought, it comes out that you've decided to quit your job and go on tour and that you don't know what will happen to us when you get back," she says, dropping her jaw and spreading her hands, staring at me wide-eyed.

"I thought we were done with all that," I say.

"Well, we are in a way," she says. "But what I'm trying to say is that whatever lies behind this way of treating people is also what lies behind your fear of intimacy and behind what Lars and Anders call your negative attitude."

I look at her, try to grin.

"Been reading your psychology books again, have you?" I say.

She looks me straight in the eye, parts her lips, shakes her head.

"See, now you're trying to dissociate yourself again," she says.

"What?"

"The way you defuse and belittle what I'm trying to tell you by branding it in advance as a regurgitation of my psychology textbooks or something," she says. "Isn't that a way of dissociating yourself, isn't that a way of preventing me from getting through to you and striking a nerve in there? No matter what I said it wouldn't get through to you, because it's all just a regurgitation of my textbooks, right?"

I don't say anything for a moment, just sit there staring at her. And my temper rises, as if something is breaking loose inside me, something heavy, as if an explosion is on the way.

"Wenche," I say, swallowing, trying to steady my breathing, trying to calm down. "For the last time, stop it," I say, looking her straight in the eye.

But she doesn't stop.

"There, you see," she says, nodding at me vehemently. "Every time I get a bit closer to you, you do all you can to keep me at bay. Shall I tell what your problem is, though?" she says, getting more and more worked up, she's off and running now, it's like she's high. "Shall I tell you?"

"No," I say, shouting, pissed off. I stare at her furiously. "I realize you've thought a lot about this over the past two months and that you've really been looking forward to telling me what my problem is, as you put it, but no, you don't have to," I say. "Put a double line under this answer and file it alongside all the other psychology assignments you've completed, but spare me. I can't be bothered with this."

But she won't quit, she keeps going.

"Your problem is that with the best will in the world you can't see how anyone could like you or love you," she says. "You try to act so cool and laid-back, taking things as they come, when you're actually the most insecure person I've ever met," she says. "You try to make out that you're the kind of guy who doesn't care what people say, but you're the most fragile character I know. You're always on your guard, as if you're just waiting for confirmation that nobody likes you. No matter how nice they are to you, no matter how pleased they are to see you, you tell yourself that they don't really like you, that somehow it's all just an act on their part! You simply can't imagine that someone might actually like you, that someone might actually love you, and that's why you behave the way you do. You refuse to let other people get close to you because you're convinced that eventually it'll transpire that they don't like you, and the idea that people who don't like you have managed to get really close to you and know too much about you, that's a threat you just can't live with." She pauses for a moment, stares at me with those glowing green eyes, gooseberry eyes. "And that's why a lot of people, including Lars and Anders, see you as being negative and kind of touchy. It's exactly the same thing," she says, "I mean, you might as well take a negative view of things and people right from the start, because that way you won't be disappointed, right? And obviously if you start out with that sort of attitude it's hardly surprising that you also find it hard to show consideration for others, it's hardly surprising that you treat your girlfriend as if she doesn't exist, and it's hardly surprising that you're totally incapable of commitment."

I stare at her, boiling inside, who the fuck does she think she is, sitting there analysing me even when I ask her not to, invading me, that's what she's doing, I feel the urge to get up and roar, yell in her face, make her face explode and her mouth crack, lean across the table and just bawl right in her face, but I don't, that's exactly what she wants me to do, wants to goad me into exploding so she can say that she's hit the nail on the head, or something along those lines.

"Are you quite finished?" I ask with a strained grin.

"For now, yes," she says.

"Good!" I say, and I don't say any more. I pick up my wineglass and take a swig, put it down again with a careless smile. Stare at those green, bulging eyes of hers and her nasty rodent-like features, those thin, cracked lips. To think that I kissed those lips, that I could bring myself to do that, stick my tongue between those lips, the thought makes my stomach turn, every kiss feels like an assault, I feel sick just thinking about it.

"Well?" she says.

"Well what?" I say, I'm seething inside, but I merely smile, act confused, and I can see by her face that this gets to her, bet she wasn't expecting this, stare at her rodent-like face, see her mouth fall open, slowly. She looks at me and gives her head a little shake.

"Honestly, Jon," she says.

"Honestly what?" I say with a gleeful note in my voice.

"I've just explained to you what I think about something that concerns us both and that I feel it's important for us to talk about," she fumes. "I would have thought you might actually want to voice some of your own thoughts on the matter."

I stare at her: those sharp, rodent features, the skinny figure, the outline of the sagging breasts under her sweater. To think that I could ever have brought myself to cup my hands round her breasts, squeezed those foul excrescences and felt them protruding between my finger and thumb, that I could do that. The very thought makes me feel sick. And that I forced myself to sleep with her, that I was actually capable of that, each time feels like an assault, and her questioning of me feels like a fucking assault.

"Don't you think so?" she says. "Don't you think I've a right to hear what you think?"

One beat, then I lean towards her, resting my elbows on my knees.

"You know what," I say, saying it with a slight quiver in my voice, trying to maintain my cool smile, but not quite managing it. "I'm not going to say one word about what I think or feel about that matter," I say. "There's no way I'm going to play the part of patient just so you can practise what you've learned on your psychology course. I don't live here any more, and if you want to start spouting all that fucking rigmarole of yours there's nothing I can do about it. But refuse to answer, that I can do and that's what I mean to do."

Silence.

"You're not well, Jon," she says. "You need help."

"No, Wenche!" I say, grinning fiercely at her. "I need a couch to crash on. The idea that I need your help is just wishful thinking on your part."

"Oh, Jon!" she cries, shaking her head. "It's sad to see you like this."

Two seconds.

"I didn't come back to you, Wenche," I say, staring at her, because I know she wanted me back, and I know that this hits her where it hurts. "I simply didn't have anywhere to sleep tonight, that's the reason, that's the only reason I'm here."

"What do you think this is?" she asks, and she looks at me, tries to look surprised and amused, but the corners of her mouth twitch slightly. She swallows – it hit home, I can tell, and I feel a malicious thrill run through me.

Two seconds.

"Would you like me to tell you how I see you?" I ask, in that tremulous voice, a voice that quivers with delight and fury. "You've had plenty to say about me, so surely I can say a little bit about you now." Pause. "You're the sort of person that eats people up," I say. "You want total control, and in your efforts to get it you invade people and go beyond all the bounds of decency. You disguise it as love of your fellow man and as a sign of your concern and fondness for other people, but in actual fact it's just an attempt to control other people. You interrogate and you question, you dissect and analyse, and all of this you do in order to gain access to the information necessary to control. That's how it seemed to me when we were together, and that's how it seems to me now," I say, glaring at her. "That's exactly what made me decide to get away from it all," I go on, "and that's exactly why I'm so happy that we're no longer together. I probably shouldn't say this, but I'm going to anyway. You may not be a psychopath, but you sure as hell have psychopathic tendencies," I say, churning, seething, inside. "And when you say that I can't imagine how anyone could love me, then I have to say that the exact opposite is true of you. You simply cannot comprehend that I would want to get away from you, or that anyone would ever think of leaving you. In your world that's just not possible, it's like there's no such option, and if, even so, anyone does leave you, or expresses dissatisfaction with you and the way you are, well, then there must be something wrong with that person, he needs help, as you just said. Jesus Christ, Wenche!" I say, I shout, straighten my shoulders and fling out a hand, glaring furiously at her. "Why do you think the friendships you make with other women only last for a year or two at most? Why do you think they're all suddenly so busy in the evenings?" I say. "Hmm? Well, I'll tell you one thing! It's certainly not because everybody but you is crazy and off their heads and in need of help, as you seem to think!"

Total silence.

"Poor you Jon," she says softly, eyeing me and shaking her head. She tries to look as though she feels sorry for me, but fails, she's on the verge of tears, I can tell, she's about to break down, and I realize that I'm enjoying this, can't help but enjoy it, I'm filled with such disgust, hate almost.

"Don't even try it, Wenche." I say, saying it straight out, grinning fiercely at her. "I know you far too well."

"Try what?" she asks.

"You know I'm right," I say. "I can tell by your face. You're trying to look as though you feel bad for me, but you're only doing that to make me feel insecure," I say, then pause.

"You sit alone here night after night with your psychology books," I say, nodding sharply. "Why in hell's name do you think that is? Why do you think all of your friends are gone? Gry, Ann-Britt, Kristine, all gone, the lot of them! Why do you think that's happened?" I say, hitting her where it hurts most, I shouldn't do it, but I can't stop myself, I detest her. She shakes her head, not about to quit, trying for as long as possible to convince me that she feels sorry for me.

"You're actually sicker than I thought, Jon," she says. "For God's sake, can't you see that? Can't you see how desperate you are? You're twisting everything, accusing me of being a psychopath just because I try to make you face up to your problems. Just listen to yourself! You're so afraid to let other people in that you'll go to any lengths to prevent it!"

I shake my head, sneer.

"Let other people in? It's not just anybody else we're talking about here," I say seething. "It's you we're talking about, Wenche. And if there's one thing I've learned from living with you as long as I did it's that no one should ever on any account let you get too close to them. No one should ever let a psychopath get too close to them. It took me a long time to learn that, but I did learn and I say again: I am not going to discuss myself and my character with you. I'm wise to all your tricks, you can't fool me, so you might as well stop trying. You're not going to get your claws into me again, I know that's what you're after, but it won't work. And, like I said, I won't be back. I came here this evening because I needed a couch to crash on and that's all."

"You're scaring me now, Jon," she says.

I just stare at her, grin furiously.

"I mean it, Jon," she says. "You're frightening me and I'd like you to leave. Please go, right now."

"Act scared if you like, Wenche," I say. "You can try till the cows come home, but you won't make me feel insecure. Those days are over."

"Jon," she says. "Please go, or I'll call the police!"

"Oh, I'm going," I say. "Don't you worry. I wouldn't dream of staying."

I pick up my wineglass and drain it in one gulp, get to my feet and stand for a moment regarding her, that nasty rodent-like face of hers and those thin lips, remember with horror what it was like to kiss those dry lips, my stomach turns at the thought.

"Poor you," I say, sneering and shaking my head. "You're the saddest, loneliest person I know!"

She looks at me and swallows, bites the inside of her lower lip, she's close to tears now, close to breaking down.

"Just go, Jon," she says.

"Christ," I say, grinning and shaking my head again. "Talk about being desperate. I can't have been here more than half an hour and you've already run through just about the whole gamut of emotions in your efforts to make me crack. Everything from honest and sincere to despairing, annoyed, afraid, and now you're going all out, resorting to tears," I say. "So, is this the grand finale? Is this where I'm supposed to cave in and become like putty in your hands? Is this where I'm supposed to start feeling sorry for you and see everything the way you want me to see it? Well, I'll tell you one thing: that's not going to happen!"

"Get out!" she screams. She raises one arm, points to the door, stares at me with big, wide-open eyes, those green, gooseberry eyes, there's madness in her eyes, and I look at her and grin.

"Bye, then, Wenche," I say, my voice cold, indifferent. And then I just go, put on my shoes, lift my jacket off the coat stand and walk out, walk off down the street, walk away nice and easy, smiling. I'll head over to the cottage in Vemundvik now, pick up some food and drink and go down to the bus station, head over to the cottage and have a few days to myself. It'll all sort itself out.

Within a month of Berit's death you had had enough of living in the same house as Arvid, so you moved in with Silje and Oddrun. You could stay with them till university started in the September.

A rift had developed between you and Arvid almost as soon as Berit was gone. He had started making all the arrangements for the funeral the very day after she died, but to everyone's great surprise you suddenly insisted that the funeral had to be a civil affair. At first this made Arvid feel sorry for you because he thought you were suffering from some form of shock. But he soon became so angry and frustrated over this that with me as a terrified onlooker he lost his legendary self-possession. You had no shame, he roared, you'd been jealous of him from the day he and Berit met and this just showed how far you were willing to go to punish him for taking your mother away from you. We were in the kitchen at your house, and I remember the little spray of spittle from his lips as he bent forward till your faces were almost touching and yelled at you that you were a total egomaniac who had always begrudged Berit and him their happiness. You tried to stay as cool and calm as always, but you were trembling with rage as you told Arvid that he had never known Berit, that she had tried hard to be the woman he wanted her to be, but she never could. And, you went on, not long before she died she had broken down in front of you and said that she felt like a stranger in her own life. She wasn't a religious woman, she couldn't stand the Christian community that she'd become a part of, and she had told you quite frankly that she was thinking of leaving Arvid and finding a place of her own. With glistening eyes and quivering voice you said that you hated yourself for not giving her your support back then, you had simply told her that it was up to her, and you'd made it clear to her that you didn't want to hear any more about it. Giving her a funeral befitting the woman she had really been was the least you could do.

Arvid didn't believe one word of what you said, he was convinced that you were only out to punish him and since he stuck as stubbornly to his guns as you did to yours there was nothing for it but to arrange two separate ceremonies: a religious service in the hospital chapel one day, and a civil ceremony in the community centre the day after.

Although it was only a couple of months until you moved to Trondheim to study, there was no way you could stay with him after that and it was a relief for both you and Arvid when Silje and Oddrun offered to let you move in with them.

I began to feel more and more uncomfortable at Silje's and Oddrun's place, although at the time I didn't know why. I was often irritable, bad-tempered even, when we were together, but since it was the very arrogance that I had once admired and envied in you that now pissed me off I was confused by my own feelings. I told you I thought you'd changed, that you'd gone from being self-confident to self-righteous, condescending and contemptuous. Now, though, I can see that it was me who had changed.

The fact was that during the last six months at senior secondary something had happened that had made me aware of things I'd noticed but never given much thought to before. It suddenly dawned on me that it was as exotic an experience for Silje to visit my home as it was for me to visit hers, and certain things Oddrun had said to me made me realize that Silje told her stories about how Mum and Eskil and I lived, that they talked about how the television was always on, whether anyone was watching it or not, that they talked about the ketchup bottle that was put out on the table no matter what we were having for dinner, about the way Mum and Eskil and I talked to one another, and about the over-furnished living room with all its ornaments and family photos and the tasteless curtains tied back with gold ribbons. Once, when I had voiced some precocious and no doubt well-rehearsed opinion on why Kieslowski was such a great director, I remember Oddrun smiling appreciatively and saying how wonderful it was that I'd turned out the way I had, considering that I'd been brought up in a house without books – which was not too far from the truth, since the bookshelf at home held only three volumes of *The Norwegian Yearbook* and a slightly larger collection of *Nordic Crime Chronicles* but Oddrun couldn't possibly have known this unless Silje had told her and in any case I didn't think she had any right to point this out it to me. I felt hurt on Mum's behalf, it was a mean thing to say, especially when she was as sick and depressed as she was.

And this may have been why I started to dislike that air of arrogance that I'd once tried to imitate and adopt. The way Oddrun shook her head sadly at the fact that so few Namsos folk ever bothered to pick all the wonderful mushrooms that they had growing right on their doorsteps, but left them to rot instead; how Silje bought *The Crying Boy* and hung it on the living room wall to give her mother a good laugh when she came home; that she spoke of the technical college as if it were a mental institution and the girls at the supermarket checkout as if they were retarded. I began to see such things as digs at my mother.

But I was also deeply resentful of my mother at that time. She never came straight out and asked me whether I could stay home and give her a hand, but the more time I spent with her and on housework, the more dependent on me she became, until it got to the point where I could tell that she simply expected me to be there at her beck and call, and this in turn filled me with an anger I was never able to express properly and didn't quite know how to deal with. I would find myself hating her when she lay on the couch watching television while I stacked firewood or washed cups, and there were times when I told myself that her friends were right when they said she made a meal of her affliction, that she wallowed in her ill health and embraced the role of victim as it allowed her to order about me and anyone else close to her. But before long this bitterness and anger always gave way to guilt, and this – along with the knowledge that I never protested when Silje and Oddrun made fun of her background and everything she represented – meant that I had an almost constant sense of letting her down.

The fact that I too had been so keen to poke fun at and distance myself from small-town people and small-town life made it even more difficult for me to disagree with them. I may have suspected that there was a difference between the contempt you and I showed for Namsos and its residents and the contempt shown by Silje and her mother, but only later did it strike me that our contemptuousness was a form of self-defence. While Silje and Oddrun made fun of Namsos because they actually did feel superior to the locals in just about every area in which they felt it was worth being superior, our contempt was a response to the contempt we felt we encountered in this small town. We were just two insecure teenagers, eager to reassure ourselves that we were worth something even though we were different, and this we did by bad-mouthing those whom we thought were bad-mouthing us.

As Silje and I grew further and further apart I became more aware of how I had sucked up to her and Oddrun and how you were still sucking up to them. I remember one occasion when we were at Silje's house while a couple of workmen were there. They had been hired to sand down, wash and repaint the house, but Silje's mother never gave them a moment's peace, she found fault with everything they did and was so condescending and so critical that even Silje looked embarrassed. Not you, though. I saw the way you glanced at her mother and raised your eyebrows when the workmen's backs were turned, as if you and she were natural allies in the company of such morons.

Even worse was the time when we bumped into an old classmate of mine on the street and took him along with us to Silje's place to play Trivial Pursuit. Silje didn't say a word when he couldn't answer the question as to which World War II commander had been known as the Desert Fox, nor when he didn't know which famous writer was associated with the Globe Theatre, but the longer this went on, the more questions he passed on, the heavier Silje sighed. The only question he was able to answer had to do with an actor who had appeared in *Police Academy II* – which threw us slightly since this wasn't the sort of question anyone we mixed with should have been able to answer, and when Silje burst out laughing he must have thought she was remembering some scene from the film, so he burst out laughing too. It was only when he saw the sympathetic look on my face that he realized Silje wasn't laughing at the same thing as him at all, and although he stayed a little while longer for appearance's sake that was the moment when he realized he wasn't welcome there. "Do me a favour, don't ever bring that dummy here again," Silje said after he had gone and to my great disappointment, I remember, you started to apologize. You, whom I had once regarded as the bravest person in the world, the one person who always spoke up if someone was being unfairly treated, not only did you not defend him, you actually apologized for bringing him to the house in the first place. We hadn't wanted to, you said, we'd tried to hint that he wasn't welcome, but he had insisted on tagging along anyway – all of which was true enough, but it didn't help matters.

When I looked at you, I saw myself as I had been not that long ago and this may have made me dislike this behaviour even more than I would have done, I don't know. At any rate, I remember how angry I was, I remember that feeling of somehow slipping into a bitter, resentful mood and not being able to get myself out of it again. I really wanted to, I didn't want to lose what we had, so I tried to pull myself together, to be the person I'd always been, but it was no use, and I found myself saying less and less when we were at your and Silje's place. I lost all enthusiasm, I no longer got any pleasure from things I'd once enjoyed, I was listless and sluggish, and while you and Silje were every bit as enthusiastic as before and tried to involve me in one project after another, I refused to play along and made a big show of being uninterested. I could be sitting in a chair, yawning and acting up, and if you asked what I thought or felt about a piece of writing or an art project you had produced or were planning to produce, I would merely say "Hmm" and pretend that I hadn't been paying attention.

All of this only served to drive us further and further apart, of course. You never said anything about wanting to end our friendship, but the signals you sent out were clear enough. You started avoiding situations in which we would be alone together and suddenly you no longer liked or you'd do down things that we had both enjoyed and that had in some way bound us to each other. Writers and bands whose genius we had extolled and whom we had spent untold hours discussing and immersing ourselves in were now, in your eyes, no longer so great, and all of a sudden you started talking about possibly going to Oslo University instead of Trondheim, where I was planning to go. It wasn't too late to change your mind, you said, and when you presented the pros and cons of these two alternatives you were careful not to cite me as one of the advantages of going to Trondheim; even when I was quite blatantly angling for you to say that you'd rather be in the same town as me you didn't mention it. You made such a point of it sometimes that I was left in no doubt: you were simply trying to tell me that I was not a part of your plans for the future.

I got over this long, long ago, of course. But sitting here in our old cottage, writing and looking back on it, I feel something of the same nausea I felt when it began to dawn on me that you didn't want any more to do with me, the chill dread that washes over you when you realize that you're not actually wanted. I remember how much it hurt to walk away from you on the day when I finally knew beyond any doubt that that was what you wanted. Every bit of me screamed to go back to you, but common sense forced my feet to keep walking.

For a long time I tried to tell myself you had backed out because you couldn't cope with the serious turn our relationship had taken. I told myself that it had scared you to discover how much you actually meant to me, I told myself that my slightly hesitant caresses and the joy I had shown when you said you loved me had made it impossible to go on pretending that what was going on between us was merely an innocent exploration of our sexuality and that you couldn't cope with the alternative; you couldn't bring yourself to admit that you were gay. That university was just around the corner, that we had talked about sharing a flat in Trondheim when we moved there, that we were going to enter adulthood, so to speak, as a gay couple, thus confirming the rumours about us, only made it all seem that much more serious and terrifying, of course, and in the end it had been too much for you.

I remember calling you once when I was drunk and cursing you for being a coward. I accused you of only having moved in with Silje in order to put paid to the rumour that we were gay. You'd never been the person you made yourself out to be, I said, you'd always done your best to appear self-assured, independent and liberated, I said, but behind that strong, silent façade there hid an anxious little boy who was terrified of what people might think or say – all of which was probably true, but it was no more true of you than it was of me and just about everybody else of our age.

Today I'm not so sure that you backed out because you were scared. I don't know, but I think you did it quite simply because you weren't gay. I don't really know whether I was gay or straight myself back then, I haven't been with another man since we went our separate ways, and during the days I've spent writing this letter it has struck me more than once that various problems I'm wrestling with now may have led me to present us as being closer to each other than we actually were. Although, I'm not sure about that either: writing this, it occurs to me that it's those same present problems that cause me to put such a negative slant on things, to give the idea that we might not have got on so well together after all. Because we did get on really well together. All the events and the conversations I've referred to in this letter seem to me like memories of a happy time, a time I miss, despite all the problems I've mentioned.

So we parted, and it was some years before I saw you again. While you moved to Trondheim to study literature, I turned down my place there and stayed behind in Namsos, not because we had split up and I was depressed or anything like that, but simply because Mum was getting worse and worse and had no one but me to help her. I had the idea that I could get a temporary job, take an external degree at night school, then move to Trondheim once we had found a way round the situation she found herself in due to her illness. But what was meant to be one year in Namsos turned into two, and what should have been two years turned into three, and so it went on.

It's almost unreal to think back on what happened to me during those years when I was living at home, how I changed. The contempt I had once shown for small-town life didn't merely disappear, after a while I almost began to cherish and value all the aspects of life in Namsos that I had once mocked. It was as if, quite unconsciously, I had gone all out to learn to embrace my own fate, and when you met me at the Wine Monopoly the night before Christmas Eve eight or nine years ago, you met a guy who, while you would never have called him a loser, you did nonetheless regard as just that: a loser, a failure, someone who had had the same urge to travel as you and many of the same dreams for the future as you, but who had never got away.

I had just stuffed a half-bottle of Finlandia into my jacket pocket when I saw you standing at the head of the queue furthest away from the door. They didn't have the wine you were looking for and the assistant had suggested another one that you didn't look too happy about, but which – a little reluctantly, but with a smile – you accepted anyway. "Oh, all right," I remember you saying, and when you'd been handed the bottles and paid for them you turned and looked straight into the eyes of a young, once plump, man with girlish features and a receding hairline, clad in a rather battered denim jacket. You, on the other hand, were wearing clothes I didn't even know the names of, but which looked like the kind of thing I'd seen in the Sunday-paper style section. Your hair was short, you looked slim and remarkably fit, which surprised me a little I remember, maybe because it didn't really seem to go with how a student of literature ought to look. We beamed at each other, shook hands and acted as if we were a little happier to see one another than we actually were. "Well, well, fancy meeting you here!" "I know! Long time, no see!" "Yeah, I know, far too long!" "Wow, great to see you!" "Great to see you, too!" And so on and so forth, talking loudly and effusively and clapping each other's shoulders. I told you I was working in the music department at Øyvind Johansen's, that I was still living at home, but that I was going out with Wenche Berg from the parallel class to ours in senior secondary and that we were planning to move to Trondheim in the autumn to study. You told me you were single, living in the Lademoen area of Trondheim and that you'd soon be a fully qualified man of letters. "So now there's no help for it, I'll have to get out there and find myself a job too!" you said, laughing.

I remember being vaguely annoyed to hear you say such a thing. It sounded to me as if you felt sorry for me for the life I was leading and that you were trying to make me feel better by talking as if we'd both soon be in the same boat. But I didn't comment on it. Instead I started to tell you about the subjects I was planning to take once we moved to Trondheim and what sort of career I was contemplating, but that fell flat as well. You smiled and nodded while I went on about my plans, but I could tell by your face that you thought it was all just talk and this only made me more annoyed. We chatted for a while longer, but once the most inconsequential, innocuous questions had been asked, we made it clear to one another that we ought to be getting on. I had nowhere I had to be, but I glanced at my watch and said, "Hmm" and you asked what time it was and when I said that it was just before twelve you looked a little startled and said, "Oops, is it that late?" But we told each other that we'd have to get together over Christmas, "have our own little party", as I put it, and even though we both knew it would never happen you pretended to be all for it. "Yeah," you said, "we really should." "Okay, be in touch," you said before we parted.

Arvid

Arvid

I raise one eyebrow slightly and try to look as though I'm concentrating, eyes fixed on the page, seemingly engrossed in my book, but Eilert doesn't take the hint this time, either. I hear him clearing his throat, hear him preparing to say something else, he's the kind of person who simply cannot understand why anyone would choose to read rather than talk, he probably thinks he's doing me a favour every single time he interrupts me. He thinks I'm reading because I'm bored and have nothing else to do, and it's up to him to come to my aid by being sociable and telling me all about his own life, about the farm in Nærøy and his wife and his two daughters, about the older daughter who's married to a doctor from Halden and who'll soon be taking over the farm, and about his younger daughter who's at university in Liverpool, studying to be a vet, blathering on about places I've never been and people I don't know. He means well, I'm sure, just wants to cheer me up, but I get so sick of it him talking almost nonstop, telling the same stories again and again, it makes me so tired.

"When are you going home?" he asks.

I stifle a little sigh, give it just a second, then I peer over the top of my book. He's propped up, half sitting in the bed, his ruddy moon face beams at me and he smiles as amiably as always, I don't think I've ever met a more amiable man than Eilert.

"Tomorrow probably, or the day after," I say, then I pause for a moment, I don't want to return the question, but I can't help it, feel almost duty-bound to ask.

"And you?" I ask.

"My younger daughter's coming to collect me this evening," he says.

I nod and smile, then I look down at my book again, trying to escape, but it's no use.

"I'm looking forward to seeing her," he says, not giving up. "Haven't seen her in over a year."

"Oh, really?" I mutter, glancing up and giving him the ghost of a smile before looking down at my book again.

"She lives in England, you see. She's at university over there, studying to be a vet," he goes on. I don't know how many times he's told me that.

"Hmm," I say, not raising my eyes.

"In Liverpool."

I glance up briefly at him, nod and smile that same faint smile, then return to my book.

"I'm dreading that drive, though," he says.

"Yes, it's quite a way," I mutter.

"I'm glad we're doing it in the evening, though," he says.

"Yes, it's a lot shorter in the evening," I mutter.

There's silence for a couple of seconds and I feel a little twinge of guilt: he's only trying to be nice, I can't talk to him like this. I look up at him and smile again, try to give him the impression that it was a little joke, but I don't think he gets it, it's not his sort of humour, he just gives me a rather bewildered look.

"I was thinking of the heat," he says. "It's murder being cooped up in a car when it's as hot as it's been lately."

"Yes, you're right there," is all I say, I can't be bothered explaining, there's no point.

"But you don't have to worry about that, living as close as you do," he says, pauses for a moment, then: "Whereabouts in Namsos do you live again?" he asks, looking at me and smiling affably and I open my mouth, about to answer, but I stop myself, he's just the sort of provincial character who'd be quite liable to drop in on a man he hardly knows. I wouldn't put it past him to look me up next time he's over for a checkup or a chemo session, and I couldn't cope with that, I'm not having that, no way.

"Fossbrenna," I say, don't feel like telling him exactly where I live, just give the name of the first housing estate that comes to mind."

"Ah, yes," he says.

"So," I say briskly, hold his gaze for a second and smile as warmly as I can, then I look down at my book, seizing the opportunity to end this brief conversation before he can say any more. I raise one eyebrow, try to look as though I'm concentrating, but it does no good this time, either, he simply can't not talk, I hear him clearing his throat again, getting ready to say something else.

"What's that you're reading, then?" he asks, nodding at my book.

"What am I trying to read?"

"Yes," he says, my little correction going right over his head. He just sits there smiling that same affable smile. I raise my book so he can see the cover properly.

"A biography of Stalin."

"Phew," he says.

"Yes," I say, "phew indeed."

"Aye, he wasn't a man to be messed with, that's for sure."

"No," I say.

There's silence for a second, and I feel laughter bubbling up inside me, but I manage to pull myself together just in time, turn the laugh into a little cough. I put my hand to my mouth and cough again to reinforce the credibility of the first cough. Then suddenly my stomach contracts, a brief and relatively mild spasm that immediately passes, but fear of the pain that's just waiting to strike promptly washes over me, my brow and the back of my neck turn cold and clammy. I quickly put the book down on the bedside table and sit there breathing rapidly and staring intently at the duvet, sit there stiff as a poker and simply wait, checking to feel whether there's more to come.

"What's the matter?" Eilert asks. "Are you in pain?"

I don't answer, I sit perfectly still and wait, and then it comes. It's like two strong hands grabbing hold of my intestines, squeezing and wringing them out like washcloths. I automatically curl up and heel over slightly, take a deep breath, squeeze my eyes shut, stay like this for a second, trying to gather myself a little, then I open my eyes and raise a hand above my head, groping frantically for the cord, feel the little plastic bob gently nudge the palm of my hand. I have to fumble around a bit before I catch hold of it, then I tug it, once and then again, short, sharp tugs. I slide down into the bed, draw my legs up to my stomach and lie there, completely rigid. It feels as though I have a huge red-hot rock in my stomach, I squeeze my eyes shut as tightly as I can, they should be here by now, I need something now. I open my mouth, take a breath, let it out and at long last the door opens and the blonde nurse comes in.

"Can you give me something?" I gasp, groan almost. I try to smile, but can't quite manage it.

"I'll be right back," she says, turns on her heel and hurries out again. I hear the suction as her sandals hit the floor, the faint schwipp as they leave it again. Then the door closes with a heavy sigh and all the sounds from the corridor are shut out.

"Oh dear, oh dear, oh dear," Eilert mumbles from the other side of the room.

I clutch my stomach and grind my face into the pillow, tensing every muscle in my body. After a few moments the door opens again and both the blonde nurse and the chubby one come in.

"It hurts so much," I say between gritted teeth. I try to roll over onto my back, but the chubby nurse places a hand on my shoulder and stops me.

"We're going to give you a Spasmofen, so just stay on your side," she says. She pulls the stool over, sits down next to me, strokes my cheek. "Not long now and the pain will be gone," she says.

"He ate his elevenses a bit too fast," I hear Eilert telling the blonde nurse. "I noticed, but I thought it better not to say anything, you know how it is," he says. "Either that or it was that water he drank a while back," he adds.

Even now he can't keep his mouth shut. The blonde nurse says not a word, I hear the quick swoosh as the curtain is drawn, hear the sound of a latex glove being pulled on, then my underpants are tugged down over my thighs and I feel a suppository slipping inside me.

"There now," the chubby nurse says. "That should help," she says. She regards me with kind, gentle eyes as she strokes and strokes my cheek. A few seconds, then I feel the suppository beginning to take effect, the pain growing fainter and fainter, and the fainter it becomes the more clearly I feel the warmth of the chubby nurse's hand. The fear gently drains out of me and I feel a calmness settling over me. I'm overcome by a sense of gratitude and I have the urge to say something they'll appreciate.

"You're so kind," is all I say.

Dear David,

I'm sitting in the shade of the big cherry tree behind the house where we lived. When I look up from the computer screen I can see right across our garden and down the avenue we drove up on that first day, the day you and Berit moved in with me, the day the two of you came home. I can picture us in the yellow Simca I had borrowed from the parish clerk because there was something wrong with the gearbox of my Volvo. I picture the way the dun-coloured dust swirled up behind us as we turned in at the postboxes and how it hung like a curtain, billowing slightly in the shimmering, sun-warmed air before settling again. You were leaning forward, I remember, with a hand on each front seat, and you whooped with laughter because I had just taken my hands off the wheel so it looked as though I wasn't really steering. You were eleven, almost twelve, and actually very keen to show that you found such things childish, but before long you always got carried away and became as were you then, eager, excited and full of life. Your mum was in the passenger seat and when she saw what I was doing she squealed and pretended to be scared and you laughed even louder and harder at that, of course. You bounced up and down on the seat and shouted at me to do it again. "No, please don't, please don't, we'll end up in the ditch," Mum begged. "Yes," you cried eagerly. "Do it, do it." And so I did, naturally I did. I took my hands off the wheel again and pretended not to be steering and you whooped and laughed in the back seat. "Oh, no, Arvid, please!" Mum cried, pretending to be even more scared. "What?" I asked insouciantly, turning to her, raising my eyebrows and acting as if I had no idea what she was talking about. "Well, keep your eyes on the road, at least," she cried, pointing straight ahead and acting terrified. I put my hands back on the wheel, turned my head slowly and looked at the road again. "What's so special about the road? I don't see anything," I said, and you roared with laughter on the back seat. "Oh, you, you daft idiot," Mum said, poking my shoulder. "Ow!" I laughed and then I glanced in the rear-view mirror and caught your eye. I smiled slyly and winked at you. "You're not right in the head, either of you!" Mum said, shaking her head and acting as though she despaired of us.

That day saw the start of what was to be the best year of my life, David. Before I met Berit I had always taken a pragmatic view of the love between a man and a woman. The way I saw it, while we humans might not be liable to fall for just anyone, there had to be plenty of people out there whom we could well learn to love and live with, and when people talked to me about the one true love, I tended to regard it as an attempt to justify the choice of partner they had already made. But then I met Berit and I realized that I was wrong. Just as the newborn baby knows its own mother, so I knew Berit. I had never set eyes on her before, but everything in me instantly told me that we belonged together and, having once met her, to say "I love you" to anyone else would have made me feel like a liar, a traitor. I would put it as strongly as that.

I looked up to her so much, I needed her, was hooked on her. If I had written something in a sermon or the "Thought for the Day" that I was particularly happy with, for example, I was not above longing desperately for praise and acknowledgement from your mum. Not that I would ever have admitted that, of course, it would never have occurred to me to read out anything without being asked, but I remember how I used to try to catch her attention by pretending to be unsure of something. "Hmm," I would murmur and cock my eyebrow. And if Mum didn't react straight away I would sit there shooting impatient glances at her to see whether she was soon going to turn round. "Hmm," I would murmur again. "Oh, I really don't know." And at long last she would respond. "What was that?" she said one day as she was bending down to pick up a towel from the pile of washing in the green plastic tub. "We-ell," I said a mite hesitantly. "It's just this little sentence here, I'm not quite sure whether it's all right or not." "Let's hear it, then," she said, and taking the towel in both hands she lifted it slightly and shut her eyes as she gave it a quick flick. It made a little crack that echoed around the room. "Oh, well, you're welcome to hear it, but ..." Mum hung the towel on the drying rack and turned to me. "People buy one thing after another and carry them all home, but they have lost the key to the house," I read, and then I lowered the sheet of paper and looked at Mum again. And she stood there, open-mouthed and smiling. "Did you really write that, Arvid?" "What do you mean, did I write that?" Inside I was crowing with delight, but I tried to look as though I didn't quite understand why she should ask this. "Well, obviously I wrote it," I added. "But it's so ... it's excellent," she said. "So you think I should leave it in?" "Yes, of course you have to leave it in," she said, "I'll be very annoyed with you if you delete it." "Ah, well in that case I'd better leave it in," I said and gave a little laugh as I turned to look at you. "What do you say, David? Better not get on her wrong side, eh, we know what would happen then, don't we?" "Uh-huh," you laughed.

It's things like that that make a person grow, David, a smile and a few words of praise from the one you love, often that is all it takes for a man to accomplish things he thought he wasn't capable of. Oh, I remember when we were doing up the basement, I remember how exhausted I was. I was so busy at work at that time and I was worn out to start with anyway, but in the evenings there was nothing for it but to climb into my green overalls and get stuck in. I can see it now, I can see the white, conical halogen lamp lying on the newly laid chipboard floor that gives slightly when you step on it, I see how it lights up the fine sawdust drifting down from the plasterboard I'm cutting, I see my shadow on the insulating material I've just put in the side wall. "Oh, Arvid," Mum would say, when I'd been at it for a while, "isn't it about time you took a break?" "A break?" I would say, acting as if I wasn't quite with her. "Yes, you must be worn out, aren't you?" "No, no, I'm absolutely fine, really!" And she would look at me and shake her head. "I don't how you do it, I really don't." "How do you mean?" I would say. "How you can work the way you do." And I would just say "Aw," and wag my head. "You're unbelievable," she would say.

Such things, such tiny drops from Berit, could give me the strength to carry on for not just one, but up to three or four hours longer than I would otherwise have done. She made me strong, David, she made me great.

During those first years I used to ask you to give me a hand when I was working on things in the house or the garden.

And you never said no, not ever. Not that you were much help, mind you. Oh, it's funny to think about it, you were bright and did well at school, but you were certainly no handyman. You simply didn't have it in you, and more than once I had to leave the room to have a quiet laugh at the sight of you wrestling with the tools until you were sweating and fuming. Hammer and saw did not seem happy in your hands, they seemed to want to go a different way from you, and when you did eventually finish a job I often had to redo it once you were in bed. I came up with a lot of weird explanations for why things didn't look quite the same when you came to check on your handiwork the next day.

"Ah, well you see, I had a bit of an accident – I knocked the paint tin off the steps," I might say when you had been painting something. "It splattered all the way up the wall and I had no choice but to paint the whole thing again." But sometimes you saw through my little white lies and then, oh, dear, I felt so sorry for you. You were a proud lad and you didn't let it show, but I could tell you were upset and then of course I tried to make it up to you by treating you like my workmate and my peer. "What do you think?" I might ask. "Should we give the doorframe one coat or two?" "One, maybe." "We-ell," I'd say, spinning it out, giving you time to change your mind. "No, maybe we should give it two," you'd say. "Yes, you know what, I totally agree," I'd say. "I think it needs two!"

And that was all it took to cheer you up. Oh, David, to have you around me as I worked, to be high up the ladder and hear the sound of your humming mingling with the buzz of insects in the flowerbed and the low drone of a distant lawnmower, to see you standing there in paint-spattered denim shorts and a baseball cap with the paint shop name on it, dipping your brush way too far into the tin of wood preservative and slapping it on willy-nilly so it ran and dripped onto the swaying flowers below, it made me so happy and, not least, it made Mum happy.

No matter how much your mum and I had loved one another she would have had nothing to do with me if I hadn't shown myself to be a worthy father for you, if I had not loved you, too. For reasons we will never know she would never say who your real father was, not to you, not to me, not to anyone, but she knew you needed a grown man in your life, that you needed a father, a man who could stand as a role model for you. I am so grateful that I was allowed to be that man, David, I'm glad of that and I think I can safely say that your mum was glad of it, too. There was poetry in her eyes when she saw us doing things together, when we were oiling the house, stacking firewood or going over your homework. She would stand a little way off, just watching us, her face shining. I'll never forget one time when it was too much for her and she started to cry out of sheer joy. We had been to the birthday party of an old evangelical friend of mine on the island of Jøa, I remember, and we were in a hurry to catch the ferry home. It was summer and the day was hot, the air shimmered over the narrow, winding country road and occasionally there would come the sharp, contained crack of a stone thrown up by the wheels striking the mudguard or the undercarriage.

"Oh, look – raspberries!" you cried, sticking one slim, sun-browned arm between my seat and Berit's and pointing to a clump of raspberry bushes on the right-hand side of the road. "Can't we stop and pick some?" "No, David, we haven't got time for that," Mum said. "Oh, just for a minute!" you pleaded. "Pleease!" "No, David, we've got to catch the ferry!" But I pulled in to the side and stopped anyway, of course I did. Berit turned to me in surprise and I cocked my head and gave what I hoped was a disarming smile. "Oh, I think we can make time for this," I said, "don't you?" A little smile spread across her face, but she quickly turned it into a pout, acting sulky. "It's funny how we never seem to have the time when I want to do something," she said with a little toss of her head. I laid my arm along the back of the seat and half turned, looked at you and winked. "Hark at her," I said, "now she's gone in the huff because we left the party before the ice cream." "Humph!" Mum snorted. "Isn't that right?" I said, smiling slyly at you. "Yep," you said and laughed. Mum turned to you, flashed you a dirty look, then faced front again and shook her head. "It's like I'm always saying, you gang up on me, you two. I'm sure you'd rather be rid of me altogether." I looked at you, frowned slightly and waited a moment. "No," I said, shaking my head. "I think we'd be in a right old mess without Mum. Eh, David, what do you think?" "Yep," you said, grinning. And Berit wiped the pretend pout from her face, turned to you and stroked your cheek. "And I'd be in a right old mess without you two!" she said, and then she turned to me, leaned over and kissed my cheek. "Yuck!" you said and then you opened the car door and fled. Mum and I had a little laugh, we stayed where we were and watched you wading through the dense and slightly dusty clump of raspberry bushes on the roadside.

"I'm so happy," she said suddenly and when I turned I saw tears rolling down her cheeks. That was the moment when she cried out of sheer joy, David. She soon pulled herself together again, shook her head and laughed at herself as she wiped away the tears. "Oh, dear, I'm so silly," she said, but I didn't think it was at all silly. She had taken so many knocks in her life that it was hard for her to believe things could be going as well for her as they were now. That was why she was crying and it made her seem genuine and beautiful, not silly.

Your mum was the least self-pitying person I've ever known, she didn't like to talk about the traumatic things that had happened to her, but sometimes, even so, she did, usually when we were lying head to toe in bed at night and she didn't have to meet my eye. With an ache in her voice she would tell me what it had been like to lose her mother at the age of six, and about growing up alone with your grandfather, Erik. He did the best he could, I'm sure, but he was a drinker, and when Berit's mother was knocked down and killed by a bus and Erik lost the one person who had been able to keep him in check, he took to the bottle more and more and became less and less able to be a father to her. According to your mum he really wasn't all that bad when he was drunk. Both then and when he had a bottle tucked away or a party to look forward to he was usually as good as gold, kind and generous. It was when he was sober, with no prospect of getting drunk, that Mum had to watch out, because at such times he was tense and unpredictable and could fly into a terrible rage at the drop of a hat. He never hit her, but he ranted and raved and told her she was useless and that he didn't see how she was ever going to get by in life. If she did something she wasn't supposed to do he would simply stare and stare at her for as much as a minute and once, when she was unlucky enough to drop a dish of boiled cod on the floor, he leaped to his feet and started jumping up and down and stamping the cod into the rug. It was farcical and if it hadn't been for the fact that your mum was only six years old and scared stiff it would have been hilarious. In fact it would have made excellent material for the Otterøya Christmas Show. Immediately after such incidents he would be devastated, full of remorse, all apologies, didn't know how to make it up to her, and this was of course a redeeming and sympathetic feature. The stupid thing was that he was always so upset and guilt-ridden that he would end up making promises he couldn't keep. He was going to buy Mum a pony as soon as he got paid, or get her a bike at least. He might even take her to Oslo soon to see the palace and say hello to the king. So it went on and all through her childhood Mum had to cope with disappointment after disappointment, each one greater than the one before. Hers was a tough childhood, David.

When Mum left school she went to live in Namsos and started training to be a nurse, but within six months she was pregnant with you and had to move back to Otterøya and Erik. There were no benefit schemes for single mothers in those days and even though Erik straightened himself out and cut down on his drinking once there was a baby in the house, he didn't get his old job with the roadworks department back. He did a bit of odd-jobbing in the town and helped out on his neighbour's shrimp boat during the season when there was a lot to do, but his income was poor and unstable and even though your mum also did occasional work during those first years it was hard to make ends meet.

The hardest part, though, was all the gossip, the jeers and the sneers that she had to put up with. Single mothers were fair game back then and she had to shake her head and laugh when she told me about the time when she got work as a cleaner for three of the posher families in town. She arranged for one of her girl friends to look after you for a few hours every day and hitched a lift on the milk van when the milkman had finished his rounds and was heading back to the dairy. It went really well for a while, because Mum's rates were reasonable, she was conscientious and hard-working, and – not least – trustworthy. These posh people used to leave earrings and small amounts of money lying about to test her, but she was honest, she never stole anything and all three families let her know that they were more than satisfied with her. One man, the manager of one of the town sawmills, even gave her a raise without her having to ask for it – not what one might have expected, since he was known for being tight-fisted where his employees were concerned. But when he and the others learned that Mum was an unmarried mother it didn't matter how hard-working and honest she was, she was fired on the spot; these grand ladies didn't want her sort in the house, who knew what temptations she might lay in their husbands' way? Thirty-five years ago that was, David, only thirty-five years. So times do change, and they change fast.

Right up until they moved out Erik had spells when he drank heavily and was difficult to live with. But according to Mum he was still a lamb compared to the way he had been before you were born, and fortunately living with him didn't seem to have done you any harm. You had many good memories of your early childhood and you laughed and were proud when you told people how "barmy" your grandfather was. You didn't know that Erik had been drunk that time when he drove the car straight through the garage door or when he played the accordion for Mum and all the guests at her birthday party clad only in his underpants, and you never noticed how your mum always seemed to have something to do in the kitchen when we had visitors and you started going on about him. You saw everything with the eyes of a child and as far as you were concerned Erik was simply a jolly buffoon.

As for me, I got on okay with Erik, but no more than that. It didn't matter how hard I tried I could never really like the man who had hurt Mum so much, and his behaviour when he came to visit us could be very annoying. He had worked as a lumberjack, a removal man and a navvy – in other words, he was a labourer and he looked exactly as you would expect a labourer to look: big, burly and with a way of talking and acting that spoke of a strange innate blend of arrogance and inferiority complex. He was confident and assertive when it came to anything practical. If there was some job to be done in the house or garden that I wasn't sure about, or needed help with, he would always lend a hand, and since there was no doubt that his skills in this area were far superior to mine his manner when he gave me tips and advice was more modest than condescending. But with things which he didn't know much about the exact opposite was the case. It was as if he were trying to compensate for his own insecurity and inadequacy by boasting and acting as if he knew it all. When he was running out of arguments and losing a discussion, for instance, he would either grin, shake his head hopelessly and act as if whatever I was saying was so ludicrous that there was no point in continuing the discussion, or he would credit me with a whole range of ridiculous, naive views, against which he would then deliver a fierce tirade, obviously in the hope of making himself and everyone else believe that he was on the offensive. Everyone there could see right through him, of course, even you, young though you were. But so good was he at fooling himself that he was completely impervious to this, and when I eventually got fed up and couldn't be bothered arguing the toss any longer, he would act as if he had put me soundly in my place. "Oh, aye, I maybe didn't have as much schooling as you, but that don't mean I'm stupid!" he would say.

And very often this was exactly what he was trying to convey when he told his stories. He was a brilliant storyteller, I give him that. If I had had even a fraction of his gifts in that area I would have had the church packed to the rafters every single Sunday, that's how good he was. But here again, as in discussions, he was hellbent on showing that he wasn't just anybody – even if he was only an ordinary working man from Otterøya, as he was wont to style himself. He put himself into just about every story he told, even those in which he could not possibly have had any part. He didn't always have the lead role, I grant you, but he always acquitted himself equally well, remarkably often at the expense of those whom he called "office rats", an epithet which covered everyone who did not do hard, physical labour. Such people lived sheltered lives, they were weak, cowardly and impractical, and in story after story Erik had to clear up the mess they made, help them or quite simply tell them to bugger off so that he, the man with the necessary muscle, courage or quick-wittedness, could take matters in hand and sort them out. I can almost hear his coarse laugh after he had told one of these yarns, almost hear that booming voice as he delivered his closing line: "That took the wind out of the chairman's sails, I can tell you!"

Naturally the tacit implication was that I too was an office rat and naturally this was one of the reasons why I found him so annoying. But at any large gathering I could always tell that I was not alone in finding him tiresome. It had something to do with the powerful urge he had to constantly put himself in the spotlight; it was quite wearing to have to sit there, affecting to be speechless with admiration at all that he had experienced, all the things he had done in his life. Although it was worst for your mum, of course. It could be downright painful for her to have to listen to this man who had ruined her childhood boasting about himself all the time. Particularly painful, obviously, when he started angling to be absolved of all the things he had done to her, as he often did, oh yes, just about every time he visited us. I can see us sitting at the round table in the living room, I see the way Erik's huge frame fills the chair, see how he twirls his black moustache. "How about that time when we pretended we were stranded on a desert island, Berit," he said on one such occasion. "On a desert island?" Mum said. "You must remember that." "No," Mum said. "That time we camped out on the sheep island," he said. He eyed her in some surprise. "When we played that we'd been shipwrecked and washed up on that beach, don't you remember?" "No, I don't remember," Mum said. "And how we were going to live off the fish we caught and the berries we picked?" "No, I don't remember any of that."

She did remember, though, of course she did. She remembered that and all the other things Erik used to remind her about, but she refused to go along with painting a rosy picture of her childhood, as she put it. Because she knew that was what Erik wanted her to do. Erik knew the sort of father he had been and he deeply and sincerely regretted that. These attempts of his to get your mum to talk about the good times which, in spite of everything, they had had together, were his way of gaining a little peace of mind. There were times when it hurt to look at them, it was such a touchy subject, this, for both of them and more than once I told Mum that she would have to try her best to forgive him, that it would make life easier for both of them if she did. But it was hard for her and I didn't want to put too much pressure on her, either; demanding of a victim that they forgive their persecutor can feel like another act of abuse, it may seem as though what he or she went through is being belittled, taken lightly, and that was the last thing I wanted.

But I remember how upset your mum was after such episodes. I remember how worried you were once when she fled into the bathroom in tears the minute Erik was out of the door. You couldn't understand what had got into her and since I didn't want to ruin the good relationship you had with your grandfather it was hard for me to explain it to you. I was at my wits' end and I didn't manage to say much except that you weren't to worry about Mum and that you must on no account think that it had anything to do with you.

But you figured it all out eventually, anyway. You would have been about fourteen, maybe fifteen, I don't remember exactly, but you were mad at Mum and me, at any rate, because we wouldn't let you go to a rock concert in Trondheim, and you threatened to go and live with your grandfather because he let you do whatever you liked. "And why do you think that is?" your mum asked hotly, slamming her hand down on the table and staring at you. "It's because he doesn't care," she screamed, "it's because your grandpa's a drunk who doesn't give a shit about you, me or anyone else, and he never has."

Nothing good came of saying that. I don't blame Mum, it's not that, it hurt her to hear you say that you'd rather live with the man who had destroyed her childhood than with her, and she couldn't stop herself from saying what she said. She simply snapped. But in the long run it led to you giving your grandfather a wider berth. You began to reflect on and reassess memories from your early childhood and slowly but surely you formed a new picture of your grandfather and possibly, indeed, of your whole childhood. All of a sudden you were no longer so keen to go to Otterøya and when Erik visited us you always made a point of being busy with your chums. Erik pretended not to notice, joked with you, asked if you were off chasing the girls again, but we could tell that it hurt him to lose you like this and that it rankled him. Mum and I did our best to play along with him, but he knew that we knew and I remember how embarrassed he looked at one point when our eyes met and it was clear to us both that we were thinking the same thing.

I tried to talk to you about it. You were in the same situation as your mum, you found it impossible to forgive him and it didn't only bother Erik, it bothered you too, I could tell. "Grandpa loves you and I know you love him, and that's all that matters," I said. But you only grunted and said, "Yeah, yeah," and tried to pretend that this was just soppy minister talk that you had no wish to hear.

You know, there were times when I tormented myself with the thought that Mum had only married me so that you and she could escape from Erik. But this was sheer fancy on my part – if she had been that desperate to get away she would have found herself some other man to move in with long before she met me. And the looks she gave me, the things she said to me, the happiness she radiated, everything about her also told me that this was not the case, it was the brooder in me that came up with this. I loved Berit and I knew that she loved me too, although I probably wasn't the easiest person to live with, especially those early years. I had lived alone until I was in my forties and had acquired habits and mannerisms which got on your and your mum's nerves, but which it was hard for me to change. Worse, though, was the fact that I wasn't used to being contradicted and overruled; that and the discovery – something of a surprise to me – that I was pretty stubborn and found it hard to admit when I made a mistake. I remember when we went fishing down at Gilten, a lake just south of Namsos. The forest down there is a maze of narrow dirt tracks running hither and yon and it's extremely easy to get lost. I had been there before two or three times, but I didn't know the area all that well. On the way home you and Mum were sure I had turned right when we should actually have turned left and that we ought to turn around and drive back, but you had never been there before, so I wouldn't hear of it. Even when we came to a sign clearly stating that we should have taken the road you and Mum had said we should take I refused to admit that I had made a mistake. Somebody must have been playing around with the signs to mislead people, it was a well-known ruse to keep the best fishing spots to themselves, I claimed, and not even when the next sign and the one after that also told us that we were driving in the wrong direction would I admit defeat. Or at least, I did admit that I ought to have turned left rather than right, as you had both said, but I steadfastly maintained that it was perfectly possible to take this road too, and besides, the scenery was much nicer and we had the whole evening ahead of us.

Worse still was the time when the bishop gave me five kilos of venison that proved to be on the turn. I refused to admit that a gift from the bishop himself could be such a disappointment, I remember, and I forced that meat down, smiling all the while at you and Mum and saying that this certainly was a far cry from dry roast beef. "A little unusual," Mum said tactfully. "Quite tangy, actually." "That's because the deer eat so many rowanberries in the autumn," I said. "Is that so?" "Did you know that, David?" I asked, smiling and trying to persuade myself and you and Mum that the venison tasted of the Norwegian countryside and that everything was just as it should be. You two weren't fooled, though, and after a while I noticed that you weren't touching the meat but were only eating the meatballs, potatoes and gravy and, childish though it may have been, I took umbrage. It was bad enough that you refused to buy my attempted explanation of the way the food tasted, but that you could sit there tucking into those delicious meatballs while I felt compelled to force down rotten venison was like adding insult to injury, and when, to top it all, Mum began to giggle, I simply lost my temper. "What are you laughing at?" I asked. I tried to keep smiling and pretend I didn't see what was so funny, but Mum knew that I knew and she giggled more and more and I got madder and madder, and she clearly seemed to think that this made the whole thing even funnier. Finally, she laid her fork down on the plate, put her hand over her mouth and laughed outright.

Generally speaking Berit had a good way with me, she joked and poked fun at me when I was grumpy and difficult, but there was never anything snide or spiteful about the way she did this, and before I knew it I would find myself seeing the funny side and laughing along with her. And because I discovered that I liked myself better when I could laugh at myself instead of getting huffy and disgruntled I found it easier and easier to do it, and slowly but surely I changed and became a better person to live with. I began to accept my own faults and failings and this made it easier to accept those of others. Oh, David, Mum turned me into the man I hadn't even known I longed to be, and she did it with love.

But even though I was less stern and dour than I had been, I was still a serious-minded man. Not that I had anything against a bit of fun and games, because I didn't – no one enjoyed a practical joke more than I did. I'll never forget the time I sucked the Cognac out of a chocolate liqueur with a syringe and injected it instead with the juice from the jar of Brazilian chillies. I plugged the hole with a little piece of chocolate fudge cake, rewrapped the chocolate and put it back in the bowl. I've never seen a face change colour as fast as that of the visiting catechist who greedily plundered our sweet dish.

Then as now, though, I was a thinker, I liked peace and quiet, I liked to contemplate and philosophize on matters great and small and I didn't need to talk all the time, even if there were several of us in the same room. Your mum found this side of me very odd, she was such a gregarious person herself and so enjoyed a good chat, and during our first years together she often thought there was a problem when I went around the house saying nothing – that I was angry or annoyed about something or other. I tried to explain to her that I was just thinking, but when she asked what I was thinking about I could never give her an answer that would satisfy her. Had I said that I was thinking about the new drain we were planning to lay or which route you and I ought to take when we went hill-walking the following week, she would have said, "Oh, right," and been content with that, but that a man could ponder the big questions in life while doing the washing-up or gazing out of the kitchen window, that she simply could not comprehend. It didn't matter that I was a vicar and that such questions were central to my education and my work, she simply did not get it, and because I didn't want her to think there was anything wrong I frequently chose to tell a white lie and say that I had been thinking about what to say at the funeral on Wednesday or in my sermon on Sunday, because that was fine, that she could understand.

And in this you and I were so alike, David. We were both thinkers. Even when you were very young you could withdraw into yourself and sit perfectly still, staring into space and thinking about one thing or another. You read a lot and like me you had a great thirst for knowledge and would not give up until you had the answers you were looking for. If Mum came across a word she didn't know when she was doing the newspaper crossword and neither you nor I could tell her what it meant, or if we were arguing about something, we would promptly turn for answers to our stock of dictionaries and reference books. "Is it really that important?" Mum would ask when we'd been at it for some time. "Heavens above, sit down the pair of you." But we couldn't rest until we'd found the answer and if we didn't find it at the time we would remember that question for later and whichever one of us did eventually come up with it could hardly wait to tell the other – especially, of course, if it was a point on which we had disagreed and it transpired that the person concerned had been right. Particularly when you were a little older we used to tease one another and pretend to gloat over having put the other in his place, it was a kind of game we played. "A-ha, so you thought Pluto had only one moon, did you?" I would say. "Oh, well, anyone can make a mistake, even you," I would add. "I do not esteem you," you would say, having just discovered Hamsun. "What are you two on about?" Mum would ask, looking at us and frowning, having long since forgotten the whole thing. "Well?" she would say. But we wouldn't answer. You would cross your arms and gaze at the ceiling as if to emphasize yet again that as far as you were concerned I didn't exist, and I roared with laughter at this little show and thought you charming and witty. "Well, tell me, what is it?" Mum would ask, raising her voice slightly, getting annoyed now. "What are you laughing at?" she would ask, eyeing me crossly, which only made me laugh even more, and in the end she couldn't help but laugh herself. I feel a surge of happiness when I think back on scenes like that: the quietly glowing embers are the warmest, David, not the raging flames, and so it is with happiness, too, it lies in the everyday things.

I open my eyes and find myself looking straight at the drawn curtains. I don't move, lie quite still and check how I'm feeling; it's not too bad, it hurts, but not nearly as much as it did this morning. I feel pretty good actually, not all that nauseous either, my mouth's not even dry. I lie still for a few moments, then roll gingerly onto my side, lift my head off the pillow and rest it on my hand, stay like this for a little while, gazing vacantly into space, give a little yawn. The air is close, it's hot and the whole room seems full of sleep. I'd better get myself out of bed, get the window opened and let in some fresh air, clear my head a little. And I do actually manage to pull back the curtains and let in some light, it looks like it has brightened up and the sun has come out while I was asleep, I can't lie here in the gloom with that glorious evening light out there. I grab hold of the duvet and pull it back. The smell of warm body wafts up into my face. I dig my elbow into the mattress and ease myself up into a half-sitting position, gently, to save my wound from hurting too much. I shut my eyes, take a deep breath and let it out, then ease myself up a little more, until I'm sitting upright. I open my eyes, gaze down at my bony legs. I still can't believe these are my legs, after all this time I ought to be used to them, but I still don't get it: that these skinny, snow-white calves, these long, slender thighs, these bulging kneecaps that look so much bigger than they are, that all of this should be part of me, that this should be me.

I swallow, still with my eyes fixed on my legs. The old me is almost gone now, nothing left but skin and bone, no wonder people look the other way when I shuffle down the corridor. It's not surprising that they pretend not to see me, I can scarcely stand the sight of myself, can't even look at myself in the mirror any more. I just stare into the washbasin when I wash my hands, and when I go to dry my hands I kind of sweep my eye across the washbasin and over to the towel hanging next to the bathroom cabinet, do all I can to avoid catching a glimpse of myself in the mirror. I can't take the sight of that gaunt, grey face. It revolts me, it's so stripped of fat and flesh that the outline of my teeth is almost visible behind my lips, my cheeks are like two small bowls turned upside down and my jaw muscles jut like thin, taut roots on either side of my face. I can't take it. And I certainly can't take the look in my eyes. Meeting my own eyes in the mirror is the worst, I don't know why, possibly because the eyes are the only part of the man I used to be that I still recognize. It has taken time and energy to reconcile myself to the idea that I'm going to die soon, and each time I see my own eyes I see the old me, and when that happens I feel as if I'm set much further back in that process of reconciliation. The sight of my eyes kindles a spark of hope in me and I don't want that, I don't want my old self to trick me into false hope. Maybe this is what lies behind the fear of meeting my own eyes, I'm not sure.

I sit quite still, and now I feel black despair creeping over me, feel my body grow somehow numb, no longer have any desire to get up. All I really want to do is crawl under the warm duvet and go on sleeping, escape into dreams, be somewhere else, anywhere but in this body, anywhere but in this head. But it's no use, I won't sleep now and besides, Dr Claussen will be coming to chase me out of bed soon. Dr Jonassen, Dr Hartberg and most of the nurses can be talked round, but come hell or high water Dr Claussen will have me trudging up and down those corridors, no matter what sort of shape I'm in.

I close my eyes and emit a sigh, open my eyes, plant both hands on the mattress and start to haul myself towards the edge of the bed. I might as well pull back the curtains and open the window a bit, let in some fresh air and some sunlight, it's bound to help a little. Am just about to set my feet on the floor when I hear the door handle being turned. Someone's coming in, oh no, I'm not up to it, I'm not up to talking to anybody right now, it's too much, I'm not in the mood. I shove myself back up onto the bed, lie down, grab the duvet and pull it up to my chin, lie very still, listening. I hear the door open, hear all the sounds from the corridor being let into the room, the sounds of voices and footsteps, laughter, coughing and the rattle of a trolley laden with cups and dishes, a brief burst of life before the door is closed and everything goes quiet again. After a second or so I hear Eilert's slippers shuffling across the polished floor and a little sigh escapes me: Eilert's the last person I want to talk to right now, I can't take all his blathering, all the stories about his family, I can't cope with it, not right now. I press my cheek into the pillow and shut my eyes, try to make him think I'm still asleep.

I hear him shuffle past me and over to his own bed, hear him open the drawer of his bedside table and take out something that rustles, a bag of humbugs it sounds like. A couple of seconds and then I hear the low click-click of a boiled sweet knocking against teeth, he gives a little slurp and says "mm" and then he starts to hum, humming the same tune he always hums, this jaunty old-time dance tune, a schottische or a polka or something. Moments pass and he doesn't let up, alternates between humming and sucking on his humbug, and now I feel myself getting annoyed, feel myself getting angry. Sharing a room with Eilert is almost worse than sharing a room with the sort of character that breaks down at regular intervals, I would almost prefer uncontrolled bouts of weeping or fits of rage to the way Eilert tackles the fear of death, this exaggerated cheerfulness, all this humming and whistling and all the chirpy chatter about his wife, his daughters and the farm in Nærøy, all the waffling he does in order to forget the mess he's in, that's just about the worst, this incessant, frantic denial of the facts, this way of escaping.

After a little while I realize I'll have to shift position, I'm lying on my arm, it's going to sleep, so I'll either have to move slightly or ease it out from underneath me. I've got pins and needles in my arm, all the way from shoulder to fingertips. I lie for a moment, then I raise my upper half off the mattress a fraction and ease my arm free, very carefully so as not to attract Eilert's attention, I just can't be bothered talking to him, can't be bothered bucking myself up and being as cheery as he always wants me to be.

And then: "Arvid."

I don't answer. I stiffen, don't open my eyes, pretend to be asleep still, pretend to just have been shifting a little in my sleep.

"You asleep?" he asks softly.

I still don't answer.

"Arvid," he says.

I feel my annoyance growing; if he hasn't tumbled to the fact that I'm awake, then he ought to keep quiet so as not to wake me, and if he has, then he ought also to have grasped that I really don't want his company and he should act as though he believes I'm asleep.

"Arvid!" he says again. "Are you asleep?"

A moment, then I give in, there's no point, he's not going to let up anyway.

"Not any more," I mumble.

"What's that?" he says.

I'm on the point of repeating it, but I stop myself, he doesn't mean any harm, it's just his way and I can't bring myself to be rude to him – no matter what, he doesn't deserve that. I smack my lips and swallow a couple of times, then I blink lazily, eye him drowsily. He's dressed in his own clothes, I see, and ready to go home, has exchanged the striped hospital pyjamas for slacks and a checked flannel shirt, stands there smiling softly with both hands behind his back. His face is burnished red and round as a bowling ball and his belly droops over a narrow brown belt.

"It brightened up while you were asleep," he says. He stands there considering me for a second, then walks over to the window. "See how nice it is," he says, raising a hand and pulling back the curtains. A golden column of evening sunlight slants across the room and over my bed and my face instantly feels warm. It's a pleasant warmth, not scorching summer heat, but the sort of gentle warmth that only the evening sun can give.

"Isn't that just lovely?" Eilert asks.

I grimace slightly, put a hand up to shade my eyes and squint at him, acting as though the sun is brighter than it is.

"Yes it is," I say, "but would you mind drawing the curtains again!"

I feel a twinge of guilt the minute I say it. I don't want to be like this, don't want to be grumpy, but I can't help it, I'm feeling down and depressed and there's nothing to do about it.

"Oh, sorry," Eilert says, and he turns, takes hold of the curtain on my side and draws it closed again. "I wasn't thinking," he says. He puts his hands behind his back again, stands there grinning at me. "Aye, well, not long till I'll be going," he says, lifts his left arm and glances at his watch. "She should actually have been here a while ago to collect me," he adds.

"Amen to that," I mutter. It just comes out and I regret it the minute I've said it. I almost blush, stare at the bed, shamefaced, wait a second and then I look up at him, smile apologetically, but fortunately it doesn't look as though he caught what I said, he seems to have an in-built shield against sarcasm, he's still smiling that same affable smile.

"But it was nice knowing you," he says.

I ease myself up into a sitting position and force a slightly warmer smile.

"Yes, same here," I say and just as I say it the door opens and in comes a slightly built young woman with a suntanned face. Her eyes go straight to Eilert and I realize that this must be his younger daughter, the veterinary student that he's always talking about.

"Ah, there you are!" Eilert says, beaming delightedly and she tries to smile back, but doesn't manage it, the corners of her mouth are turned down and she's close to tears, she hasn't seen Eilert in over a year, he told me, they haven't seen one another since he fell ill, so it wouldn't be all that surprising if she were to cry. She stands there looking at Eilert for a moment, then she sort of glides into the room, sorrow emanating from the very way she walks. Her arms hang limply by her sides, she looks almost as if she is moving by remote control. She goes up to him, puts her arms round him, rests her chin on his shoulder and clasps her hands behind his broad back. They stand there like that, swaying back and forth for a few moments and then she starts to cry, her narrow shoulders tremble and she buries her face in Eilert's shoulder.

"There, there!" Eilert says. "There, there!"

They stand there hugging and swaying. Eilert pats her back to soothe her as she cries and cries.

"Oh, Dad," she sobs, "dear Dad."

"There, there," Eilert says again.

A few moments pass. Then:

"Are you angry with me?" she asks. She sniffs, lifts her chin off his shoulder and takes a little step back. Her face is anguished, torn apart by grief and her eyes plead with him.

"Angry? Why should I be angry?" Eilert asks. He wrinkles his brow, acts as if he has no idea what she's talking about, but his voice is a little too astonished to be credible, he may not be angry, but he knows very well what she's thinking of and what she's referring to.

"Because I didn't come home earlier," she says and swallows.

"Oh, sweetheart, no!" Eilert says. He raises his eyebrows, drops his jaw and tries to look even more flabbergasted.

"I should have come home the minute I heard you had cancer," she sobs.

Keeping the flabbergasted expression on his face he looks her straight in the eye for a couple of seconds, shaking his head gently.

"Now, now, don't talk daft, Helene," he says and he gives a little laugh, acting as though this is so utterly preposterous that he has to laugh, although he has had the same thought as his daughter, I can tell, has wondered whether she was going to come home to see him, but he tries to make it look as though he's never heard anything so ridiculous. She doesn't say anything for a moment, she tries to hold his eye, but with no success, her face crumples, her eyes fall closed and she wraps her arms around him again, digs her fingers into that broad back and clings to him, presses her face against his shoulder and cries her heart out. "Yes," she sobs, "I should have come home straight away, I should have come as soon as Mum called and said you were ill, now we've hardly any time left together." And when she says that, Eilert raises his chin. He takes a great, deep breath, filling his lungs, and stands there with his round, bewildered eyes staring into space. He looks close to tears himself, the corners of his mouth twitch slightly, but he swallows hard and composes himself.

"Helene, pet, you had your studies to think about," he says.

"What does that matter compared to this?" she sobs.

"Hey!" Eilert says, introducing a stern paternal note in his voice now. "Don't say things like that," he says, "If you'd neglected your studies because of me, then I'd have been angry, then I'd have felt guilty too," he says, he's not about to give in, he's defending the choice she made, taking the guilt off her shoulders so that she'll be able to carry on after he's gone, and she cries and cries and cries both because she's heartbroken and because she's relieved by what she hears. I just sit here staring at them, feeling rather touched, because it is touching to see Eilert summon up such strength, to witness all this love.

"And anyway, you might not be rid of me as soon as all that," Eilert goes on. "I'm every bit as tough and stubborn as you, you know," he says and then he gives a little laugh, trying to make a joke of the whole thing.

"Oh, Dad," his daughter says and they say no more, they simply stand there clinging to each other, big fat Eilert and his slip of a daughter. They put their arms around each other and I sit and watch them for a few seconds more, then I swallow and look down at my bed, don't want to seem rude either, don't want to intrude. I ease myself up in the bed, I should let them have the room to themselves until they recover, should let them be alone. I push back the duvet, slowly swing my legs over the edge of the bed, slide forward a bit, place my feet on the floor and stand up, carefully, to save my wound from hurting too much. I lean forward, pull the curtain round the bed, pick up the pale blue, striped pyjama trousers that are hanging over the spindle-back chair, then I sit down and draw them up over my legs. I don't stand up right away. I sit still for a moment and catch my breath – I get out of breath so quickly, it doesn't take much at all. A couple of seconds, then I raise one hand and put it to my head, it must be months since the last wisp of hair disappeared, but I still find it odd, it feels like laying my hand on a bent knee. I cast a quick glance at Eilert and his daughter, they're still standing there hugging each other, he's rocking her gently from side to side, saying nothing. A second more, then I brace my hand on the bedside table and heave myself upright with a faint sigh. I work my feet into my slippers, draw back the curtain and head for the door.

In 1986 we took a new organist at the church. His name was Samuel, he was from Oslo, and to begin with, because he had no friends or relatives in Namsos, we often invited him over. But I took an immediate dislike to him. For one thing, he was a former volleyball player and desperate to demonstrate how fit and athletic he was. When he visited us he didn't use the gate like everyone else, instead he hopped lightly and gracefully over the fence. And when he tied his shoelaces, so keen was he to show off the rippling muscles in his forearm that anybody would have thought he was making fast a hawser rather than a pair of laces. What was worse, though, was that as an Oslo man he looked down on us Namsos folk. As far as he was concerned Namsos was not a part of the real world, so it seemed, but a kind of north Norwegian fairyland inhabited by grunting weirdos who lived on porridge and answered in words of one syllable when spoken to, and he never missed an opportunity to talk and laugh about people and incidents that reinforced this distorted image of provincial Norway. He was condescending and smug and since he was not bright enough to see that he had no reason to be either he was also extremely sure of himself, and this in turn made him seem charming and attractive to a lot of women, including your mum. It pains me a little to write this, David, but shortly after we first made his acquaintance I noticed that she started smartening herself up if he was paying us a visit. And if he showed up unannounced she would always pop into the bathroom and emerge smelling faintly of perfume or wearing a little more eyeshadow than she had been five minutes earlier. Not only that, but when he was there she talked and acted rather differently, I noticed. She toned down her accent, said "fish" and not "fesh", she laughed at things she wouldn't normally have found funny and she was more alert and attentive than usual, her eyes shone with a very particular light.

There were times when I got so jealous that it felt as though my insides were being tied in knots, but I never said anything, not to Mum or anyone else, possibly because I was too embarrassed, possibly because I was too much of a coward, I don't know. In any case, instead of confronting her I withdrew. The only thing I did actively to put an end to it all was to stop inviting Samuel to the house; that and to lie, if he called to arrange something with us, and say that we would be away. Not that it did much good.

It was about this same time that you started going around with Jon and Silje. Jon was tall and skinny and pale, almost chalk-white. He always wore this chain around his neck with a death's-head on it and from the kitchen window I would see him stopping on the front step and tucking it inside his shirt before he rang the bell, probably to save me, a vicar, from seeing it. Initially I found this quite funny, rather sweet even, he wanted to look tough, but he didn't even dare to be seen wearing something as innocuous as a death's-head. He was also afraid to swear if I was within earshot, and if they happened to be sitting chatting in the same room as me I noticed that he tried to give the impression of being both a non-smoker and a non-drinker. It wasn't long, though, before his insecurity began to seem anything but funny and sweet. It hurt to look at him sometimes. David, he wasn't insecure in the way that most normal teenagers are, with Jon it was an affliction, a sickness. When he spoke to people he never met their eye and no matter how smiling and friendly I tried to be he would look anywhere but at me when we were talking. He was, of course, painfully aware of this himself and occasionally he would force himself to make eye contact, but after no more than a second or so he always dropped his gaze again. And his voice was liable to crack at any minute. I only had to ask him how he was getting on and even though everything was as usual and nothing out of the ordinary had been happening, when he replied it sometimes sounded as if he was about to dissolve into tears of pain and grief. At first I thought it had something to do with me, but as it turned out he was the same with everyone. He was so fragile, so close to breaking point all the time. It was worse when there were a lot of people present, as there often were at our house; when he walked into the living room with you he would try to make himself as invisible as possible, and on those rare occasions when you had time to sit down for a moment he seemed terrified that someone might speak to him. He would kind of curl up in his chair and sit there staring at his lap, not saying a word, and if anyone did speak to him his face would turn brick red and he would make some sullen, almost antagonistic response. Not that anyone took offence, of course. His discomfort was written all over his face, as Mum used to say, and I think everyone felt sorry for him.

I liked Jon, he was a good lad, he was nice and basically harmless. But he was incredibly impressionable. He looked up to you and Silje and I saw how his face changed when you laughed at something he had said or done, how it perked him up, and how he strove to reap even more laughs or even more compliments. He was so easily led, so easily manipulated. "You're not right in the head, you," Silje might say when she wanted him to do something he wouldn't normally have done, and Jon was weak-willed enough to give in and endeavour to live up to her picture of him. "You wouldn't dare," Silje would say, and despite his fears Jon would do whatever it was she said he didn't dare to do. Matters were not helped by the fact that he had a crush on her and that she exploited this situation for all it was worth. Not only did she get him to play the fool and act the goat sometimes, just to give her something to laugh at, on several occasions I witnessed her getting him to run errands for her. "Could you bike down to the video shop and rent such and such a film?" "Pop down to the corner shop and pick up some sweets for us, would you." That's how she went on. To begin with Jon usually tried to make out that he wasn't someone she could just order about as she pleased. "Do it yourself!" he would cry and then give a surprised laugh, designed to make it sound as if he had never heard such cheek. But it was never long before he did an about-turn: "Oh, all right, then," he would bluster. "I'll take a run down to the video shop. Since you keep going on about it," he would add and then he'd look at Silje and laugh.

What I took to be an echo of my own unhappy teenage crushes ran through me when I overheard such exchanges and even though they were sweet and rather amusing I sometimes cringed in my chair. I could scarcely stand to listen to them. When Mum, on the other hand, witnessed such scenes they simply confirmed for her the impression she had already formed of Silje. Where, at times, I saw a teenager struggling to conceal the fact that she was anxious and unsure of herself by adopting a pert and somewhat overconfident manner, your Mum saw, and I quote, "a cynical, manipulative, shameless little tart". I remember being mildly surprised to hear her using such language of a friend of yours and even though Mum was startled by her own words and even though we had a bit of a giggle about it afterwards the shock of it stayed with me for some time. To me Silje was a vivacious girl, full of laughter and life and ideas, almost always smiling and cheerful without in any way seeming naive or shallow. Quite the opposite, in fact. She always came over to have a chat with me when she called at the house and at such moments she was invariably interested and attentive. She was not a religious person, but she was so curious about the ministry, about my beliefs and my thoughts on the big questions in life that I detected more than a hint of a religious longing in her, and – partly, no doubt, for this very reason – I can only say that it was a pleasure to talk to her. She was intelligent and articulate, and despite the fact that I was occasionally taken aback by her bluntness and her boldness she was such a fascinating and rewarding conversationalist that I had been known to put off doing other things simply in order to finish our discussions.

Mum, on the other hand, did her best to avoid her. Her face took on a rather sour expression whenever Silje visited the house and she could become almost childishly fractious and contrary, especially if Silje was the centre of attention. While the rest of us laughed at some witty remark Silje had made, Mum would sit there looking determinedly po-faced; if Silje suggested that we do something, your Mum would always be against it, and if we were having a discussion and disagreed over some point, you could be one hundred per cent certain that Mum would side with whoever disagreed with Silje. It was so obvious it was almost comical.

To begin with I thought she was simply jealous, and although it was a tricky and a touchy subject I felt I had to let her know that it had not gone unremarked, before it went too far and she made a fool of herself. I remember one time when we were in the living room and you and Silje and Jon were playing croquet in the garden. Silje was wearing a white miniskirt that flew up in the wind from time to time. This, combined with the fact that Silje sometimes looked like a rather languid prima donna who felt that the world was altogether too dull and boring for her, prompted your mum to suddenly hiss: "Look at her! There she goes, trying to do a Marilyn Monroe again, bending over and going all misty-eyed, the little tart!" "Berit," I said, "she's playing croquet, it's perfectly normal to bend over like that when you're playing croquet." Mum turned to me, studied me for a moment or two, then gave an exasperated shake of her head. "You'd have to be a man – and a vicar – not to see that that pose of hers is carefully calculated and planned," she said caustically as she turned to look at you three again. "Berit," I said, trying to keep a smile on my face, "they're just friends." She didn't get my meaning at first, but when it dawned on her she gave me a look that was so cold and indignant that I never again dared to suggest she might be jealous.

Instead, I tried to convince her that you got a lot out of being with Silje and Jon, because you did. All three of you were interested in the arts, and you inspired one another, learned from one another. You wrote poetry and short stories that I sometimes had the pleasure of hearing you read aloud to one another in our garden. You wrote and performed music which, to be honest, didn't give me quite so much pleasure and – not least – you held lots of long conversations in which you discussed everything under the sun: politics, religion, art and literature, everything. And not a Saturday went by without you coming home with a little pile of books you had borrowed from the library. I regularly heard you telling the other two about what you had read since you last saw them – often books and authors I had never heard of and almost always literature of the gloom-and-doom variety, or so it sounded. At first I wasn't overly concerned about this, I would hear you sitting here, at the same stone table I'm sitting at now, holding forth on nihilism and the pointlessness of life, but I simply took this as a youthful flirtation with certain relatively extreme theories. The pessimistic view of life, which you professed to embrace, did not accord with the ardour, enthusiasm and exuberance that you usually displayed, nor with the confident, well-balanced person I knew you to be, and I interpreted all of this merely as an attempt by three young people to form their own identity by becoming adherents of philosophers whom no one else of their age would have heard of. There were, in fact, some signs that this was indeed the case, that the idea was to create the impression of being well-read, of being intellectual. When you were expecting visitors I noticed, for instance, how you picked out certain books and magazines and placed them where anyone entering the room would be sure to see them, usually lying open at pages with passages underlined or notes in the margin, and usually scattered around somewhat haphazardly to make the room look like the chaotic study of a scholar. And when you and Jon and Silje were talking I would frequently hear you trying to impress them by dropping great names from the worlds of philosophy and literature. You were forever referring to Nietzsche and Schopenhauer, but even though you cited them so naturally, almost as if you were speaking of close personal friends, I was pretty certain that you had not read anything by either of them. You might have borrowed their books from the library and you might even have dipped into them, read the odd passage, but not in any depth and not to any great profit, you were too young and immature for that, after all.

So, even if I wasn't exactly pleased to find you so preoccupied with death and corruption, nihilism and pessimism, I couldn't help chuckling to myself. I had great respect for all three of you, you were far more on the ball than I had been at that age, but there was also something charming, sweet and funny about your eagerness to seem so much gloomier than you actually were. Not that I ever said this to the three of you, of course, I would never have made fun of you. But I did mention it to Mum a few times, because she was worried about you being like this. "It'll pass, Berit," I said, "it doesn't go that deep, he's seventeen, he's out there exploring, but he'll come home again."

As it was, I had other things to worry about just then. I had a suspicion that Mum and Samuel had started seeing one another behind my back and there were times when I felt torn apart by jealousy. I had no proof, but if we met Samuel after not seeing him for a while, certain remarks made me wonder. Like the time when we bumped into him in the street and your mum said, "Oh, by the way, that Isabel

Allende was excellent." "See," Samuel said, "I told you you'd like her. What did you read, *Eva Luna* or *The House of the Spirits*?" Afterwards, once we had gone our separate ways, I asked Mum as casually as I could when she and Samuel had been discussing Isabel Allende. She shrugged and said airily that he had mentioned some authors he liked at the dinner party at the catechist's house. "Oh, I don't remember that," I said with a wry little grin. "Well, you were probably in the loo or something." "No, I don't remember going to the loo either," I said. "What is all this?" she laughed. "Are you giving me the third degree?" "No, of course not," I said and tried to laugh too.

The fact that your mum suddenly started reading novels was, to me, suspicious enough in itself, since she had never shown any interest in books before, and when she also began to "sample a bit of classical music," as she put it, I was left in no doubt that she was trying to change in ways that would please Samuel. As with so many organists, Samuel's favourite composer was Bach and one day, quite out of the blue, Mum came home with the first three *Brandenburg Concertos*. On the rare occasions when she put on some music it was usually one of those old compilation tapes of country and western music or old rock tunes and only once had I seen her actually buy a record – when Namsos-born rock musician Åge Aleksandersen's *Light and Warmth* came out. And now here she was, carting Bach home, and on CD at that, a medium that was still very new and that your Mum had hardly dared touch, being, as she said, such a "technological ignoramus".

I tried to console myself with the thought that she would have done more to cover up her moves toward Samuel if my suspicions were well-founded, that it was so blatant made it seem less than likely. But it was never long before jealousy and suspicion would come creeping back; it had got to the point where they had thrown caution to the winds, I told myself, it had got to the point where they could no longer control it themselves. Oh, that was a terrible time, David, I was so desperate, in such agony and torment.

For all that you were so keen on the arts yourself, you only sneered at Mum's sudden interest in books. As a teenager you were bound, of course, to scoff at and reject anything Mum and I liked, and you rolled your eyes at Isabel Allende, denouncing her writing as a load of Latin American claptrap. Bach was good, obviously, you allowed, a genius, but you couldn't refrain from adding that that particular recording of the *Brandenburg Concertos* wasn't rated all that highly. You rarely listened to classical music, as far as I knew, but you made it sound as though you were an expert on Bach and both Mum and I realized that you must have looked this up in some book or other after she bought the CD. We didn't say anything, though, we had sense enough to know that you needed us to rebel against. Indeed for a long time I also let you think that we differed more in our personalities and opinions than we actually did, reluctant as I was to interfere with what I saw as a natural youthful rebellion. When you played music that I in actual fact thought was pretty good, I would shake my head and mutter "What a racket", and when we were discussing the Israeli–Palestinian conflict I tended to make myself sound more pro-Israeli than I actually was.

But there came a point when your youthful rebellion became so extreme that there was no need for any of that sort of play-acting on my part. The gap between you on the one hand and Mum and I on the other became stark reality, so to speak. We might have commented on and been critical of the pessimistic view of life that you and Jon and Silje had adopted, and we might have sighed in frustration at the attendant unhealthy and somewhat decadent lifestyle, but it wasn't until you began to build up a small collection of bones and teeth that it came to a confrontation of sorts. When Mum was making brawn for Christmas, you retrieved the pig's head from the bin and took it up to your room. When you and Jon came across the carcass of an elk in the forest you filled your rucksacks with the bones and brought them home and once, when you had gone sea fishing with a neighbour, you came back with the jaw of a catfish and the feathery backbone of a large skate that the two of you had filleted. Slowly but surely, what had once been a boy's room with posters of rock bands on the walls was transformed into something resembling a place of sacrifice where you and Silje and Jon would sit in the glow of the candles you had set in tall candelabra, listening to dirge-like chants and talking late into the night. At first your mum thought your collection of bones represented a revolt against me, a man of the church, and she was furious on my behalf, lambasted you for not appreciating all I had done for you. I remember being surprised by the ferocity of her outburst, and although I have to admit I was pleased to hear her defending me and showing concern for me at a time when I was frightened of losing her to Samuel, I had to take her aside and try to calm her down. She was not readily pacified, though, and it did not get any easier, she grew more and more fretful until it got to the stage where she became overprotective of you, she started setting unreasonable limits for when you should be home in the evenings, what you were allowed to read or watch on television and so on. Naturally everyone thought that I was behind this, that this was the stern, finger-wagging vicar trying to keep his stepson on the straight and narrow, but it really wasn't. I backed Berit to the hilt and sided with her in any discussion or row with you, of course I did, this was a firm rule with us, but more and more often when I was alone with her I found myself criticizing her for going too far, for being too hard on you. I told her she didn't need to be so afraid of letting you go, that we had instilled you with good solid attitudes and values and that you would be fine, this was simply a perfectly normal teenage rebellion. But she wouldn't listen to me. She was convinced that Jon and Silje were a bad influence on you. There was something wrong with you she said, she could tell, you were moody and sullen and she also felt that you had grown cynical and apathetic. You no longer went by the rules and the limits we set and you didn't seem to care. "Be back by eleven," she would say, "it's a normal school day tomorrow." "Okay," you would say and then come trailing in at half-past two. "It's like I don't exist," she said to me, "he's lost his way and I feel so helpless."

Then one day something happened that made me feel just as uneasy. We had always been at pains to respect your privacy, we never opened drawers or cupboards where you were likely to keep things you didn't want us to see, but on this particular day Mum accidentally bumped that set of little drawers on top of your desk with a mop, knocking it onto the floor. Several of the drawers fell open and their contents spilled out onto the floor. In one of the drawers was a small plastic bag with a label on it which said something like: "roughly two and half kilos of the person I am at any given time is dead skin. Here is a little bit of the person I was on 14/6/1987" and next to this lay some flakes of shed skin, probably from the soles of your feet. In another drawer lay a bag with a label saying, "not a single tiny molecule is left of the person I was about nine years ago, not a single tiny molecule of the person I am now will be a part of me nine years from now. Here is a little bit of the person I was on 29/9/1987", and inside were some of your toe- and fingernail clippings. And so it went on, you had kept locks of hair, eyebrow hairs, beard stubble, pubic hair and clumps of reddish-brown earwax, all packed in small, clear plastic bags bearing yellow labels, on each of which you had written a line or two.

It was almost like being in a thriller movie, to suddenly come upon this. Like being in the sort of revelatory scene in which some character turns out to be not at all who you thought they were, and if we weren't exactly in a state of shock our faces were certainly pale and grave as we stood there reading the various labels. Neither of us said anything straight away, we even shrank from meeting each other's eyes, I don't quite know why, possibly because deep down we did not want to accept what was happening to you, and because we knew that the anxiety in the other's eyes would make it impossible for us to tell ourselves that everything was really all right.

From then on Mum was convinced that you were mentally ill and she found it impossible to stay calm when we raised the matter with you. She swung between begging you to seek help and threatening all sorts of sanctions if you didn't. We wouldn't give you the money for driving lessons as we had promised we would, she said, and there was no way you would be allowed to go to Denmark for the Roskilde Festival. "But why is it worse for me to stick some locks of my own hair in a plastic bag than for you to stick them in a photo album?" you asked. "I mean, it comes to the same thing." "Oh, but David – toenails?" Mum cried. "Why is saving toenails worse than saving hair?" you asked. "They're both leavings from my own body, they're both reminders of the person I was at a certain point in time."

I couldn't help it, I thought you put your case very well and you were so relaxed and sensible in the face of all this that I felt much easier in my mind after this conversation. Later I would find myself thinking that at that moment I was on the verge of being sucked into your universe, that the limits for what I defined as normal were being pushed out further and further and that I was simply coming to accept more and more of who you were. But I was still concerned enough to accompany Mum when she insisted on going to see Jon's and Silje's mothers, to discuss the situation and discover whether there was anything they could do before things went seriously wrong.

Grete, Jon's mother, didn't seem particularly upset by what Mum told her, although she pretended to be: "What are you saying?" she asked, feigning shock. "Oh, no, now you've got me worried," she said, but she was only saying it because she thought that was what we expected her to say, as I realized when I saw what passed between her and Jon's brother, who was sitting in the background with a barely concealed grin on his face. Just when Mum was at her most distraught I noticed him and his mother exchange a glance and I saw Grete struggling not to laugh. They evidently thought Mum was hysterical and rather than being alarmed they actually seemed to be enjoying the whole business. Not long after this, the catechist told me that he had overheard Grete in a café in town, declaring to her women friends that you were "going to pot," as she put it. In an attempt to appear concerned and responsible she had said that she was going to do everything she could to keep you away from Jon in future, but most of her talk was about Mum: "Seems life isn't all a bed of roses for that

Berit, even if she did marry the vicar," she had said. "They're actually no better than us, no matter what they might think."

Oddrun Schiive, Silje's mother, wasn't worried by what we had to say either, quite the reverse. "But that's great," she said when we told her what we had found in your drawers. "If you ask me, you should be proud to have a son who doesn't want to be one of the common herd, I'm certainly proud of Silje for being able to think for herself and daring to do so," she said. Well, we might have guessed she'd say that, she was known after all for presenting herself as the artistic sort with alternative views on everything and anything. For example, when asked she always said that she worked in the arts, when in fact she had a job in the Arts Centre café, and apart from selling art posters and tickets at the various events at the centre there was no difference between that and waitressing in the café at the local department store or shopping centre. Rumour also had it that her interest in the arts was really just a front, that it was part of an act designed to render her drinking more respectable and a little less shameful. "As if it's somehow more acceptable to swan around with bleary eyes and flushed, puffy cheeks if you're a Bohemian doing something in the arts than if you're an ordinary working woman waiting tables in a café," as the catechist remarked.

Actually, all the partying that went on in that house was one of the reasons why Mum and I were not happy about you spending so much time there. It was one thing to go to parties with kids of your own age – not that we were all that happy about that either, but we accepted it as long as it didn't get out of hand and didn't happen too often – but drinking with Silje's mother and her raggle-taggle bunch of friends weekend after weekend was a very different matter. Mum knew most of the people who frequented that house and according to her they were a sorry shower of middle-aged men, all of whom had at one time dreamed of being musicians, painters or writers, but had wound up as drunken youth workers or supply teachers in Norwegian and music who probably felt younger and less like failures when dispensing their so-called wisdom to you and Jon and Silje.

But all the partying with Oddrun and all those men with potbellies and grey ponytails was just part of it. What dismayed Mum most and also caused me to become seriously worried were the changes in your behaviour. You became more and more moody, you weren't your old cheery self, never animated and eager, although you could still show passion and enthusiasm, but always in a rather grim, resentful way. Even more disturbing was the way you and Silje and Jon had begun to isolate yourselves. Previously, the three of you had at least had some contact with other young people, but now it seemed to be you three and you three only, hardly anyone else ever phoned you and if anyone did you lied and said you were busy, or you asked us to say that you weren't home; you couldn't be bothered talking about football and females and how plastered this person or that had been at the last party, you said, your old pals bored you.

We tried to talk to you about this, but it got us nowhere, which was probably as much our fault us yours. Mum was so distraught that she simply could not contain herself. She may not have got hysterical, not exactly, but it still always ended in tears, entreaties and threats, all of which merely defeated the whole purpose, of course. You responded by sighing and asking if she was about done, which only made her even more frantic and upset and such sessions usually concluded with you getting up and walking out. We had always been able to talk to one another, you and I, we were quite alike, both of us thinkers, and I believe you appreciated the fact that I treated you like an adult and didn't try to act young when we had a conversation. Well, I had seen where that approach got you. Samuel didn't realize, you see, that there were certain unwritten rules concerning who could and who could not use words like "dig" and "cool" and "awesome". He thought that by talking like this he could become one of the gang, be accepted by the kids in his confirmation classes and the Ten Sing choir and he couldn't understand why he met with contempt, why the kids laughed at him behind his back.

But even though I kept a cooler head than your mum and even though I treated you like an adult, I still couldn't get through to you. Maybe I behaved too much like a psychotherapist or a psychologist in my efforts to understand what was going on in your head, maybe you found the whole situation too unnatural and stupid, maybe you felt there was too little conversation and too much questioning and maybe that, in turn, made you feel like a little boy and not like the young, independent man you so wanted to be. Maybe you found it humiliating and hurtful, I don't know. At any rate you would sit there yawning and looking at the clock, making a big show of not being interested, and afterwards Mum and I would be as worried and confused as we had been before we spoke to you.

Hospital, Namsos, July 4th 2006. Reconciling oneself

I open the door and step out into the corridor, look back and see Eilert and his daughter pulling apart. Eilert straightens the collar of his checked flannel shirt and says that it'll be good to get home all right, and his daughter tells him they can't wait to have him home. "Mum's not the same when you're not there," she says. "She's restless, she just wanders around the house and doesn't know what to do with herself," I hear her say before I close the door behind me. I stand for a moment looking round about. It's quiet and pretty peaceful out here, there's a porter up a stepladder, changing a flickering fluorescent tube and the chubby nurse from earlier on comes along wheeling an empty bed. She stops and waits for him to finish so she can trundle on. They look at one another, exchange a few words and I seize the chance to slip past. I'm not up to talking to anyone right now, just want to be alone. I make my way towards the lift, slowly, stiff-legged. I'll take the lift down, go for a little stroll, sit down on one of the benches and enjoy the last of the sunset.

But then the door of one of the rooms opens and out comes Dr Claussen. He turns, says something to a patient in the room and I stop short, glance around for somewhere to hide, I'm not up to talking to Dr Claussen either, can't take his fussing, he has his back to me, still talking, he hasn't spotted me yet, so I nip round the corner and down a side corridor, going as fast as my feeble legs will carry me. I walk all the way to the end and stop, stand there: I'll just have to wait till Dr Claussen has gone past. If he sees me I'll simply say that I took a wrong turn, or maybe that I'm looking at that painting. On the wall in front of me there's a large picture of a man and woman walking hand in hand along a beach, smiling and looking happy, looking blissful. All the pictures in the unit aim to exude an air of bliss, aim to present some sort of idyllic scenario. They're probably supposed to make the unit seem more homey, but they have the exact opposite effect, on me at least, because when I look at this picture I see it for exactly what it is. I see it as an attempt to make me forget that I'm ill, an attempt to help me escape from what I cannot escape. Actually it reminds me of the titbit that the driver of the slaughterer's truck gives the cattle to steady them as they're herded into the truck. I remember this from when I was a little boy and used to visit my grandfather's farm: the driver leaning on the rail of the short ramp leading up into the back of the truck, luring and coaxing the most restive beasts with sugar lumps, and how those stupid cows let themselves be fooled. At such times cattle can sense the horrors that lie ahead, I don't know how, but they do. All animals on their way to the slaughter can sense that something terrible is about to happen and yet it takes no more than a little lump of sugar for them to settle down and climb into the slaughterer's truck, one lump of sugar and they act as if they're on their way to summer pasture. That the people responsible for the decor in here treat me in much the same way as those cattle annoys me, I realize, it makes me feel even more agitated than I was to start with because when faced with such blatant attempts to make me feel at home, such blatant attempts to get me to stay calm and composed, I take it simply as a sign that those of us who have wound up here really do have cause to be worried and afraid. I gaze at the picture, at the happy couple strolling along the beach barefoot with the waves lapping lightly at their toes, and all of a sudden I have the urge to poke my finger through the canvas, have the urge to make a little hole in the painting and ruin it.

Then I hear a voice say: "Arvid." I give a little start, spin round and there's Dr Claussen, his glasses perched on the tip of his nose. He ducks his head slightly, eyes me over his specs.

"Oh, hello," I say and start to walk towards him.

"So, have you been up and walking about as we agreed?" he asks.

"A bit," I say.

"Are you sure?"

"Of course."

He doesn't say anything for a moment, holds my eye, as if weighing me up. A couple of seconds, then I let out a little laugh, a laugh that's as good as an admission that this is not entirely true and he immediately understands the significance of this laugh, I can tell by his face. He doesn't laugh, though, he looks at the floor and removes his glasses, and only now do I notice that he has his glasses on one of those cords. He lets them fall from his hand to dangle on his chest and stands there looking at me.

"As a former vicar who has had a lot to do with people in difficult situations you know this as well as I do, of course," he says. "But I'm going to say it anyway. You are sick, Arvid, but you have to remember that you're not just sick! I know it sounds like something you'd read in a woman's magazine, but you really do still have to make the most of the time which you have left," he says. "And it will take you a lot longer than necessary to get to the stage where you can go home if you don't get up and about more than you're doing."

"I know," I say and force a little smile. "I'll try to do better," I add.

He holds my eye for a second or two.

"Good," he says, then he raises his glasses and pops them back onto his nose, turns on his heel and walks off down the corridor. I stay where I am, following him with my eyes, stay perfectly still. He'll be going off duty soon, then he'll be going home to his family, exactly as I used to go home to my family after telling someone much the same as he has just told me. "I've been in your situation, but you've never been in mine," I say under my breath. "If you only knew what it really feels like," I mutter as I start to walk. As if I haven't done all I could to shake myself out of this frame of mind, as if I haven't tried to extricate myself from this image of myself and dredge up sides of myself other than this, the sick Arvid. To begin with, each day was one long struggle to do just that, behind almost everything I thought and saw and did was an awareness that I mustn't only be sick, that I would only get worse and that I might not get well again if I didn't pull myself together and dredge up a little of the old Arvid. But no matter what I did or thought or said it did no good, the sicker I became the more of my image of myself my illness occupied and now, when I can't even look myself in the eye any longer, the exact opposite is the case: now I want to have as little to do with my old self as possible. The old Arvid has the same effect on me as the pictures in these corridors, every time a little of the old Arvid starts to rise to the surface I have the idea that that I'm simply trying to escape from what I cannot escape, every time I feel happy or enthusiastic or light-hearted a little voice inside me tells me that this is merely a sign that I haven't succeeded in reconciling myself to what lies ahead and if there is one thing I must do, it is to reconcile myself.

I turn the corner and walk over to the lift, slowly and with my stiff, somewhat unsteady gait. Then I hear a crash and a scream. There's a moment's silence and then Eilert's daughter comes running out of our room. "Doctor!" she screams, "Doctor!" She doesn't even see me, her eyes are wide and staring as she runs straight past me and on down the corridor. And here comes the chubby nurse, emerging from the staffroom with her mouth full and half a slice of bread and cod roe in her hand. She stares at Eilert's daughter in alarm. "My dad's collapsed, he's all blue in the face," Eilert's daughter screams. She looks at the chubby nurse and points to our room. The nurse lays her slice of bread on a steel trolley and sprints down the corridor, she flings open a door and says it's an emergency. "Guttormsen in room 301," she says, then she steps aside and first Dr Hartberg then Dr Claussen dash out. Like gladiators when the gate is raised they leap through the door and along the corridor, grim-faced, their white coats open and blown back, flapping like the capes of a couple of superheroes. "Hurry, please!" Eilert's daughter wails and I step out of the way, flatten myself against the wall to let the doctors past, stand there watching all the commotion. Eilert's daughter holds the door of the room open for the doctors and I catch a glimpse of her father. He's lying on the floor, blue in the face, the gnarled veins on his temples are thick as pencils and his eyes are bulging out of his head like little glass domes. Eilert is going to die, I can tell, there's nothing the doctors can do here, I can't take it in, it's all over for Eilert.

"You'd better stay here," the chubby nurse says, placing a hand on Eilert's daughter's shoulder as the girl makes to go back into the room. "Come here," she says and she pulls Eilert's daughter to her, holds her and strokes her hair. I stand there staring at them for a second or two, see how utterly distraught Eilert's daughter is. She throws her arms around the nurse and buries her face in her shoulder, sobbing with despair, her fingers clawing at the white tunic and making faint scratching noises before they dig into the nurse's back. "Oh, please don't let him die," she sobs, "please don't let him die."

I stare at her and swallow. I ought to go now, I've no right to be here, watching this, it's too private, but still I stand there, stand bolt upright, staring at the young woman weeping like this for someone she loves, weeping for her own father. A couple of seconds, then it's as if I somehow break free of myself, come to my senses, and I start to walk away. I walk towards the lift, slowly and with my faltering, unsteady step. But how can Eilert die like this? It can't have anything to do with his illness, I don't understand it.

"Oh, my God," I murmur, raising one hand and running it over my smooth scalp. I give a faint shake of my head, my jaw drops slightly and I carry on along the corridor with my mouth half open and my eyes wide. A few moments pass, then slowly the thought creeps over me that I'm not actually as sad and shocked as all this posing and posturing would suggest. It's awful to think of Eilert lying there dying, but I'm not as sad as all that. "I'm actually not nearly as sad as I would have thought," I mutter, and immediately feel a twinge of guilt; guilt because I'm affecting to feel more sorry for Eilert than I actually am, guilt because I don't feel more sorry than I do.

"Well, this is a hospital, after all," I mutter, "and it doesn't exactly come as a shock if someone dies up here. I mean, they're prepared for it." And this makes me feel a little less guilty, I can tell. I don't think my death would have been a bigger blow to Eilert than his is to me, we hardly knew one another, and I'm sure he would have forgotten me as quickly as I'll forget him. I make my way up to the lift, press the "Down" button and wait, watch the red numbers marking the lift's progress. "As quickly forgotten by Eilert as by everyone else," I mumble to myself. Then the lift door glides open. Fortunately it's empty, because I realize that my eyes are wet, I feel the tears beginning to well up. No, this won't do, I can't stand here blubbing, somebody might get in, I need to pull myself together. But it's no use, the tears well up and I feel a cold trickle down one cheek. "Poor Eilert," I say. "Poor Eilert," I say again and I try to picture Eilert as he was only a short time ago, try to picture that jovial face, hear that bright, cheery voice. "Poor Eilert," I say for a third time, but I can't kid myself, I know I'm only saying it because I'd rather cry over Eilert's death than over my own plight. "And I was so rude and mean to him," I mumble, not about to give up, trying to get out of having to blame myself. But it does no good, it only makes matters worse because the way I behaved towards Eilert only serves to highlight what my problem is. I'm not that stupid, I know why I was so rude and mean to him, obviously it wasn't only because I was sick and tired of him talking so much, talking and talking and always about the same things, it was just as much because I envied him his wife and the two daughters he was forever going on about, I realize that. When he talked about his family it reminded me that I also needed someone to live for and that's why I was so rude and spiteful and tactless. Because what I needed more than anything else was someone to live for, someone to whom I could show the old me. Just as Eilert was being the old Eilert for his youngest daughter only a moment ago, I suppose I need someone for whom I can be the old Arvid. Just as Eilert could appear strong for her, I suppose I need someone to appear strong for. It's because I haven't had that, you see, that my illness has been able to gain control, gain the upper hand. The main reason why the old Arvid disappeared as fast as he did, that the illness was allowed to become so dominant when the new Arvid came into being, was that I had no one with whom I could be my old self. I haven't had anyone for whom I could appear cheerful and full of fight, and it's this and not the disease itself that has made me the man I am today. I've always tried to convince myself that I was merely facing the facts, that this new Arvid is simply a result of an attempt to reconcile myself to reality. But that's not so, rather the reverse. This supposed willingness to reconcile myself to my own fate is merely another attempt to escape, merely an attempt to avoid admitting to myself that the old Arvid has no one to live for. "Oh, God, how maudlin can you get," I say, then I shake my head briskly and wipe the tears from my eyes. "That'll do, Arvid," I mutter, shaking my head again impatiently. I try to laugh a little at myself, but I can't, my mouth pulls out of shape and I have to bite the inside of my cheek to stop myself from crying even more.

Namsos, July 19th–21st 2006

One day I overheard the verger and the parish clerk talking in shocked tones about some man who had apparently had a child by a woman little more than half his age. They were sitting in one of the back pews in the church drinking coffee and they didn't notice me standing in the doorway, catching a breath of fresh air. And that I'm glad of, because when it became clear from their conversation that the man in question was Samuel I am ashamed to report that I was so overjoyed that I was unable to stifle the little burble of laughter that escaped me.

I guessed that this would come as a bit of a blow to Mum, but even when we were sitting at the dinner table that evening and I was waiting for the right moment to tell her what I'd heard, I couldn't help gloating. "I feel so sorry for Samuel," I said, sounding as if I meant it. "Oh, why?" Mum asked, but even as she said it I realized that she already knew all about it, I could tell just by looking at her. She made a half-hearted attempt to look puzzled, but she was clearly vexed at being confronted with this news and while I was telling her about it she kept her eyes fixed mainly on her food and said "Hmm" and "Oh, dear". I should have stopped myself, of course, and asked her how long she had known, but I couldn't bring myself to do so and she couldn't bring herself to admit that she knew, especially since she had initially tried to give the impression that she didn't. So we both endeavoured to act out this little charade as best we could and I was just about to change the subject when you suddenly announced that you had heard Samuel was a randy old goat. Everything immediately went very quiet. I tried to gauge from your face whether you actually knew anything and whether this remark had been meant as a sarcastic dig at Mum and me, but I don't think it was because you looked at us in amazement, obviously wondering what you had said. Mum struggled hard not to let her feelings show, she went on eating, but her face was grim and clouded and when you giggled and asked what exactly you had said wrong, she turned to you and said with inordinate asperity that she would thank you not to use such language at the dinner table. You blew up at her and asked if she was going to tell you how to talk now too, and this brought the conversation round, yet again, to how you had changed and how worried we were; to the need for limits and you having obligations as well as rights, and so on and so forth. Eventually you said: "Please may I leave the table?" then you got up and walked out. Your mother sat where she was, shaking her head and close to tears while I went after you and asked if you wouldn't please come back so we could talk. "Talk?" was all you said, and you grinned wryly as you tied your shoelaces with sharp, fierce tugs.

Worse was to come, though. One day I came home from work to find Mum crying in your room. Her eyes were red and swollen and when I asked what was wrong she didn't say anything, just shook her head and pointed to your bed – and there was your diary. "Read that," she said. I knew of course that by reading your diary I would be overstepping the mark, but given the gravity of the situation I had no choice, and what I read and what I saw there made my blood run cold. The countless poems about death, decay and corruption were one thing – those and the almost morbid fascination with everything that was dark and destructive, the innumerable detailed drawings of forms of torture and methods of execution, the way you romanticized suicide and attempted to justify it by means of warped interpretations of Camus, Zapffe and Schopenhauer. All of this was dreadful and disturbing, of course, but I found it hard to take it as seriously as I ought to have. I couldn't get it to fit with the person that I knew you to be, deep down. Still I construed it as a youthful flirtation with extreme theories and standpoints.

What did cause my legs to give way, though, forcing me to drop down onto the bed next to Mum, was a brief description of something that had happened once when you and Jon were out walking in the hills: you had met a girl (mentioned by name in the diary), she had got lost and you refused to tell her the way home until she had sex with both of you. I can't remember ever having read anything, before or since, that has left me as stunned as that entry in your diary. It was so brutal and vicious that I felt like throwing up after I had read it. I had barely recovered from that shock when we confronted you with it and you dealt us another shock. It wasn't true, you said. You were angry and on the offensive. You told us you had been wondering how far we were willing to go to control you and that certain entries in your diary had been written to find out just that. The incident with the lost girl was all lies, you said, we could phone her and check if we liked, you had simply decided to write something so terrible that, if we read it, Mum and I would find it impossible not to confront you with it, thus giving ourselves away. "Well, now I know I can't trust you any more than you trust me," you said. Mum and I didn't know what to say, and a moment later, when you turned and walked out, we felt we were losing you for ever. We didn't know what to do and in frustration I turned on Mum and said that now she really had to tell you who your real father was.

For some time I had had a vague and possibly mistaken idea that your real father had something to do with all this. The man in whose image you were actually supposed to shape yourself was absent. Indeed, not only was he absent, you didn't even know who he was, and I had an idea that this had led to you having an identity crisis much more drastic than the usual crises of identity experienced by all teenagers.

You had always said you had no great desire to know who he was. You used to snort scornfully when you heard stories of people who had grown up knowing nothing of their origins, because no matter whether these stories were presented in the form of novels or films the question of the central character's real mother's or father's identity was always made out to be the most crucial question in his or her life. According to these accounts, anyone who didn't know the names of their birth parents could never be happy, they would always feel that something vital was missing and that, whether they knew it or not, their life would be one restless hunt for their roots. This search might be disguised as a constant hunt for new sexual partners or the ultimate high or all manner of religious experiences or political and ideological father figures, but in the end it always boiled down to the same thing: the search for one's biological origins. But, you used to say, all of these were nothing but displays of sentimentality, they had little or nothing to do with reality. Naturally you did sometimes wonder who your father was, but this was not and never had been something you thought of every day, you got on perfectly well without knowing who your real father was.

I have to admit that it was good to hear you say this, especially when Jon and Silje were there. I loved you like my own son and there was a part of me that wanted you not to miss your real father and wanted everyone around us to hear you say as much. Now and then I might have had the suspicion that this was exactly why you said it, that you knew I cherished a desire to be all you needed and that this was your way of letting me know that I was. To me this was a declaration of love so powerful that I found it hard not to show how happy it made me.

But hard though it was for me, and even harder for your mum, this situation was so serious that I had no choice but to raise the question of your paternity with her. I had tried once before, not long after we met, but her reaction back then had left me in no doubt that your real father was a no-go area. And gentle though her dismissal of the subject had been, it was also so firm and clear that I decided to leave it at that for the time being. I hoped and trusted that she would eventually find it easier to tell me about it. I thought perhaps she harboured a secret that she felt you could not cope with hearing until you were a certain age, or that she wanted to put off saying anything until we had been together long enough for her to feel sure that I would never abandon her, no matter what she told me. Whatever the case, I had made up my mind to ask her again before we got married and I probably would have done, if she hadn't beaten me to it and made it a condition of marrying me that I let that particular question lie for ever. In love as I was and willing to forgo anything for love of her, I promised never to ask again, and I actually succeeded in keeping that promise until the day when you stormed out because we had read your diary.

You had no sooner slammed the front door than I turned to Mum and said that it was time you were told who your real father was. I hadn't planned on saying it, it just slipped out and I remember giving a start as I said it. Mum, on the other hand, acted as if she hadn't heard what I had said. She had the same sad look on her face that she'd been wearing before I said it. At first I thought she was pretending not to have heard, thus giving me the chance to get it out of my system by behaving as if I had said something other than what I had actually said, but that was not the case, as I discovered when I plucked up the courage to repeat it. "I don't know what we're going to do," was all she said, and there was nothing in her voice or her expression to suggest that she was putting on an act. She didn't respond at all to what I had said, it was as if she had an in-built psychological mechanism that prevented her from taking in anything associated with your biological father and I remember what a strong impression this made on me. I used to have a friend who discovered that his wife was psychotic and he described to me what it was like to see the person he loved most in the world become a total stranger to him. It wasn't until the moments after I had mentioned your biological father to your mother that I finally understood what he had meant. I never spoke to your mother about this episode, I never saw her look like that again and I tried to forget that this side of her existed. Nor did I ever mention your biological father again. I tried to tell myself that there were times when it was better not to know and all the signs were that this was one of those times.

Later it would occur to me that Mum and I only used you as an excuse for staying together when our marriage was falling apart. Compared with parents who have drug addicts or delinquents in the house, or anorexic kids for that matter, we really had little to complain about or to worry us and it struck me that, each in our own way, we blew your problems out of all proportion and made the situation much worse than it actually was. By standing by you I wanted to show that I was a worthy father for you and a good family man; the more troubled I made you out to be, the better I would look and consciously or unconsciously the aim was always to show Mum that I and not Samuel was the man for her.

Mum, for her part, overdramatized your problems because, having been let down by Samuel she wanted to find her way back to me, or so I thought. She was also genuinely worried about you, of course, but when Samuel told her that he was having a child by another woman she turned your problems more and more into a project that she and I had to accomplish together, a project that would bind us to one another and help us to save the marriage that she had been about to walk out of. Because the more I thought about it, the more convinced I was that she had seriously been considering leaving me. I would sit alone, thinking, and I came up with clue after clue to support this theory. The disproportionately fierce animosity she felt towards Silje, for example, stemmed from the thought that such a "rude, shameless little tart" possessed all the qualities that Mum herself would have needed to possess in order to leave me for Samuel, so every time she saw Silje she was reminded of her own shortcomings. She was, I concluded, quite simply jealous of her. Something similar had happened when you built up that bone collection and your mum took you to task for not being grateful for all I had done for you over the years. Mum was eternally grateful to me for having rescued you and her from a life with Erik, and since it was this same gratitude that prevented her from leaving me for Samuel it hurt her to see how you could take me so much for granted. She envied you that ability.

At brighter moments, though, I saw what had happened in a very, very different light. The challenges we had been faced with as a family when you were a rebellious teenager may not have been huge compared to what other families had to cope with, but if you looked at the bigger picture, for many years we were almost outrageously happy and hence, when we did encounter problems and challenges, they seemed greater than they actually were, or so it seemed to me. As if that weren't enough, at some point the past seemed to catch up on Mum. Her childhood had been a catalogue of disasters and it was as though she had begun to doubt that the happy life she had with you and me could last. She seemed almost to be preparing herself for fresh disasters to strike and, since she regarded what was happening to you as the start of just such a disaster, she felt both desperate and afraid. Samuel had nothing to do with this, I would tell myself, he had been nothing but a passing fancy, an infatuation that had eventually run its course, as such infatuations tend to do.

At other times it has crossed my mind that you and Silje and Jon really were getting into deep water and that our concern was not merely justified, but possibly not as great as it ought to have been. More than anything, it was Jon's attempt to kill himself that made me think this. It was his mother who found him. She suffered from some sort of neuromuscular disease and had got up in the night to take a painkiller only to discover that several bottles of pills were missing. At first she had thought Jon's brother must have taken them when he had called at the house earlier that evening: he was a drug addict just like their father and if she hadn't heard the sound of music coming from Jon's room she probably wouldn't have gone in there at all. He was still conscious when she found him, but the pills had begun to take effect and fortunately he was too dopey and confused to stop her calling the ambulance.

I don't think any of us realized how fragile, sensitive and highly strung Jon was and how easily he could be manipulated and led on by things you and Silje said and did. It wasn't your fault that he tried to take his own life, of course. He was a troubled and tormented soul and who or what was to blame for that I don't know. For you, the fascination with death and destruction was probably just an innocent exploration of yourself and of the big questions in life, but for Jon it was the proverbial last straw. Maybe he wanted to impress the two of you, maybe he felt small and insignificant or maybe he wished to show that of the three of you he was the one who dared to do what you and Silje only talked about.

You and Silje gradually lost touch with Jon after that, as I recall. He was deeply ashamed of what he had done and even though it had been his own choice to swallow those pills he was well aware, of course, that the company he kept had also had something to do with it, so it was understandable that he wanted to distance himself somewhat from you two. Oddly enough, this close encounter with death also prompted you to abandon your warped philosophizing and all it entailed. Not overnight, obviously. I think that in some way you would have regarded that as a loss of face. Slowly but surely, though, you began at any rate to gravitate away from the person you had been before Jon's suicide attempt. Your youthful rebellion was over and you were on your way home again.

Hospital, Namsos, July 4th 2006. Home again

The lift is starting to slow down, so now I really will have to pull myself together, I don't want to be caught blubbing here if somebody gets on, so I hastily tug my sleeve down over my hand, raise my hand to my face and dry my tears. A couple of seconds, then I hear the long hiss of the brakes followed by a high, grating whine as the lift comes to a halt. It gives a long shudder, then a little lurch before it stops completely and the doors slide open. I step out, walk slowly past the reception desk and down to the entrance. Someone has left a newspaper on top of the rubbish bin outside the kiosk; I pick it up on the way past, it's always good to have a paper to hide behind when you don't feel like talking to anyone. On the other side of the entrance hall I see a bloke from the room next to mine, he looks across at me, smiles and nods, but I don't nod back, I run my eye vacantly around the entrance hall and pretend not to see him, I don't want to risk him coming over, I'm not up to that, I'm in no mood to talk to anybody right now. I walk out into the warm summer evening. There's an empty bench under the lilac tree so I stroll over to it and sit down. I shut my eyes and breathe in through my nose, smell the sweet scent of new-mown grass. I sit like this for a little while, then I open my eyes, lay the newspaper on my lap and open it.

And suddenly I'm looking straight into David's eyes. "David," I cry out and I snatch up the newspaper in both hands and bring it close to my face. I haven't seen him for years, not since he moved away from the town, but that's him in the picture, there's no doubt about it, that's David. But what on earth is he doing in the paper, what does it say, he's lost his memory? I feel my mouth fall open and I crease my brow, try to focus and rapidly skim the newspaper report, read that he has lost his memory, that he doesn't know who he is, his past has been erased and everyone who knows or has known him is urged to contact the authorities so that he can be helped to discover who he is. I tip my head back slightly, look up at the sky and shake my head, sit like that, open-mouthed, for a couple of seconds. "Oh, my God!" I murmur.

Well, I'll have to do my bit, that's for sure, there weren't many people who knew David as well as I did when he was younger so I'll have to do all I can to help with this. "I'll help you, David," I murmur solemnly, and as the words leave my mouth I feel a surge of eagerness, I feel so eager to get on with this task, and I'm conscious that it makes me happy again just to know that I'm still capable of feeling such eagerness. I feel filled with a strange sense of happiness, something akin to relief. "So there is a little of the old Arvid left," I murmur and even as I say it I realize that I've been given the very thing that I have just been shedding tears over, because it was gone. Only a moment ago I was standing in the lift, crying because I no longer had any of the old Arvid in me, because I had no one to care for and show my positive qualities to, crying because this had turned me into a sick man and nothing but a sick man. But suddenly everything has changed, I think. Suddenly I have someone for whom I can be the old Arvid. David has lost his memory, he has no idea who he is and he needs me to tell him.

I lower the newspaper onto my lap, sit there staring into space for a couple of seconds, feel myself filled with a strange, faint sense of happiness. "Ah, no," I say, and I feel a sneaking twinge of guilt, feel guilty for sitting here feeling happy when someone who was once very close to me has been struck by such a tragedy. "Poor David," I say, shaking my head. "Poor David," I say again and it helps, I can feel it, feel the guilt ebbing away. A second, then I get to my feet and start to walk back to the entrance, because now I have to hurry, I have to hurry along to the computer room, have to hurry up and write an email to ask how to proceed. The best thing would probably be to write down everything I remember, put it all down in writing and post it or email it, that would be best, I suppose, but I can ask the psychologists what they think, take their advice. There could be all sorts of considerations that I'm not aware of, I'm sure there must be both practical and more psychological aspects to be taken into account in such cases, I'll have to remember to ask about all that sort of thing, find out about it, it's important, I mutter to myself, then the doors slide open and I stride into the entrance hall, going as fast as my feeble legs will carry me, and there's the computer room, I can see it, down at the end of the corridor. I feel so fired up, I can scarcely remember the last time I felt so inspired and it's so good to have something as important as this to do, it feels so good to matter to someone, to be allowed to give something of oneself to another human being. "It sounds so banal, but you don't realize how true it is until you've been hit by loneliness," I mutter under my breath, "you don't realize how dependent you actually are on other people until you've felt what it's like to be lonely," I mutter and I give a little laugh, laughing at the banality of what I'm saying. "Ah, no," I say, "no, that's enough now," I mutter, because I can feel the guilt returning. "This person who was once my stepson, the boy I loved as if he were my own, little David, has been struck by tragedy and here I am feeling happy again," I mutter and I give a little shake of my head, shake my head to salve my guilty conscience. "Yes," I mutter, "but it's not the fact that David's been struck by tragedy that has fired me with such enthusiasm. Surely it must be possible to differentiate between the tragedy itself and the joy I feel at being able to help," I mutter. "The tragedy has already struck, so what better than to throw myself into the task with zeal and enthusiasm. It's not as if I'm feeling happy because this misfortune has befallen David," I mutter and I'm conscious that what I'm saying is true, it's true, and this in turn makes it even more alright to feel happy. This new fire, this spark that was lit when I read about what had happened, well obviously I have to tend it and keep it burning, I have to do it for David's sake, and I have to do it for my own sake, this task comes almost as a gift to me. Only a little while ago I was blubbing in the lift because I believed I had no one to live for, and then, out of the blue, I'm given this. I've never seen things in this light before, never give any real thought to how much influence other people actually have on who I am as a person. Well, obviously I had thought about it in a more superficial way: there can't be many people who talk as much about brotherly love as we clerics; in all my years in the ministry, in sermon after sermon, talk after talk I wrote and spoke about loving thy neighbour and yet I don't think I had ever understood what it meant, not until today, not until I was standing blubbing in that lift, not until it struck me that the absence of any close kith or kin has probably had as much to do with how I've changed as my illness. And no sooner had I come to the conclusion that what I missed most of all was having someone to live for, no sooner had I told myself this than it was given to me, the very thing I was crying for. "And if that isn't a gift I don't know what is," I mutter. "No, it's more than a gift, it's a miracle," I mutter as I sit down in front of one of the computers and even as I hear myself say this an avalanche sweeps through me, a long avalanche of joy, because suddenly I see it, I see it all so clearly and distinctly, suddenly I see that it is God who has granted me this gift and that is Him who has worked this miracle. I see it and I feel this almighty force running through me, feel my whole body being filled with the power of the Lord and I can only sit here, incapable of speech, incapable of movement, because this, this is the greatest gift of all, I am with God, again, I have come home to Him once more. In the blink of an eye I've been shaken out of the life I've led for the past year and into a new life with God. Since I became ill I don't know how many times I've prayed to God for a miracle, it's years since I resigned my ministry and forsook the Lord, but in my despair I prayed anyway; weeping and with clasped hands I've begged and pleaded for him to make me well again, but I've never received a single sign, not one, not until now, not until today, not – it strikes me – until I prayed for a miracle regarding something other than being cured of my illness. The minute I did that, God revealed himself to me, and that very fact is significant. "This can't be a coincidence," I mutter excitedly and no sooner have I said this than I realize what it is God has been trying to show me – well, what was it I was praying for, what was it I was crying for in that lift and saying that I lacked: someone to live for, a neighbour to love. "The nature of brotherly love, that's what this is all about," I mutter, "what it means to love they neighbour and how much it's worth, that's what it's about."

I raise my eyes, tilt my head back instinctively and gaze at the ceiling. "Thank you, Lord," I whisper, then I swallow and wait a moment. I feel my mouth widening into a little smile, then I straighten my head, face front again. I smile and feel myself being filled with joy and gratitude. And now I'm going to write an email and ask how I can best help David. I may not have that much time left, a month perhaps, or possibly six months, Dr Claussen said. At any rate, whatever time I have left I'm going to use to help David. "Help David and help myself," I mutter. Because by helping David I'll be helping myself too. Having someone to live for is what makes us human. It's banal but true, if we have no one to live for we cease to exist; the old Arvid disappeared when he lost those closest to him and only with God's help can he rise again. By praising God and all His works I have been reborn; to love thy neighbour as thyself is to praise all that God has created and all that God is and only through this can we find salvation.

Namsos, July 23rd–24th 2006

On the morning of August 11th 1989, as she was trying on a new pair of shoes in Ole Bruun Olsen's shoe shop, your mum's aorta burst and she keeled over and died.

While she was still alive I had occasionally tried to imagine how I would react if she died before me and when I did this I had felt a certain light-heartedness that I was reluctant to acknowledge and that always made me feel guilty. I knew of course that I would be devastated if I lost her, but the thought of being able to do exactly as I pleased and of being spared some of the obligations that come with marriage did sometimes seem tempting and exciting. But when she really did die there was none of that whatsoever. I didn't feel so much as a glimmer of excitement, no thrill at being free, neither immediately after her death nor when I was starting to get back on my feet. Losing her was just terrible. In order to make the loss easier to bear I tried to convince myself that she hadn't really loved me, that she would have left me and gone to live with Samuel if he hadn't let her down. But it didn't work, she had got over Samuel a good while before she died and if there was anything at all to forgive I had long since forgiven her. As she had always forgiven me for the mistakes, big and small, that I had made. I remember

I also tried to make myself angry with her by thinking back on the things about her that had irritated me: a strategy I had heard counsellors recommend to people coping with the breakdown of a relationship. I thought of how often she had tried to make me feel guilty by being in such a hurry to do things that were actually my responsibility, but which she felt I didn't do soon enough. I thought of how bright and bubbly she could be, giggling at the silliest things when she was with some of her women friends, and how she would simply become brighter and bubblier when she saw how this annoyed me. I thought of how she snored, how she smoked on the sly, and of how she mispronounced certain foreign words or used them in the wrong context and how it always embarrassed me when other people heard her do this. But since that was the worst I could come up with, this strategy actually had the opposite effect. The fact that I could only come up with such petty failings simply served to underline how well Mum and I had got on and this made my grief all the greater. I balk at writing this because more than once since then I have found myself thinking that it was such a ridiculously sentimental thing to do, but I actually kept the pillow on which she had dreamed her dreams. Every single night for one or possibly two years after she died I slept with my head on her pillow, hoping that with its help I might meet her in my dreams.

I still think it's a lovely thought, however sentimental it might be, but it was also a symptom. I didn't realize it at the time, but looking back on it I can see that it was also one of many signs that I was no longer capable of living among the living, so to speak. It was not only Mum who departed this world on that August day in 1989, the man I had been for as long as I had known her and you also departed this world. Because it's trite but true: when there is no longer anyone to document our life, when there is no longer anyone to tell the funny stories of how stubborn we are or how grumpy in the mornings; when we no longer have anyone who will laugh when we tell a joke or get mad at us when we are bad-tempered: when we no longer have anyone to remind us of who we are; when we no longer have anyone to encourage us to be the person we can be, we crumble away to nothing. Even Arvid the Christian crumbled away to nothing in the weeks and months that followed. Although, I don't know whether this was due purely to the loss of Mum, it certainly wasn't as if losing her rendered me incapable of believing in a good and a just God – nothing so banal. My loss of faith was possibly more a sign of the secularization that was taking place all around us. As a vicar I had had plenty to say about yuppiedom and dancing round the golden calf. I had warned against the growth of materialism and been concerned about the flight from the world of the spirit, but I did not see that I too was a part of the society and the times in which this was happening. I wasn't merely a vicar who could and should help reverse this trend, I was also a small individual, and one who was equally affected by this same development. But it wasn't until after Mum died that this was really brought home to me. When I stood in the pulpit for the first time after returning from sick leave I remember being struck by how empty the church was. There probably weren't any fewer people there than there had been before my leave of absence, but after my time away it seemed so to me and this triggered a train of thought in my mind. It was as if during my brief absence God and all the godly had left this world, they had fled in all haste, rather like the Jews during the war, and here I was, standing in a large and almost deserted church, talking as if nothing had happened. I looked at the cross, at the altarpiece, at the font and all the beautiful paintings on the walls and suddenly I saw myself as a bewildered museum director. I was coming to the end of one of the first sermons I had given since returning to work and suddenly I had this image of myself as a museum director who thought he was living in the age from which his museum exhibits dated. Nothing outrageous happened, I finished the sermon as normal and I gave several sermons after that. But I could not get that image out of my mind and this sense of not being a part of my own time, of not living in the same age as all the people I saw round about me every day, filled me with an overwhelming dread. I would wake up in the middle of the night drenched in sweat and ask myself what I was really doing with my life. Suddenly and without any warning this question would come into my head; it happened more and more often, I was given no peace. I tried putting it down to a perfectly normal mid-life crisis and I laughed at myself, told myself I ought to buy a motorbike. But it did no good, it was only a stupid attempt to take the sting out of the question and I couldn't fool myself into thinking anything else, the situation was too serious for that. I hardly slept at all any more, many a time you were woken in the middle of the night by me talking to myself downstairs in the living room.

"Who are you talking to," you asked me once. "Hmm?" I looked up to see you standing there in nothing but your underpants. You scratched the fine line of hair running downwards from your navel. "Who are you talking to?" "Oh, I was just having a little chat with myself," I said, trying to smile. "At least that way I'm always in the right!" I added, as if such a stupid crack would make it all seem slightly less worrying. You neither smiled nor laughed, you simply shook your head, then you turned and went back up to your room without saying a word.

It's dreadful to think that you had to witness everything that I went through at that time, David. Eventually it got so bad that I had to see a psychologist and it was after many long sessions with him that I decided to give up the ministry and accept the job of accountant. After that things started to improve slightly. Not only was I relieved to finally have made my decision and not only was I sure that I had been right to resign my vocation, I also felt it was good to work with something as concrete as accounting, where I could put a double line under the final balance and go home for the day. I needed that.

Still, though, something wasn't right. I was functioning on a day-to-day level. I went to work, earned money and did whatever had to be done in and around the house. But I did it joylessly, reluctantly. Where I would once have pushed myself to work on for an extra hour or two just for a word of praise or an admiring glance from Mum, now I was more liable to stop an hour early. I put off cleaning the house and washing the dishes until I couldn't put it off any longer, even though I had much more spare time than I had had as a vicar, and I no longer put on a smart shirt at the weekend, as I had done when Mum was alive. I didn't even make myself something a little more special for dinner on Saturday evenings. It was a life devoid of cheer and magic, I was not so much living at that time as simply surviving.

So it wasn't surprising that I saw less and less of you, or that you eventually moved in with Silje and her mother. Only vestiges remained of the man I had been and you needed more than that, you needed a good male role model, a man you could look up to and strive to emulate, and I was unable to be that for you back then.

Now, though, I have regained something of the old Arvid. I won't go into all the details except to say that what I have tried to do for you with this letter you have already done for me. You have brought to life a little of the man you knew when you were about ten or eleven and moved into the vicarage with your mum. This may even have left its stamp on what I've written here, you may read this letter and recognize aspects of the man I was then, something about the tone, the tenor, something about the mood, I don't know, but I can hope.

You know, I'm often been unsure of exactly how to phrase things here. I have sometimes felt like a mad scientist, playing at being God and attempting to create an ideal new human being. I have felt tempted to fill you with false memories, not because I wanted to present myself as better than I was, but because I had a burning desire to present you as someone who believes in God and thereby turn you into someone who believes in God. I admit it, there was a part of me, especially when I began this letter, that was desperate to make a Christian of the person you are now by leading you to think that you had always been a Christian. I'm not going to dwell on this, but I was in a kind of ecstasy when I started writing and my missionary zeal may well have had something to do with this. As I wrote, though, it became more and more clear to me that I loved you exactly as you were and that it is the boy you were that I miss. Just at this moment the mere idea that I could have contemplated improving you fills me with shame. As if I could have done that. Talk about arrogant.

But let me close this letter as I began, David. As a Christian I believe that everything ends with us coming home, so let me close with our homecoming, with the first day of what were to be the best years of my life. I can see myself in the yellow Simca I had borrowed from the parish clerk, I see the heavy green branches hanging over the road, the shadows of the leaves softly flickering over the yellow gravel and Berit's red hair fluttering lightly in the draught from the half-open car window. "Are you excited?" Mum asked. "Yes," you said. "Any minute now we'll see it," she said and then she turned to you and smiled. "But ... what have you done to yourself?" "Done to myself?" you echoed, not quite understanding what she was talking about. "There," she said, nodding at you. "Your finger, you're bleeding." "Oh, that. I had a bit of an accident, that's all, cut myself with my pocketknife." "Oh, no," Mum said, "does it hurt?" You raised your eyebrows and eyed her quizzically. "What, that?" you said. "No!" "Are you sure?" Mum asked. But you just laughed and didn't even bother to answer. "Women!" I said. I shot you a glance in the rear-view mirror and shook my head. "Hey, you!" Mum cried in that pretend-cross voice of hers and punched me on the shoulder. I laughed and shot you another glance. "The weaker sex, eh, David?" I said. "Yep," you said, laughing back at me. Mum turned and glared at you, then faced front again, sat there shaking her head. "See, I told you. You two are always ganging up on me." I looked at you in the mirror and winked, and you smiled back. "Look, David," Mum said. "There's the house." You didn't say anything right away, simply sat with one hand on each front seat gazing at the rambling red-brick pile which was to be your home from then on. The car wheels crunched over the gravel as we drove up in front of the house, the neighbour's elk hound barked fiercely a couple of times, but he was old and tired and soon fell quiet again. We climbed out of the car and stood looking at the house. Behind us the car engine clicked and clunked: we could hear the flies buzzing about over in the flowerbed and I remember that the backs of my knees and thighs were damp and sweaty from sitting in the boiling-hot car. "Here you are, David," I said, pulling the door key out of my shorts pocket and handing it to him. "Go up the stairs, turn right and you'll come to your room." "Oh, yeah!" you whooped and off you raced across the drive. Mum and I watched you for a few moments, then we turned to one another and smiled. "Do I get a kiss?" Mum said softly and as I bent down to kiss her we heard a long "Yuck" from you on the front steps. I can hear it now, David, I can hear it and see it and it reminds me that loving gestures are handed down through the generations. One day, when you kiss your own wife and are good to her, I would like to see that as an echo of the time when I kissed Mum and was good to her. And one day, when you tuck in your own child and tenderly kiss its cheek, I would like to see this as an echo of the kisses and caresses Mum and I gave you at bedtime when you were small. That, I hope, is how I will live on in this world, through the kisses and caresses I gave to you and to others. Anything else of myself that might remain is of no interest to me.

Silje

Silje

I look at Mum and I look at Egil and Egil's talking and Mum's listening to what he's saying and I smile at them and act as though I'm paying attention. I put my hand to my mouth and stifle a yawn, never taking my eyes off them. It's like I'm looking straight through them and on through Mum's flat, but they think I'm looking at them, they think I'm paying attention, and I open my mouth as if to say something, then close it again as if I've decided not to say it after all. And Egil talks and talks and Mum murmurs "Oh, really," and takes a sip of her brandy, then murmurs, "Mm-hmm" and takes a little sip of her coffee, and I pick up my coffee cup and take a sip of my coffee, then put the cup down with a little chink. "Will you run the girls down to the bus station afterwards?" The words blurt out of me and Egil turns to me, taken aback, and I look at him and I realize that he hadn't quite

213

finished talking, I realize that my question came right out of the blue. "Er," says Egil, gazing at me wide-eyed and a little laugh escapes me, but he doesn't catch it, he has turned to Mum, he shoots her a puzzled glance, but Mum avoids his eye, she looks as if she's just happy not to have to listen to him any more, she's tired of all his talk, and she leans quickly over the table and drains the last of her brandy and I hear the hum of the fridge out in the kitchen.

"Oh, come on, Silje," Egil says. "It's only a fifteen minute walk to the bus station," he says. "I don't like them walking down there on their own after dark," I say. "Oh, come on, Silje," he says again, tilting his head to one side and smiling at me. "Okay, okay, then I'll have to take them," I say, eyeing him a little wearily and he gives that sweet smile of his and winks gently at me. "No, no!" he says. "I'll take them," he says and he cocks his elbow, angling his hand towards his knee, and his watch slides out of his shirt sleeve and hits his slim wrist with a faint clink, and Egil looks at his watch and says, "Hmm" and thinks for a moment. "I can run them down there before I go to work," he says. "Fine," I say, and I look at Egil and smile.

"Damn," I hear Mum say. I turn to look at her and see that she has spilled coffee over herself. She's sitting with one hand hovering in mid air and coffee dripping from her fingers. "Fetch me a wet cloth from the bathroom, Silje," Mum says, her eyes never leaving her dripping hand and first one moment passes, then another moment passes and I just sit there and then Egil gets up. "I'll get it, Oddrun," he says briskly and I notice that his suit jacket is covered in stray hairs again, I picked them all off before we got in the car, but it's almost as thick with them again, and Egil nips out of the living room door and strides off down the hall.

"Nothing about me works any more," Mum mutters crossly. "I can't even drink my coffee without spilling it," she says, and that's all she says and I just sit here looking at her and a moment passes and now I have to pull myself together. I take a deep breath, blink a couple of times and feel myself waking up slightly. Then I look at Mum and it's as if only now do I really see her. I see her slack, purplish cheeks, see the dark bags under her eyes. With those cheeks and those bags under her eyes she looks a little like a bloodhound. I smile hesitantly at her. "Oh, we all spill things sometimes, Mum," I say. "Humph!" she says, whirling round to face me, her slack cheeks quivering slightly as she turns, and she eyes me indignantly. "Stop that," she says. "You can't fool me into thinking that I'm younger or fitter than I am," she says, and just then Egil comes back into the living room. "There weren't any wet cloths in the bathroom," Egil says and he stands there looking at Mum and Mum looks at him and frowns. "What?" she says. "There weren't any wet cloths in the bathroom," Egil says again, "only dry ones," he says and I look at Egil and suddenly I realize that he's joking and I start to laugh and it feels good, the laughter seems to loosen something inside me and I feel myself waking up a little more and I look at Egil and laugh and Egil looks at Mum and laughs, but Mum doesn't join in. "I'm only kidding, Oddrun," Egil says and he flicks a hand at Mum and grins. "I'll go and wet a cloth and bring you it," he says and he turns and leaves the room again and I stop laughing and look at Mum and Mum looks offended.

"Oh, Mum," I say, putting my head to one side and regarding her. "It was a joke," I tell her. "Oh, I'm sure," she says. "Hey," I say. "Yes, yes," she says and a moment passes and I feel the life ebbing out of me again and I take a breath and sigh, pause, then force a little smile. "Well, Mum, was it fun to see the old house again?" I ask but she doesn't answer. "Hmm?" I say and she turns to me again and looks at me with that same indignant look on her face. "Humph!" she says. "You've asked me that five times since we got back," she says. "Do you want me to say how grateful I am to you for taking me there, is that why you keep going on about it?" she says and a moment passes and I feel myself getting upset now. "No, I've no such hopes," I say, it just comes out and I look at her and give a weary little smile. "What?" she says, frowning and glaring at me. and I'm about to repeat it, but I don't, I can't be bothered arguing with her, can't be bothered starting anything. "Nothing," is all I say, still smiling that weary little smile. "Anybody would think it was you, not me that was getting old, with all the questions you ask," she says. "Yes," I say, saying it with a little intake of breath, saying it with a little sigh, and I feel myself growing more and more fed up with her. Then Egil comes back, this time with his fingers wrapped round a cloth, those slender shopkeeper fingers, and he hands the cloth to Mum. "Here you are," says Egil. "Thanks," mutters Mum.

"Well," Egil says lightly, glancing at his watch, "I'd better be on my way if I'm to drop the girls off at the bus station before I go to work. He looks at me and smiles then turns to Mum. "Right, then," he says. "Well, thanks for coming with us today, Oddrun," he says. "Thanks for taking me," Mum says. "Are you quite sure you can't take the time off, Egil?" I ask, eyeing him beseechingly. I know very well that he can't take the time off, but I ask anyway and give him a rather strained smile. "Yes, Silje," he says. "Oh, please," I say. "The kids will be out and we'd have the whole evening to ourselves," I say. "It's been so long since we had an evening to ourselves," I say. "We could go out. Book a table at Credo maybe and have dinner together, share a bottle of wine?" I say. "A romantic evening, just the two of us," I say, and I hear what I'm saying and I don't really know why I'm saying it, I don't even feel like going out. "Silje, please," he says and he looks at me, smiles gently at me and I smile wanly back. "No, never mind," I say. "Some other time, eh?" he says. "Anyway, it's not that long until we're off to Brazil and then we'll have a whole two weeks to spend together, just you and me." "Yes," I say. "And play golf," I add. "Hey," he says, "I promise not to overdo the golfing this time," he says, looking at me. "Okay," I say and a moment passes and I close my eyes and nod, then I open my eyes and give a faint smile and he tilts his head to one side and smiles back. "Hey," he says. "Don't go making me feel guilty," he says. "No, of course not," I say and we look at one another and a moment passes. "A three-course dinner at Credo," I say, it just slips out. "Oh, come on," I say quickly and I crease my brow and send him a coy little look. "Silje, please," he says and he flashes me an indulgent, almost paternal smile, holds my gaze for a couple of seconds, then bends his head and plants a kiss on my forehead, "Bye-bye, then," he says. "Bye," I say, then Egil turns to Mum. "Bye, then, Oddrun," he says. "Bye," Mum says.

And Egil turns away. His back is covered in stray blond hairs, he sticks a hand into his suit trouser pocket, jingles his car keys as he walks out of the door and Mum and I sit there, staring into space, and the fridge hums and hums, and I pick up my cup and and drink the rest of my coffee, then set the cup down on the table. "He works a lot," Mum says. "We both work a lot, Mum," I say, giving her my weary little smile. "Yes, I suppose you do," she says. "I worked till half-past ten last night," I say. "Yes, well," Mum says, "I don't know why, but there it is," she says. "You're rolling in money, but you can hardly ever afford to take a break. I don't know what you want with it all," she says, "all the stuff you buy," she says. "No," I say, and I look at her, still with that weary smile on my face. I can see that my smile irritates her. "I don't know how you can get any pleasure out of it all," she says. "It's not as if you've time to spend any of it anyway," she says. "No," I say, saying it with a little intake of breath, saying it with a faint sigh, keeping the smile on my face. I can see that she's getting more and more irritated and I realize I get a little kick out of the fact that she's irritated. I'm so sick of listening to her harping on about this, it'll do her good to see that I don't care. "And yet you always want more," she goes on. "You're never content," she says. "No, you know what, we never are," I say. "And the kids are becoming exactly the same," she says. "Don't start complaining about the kids, Mum," I say, smiling that weary smile. "I'm not," she says. "It's not their fault they're spoiled." "No, it's my fault, of course," I say. "That's not what I said," she says. "But it's what you meant," I say. "Well, you do have a certain responsibility for how your kids turn out, don't you, as all parents do?" "Of course," I say. "Just as you have a certain responsibility for the fact that I've turned out the way I have," and I hear what I'm saying and how much anger there is in what I say and I search inside myself, to check whether I really have so much anger inside me, but I feel more tired and indifferent than angry and I smile wearily at her. "Oh, no," Mum says. "It's your father who's most to blame for that," she says and I hear what she's saying and I know she's saying it to provoke me, because she knows I hate to hear her criticizing Dad. "Yeah, yeah, if you say so," is all I say and I smile that weary smile and I close my eyes then open them again and I picture how calm I look as I do this and I can see that Mum is getting more and more irritated.

"It was beyond belief the way he spoiled you," she says. "Yeah, right, " I say. "It's Dad's fault that my life is such a mess," I say and for a second or two there is total silence and I feel myself getting more and more upset and I close my eyes, I draw breath and let it out again with a little sigh. Then I open my eyes and look at Mum again. "Why are you like this, Mum?" I ask in a slightly exasperated voice. "Here we are, Egil and I, trying to be nice to you, taking you to Namsos to see the old house again," I say, "and then you carry on like this," I say and I hear what I'm saying and I really can't be bothered bringing this up right now, but I do it anyway, it just comes out, all unbidden and there's nothing for it but to let it come. "Are you trying to make me feel guilty now?" she asks, smirking at me and I look at her and sigh, then I pause for a moment. "No, I'm not that ambitious," I say, with a sad little laugh. "No, because I don't have a conscience, do I," she says, and she gives that smirk and I realize that I can't take this, not right now, and I raise my eyebrows, look down at the table and sigh again. "Humph," I say, then I look up at her again. "Let's stop this now, Mum," I say. "By all means, let's stop," she says. "Oh, Mum, please," I say, putting my head to one side and eyeing her imploringly, and a moment passes and I picture how weary I look when I do that. "What?" Mum says. "I was only saying that we'll stop it," she says and gives that little smirk of hers and I give my weary smile and nod at her. "Good!" I say. "I fancy some more coffee," I say. "Shall I go and get us some more?" I ask. "No, thanks, I've had enough," she says. "Okay," I say.

And then there's silence and Mum looks at me, smirks at me. "But there's nothing to stop you getting a cup for yourself," she says. "No, no," I say, "I don't need any more, either." "No, you don't need any more. But you fancied some more," she says. "Yes, I know, but it doesn't matter," I say and Mum smirks at me and shakes her head. "Sometimes you look and act as if it was you that nailed Christ to the cross," she says. "Do you realize that?" she says and a moment passes and I feel myself growing more and more sick of her, it's like she's sucking all the strength out of me and I'm growing tireder and tireder and I give her that weary smile again. "No, I didn't realize that," is all I say. "You look so burdened with guilt it's just not true," she says. "Is that so," I say, still smiling. "Have you any other holes to pick in me while you're at it, because if you have I'd be grateful if you'd just tell me," I say. "Because then, you see, I'll know exactly what I ought to work on," I say. "Well, well, it's good to know you've still got a bit of spirit, Silje," she says. "So there is a little bit of you left," she says, smirking at me, and there's a moment's pause and I'm getting more and more sick of this and I look at her and sigh.

"Oh, Mum," I say, trying to sound sincere. "Please stop," I say, but she doesn't stop. "You haven't shown nearly enough spirit over the past few years," she says, smirking at me. "Oh, that's good, coming from you," I say and a sad little laugh escapes me. "If there's anybody who's tried to teach me what nice girls should and should not do it's you," I say. "Hah," she says, "I allowed you more freedom than most parents give their daughters," she says. "After Dad died, yes," I say. "You couldn't be so strict with me once you'd made up your mind to realize yourself and live life to the full," I say. "I'm talking about when I was younger," I say. "Yes, well it was up to me to keep you in check, I had to be a bit strict, what with the father you had," she says. "It was beyond belief the way he spoiled you," she says and I hear what she's saying, now she's trying to get at me by criticizing Dad again, and in my mind I see my dad, dear sweet Dad, and I realize how sick of her I am, I realize how weary I am and how weary I must look, I picture my drawn face and tired eyes, and picturing this makes me feel even more weary. "You know what, Mum," I say. "It's no fun coming to see you when you're like this," I say. "It doesn't matter what I do, all I get from you is a smirk or some negative comment," I say. "Nothing I do ever pleases you," I say and I hear what I'm saying and I hear how much hurt there is in my words and it's as if my words bring out an ache in me, an ache that seems to wake me up. I look straight at Mum, a couple of moments pass and I'm feeling more and more awake. It's as if I'm actually seeing her now, seeing how mean she can be. It's as if I'm only now fully awake.

"I'm doing the best I can, Mum," I say. "I'm sure you are," she says and I hear what she's saying and I feel my mouth fall open as I hear her say it and I just sit there looking at her, because I don't know how she can say such a thing and I don't know how she can be so mean to me and I don't quite know what to say, don't quite know what to do. Moments pass and there's silence, then suddenly she starts to cry and it shocks me to see this, I can't really remember ever seeing Mum cry before, but now suddenly she's sitting there crying, strong, tough Mum, and I feel a flicker of unease.

There's silence and this feeling of unease grows inside me, I feel cold all over and I don't really know what to do, don't really know what to say, but I get up and go over to her and I lift my hand to stroke her hair, but I don't do it, I can't remember ever touching her in that way before and I can't bring myself to do it. I lower my hand and lay it on her shoulder instead and I feel a wave of revulsion wash over me as I do this, I can't just stand here like this, so I pat her shoulder lightly, once, then again, then I take my hand away.

"Don't cry, Mum," I say, swallowing, and then I just stand there, not knowing what to do, not knowing what to say. Then: "I don't want to be like this Silje," Mum says and I hear what she's saying, but I've never heard Mum talk like this before, this is serious and the feeling of unease grows and grows. "I get so sick of myself," she says, and she cries and shakes her head, and her slack cheeks quiver slightly when she shakes her head and the dark bags under her eyes quiver slightly when she shakes her head, I stare at her and there's silence. I take a breath and let it out again, lift one hand and run it through her hair.

"You spend too much time alone, Mum," I say, then I walk hesitantly back to the couch, sit back down on the couch and eye her as affectionately as I possibly can. "You ought to get out more often and meet people," I say and a couple of moments pass, then Mum wipes away her tears and she stops crying and I look at her, relieved that she's stopped crying. "Oh, and who would I meet?" she asks, and I hear what she's saying and I feel even more relieved when I hear her pick up this new strand I've introduced. "I don't know anybody any more," she says. "They're all gone," she's says. "I'm the only one left," she says.

"Oh, I'm sure you could make new friends," I say, giving her a rather tentative smile. "At my age?" she says with a sad little laugh. "Just you wait till you get old and you'll find out," she says tartly. I look at her, conscious of feeling relieved that she's back to normal, and I give her a slightly more affectionate smile. "Tell you what, Mum," I say, trying to sound more cheerful. "There's live jazz at one of the cafés in the old town every Wednesday afternoon," I say. "Why don't I pick you up tomorrow and take you down there?" I say. "No," she says, narrowing her eyes and shaking her head. "Why not?" I say. "You'd really enjoy it, I'm sure you would," I say. "Humph," she says. "No, Silje," she says, "I don't feel like it," she says, looking crosser and crosser, and I look at her, and I'm conscious of feeling happy and relieved that she's back to normal. "But you can't just sit at home alone all the time," I say. "That's why you're feeling so low," I say. "Stop it, Silje," she snaps. "Yes, but Mum," I say, then I pause and she glances off to one side and down at the floor, looking cross and troubled. "Know what?" I say. "When we were in Namsos today, so many good memories came flooding back," I say. "I know those days are over and that things can never be the way they were," I say, "but I wish you could call up just a little bit of the person you were when we lived there."

"As if you've any idea who I was," she says. "As if you know anything at all about what life was like for me back then," she says, and I stare at her, what's she on about now? "He could be a proper tyrant sometimes, Silje," she says. "Tyrannical in a kind way, but a tyrant all the same," she says, and I hear what she's saying and for a moment I just sit there looking at her and that feeling of unease is back – I mean, what is all this? "If you only knew," she says. "You've no idea what it was like," she says. "You've no idea what it was like to have no say whatsoever in your own life. You've no idea what ... he was a ... you think he was such a saint, but he ... you've no idea," she says, and I hear what she's saying and unease washes over me and again I go cold all over and I stare at her. This isn't something she's blurting out simply because she's angry and bitter, this is serious, she really means it, but she's never talked about Dad like this before, and in my mind I see my dad, my dear, sweet dad. " I haven't missed him," she says, "not for one second," then she pauses and she looks straight at me and I look at her and I swallow once, then once more, I can't take this, it's too much, and I look at the floor, then up at her again and I try to smile and stay calm.

"Mum," I say, saying it softly and almost imploringly, and I close my eyes, then I open them again and give her a faint smile, but she won't let up. "God, how I hated that man," she says and I hear what she's saying and my heart beats a little faster, my pulse races a little faster and the unease grows inside me, because I can't bear to hear this. "Mum!" I say. "That's enough," I say, and I blink, blink as steadily as I can, and smile that faint smile. "Enough?" she says. "You're the one who started going on about how things were back then," she says, "so you'll just have to put up with hearing my version, too." "No, Mum," I say, "I don't have to," I say. "If you'd known a bit more about what it was like to be married to him you might have understood me a bit better, too," she says. "Mum," I say and my heart is beating faster and faster and my pulse is racing faster and faster, but I keep that faint smile on my face and I blink as steadily as I can. "Mum," I say again, "I'd really rather be spared the intimate details of your marriage," I say and I smile steadily at her. "I'm your daughter, his and yours." "But don't you understand that I need to give you a more nuanced view of your father and me?" she says, never taking her eyes off me. She's demanding a response from me, but my heart is beating faster and faster and I avoid her gaze, I look this way and that. You don't understand that ..." she says. "Yeah, well go talk to somebody else about these nuances of yours," I cry, my face twisting into a sneer, and I look her straight in the eye, almost starting at the force of my own aggression. "If it's that important to you," I mutter crossly, and I glance sidelong at the floor and there's silence. "Don't be silly, Silje," she says. "I don't care what other people think or say about me," she says. "But you, you're my daughter," she says and her voice is brittle again, suddenly she's close to tears again and I look at her and swallow and now I'm close to tears as well. "And it hurts to know that you see me the way you do," she says. "It hurts, because it's ... unfair!" she says. "You've no idea what it was like to be me, all those years," she says, and then she pauses and I can tell that she's crying, and I also feel close to tears, but I will not cry, I can't get into this with her, I won't have it, can't handle it. "Do you know how he used to control me?" she asks. "Don't you hear what I'm saying," I cry, a cry that bursts out of me all unbidden, and my voice is both frantic and furious and I stare straight at her and a moment passes. And she looks at me, saying nothing and there's such sadness in her eyes. I feel a wave of guilt wash over me and I gaze at the floor and I raise my hand, run my hand through my hair, then I look at her and sigh. "Sorry, Mum," I say. "But," I say, then I pause and I run my hand through my hair again. "I'm here for you, no matter what," I say and I hear what I'm saying and I hear that what I'm saying is true. "But I won't listen to you bad-mouthing Dad," I add. "I'm his daughter, too," I say, then I pause, regard her tenderly, try to smile at her. "Mum," I say, "why don't we ... let's stop this, both of us," I say, a note of reconciliation in my voice, and a moment passes, then she sniggers at me. "Yes, why don't we do that," she says and suddenly she's smirking again, and it's a sad smirk. "Let's talk about something nice instead," she says. "The weather or something," she says. "Mum, please," I say, eyeing her imploringly, and she looks at me, feigning astonishment. "What?" she says. "Isn't that what you want?" she says. "Easy and uncomplicated," she says. "The minute things get a bit difficult you shy away. Over the years that's how you've become," she says and she looks at me and smirks and I look at the floor and a sigh escapes me and I realize how weary I am, I realize how sick of this I am, and the fridge hums.

Trondheim, July 8th–9th 2006

Dear David,

I'm sitting here in Mum's flat, and since I only have these first lines of my letter left to write I've made so bold as to open one of the wines she bought in St Emilion in the late Eighties. After listening to her holding forth on everything from soil and temperature averages to viniculture and wine-growing traditions in that particular region of France we were more than keen to sample it, I remember, but because the wine was young and hadn't yet achieved its full potential, as Mum put it, we had to content ourselves with listening to her detailed and elaborate descriptions and from them gain some impression of how wonderful this wine must be. But it has now achieved its potential and as soon as I've put a full stop to this sentence I'm going to switch off my laptop and pour myself a big glass, and as I raise it to my lips and take that first sip, fantasy and imagination will meet reality and then we'll see which is the stronger of the two.

The first drafts of this letter that I wrote were all attempts to write much in the style of the short stories I produced in the late Eighties, back when we were close friends and sweethearts; when time was on our side and we were determined to become artists of one sort or another. Since we also acted as each other's consultant and you read virtually everything I wrote, I had some hope that replicating my writing style from those days would be as effective a way of triggering your memory as descriptions of things we did, people we knew or the world in which we lived. But just as I can imagine Jon would find it hard today to play the bass the way he did when he was eighteen, I found it difficult to write the way I had when I was eighteen, and even when I've tried my hardest, even in those passages where I feel I've been most successful, my writing has been coloured, both in form and in content, by the life I've led since we lost touch. The rawness, the intensity and the passion I had at the age of seventeen or eighteen are gone for ever, or at least: not gone, I sense that I still have all of that in me, but as an academic and almost middle-aged woman (God help me), I no longer have the naivety necessary in order to give rein to it. I feel as though I've been consigned to a language that forces me always to have reservations and, as I'm doing now, prove to myself and everyone else that I've given great thought to everything I do, say and write. I don't know when I became like that and I don't know why I'm like that, but even though I am like that I hope this letter will contain enough imprints, leavings and traces of the Eighties for you to recognize something of that time and follow the trail back, as it were, to the person you were. And in so doing learn more about who you are.

I'll start with the time when we saw an orange Audi 80:

You were hungry, and since I lived closest, we popped into my house so you could grab a sandwich before we went to the cinema. Mum was at the Arts Centre and I thought I had the place to myself, but I'd forgotten that my gran was coming to visit and when we walked in she was in the kitchen, having a footbath and reading the local paper. Her white old-lady legs stuck up out of the lead-grey zinc basin like spindly flower-stalks in a vase and her long, lank hair hung down over her shoulders. She smiled cheerily when she saw me, but for some reason I was overcome by embarrassment, and no matter how fond I was of her, no matter how proud I was of her, I couldn't bear the thought of you seeing her, so I turned on my heel and pushed you gently but firmly back down the hall, trying all the while to come up with some excuse to give you later.

But there was no need, because once we were back out on the front step something happened that made us forget all about the sandwich and the rude way I had stopped you from entering the house. On the other side of the street, parked next to the telephone box with its engine running was an orange Audi 80. Through the half-open window on the driver's side we saw a woman in her early forties light a cigarette, flick the match out of the window, glance in the mirror and pull slowly out onto the road. Initially I thought it was the way she had inhaled, drawing so deeply on the cigarette, hollowing her cheeks and causing her eyes to bulge slightly, that made her look like the panic-stricken figure in Munch's *The Scream*, but when her face still looked the same even after the coil of smoke had left her gaping mouth I realized that she actually was panic-stricken. At first I thought she must have spotted something shocking happening behind us, that our house was on fire, or that a plane was about to crash into the estate, or whatever. But when I spun round to look, my heart already pounding, I could see nothing out of the ordinary. I promptly turned round again only to discover that it was you she was staring at. She didn't stop or slow down, but as the car rolled slowly past, she kept looking further and further back over her shoulder, straining not to lose sight of you, and only once she was almost on the bend and a car pulling out from the right had to beep its horn to warn her to stop and give way did she turn to face the front.

We stood perfectly still on the steps, staring after her until the car had disappeared around the bend and she was gone forever. When I asked you who on earth this woman was you told me you had no idea, that you'd ever seen her before in your life, and this moved me to remark – off the top of my head and with a little laugh – that it might have been someone who had seen your dad in you (your mother never revealed who your father was, not to you or to anyone else). "Yeah, maybe," was all you said, and then you laughed.

Gradually, over the next few seconds, it began to dawn on me that what I had said was not, however, altogether out of the question and when I saw how your eyes changed as this dawned on you too, I realized that the longing to find your real father was stronger than you had ever let on. But when I asked you what you were thinking, you simply shrugged and said you weren't thinking of anything special, and when I held your gaze to somehow show you that I knew you weren't telling the truth, you raised your eyebrows and looked quizzical, and that was enough to stop me asking any more questions.

My gran was every bit as blithe and cheery when I popped back into the kitchen moments later to get you something to eat, and even though she must have known that I had pushed you out of the house because I was embarrassed by her, she never said a word about it, neither then nor later. Dear, wise Gran. For some reason, whenever I thought of her

I pictured a little tree stump, and when I told you this you said you knew exactly what I meant, only then to add: "You can always count on a stump." I remember thinking this was an odd, but lovely, thing to say.

The time when we ran away from Jon:

We thought Jon was taking a rest before the party and we only meant to give him a bit of a fright, but we never got that far because the sight that met us when we climbed up onto the stack of timber, popped our heads over the windowsill and perched there like roosting chickens, peering into his room, was so at odds with what we had expected to see that we simply forgot everything else and fell into a weird, open-mouthed trance.

Stark-naked and glistening with sweat, he was hunched over the big, brown double bass, like a weary drunk draped round the shoulders of his boozing buddy. The room was filled with a rich, low, dark, vibrant note that went on and on, a note that for some reason I sometimes find myself remembering when I drink red wine from Rioja. His eyes were closed and his hand hovered over the quivering string like the talon of a bird of prey, stiff, his index finger sticking out slightly, all set to pluck again. But he didn't pluck, he let the note die away completely, holding a pause that seemed to chisel a trench in the music, and we stood there on the green-tinged, rain-soaked and somewhat slippery stack of timber, rigid and motionless.

Had I been as much of a romantic as my husband thinks and says I am, I could have embellished the truth a bit and said that we climbed quietly down from the stack of timber, that we made our way thoughtfully out of the garden and round to the front door, and that I said something "nice" before we rang the bell: that we didn't need to tell Jon we had seen him or, even "nicer", that Jon was going to be a great musician some day (which seemed, in a way, quite likely).

But I'm not as bad as my husband thinks. We stood stock still atop the timber for a while longer and then, after exchanging glances and a quick grin, I slid a hand under the windowframe and very gently tipped the window up just far enough for us to slip our heads under it, place our elbows on the sill and lean into the room.

We didn't say a word. Not even when, after some moments, Jon noticed us and his normally pale face turned bright red. We merely hung there staring straight at him, bursting with laughter. And by the time he closed the curtains with a sharp tug (so the contours of our faces must have shown clearly through the filmy, but opaque fabric), when still not a word had been said, by us or by him, it was hard to say anything at all. We did our best not to laugh out loud as we walked round the house to the front door, but we couldn't stop ourselves and he was mad as hell when we walked in. You had to spend half an hour soft-soaping him and coaxing him before he would come to the party, because suddenly that wasn't so important any more, and no sooner had we got there than he wanted to go home again, but when he said this, much to his dismay you merely shrugged and said "fair enough".

He didn't leave, of course. Instead he got drunk and became a real pain in the ass and when we were heading home in the early hours and he had to pee, we didn't stop and wait for him, we just kept walking, and once round the bend and out of sight we left the path and ducked into a grove of birch trees, their branches already thick with new leaf. It was rather like walking through a green waterfall, and I distinctly remember thinking of some film in which two lovers do just that, possibly *The Blue Lagoon* which had been one of my favourite films a few years earlier. When we emerged on the other side you put a finger to your lips and said, "Shh," and a moment later we heard Jon go stumbling and mumbling by, looking and sounding as funny as a drunk man in some crappy comedy. A moment later he started calling our names, softly at first, then louder and eventually with anger and a touch of desperation in his voice. "He doesn't how to get home," you whispered to me.

I don't remember ever feeling bad that we weren't always nice to Jon, and I don't think you did either. Quite the opposite, really. Jon was so self-centred and so full of self-pity sometimes that we felt it was all he deserved. And besides, he was such a wimp, so pathetic and helpless when it came to anything but music that it annoyed us and got our backs up, and we felt it served him right when we, or usually I, disregarded his touchiness and told him straight out that he had to get a grip. We even took a sort of pleasure in asking him to do things we knew he didn't dare to do, or thought were beyond him: anything physical, for example, or going up and speaking to strangers, not because we were bad people and loved to see him screw up, but because it was as much laziness as lack of ability that caused him to balk at even trying, and because it pissed us off the way he took it for granted that we would take care of all the things he didn't feel up to doing.

The reason why, even so, Jon hung around with us as much as he did and why, in spite of everything, he fitted in, was simply that he was the sort of person you might come upon playing the double bass stark-naked (paradoxically, perhaps, considering that we laughed at the sight of him). I don't know whether this nude bass playing was one of his countless experiments or whether he had simply come out of the shower and been so overcome by the sudden urge to play that he forgot to get dressed first, but the very fact that he did what he did, stone-cold sober and not in any attempt to seem "crazy" to anyone (as would have been the case if one of the other boys in our class had pulled a similar stunt) was nonetheless one of many signs that he possessed the same uncompromising passion and commitment that I remember you and I possessing back then.

Like all other kids our age we may at times have tended to affect a certain nonchalance and apathy, but unlike a lot of other people, especially the girls I knew and hung around with sometimes, I think it's fair to say that we had a gift for immersing ourselves totally in things and actually believing that what one does really matters. When we wrote stories, when we wrote and played music or produced one of our sometimes rather obscure art projects, we could keep at it for hours on end without a thought for food or rest or whatever else we had to do and we worked with a concentration and an intensity so profound that, sometimes at any rate, we attained that glorious state of mind in which you lose yourself completely in something else, something bigger. These days it's very rare for me to become immersed in anything. Writing the first sections of this letter is actually the closest I've come in a long time to being totally immersed.

The first time we shagged:

The first thing we noticed was that something had startled the birds. They flew up in a flurry from the branches on which they'd been perching, much like a handful of sand and grit flung into the air by a toddler in a sand box. One, possibly two, seconds later we heard a kind of rumbling noise that swelled in a fraction of second into a deep, dark booming. When we looked round to see what was happening, my eyes were forced shut, I felt my fringe lift slightly and the skin of my face seemed to draw back and sit more tightly over my skull.

Looking back on it now, that one second in my life was not unlike standing at the side of the road when a trailer truck thunders past and the back draught hits you so hard that it almost blows you off your feet. But we weren't standing by the side of the road, we were in the middle of a grove of trees, each clutching a bunch of wood anemones (it was my gran's eighty-fifth birthday the next day and I had promised to help with the table decorations) and what we saw rushing towards us was quite clearly not a trailer truck, it was what was to become known as the Holseth Landslide.

When I opened my eyes and saw the landslide sweep past us – rather like a dog's tongue slipping out of its mouth and reaching down to lap something off the ground – I instinctively grabbed hold of your arm and screamed in terror. I felt the earth beneath our feet kind of contract, once, then twice, and straight ahead of us, about four or five yards away, I saw the ground crack open with appalling speed, rather like a piece of clothing being torn apart. Great clumps of soil broke loose and toppled into the slide and the tree in which you and some of your chums had built a tree house complete with rope-ladder when you were about eleven, as part of the Red Indian camp you made out there, was left hanging more or less in mid air with its roots, like long fingers, scrabbling to gain a purchase and return to the ground in which only a moment ago they had lodged.

But the worst of it was, of course, that the landslide took with it the Holseth family's new house. It was almost as if we were looking at a painting of a house and someone came along, lifted the painting off the wall and carried it away. All of a sudden the house seemed to come adrift and sail off as we stood there gaping, following it with our eyes until it was no longer a house, but a pile of timber lying at the bottom of the slope, with boards and beams sticking out in all directions like potato straws in a bowl.

What we didn't know, though, was that Ida Holseth was at home at the time and that, strictly speaking, only a wall prevented us from seeing her depart this life. The first we heard of this was when her husband got back from the shopping centre half an hour later and broke down completely in front of the whole neighbourhood. Only fifteen minutes after that, however, when the reporter from the regional television news asked us for our version of what had happened, you said that as the landslide swept past you heard laughter coming from the open living room window. You told this same story again a little later when we were interviewed for the local paper, and to all of the neighbours who came round, wanting to know what it had been like to experience the landslide at such close quarters. I hadn't heard this alleged laughter and you hadn't said anything about exactly how it had sounded but eventually, whenever I thought about the landslide, I seemed to hear a cold, shrill, hysterical laugh.

That same evening, up in my room, while Mum was hoovering the living room down below us, we shagged for the first time and I remember that as you came you let out a great groan that really seemed to come from deep in your stomach. I didn't say anything about it, but I remember feeling a twinge of guilt afterwards, not because we had had sex, but because we had done it on the day that Ida Holseth died, and because I had the vague feeling that that in itself was somehow disrespectful. But without knowing exactly why, I am also convinced that I would not have crossed the line and shagged you on that particular day had it not been for the Holseth Landslide and Ida's death. What I remember most clearly, though, is that when I pulled your jeans down to your ankles and was able to take a close look at you, your balls reminded me of great tits and the way they puff themselves up in the winter. This inspired me, by the way, to write a poem entitled "Great Tits are Tiny Mouthfuls in the Snow".

Trondheim, June 23rd 2006. What's for dinner?

"Okay, so dinner next Sunday," Trond says. "Talk to you then." "Great," I say. "Bye," Trond says. "Bye," I say, and I put down the phone and go back to the kitchen. I pour batter onto the waffle iron, close the lid and hear the soft sizzle as the batter is squeezed between the plates. A moment later I hear the front door open and then I hear Egil cough and I press the lid down a little harder and hear the sizzling increase.

"Hi," Egil says behind me, in a voice designed to let me know that he's tired, but I can't be bothered giving him the sympathy he's after, he's never exactly attentive and supportive when I'm tired so I don't feel like being that way for him. A moment passes and I still haven't answered him, and I'm still standing with my back to him.

"Hi, I said," Egil says, a little louder this time, and I turn and look at him. He's standing there with his briefcase in his hand, his shoulders covered in stray hairs again, and I promptly turn away. "Hi," I say, and I hear how tired my voice sounds, I sound far more tired than I actually am, sound much more tired than Egil. "What are you doing?" Egil asks. "Making waffles," I say, but I don't turn round, I keep my eyes on the waffle iron. "Now?" he asks and

I hear him shoot his watch out of his shirt sleeve and I know that he's wondering what's happened to dinner, and I say nothing about dinner being in the oven. "But it's dinnertime," he says and I can tell that he's cranky and irritable and I feel myself getting cranky and irritable too. If only he knew how tired I've been feeling lately, maybe not quite so tired today, but he couldn't possibly know that and he's got no right to be cross. "Yes," I say shortly and the moments pass and I still don't say anything about dinner being in the oven. I pick up the butter knife, slip the finished waffle off the hotplate, then close the lid and turn to face him, and he's standing there staring at me, looking cross and confused. "Well ... er," he says, shaking his head and widening his eyes. "So, what's for dinner?" "Waffles!" I say, it just slips out, and I turn my back again and gaze down at the waffle iron. It sizzles and grey steam rises to the ceiling. "Ha-ha," Egil says, in a way that says he doesn't find this at all funny. "No, really," I say and I hear what I'm saying and I don't know why I say it, I just do, and I turn to face him, give him a rather cold, indifferent smile. "We're having waffles," I say, and I turn away again. "The kids aren't here for dinner this evening," I say. "So I thought we'd have something simple for once." It sounds as if I mean what I'm saying and I realize I'm enjoying this. "Cut it out," Egil says. "We're not having waffles," he says. "Yes, we are," I say. "Really," I say and I turn to him again and I look at him and I give him a cold, indifferent smile. "And anyway, I'm tired," I say crisply, and a moment passes and I get a little kick out of being the first to say I'm tired. "I hardly slept at all last night and I can't be bothered making anything fancy," I say. "Yes, but we can't have waffles for dinner," Egil says. "Well, we have pancakes for dinner," I say. "Yes, but that's not the same," he says. "Oh, yes it is," I say, "there are exactly the same ingredients in pancake batter as there are in waffle batter." I hear what I'm saying and it strikes me that what I'm saying is actually true. "Eggs and milk and butter and a little sugar," I say. "Stop it, Silje," Egil says. "I don't eat waffles for dinner," he says. "Why not?" I ask, and I look at him, try to look a little puzzled, and he stands there searching for something to say, but he can't think of anything to say, and I realize I'm enjoying the fact that I've got him stumped. "Well, you eat pancakes," I say. "Yes, but pancakes and waffles are two different things, I tell you," he says. "You put jam on both," I say and I hear what I'm saying, and it's true what I'm saying, I'm actually right, and I'm enjoying this more and more. "Yes, but ..." he says. "And you put sugar on both," I say. "Yes, but that's neither here nor there," Egil grumbles. "Waffles aren't dinner," he says, and I look at him and I realize it annoys me that he will not accept the idea of waffles for dinner but can't say why not.

"If we can have pancakes for dinner, we can have waffles for dinner," I say. "The only difference is the name," I say. "They contain the same things and you have the same things along with them," I say. "Oh, yes?" Egil says. "What about pea soup?" he says. "Would you have pea soup with waffles?" he asks, and I can tell from his voice that he's pleased with this question. "I've never tried it, but I'm sure it would be good," I retort. "It goes very well with pancakes after all," I say and I hear what I'm saying and yet again I'm struck by the truth of what I'm saying and I look at him and he just stands there, lost for words, and yet again I get a kick out of having him stumped. A moment passes and then he gives a sigh. "Stop it," he snaps. "You're not serious?" he says. "We're not really having waffles for dinner?" he says, giving me a look of indignation and dismay, and I'm growing more and more annoyed, he hasn't come up with one good reason for not having waffles for dinner and yet he's so sure he's right. "Yes," I say, "we are having waffles for dinner," and I look at him and he looks at me for a moment or two. Then: "Well, in that case you'll be eating alone," he says crossly, then he bends down, sets his briefcase on the floor with a loud thud. "I want a proper dinner," he says, straightening up. A moment passes and it annoys me intensely that dinner is in the oven; if dinner hadn't been ready and sitting in the oven I wouldn't have given in on this. But: "I'm only kidding, Egil," I say sulkily and I feel myself getting even angrier as I hear myself say it, I sort of have to admit that he's right, even though he's not right, and that is so annoying. "The waffles are for after dinner, with coffee, and dinner's in the oven," I say and after a moment or so I hear Egil give a little sniff and I turn and look at him and see how angry he looks, and I get a kick out of the fact that he's as angry as he is, don't feel quite so angry myself when I see that he's this angry.

"Oh, don't be angry," I say, trying to sound a little less angry than I am, trying to make it seem that he's the angry one here. "I'm not angry," he says. "It was just a joke, Egil," I say. "Yeah, yeah," he says and I can tell by his face that he's getting angrier and angrier and I realize I'm enjoying this more and more, and I raise my eyebrows, pretend to be dismayed that he should get so het up over such an innocent little joke and I look at him and give a little shake of my head. "For heaven's sake, Egil," I say, exasperated. "What?" he asks. "Well, I can tell that you're angry," I say, and it feels so good to know that for once he's angrier than me. "Would you stop saying that I'm angry," he says. "Because if there's one thing that will make me angry it's that," he says and he says no more and I regard him for a moment or two, then I give a despairing shake of the head and turn away.

"Can I switch off the lamps?" I hear Egil ask and I turn to look at him again and he's pointing to the lamps in the living room and he's giving me a look intended to let me know how hopeless I am, how thoughtless I am, having the lamps on when it's light outside. "Well, can I?" he asks and I look at him and my annoyance grows, I grin, give a little shake of my head and turn back to the waffle iron. "Oh, all right, Egil," I say. "You can switch off the lamps," I say and my voice is almost soft when I say it. "I simply don't see the point of having all these lamps burning in the middle of the day, when the sun's shining straight into the room," he says. "No, of course not," I say and I hear how airy and indifferent my voice is, and I smile as I check the waffle, knowing full well that it annoys him all the more when I'm all smiles and indifference. "I'm sick and tired of reminding you about this," he mutters, and I hear the little click as he turns off one light switch, then I hear him stride briskly across the room, hear the click as he turns off the other switch.

"Ah, but maybe that's what your father used to do?" he says, right out of the blue and I hear what he says and the moment he says it I feel a surge of ice-cold fury and I turn round slowly and stare straight at him. "What?" I say, my eyes never leaving his face. "Well, isn't that what you're always saying?" he asks. "That's what Papa used to do," he says. "Papa always used to say that," he says, and he looks at me and I don't take my eyes off him, and then it seems to dawn on him what he has said.

"Oh," he sighs. "I'm sorry, Silje," he says. "That was a horrible thing to say, I didn't mean it," he says, and I stare straight at him for a second or two, then I turn away without saying anything and a moment passes, then he comes over to me, puts his hands on my shoulder, and I feel those long, slender shopkeeper fingers of his closing gently over my collarbone. "Hey," he says, and I can tell by his voice that he really is sorry for what he said. "Silje," he says, then he pauses, but I don't meet him halfway, I just stand there, smiling my cold, indifferent smile. "Silje," he says again. "Yes, yes," I say and my voice is cold and indifferent. "Sorry," he says. "It's okay," I say, and I'm stiff and still and he runs his hand over my shoulder. "I didn't mean it, honestly," he says. "No, of course you didn't," I say. "Don't be like that," he pleads. "I've had a lot on my plate at the shop recently," he says, "and Mum has been even more difficult than usual," he says. "But I really didn't mean to take it out on you," he says. "No, of course not," I say. "Silje, please," he says. "Oh well, as long as you didn't mean it, then that's fine," I say and I pause. "But if there's a problem don't you think it might be better to speak to your mother, rather than taking it out on me?" I say. "I know," he says. "I just don't have the heart to," he says, and a moment passes and I grin and shake my head slightly at what he says. "It's no more than I can handle," he adds. "All right," I say and I smile that cold, indifferent smile. "But I'm not sure she can handle being told that she's no longer of any use," he says. "That shop has been her whole life," he says. "Yes," I say with a little intake of breath. "Oh, Silje, come on, you understand, don't you?"

he says. "Of course I understand," I say and moments pass, then I hear Egil sigh, then I hear him walk back into the living room and I hear the faint creak as he sits down in the wicker chair.

A moment passes. Then: "So where are the kids?" Egil asks, and I can tell from his voice that he's trying to unbend, but I'm not playing his game, I just stand here, don't answer him. "Hmm?" he asks, and a moment passes. "They're at a concert in the church," I say. It just comes out and I hear what I'm saying, and I don't know where I got it from, this concert, and I'm amazed at what I'm saying. "Oh?" Egil says, looking even more amazed than me. "What concert's that?" he asks and I hear the rustle as he lowers the newspaper onto his lap and I can tell that he's sitting there staring into space while he waits for me to answer, and a moment passes. "Something by Vivaldi," is all I say and I hear what I say and I hear how genuine it sounds, and I've no idea where all this is coming from, where I got the idea of this church concert. "Gosh," Egil says. "What?" I say. "No ... it's just that I didn't know they liked that sort of music," he says. "Ah, well, " I say. "I mean, Vivaldi – it's not exactly what they normally play in their rooms," he says and I hear what he says and he's right in what he says, but he's spent so little time at home recently that he can't possibly know whether he's right or not. "Oh, they do play classical music sometimes," I say. "Do they?" he says. "I've never heard it," he says. "No," is all I say, and there's silence and then I hear Egil sigh. "I know I haven't been home much lately, Silje," he says. "But I'll make it up to you," he says. "Fine," I say. "Hey," he says. "No, if you're going to try to make it up to me that's fine," I say and I hear how spiteful I'm being and I lift the waffle iron lid, pick up the butter knife, ease the waffle off the metal plate and place it on top of the other waffles.

"And anyway, the kids are getting big now," he says, "they're becoming quite independent," he says. "Oh, yes," I say and my voice is cold and indifferent. "Oh, don't be so brusque," he says. "Oh, so I'm being brusque, am I?" I ask. "Yes, Silje, you are being brusque," he says, and he's starting to sound exasperated. "Oh, I'm sorry," I say. "Oh, come on, Silje," he says. "Can't we ... I didn't mean what I said about your father," he says. "I'm sorry," Egil says. "You already said that," I say. "I thought we were finished with that," I say, and a moment passes and the only sounds are the sizzle of the waffle iron and the rustle of the newspaper, and I suddenly remember that Trond just called and I realize I'm looking forward to saying that Trond will be coming on Sunday after all, it's childish to be looking forward to telling him something that will make him mad, but I can't help it, I turn to Egil.

"Oh, by the way," I say, "Trond called." "Oh," Egil mutters. "He's coming on Sunday after all," I say, and Egil shuts his eyes and gives a little grunt. "Humph," he sighs and I feel a sweet ripple of malicious glee run through me as I say it. "Humph?" I ask, injecting a note of surprise into my voice. "Yes, humph," he says. "I'd been looking forward to a nice, quiet Sunday dinner for once," he says. "Well, you could try toning down the big brother act," I say and I hear Egil give a scornful little laugh. "Ah, so it's my fault, is that what you're saying?" Egil asks. "Not at all," I say, grinning. "It's all Trond's fault, I'm sure," I say. "Well, yes, actually I believe it is," Egil says and a moment passes, then, "Ah," I say with a little intake of breath and I hear how sarcastic I sound when I say it like this.

"You're not going to start making excuses for him again, are you?" Egil says. "No, no," I say, saying it in a bright, airy, ironic voice. Oh, come on, Silje," he says. "It's commendable of you to show concern for him, but ... more than anything what Trond needs is for people around him to tell him in no uncertain terms when enough is enough," he says. "Oh, right," I say and there's silence for a moment, then I hear Egil lay his paper on his lap again. "Silje," he says. "Please, just drop it, will you?" he says. "Can't we be friends?" he says. "Oh, all right," I say. "Humph," he grunts and then I hear him laying the paper on the table and I hear him getting up from the wicker chair and walking towards me and I pour batter onto the waffle iron and put the ladle back in the bowl, then I go over to the kitchen cupboard, take plates and glasses from the cupboard and start to lay the table.

"Are you setting places for the kids, too?" I hear him ask, and I hear how surprised he sounds, and I turn to him, I look at him and I see his surprise simply grow and grow, but I don't feel put out, I'm perfectly calm and relaxed and I give him my indifferent smile. "Yes," is all I say as I set down the last glass, feeling light and careless and almost happy in a strange sort of way. "But," Egil says, and I can hear how flummoxed he is. "But aren't they at a concert?" he asks. "At a concert? No," I say, and I'm struck by the casualness with which I say this, and I cross to the drawers, take cutlery from the top drawer, walk over to the table and lay out the cutlery, then I look up at Egil and smile that indifferent smile again.

"But you said they were," Egil says, and I look at him and I don't think I've ever seen him so flummoxed before, and I realize I get a kick out of knocking him so much off-balance. "But you said they wouldn't be having dinner here this evening," he says. "I know," I say, and I look at Egil and smile and he just stands there gaping, and a bubble of laughter breaks loose somewhere inside me and the laughter sweeps through me like a landslide and he looks so flummoxed that I almost laugh out loud, but I don't, I simply look at him and smile. "But," he says, then he stops and he looks at me and gives his head a little shake. "But ... what was all that about the concert?" he asks, and I look at him, smiling that indifferent smile, and a moment passes and now I have to answer and I might as well be honest. "It just came out," I say with a little shrug. "And I thought it sounded so good that I didn't want to say it wasn't true," I say, setting down the last fork, and there's silence. "It's nothing to get upset about, is it?" I say, looking at Egil and smiling again. "No ... not really," Egil says and he pauses, gives another little shake of his head. "But it's kind of an odd thing to lie about, don't you think?" he says. "Yes, I suppose it is," I say, and I smile that same smile and I see Egil's mouth drop open again and I can tell that he's searching for words.

"Tell me," Egil says, and he looks at me and he can't rid himself of his confusion, he just stands there gaping and the laughter resounds right through me. "Are you losing your mind?" he says. "Maybe," I say and a moment passes. "Silje," Egil says, raising his voice slightly now, and he eyes me gravely and I eye him in return and I smile at him as calmly as I can. "Yes," I say. "What's the matter?" he asks. "Nothing's the matter," I say. "You ... you're acting so strangely these days, " he says. "Oh, do you think so?" I ask. "Yes, I do actually," he says. "I wish I could agree with you," I say. I don't know quite what I mean by what I'm saying, it just slips out. "And what on earth is that supposed to mean?" he asks, looking at me with those bewildered eyes again. "Nothing, Egil," I say. "I'm probably just trying to make myself a little more interesting for you," I say and I look at Egil and smile, and he looks at me and a moment passes and all at once he starts to laugh. "You're so weird," he says. "Oh, well, if you say so," I say. "Do you love me even though I'm weird?" I ask. "I love you because you're weird," he says, and then he comes up to me, puts his arms round me and hugs me.

"And you're simply getting weirder and weirder, it seems!" he says. "So you don't think I'm boring?" I say, and I hear myself ask and I've no idea where this question comes from. "Boring?" Egil says. "There's a lot I could say about somebody who spins yarns like the one you just spun," Egil says, "but one thing you're not is boring," he says. "Well, do you think I'm too dependent?" I blurt, and I look at him and I wonder where it comes from, all the stuff I'm saying, it's almost as if it's not me who's talking, it's as if someone were talking through me and I almost wonder whether I actually am too dependent, I mean it must come from somewhere, all this, and maybe I'm right, maybe I am too dependent. "Why on earth do you ask that?" Egil asks, his eyes searching my face. I smile at him and shrug and a moment passes.

Then: "Is it Oddrun, has she been saying things again?" Egil asks. "No, of course not," I say and Egil looks at me, and gives a sly little smile, and I can see that he doesn't believe me. "Did she say you were too dependent?" he asks and he laughs and shakes his head. "No," I say. "Yes, she did," Egil says. "I can tell by your face," he says. "Ah, then she must have done, mustn't she?" I say. "Christ," he says and he laughs again. "You shouldn't take everything she says to heart, Silje," he says, and he looks at me and I look at him and I can't be bothered contradicting him again, I can't remember Mum ever saying that I was too dependent, but it doesn't matter, it makes no difference anyway. "It's just that ... when she delivers one of her salvoes it's herself she's talking about, you know," he says. "Herself?" I say. "Silje," Egil says, and he tilts his head forward slightly and regards me almost paternally. "Too dependent ..." he says. "I would have thought that was a description more suited to women of Oddrun's generation than to women of yours," he says. "It's the woman she was when she was young that she's accusing of being too dependent," he says. "It's a perfectly normal psychological mechanism, a way of mourning the fact that she didn't have the life she so much wanted to have back then," he says. "You've told me yourself how much it bothered her that she didn't dare to live her own life until she was well up in years," he says. "Not until your father died," he adds.

"What a lot you know," I say, and I look at him and I smile that indifferent smile. "Hey, Silje," he says. "Don't start that again." "No, no," I say. "Okay, but do you think she's right?" he asks. "I don't really know," I say. "But," Egil says, then he stops himself and looks at me, laughs and shakes his head. "Well, if so, in what way would you say you were too dependent?" he says. "You have so many options open to you," he goes on, "all you have to do is get out there and make the most of them," he says. "Yes, I suppose so," I say and then there's silence and we just stand there looking at one another. "Oh, for heaven's sake, Silje," he says. "What's stopping you?" he asks, and he spreads his hands. "Have I ever stopped you from doing anything you wanted to do?" he asks and he looks at me, waiting to hear what I'll say, but I don't really know what to say, it's as if someone is talking through me and I'm just standing here waiting to hear what I'm going to say. "I don't know what's stopping me," I say. "Well ... er, what would you like to do?" he asks. "I don't know what I'd like to do," I say. "I just sort of do the things you're supposed to do," I say and I hear what I'm saying and I wonder where all this is coming from. "Is that what you mean when you say you're 'too dependent'?" Egil asks. "Maybe," I say, and then I pause. "I've never really thought about any of this before," I say, and I see how bewildered Egil looks and a moment passes and then I start to laugh and Egil just stands there staring at me, then he shakes his head. "What on earth's the matter with you?" he says. "First making up stories, then beating yourself up like this, and then ... what is all this?" he says, looking helpless and I look at him and laugh and Egil raises his eyebrows and shakes his head and then he starts to laugh, too. "Oh, God," he chuckles and he runs his hand through his thin hair. "I think it's just as well we're off to Brazil soon," he says, "I think you need a little holiday," he says.

Trondheim, July 10th–12th 2006

The time I devised an experiment:

I have no more idea of how we got up there than of what we were doing there, but at any rate we were standing on the top of the corn silo, gazing out across Namsos town centre. To begin with the cars reminded me of guinea pigs and then, because of the way they were darting up and down the narrow, maze-like streets, of rabbits in an experiment of some sort, and this may have been what led me, just after this, to come up with the silly little phrase that I would later use as an amusing, off-the-cuff test as to whether I found a man interesting or not. In any case, I suddenly turned to you and asked what was the first thing that came into your mind when I said "bunny in the bush", and when you replied simply and with a perfectly straight face that you pictured a rabbit with an Afro, I let out a happy ripple of laughter, and I think I was even more surprised than you when I then came straight out and told you I was in love with you (boring men obviously pictured a twat surrounded by a bush of pubic hair). Lightly, with a smile and the hint of a shrug, you said you were a little in love with me, too, and after looking each other in the eye for two, maybe three, seconds, we both laughed. We didn't hold hands afterwards. We didn't say anything either. We merely stood gazing out across the town, smiling, with the wind in our hair. I clearly remember an SAS plane slicing across the grey sky.

The time when I had a nightmare:

The day before we left, over at Jon's house, we'd watched a stupid film on video. There was one scene in which eight black-clad special-force cops jumped out of a helicopter and slithered down ropes onto the roof of a warehouse where some aliens from outer space were hiding. In my nightmare these were transformed into eight spiders, all spinning their threads and lowering themselves onto the roof of the mountain tent in which we were sleeping, exhausted after trudging for miles through a soggy, sucking bog. I don't suffer from arachnophobia and I never have done, but in my dream, probably because of the green Ajungilak sleeping bag I was tucked up inside, I had turned into a plump green grub and I was absolutely terrified because the spiders were going to eat me. On the few other occasions when I've had nightmares the fear has subsided as soon as I opened my eyes, but not this time. When a little gust of wind set the canvas billowing and a couple of drops of condensation fell off the inside of the tent roof, landed on my brow and woke me up, I was sure they'd been dislodged by the weight of the spiders, and when I sat up sharply the sight of the sleeping bag only confirmed, as it were, that I really did have the slippery green body of a grub. I went into absolute hysterics; screaming and wriggling exactly like a grub I wormed my way frantically out of the tent (which I had now got it into my head was my chrysalis), then I rolled down the gentle slope to the kingcup-fringed lake. I lay there on the bank on my back, panic-stricken and perfectly still, so the spiders wouldn't find me. What were actually crows in the treetops looked to me like blueberries dangling high up in the heather and I was sure that the plane cutting across the deep-blue sky was a white bird.

I don't know how long I lay like that, wide-eyed and rigid with fear (probably no more than a second or two), but when you called my name, once and then again, the dream began to loosen its grip on me. Little by little the countryside took shape around me, in much the same way that toads and trolls revert to being trees and roots when the fog lifts, and by the time you dropped to your knees beside me and I saw your big, worried face come floating down towards me (rather as I imagine a father's face would seem to a feverish child as he bent over its cot to feel whether it was hot), I was almost wide awake.

I couldn't help crying when I told you about my dream and how terribly frightened I had been, but as the knowledge that it had only been a dream took root in me the tears gradually gave way to giggles, and as I sat there hiccuping and giggling I found myself feeling something of what I had felt after Dad's first operation was safely over and we thought he was going to be okay after all. The fear and despair I had felt in the hours before and during the operation had still not entirely left me, but I was imbued with an indescribable sense of relief and joy, and in this intermediate state I was filled with gratitude and overcome by a powerful, almost heady urge to be good and sincere to everyone around me. No, more than that. As I recall, I was filled with a conviction that the world and all mankind were essentially good and that nothing was stronger than love.

I had much the same feeling this time too, albeit in a far milder form, and once we were back inside the tent, lying side by side in our sleeping bags with our hands behind our heads, everything in me told me that I loved and trusted you. As a result I was unusually open with you and this must have rubbed off on you because, after we'd been talking for a while, when I happened to say that I didn't mind the fact that my mum had slept with so many different men, you said that at least it was better than trying to escape from her own sexuality the way your mother did.

As far as you could tell, Berit seemed to find sex and everything to do with sex disgusting and she cultivated the habits and manners, values and norms that would save her from talking about it, thinking of it and most certainly from having it. This problematic attitude to sex was also, you suspected, the reason why she had married Arvid, because not only was he a clergyman and hence particularly wary of being accused of not being sufficiently respectable or proper – something which made him easy to control sexually – he was also, as a person, almost asexual. He was snobbish and pernickety and could be shocked and appalled by the merest glimpse of a bare breast on television, you told me. And then, with your eyes fixed on the billowing tent roof, you said you were afraid that Berit's aversion to sex might stem from the fact that your real father had been a sexual molester who had raped her and got her pregnant. This would explain why your mother refused to talk about him and why she was so dead set against revealing his identity. It would also explain why the unknown woman in the orange Audi, who – according to this same theory – was another of your biological father's victims, had looked so horrified when she caught sight of you outside our house; she had, as I happened to remark when we were standing there on the steps, seen something of your father in you and thus relived the rape to which she had once been subjected.

After a half-hearted attempt on my part to remind you that this was, after all, pure speculation, I remember that we lay for some moments in silence. The conversation had begun and ended somewhat abruptly and this, together with the seriousness of the subject matter, had left me feeling dumbfounded and confused, as were you I realized when I turned and met your eye (you're not the most open person I've ever met, to put it mildly, and you probably hadn't planned to say what you had said). The rather comical aspect of the situation, with the two of us lying there feeling equally perplexed by the turn the conversation had taken, prompted us both to burst out laughing, suddenly and at exactly the same moment, and shortly afterwards, when we crawled out of the tent and made a start on the day, we were feeling on top of the world.

We tried to do a bit of fishing before breakfast, I remember. There was a slight breeze and our red-and-white styrofoam floats were nudged back and forth by the choppy little ripples on the water. Every now and again we had to reel in our lines and cast again as the wind caused the floats to drift slowly but steadily into the shallows, among the reeds that stuck up out of the water here and there, rather like hair after a botched hair transplant.

One of the countless times we performed for Mum's guests:

The neck of the double bass jutted through the thin, faintly rippling veil of cigarette smoke, not unlike a mountain peak rising out of the morning mist, and as Jon's fingers loped like lumbering bear paws over the strings, Mum's guests sat listening, mildly pissed on red wine, their ears wrapping themselves around the notes and cherishing them the way mussels close around their pearls and cherish them (wow, so beautiful). You were next to Jon, standing perfectly still, your arms hanging by your sides, head bent, eyes fixed on your feet, and your long hair hanging down on either side of your face like heavy curtains. Then, as Jon suddenly switched tempo and his fingers changed from loping bear paws into pelting kangaroo feet bounding across the strings, you raised your right hand, clenched the mike – much as a mafioso would slap his hand down on the shoulder of a man he wanted to put the frighteners on (menacing in a matey fashion) – snatched it up to your lips and wailed out the lyrics I had written, lyrics I thought I had kept and which I have therefore spent the whole of this morning searching for, although I had actually made up my mind not to leave Mum's flat for a while yet.

But like so much else from that time those song lyrics must have been lost during one of the many moves I've made in my adult life and the only lines I remember clearly are "They've put Pan-flute railings round Vivaldi and walled the bugger up in brick / we're gonna blow up the supermarket, 'cos the whole thing makes us sick" – lines that I can tell could only have come from me and no one else, but which are also so strongly coloured by the youthful rage, intensity and sense of commitment that we possessed back then that they nevertheless seem foreign to me today, now that I have – sad to say – become such a thoroughly tragic figure that in my darker moments there's another line I wrote which I feel sums me up perfectly: "She is a star, she shines, but her light died long ago."

Mum and her friends belonged to a world where the emphasis was on creativity and originality and even though some of those present must surely have detected the amateurishness of the lyrics, the music and the performance, they clapped and cheered wildly when we were finished; applause which you, whose ambitions inclined more towards fine art and literature than to music, appreciated, but no more than that, but which Jon, as usual, allowed to go to his head. He spent the rest of the evening going around fishing for more compliments, and he received plenty to begin with, but there were limits to the praise people were prepared to shower on his bass playing, and eventually – although he wasn't aware of it – people started doing their best to avoid him. They suddenly found they had to go to the bathroom when he came over or they pretended not to notice when he tried to catch their eye, and later in the evening when everybody was drunk and no longer as strictly bound by the rules of good behaviour, one of Mum's friends lost patience with him and told him to go to hell. That woke Jon up and jolted him out of both his alcoholic haze and his ego trip. He hung around for a while with an anguished little smile on his face, saying nothing, but eventually the embarrassment became too much for him, he pleaded a headache and left the party, looking like a wounded animal, as he always did when things went the slightest bit against him.

Actually, it was cowardice and lack of backbone that prevented him from becoming a serious musician. Instead, he wound up as a youth worker and bass player with various useless Trøndelag rock bands (or at least that's what he was doing when I ran into him some years back). He used to say that he had turned down a place at music school because he had to stay home and look after his mother, but although she may sometimes have been ill, she wasn't as sick as all that and you and I both knew that this was simply a good excuse for not trying to make a go if it with his music. He exasperated and infuriated us, but we tried not to let it show, because that was exactly what he wanted. He loved to see and hear people lamenting the fact that he wasn't making the most of his gifts. I've never seen him happier than when some guitarist hero whose name I've forgotten (a long-haired jazz musician who held a workshop in Namsos) told him that he could have been one of the very best if only he had put his mind to it.

Writing this it occurs to me that it was much the same story with all of Jon's half-hearted suicide attempts. Unlike you and me, who understood the importance of making choices and knew that it is actually possible to break out of the patterns ingrained in one since childhood, Jon regarded himself as purely a product of his environment and it may have been all of the maudlin sentimentality and self-pity that this victim mentality brought with it that made him threaten to take his own life every now and again. You and I knew, of course, that he was only looking for attention and sympathy and that he would never dream of killing himself, but this was not something we could discuss with anyone else – we would have been considered cold and callous. But then he went and ruined my eighteenth birthday by locking himself in the loo and threatening to slit his wrists with a razor blade. That did it, I'd had enough, and with everyone else at the party listening in I grinned and yelled, "Go right ahead, but be quick about it because there's a lot of beer to be flushed out in there tonight." I don't think Jon ever forgave me for that. He tried to make out that he'd been a lot drunker than he actually was and that he didn't remember a thing (as usual), but the gap that had already opened up between us grew even wider that evening.

The time when a fat middle-aged woman hurled a sour remark at us:

The boathouse had just been oiled and a little metal ladder covered in old paint stains was still propped against its wall, so we'd been able to climb up onto the roof, dripping wet after our swim. We lay on our backs on the rough, black, sun-baked roofing felt, you with your hands under your head and me with my arms by my sides. The warm breeze brushed my slightly goose-pimpled skin and, while my hair, which was long and caught back into a red band, was still wet and lay cold and rather heavy on my shoulder, my bikini was already dry, as were your blue Adidas shorts by the way – I noticed this when I turned my head slightly to check whether your dick was making a bulge in the flimsy material but, disappointingly, it wasn't.

I almost asked you whether the water had been really cold, but I had learned that you had to be very careful when it came to joking about the size of somebody's dick, so I restrained myself. Instead I turned my head the other way and gazed out across the sparkling blue sea, to where a motorboat carrying two boys in red life vests was chugging by. As they passed the boob-shaped skerry where the gulls nested, the birds began to dive-bomb them, swooping down over their heads, then up into the air again in long, sweeping curves, then dive-bombing the boat again, shrieking and plummeting from high above and scaring one of the boys, who put his arm up as if to shield himself. I nudged you and laughed and when you lifted your head off the roof a fraction and shaded your eyes with your hand to take a look I said something about the mother gull wanting to protect her young. This may have been what prompted you, shortly afterwards, to start talking about your mother and how she wouldn't tell you who your father was.

I had always had the idea that you preferred not to talk about your real father, but you had now broached the subject with me twice in a relatively short space of time and I took this as a sign that you were thinking about him a lot just then, a suspicion which was indirectly confirmed when you told me the following story.

On one of the first days of the Namsos Fair you and Jon had stopped at one of the many stalls selling old military gear, and when you came home from the fair with a pair of army boots and a jacket with three stripes on the shoulders that gave you exactly the cool, freaky look you were after, Berit flew into a quite unexpected fit of rage and snapped at you to take that Nazi get-up off that very instant. According to you, she had been almost as taken aback by her own angry outburst as you were and a second after saying what she had said she had tried to smooth things over with what you described as a very unsteady and anxious laugh (as if it had been a joke). You had asked what the hell was the matter with her and she had said nothing was the matter. Then she had simply turned away and you had stomped upstairs to your room, not quite knowing whether she was laughing or crying.

This incident was by no means unique, you told me. You had never given it much thought before, but Berit had always reacted in unexpected and, for you, inexplicable, ways when she saw you in certain situations or circumstances. She thought, for example, that it was disgusting when you did this, you said, jutting your chin out and up, as if to stretch your jaw a little or smooth out the skin of your throat. And she had to look away when you did this, you went on, curling your upper lip slightly and inhaling deeply through your nose (as if you had a cold).

There was a connection, you believed, between such responses on her part, her sudden fury at the sight of you in army gear and the identity of your biological father. In the same way that the unknown woman in the orange Audi had relived her rape on seeing a young man she had never laid eyes on before, so your mother relived her rape on seeing you in situations in which you looked particularly like your father.

"So now you're on the look out for a middle-aged army officer with a facial tic?" I remember asking and you roared with laughter for so long that eventually we heard a crabby, tobacco-roughened woman's voice down below say, "Yeah, yeah, we hear you. The whole bloody beach can hear what a great time you're having." We immediately pushed ourselves up onto our elbows and peeped over the edge of the roof. Beneath us we saw three flabby white women in their late thirties lying on their stomachs on the rocks. The backs of all three were slightly bowed, their upper bodies raised half off the rock, and this – along with the damp, glistening skin, stretched so tightly over the flab that it looked as though it was about to burst – made them look like three sea lions, all set to slip into the water.

Cheeky and fearless as we were, and somewhat provoked by this sour remark, we started firing snide comments back at them. I find it a bit scary, though, to think that at the age of eighteen I knew exactly how to get at women the same age as I am now, because while you, as a young man, could only venture a rather silly remark about periods and PMS, I sat up to give them a good view of what was then a slim, shapely figure with firm breasts peeking out of my bikini top, smiled wryly, and in a loud, clear voice said: "Well – I didn't know you got sea lions this far south."

I remember one of the women responding to this by trying to act as though she thought we were ridiculous, but she was far too hurt and het up to carry it off, and her affected laugh gradually petered out into a seething, impotent hiss.

The time when Berit turned and looked at us:

Arvid was mowing the lawn, Berit was painting the garden gate and we were sitting at the little stone table under the cherry tree, our heads bowed over my notebook, on which I had just spilled coffee, washing away some of the writing and turning the words into a gritty blue mess, all but impossible to decipher. "It's kind of like when you're out paddling and you disturb a flounder," I remember saying, and when you asked me to explain what I meant and I described how a flounder will dart off across the sea bottom, sending the sand swirling up and turning the water round your bare feet all cloudy and muddy, you shifted your hand until it was almost touching me, and I remember the lovely warm feeling that flowed up my arm when your fingers grazed mine. But the next moment, when Berit laid her brush across the top of the paint tin, stood up and turned to us, you drew your hand away again, kind of casually. "I'm a bit tired," I remember you saying, then you sat back in the camping chair, stretched your arms over your head and yawned.

But, contrary to what you obviously thought, Berit wasn't jealous. I realized this when, since she found it hard to talk to you about such things, she came up to me a few days later and asked if we were using contraception. She was smiling and almost friendly in a kind of all-girls-together way, and when I nodded and said that, yes, we were (you were very careful about using a condom, far more careful than I was), she put a hand to her chest and let all the air out of her lungs in one breath, as if very relieved. "I know what it's like to have a baby when you're young and I wouldn't exactly recommend it," I remember her saying, and before we parted she made me promise not to tell you about our little chat. "He'll only think that I'm trying to control him," she said, and she winked slyly at me as she added: "You know what he's like, he does so want to be free and independent."

And it may have been this as much as the fear of Berit being jealous that moved you to pull your hand away when she turned to us. Because it wasn't just that you didn't want your mother to regard us as a couple, you didn't want anyone regarding us that way, and when I asked you why not, you always came out with some tired old line such as: "I don't want to be tied down, or not yet anyway."

Trondheim, July 3rd 2006. Dinner at Silje's and Egil's

We sit at the table, eating, and no one says anything. I hear
Else's knife scraping her plate and on the other side of the
table I hear Egil say, "Mm," and I hear the glug-glug of wine
being poured into a glass and I see that it's Trond who has
refilled his glass and Trond sets the bottle down on the table
with a little thud, then he looks at me as he raises his glass.
"I'm sorry I couldn't come on Thursday," he says, his voice
deep and slightly husky. He takes a big swig of his wine,
tucks his long, thick hair behind his ear and leans over his
plate. "That's all right," I say, looking at him and smiling.
"I heard it was a good funeral," he says, then he takes a big
mouthful of fish and eyes me with interest as he chews.
"Yes, it was," I say, and I picture the funeral, I picture all
those sad, sombre faces and in my mind I hear the voice of
the earnest, stammering vicar. "Yes, the funeral went well,"
I say and I chuckle at my rather frivolous choice of words,
then I look at Trond and smile, give a little shrug. "It was
like any other funeral," I say, and Trond nods and smiles
back. "So how are you doing?" he asks. "Oh, I'm fine," I
say, "although it was a bit sudden," I add, and I look at him
and give a little wag of my head and he smiles warmly as
he takes a sip of his wine.

"The strange thing about your parents dying, though," I say, "is that you start thinking of yourself as being next in line," I say. "It's like in gym class at school, suddenly you find yourself at the head of the queue and it's your turn next," I say with a little laugh. "Yep, you've got to live while you can," Trond says, and he too gives a little laugh. "Yep," I say and I lean over my plate, take a little bit of my fish, then look up at Egil, and now I see that Egil is sitting there staring at me. He gives me a wry little smile. What is it this time, what's he looking at me like that for?

"She was your mother, Silje," Egil says, and a moment passes, and I look at him and I frown. "What's that supposed to mean?" I ask. "I just think you could show a little more respect," he says. "It was like any other funeral," he says, staring at me, still with that wry smile on his face and there's silence for a moment and I glance across at Trond and Trond looks straight at Egil and I glance across at Else and Else lowers her eyes and straightens the napkin on her lap. Her long narrow face is suddenly tight, she looks rather aggrieved, looks a little put out, and a moment passes and then, all at once, I realize what this is about, it's not me but Else that Egil is addressing, it's not me but his mother he's talking to, and I turn to Egil and hold his gaze and I feel myself growing annoyed.

"Yes, well," Trond says suddenly, and he looks at Egil. "We all know how fond you are of Mum, Egil," he says, just like that, and I almost jump when he says it, and there's total silence for a moment and I feel a little ripple of delight run through me, it'll do Egil and Else good to hear this, there's silence and Else purses her lips and becomes even more tight-faced. She's breathing a little faster than usual as she straightens the jacket collar of her beige trouser suit and Egil is looking daggers at Trond. "What?" Egil says and Trond grins and shakes his head. "Nothing," he says, and there's silence again and a moment passes.

"Could you pass me the salt, Egil?" Else asks and I stare at her, she still looks strained and aggrieved and I realize she's starting to annoy me. I turn to look at Egil and he lays his knife and fork on his plate, his face looking so tight and stern, and he lifts his chin slightly as he reaches across the table and curls his slender, white shopkeeper fingers round the salt cellar. I notice how finicky and feminine this action makes him appear, it's almost disgusting how unmasculine he is. "Here you are, Mum," Egil says. "Thank you," Else says, and I look at Else, then I look at Egil and I'm struck by how alike they actually are, with the same clean-cut features, the same brilliant white teeth, the same narrow shoulders and the same slender fingers.

"What are you grinning at?" Egil snaps and he looks up at Trond and I turn and look at Trond and Trond chuckles and shakes his head. "Nothing," he says, raising his eyebrows slightly, and he chuckles as he drinks the rest of his wine, then he refills his glass and there's silence and I look at Egil again and yet again I'm struck by how alike he and Else are. I've always known that he looked like her, but not that he looked so much like her. I feel almost as though I'm seeing Egil in a new light, almost as though I'm seeing him for the first time; I don't take my eyes off him and the moments pass and then he suddenly looks straight at me.

"What?" he says, and a moment passes and I simply sit there staring at him. "Silje," he says a little louder and he frowns and shakes his head and a moment passes and then I seem to come to my senses a little. "Yes?" I say. "You're giving me such a funny look," he says. "Am I?" I say. "Yes," he says and there's silence and I don't take my eyes off him. "No, really – what is it?" he says. "Nothing," I say, giving him a rather stiff little smile. "Nothing?" he asks. "Just something I thought of," I say. "Ah, so there was something, then," he says, and a moment passes and it annoys me that he's so persistent, sitting there giving me the third degree when we have guests, and my annoyance grows. "I'm simply trying to say I don't want to tell you what I was thinking." It just comes out and I almost jump at what I'm saying, and Egil flinches as I say it and there is total silence and Egil stares at me, shocked and furious, and I look him straight in the eye, and I can tell that he expects me to back down, he expects me to lower my eyes, but I hold his gaze and I smile a stiff little smile, and a moment passes, and one of us is going to have to look away soon, we can't go on sitting like this, not when we have guests, and another moment passes and Egil is looking more and more furious, but I don't back down, and Egil leans over his plate and goes on eating, eating a little faster than usual, and I can see how furious he is and I realize that I'm enjoying this and I carry on eating and there's an awkward silence and the moments pass.

"This sauce is delicious," Else says, then there's silence again and the moments pass, then Trond starts to laugh, and his laugh is deep and husky and Egil lays his cutlery on his plate, sets it down a little more firmly than normal and glares at Trond. "What exactly is all this?" Egil asks, blinking steadily at the end of this sentence, blinking as if to command respect, and I look at his slender wrists and clean-cut, feminine features, and I find it hard not to laugh, he's so unmasculine that it's funny when he tries to seem intimidating. "What is it?" Trond asks, and he chuckles and shakes his head. "I don't really know," he says. "But one thing's for sure – nothing's changed." "Trond!" Else says, giving Trond a shocked look, then her shock turns to anger, her upper lip tightens into a fan of fine, vertical creases, and she stares at Trond, and Trond stares back at her. "Yes?" he says, and he smiles at her with feigned tenderness. "Behave yourself," Else snaps. "I'm to behave myself?" Trond says. "Yes, you," Else says. "But what did I do?" Trond asks. "Behave yourself," Else says, a little louder this time, then there's silence again and the moments pass. "But this sauce is delicious," Trond murmurs, and he looks at his plate and grins.

"Hey!" Egil snaps, jerking his head at Trond. "We didn't invite you dinner just so you could flash that mocking grin of yours," Egil says. "I didn't exactly come here for a laugh, either," Trond says, still grinning. "What's that supposed to mean?" Egil asks. "What do you think it means?" Trond asks. "You can leave whenever you like, you know," Egil says. "Oh, thanks," Trond says. "But if I can just finish eating first. I'm hungry," he says, and a moment passes and I just sit there gazing at them and Egil is looking daggers at Trond and Trond drinks the rest of his wine, tucks his long, thick hair behind his ear, picks up the wine bottle and refills his glass, and Egil snorts, shakes his head angrily, leans over his plate and carries on eating and for a little while everyone concentrates on their food and there's silence.

Then: "Trond, do you mind!" Egil snaps, eyeing Trond sharply. "Huh?" Trond says. "Do you think you could possibly show some manners," Egil says. "Oh, what now?" Trond asks. "You're smacking your lips," Egil says. "Oops, sorry, I forgot where I was," Trond retorts sarcastically.

"Spare me your sarcasm," Egil says. "Sarcasm?" Trond says. "I wasn't meaning to be sarcastic, it's just that for a second there I actually felt at home," he says. "But it won't happen again, brother mine," he says and I simply sit there listening to them, simply sit there looking at them and I see how angry Egil is and Egil glances wearily at Else as if signalling to her to take over, and Else takes over.

"Trond, I think you should apologize," Else says. "What for?" Trond asks, and he looks at Else and smiles and Else glares at him. "You're getting more and more like your father," Else says. "Well, thank heavens for that," Trond says. "At least he lived till he died," he says. "And what's that supposed to mean?" Else demands. "Oh, nothing," Trond says. "No, go on, say it," Else says. "It was nothing, I said," Trond says. "Lived till he died," Else says, and she sniffs. "If you mean to say that he was, and you are, more alive than anyone else in this family, may I just remind you that it's us and the work we've put into that shop that made it possible for him to live the way he did, the way you would so like to live. If it weren't for us there wouldn't have been so much as a peep from either of you, because you'd have had to work and earn your living," she says. "Like other people have to," she adds. "Yeah, right," Trond says. "Yeah, right?" she says. "Are you saying that's not true?" she says. "Oh, sure," Trond says. "Keep a civil tongue in your head when you talk to me," Else says. "I was only saying you're right," Trond says. "If it weren't for you I'd have had to work," he says. "I mean, what I do isn't work, is it?" he says smiling at Else, and Else is getting more and more het up. "You keep a civil tongue in your head," she says again. "I'm only saying you're right," Trond says. "I'm a layabout and a leech, and I should be eternally grateful to you and Egil for the fact that I even exist," he says. "To you especially, of course," he adds.

"Oh, please!" Else says. "Don't make a bigger fool of yourself than you have to, all I was asking for was a little respect," she says. "Is that too much to expect?" she asks. "Respect?" Trond cries. "Do you think you're showing respect for me, talking like that about what I've chosen to dedicate my life to?" he says, staring straight at Else. "Do you think you're showing respect when you insinuate that the rest of us at this table, who have chosen to do something different with our lives, are less alive than you?" Else says. "I'm the one who actually finances this choice of yours," she adds. "A-ha," Trond says. "So that's it. I knew it," he says and he shakes his head, grinning furiously. "Well, one thing's for sure," he says. "Gone are the days when capitalists still had a certain refinement," he says. "Oh, please," Else says, making a face designed to let Trond know he has said something stupid. "I know you miss your father, but now you're being pathetic," she says. "I miss my father?" Trond cries. "I know you miss your father, but if you think he was more refined than anyone else here, then you're wrong," Else says. "The time he spent tapping away at an old typewriter up in his study had very little to do with refinement," she says. "He did it because he was always too drunk to work," she says. "Yes, and is it any wonder?" Trond says. "So it was my fault he drank, was it?" Else says. "No, not just your fault, I'm sure," Trond says. "But it wasn't without its ups and downs, your marriage, was it?" he adds, looking Else straight in the eye and grinning, and Else glares at him and I simply sit there looking at them. I might as well not be here at all, they're talking so fast and so fiercely, they seem almost to have forgotten that I'm here, they're so engrossed in one another, it's like they don't even see me, and neither of them will back down, they just keep going.

"Oh, apropos relationships, Trond," Egil says, suddenly breaking in, and now he's the one who's grinning. "D'you think we'll get to meet the new woman in your life before she, too, is history?" he asks. "I'm not sure I want to subject her to that?" Trond says. "I happen to care about her, you see," he adds. "Yes, well, a culture shock like that – it's no joke," Egil says. "No, for once I have to agree with you," Trond says. "What was it you said she does?" Egil asks, looking at Trond and grinning, and Trond stares at Egil, grins angrily back at him and I simply sit there looking at them, I'm a spectator, I'm their audience. "Do you really think I'm embarrassed by the fact that she works as a waitress?" Trond says. "Do you really think I care what she does for a living?" he says. "Good heavens, no," Egil says. "I really don't think you do?" Egil says. "I'll tell you something," Trond says, "she's a far better person than you are. I can't even begin to describe how much better," he says, and he glares at Egil and Egil looks at him, and Egil forms his lips into a big "O". "Ohhh," he says. "True love," he says, and he gives a little laugh. "Now I understand," he says. "I doubt that," Trond says. "I doubt if you're capable of understanding any of it," he says. "Ah no, of course, only writers like yourself can do that," Egil says, grinning again and shaking his head, then his expression suddenly changes to one of weary disdain. "Dear, oh dear," he sighs, his face falling into heavy folds: "When are you going to leave adolescence behind?" he says. "When are you going to grow up?" he says. "When am I going to become like you, you mean?" Trond says.

"Never," he says, giving Egil a steely, indignant smile and Egil laughs and shakes his head again. "Never," Egil echoes. "I want to live my own life," he says, putting on a funny voice. "I want to be free," he says and he grins again.

"You know what," Trond exclaims, glaring at Egil, "you're so fucked up you simply can't imagine how anyone wouldn't want to be like you," he says. "That's right," Egil says. "I've been corrupted by filthy lucre and lost sight of what really matters in life," he says, still grinning. "Yes, you have," Trond says. "And your saying it in that sarcastic tone won't make it any the less true," he says, glaring furiously at Egil and Egil grins furiously back at him. "For God's sake, Trond," Egil says, staring at Trond and shaking his head, "You're the one who's lost all focus in your life," he says. "Oh yes?" Trond says. "Yes," Egil says. "You've no goals in life," he says. "Or no long-term goals at any rate," he says. "Listen to Mr MBA, listen to him!" Trond says. "Long-term goals," he says. "Yes, well, you keep chopping and changing," Egil says. "One minute you're working in the firm with Mum and me, the next you decide to study medicine and become a doctor, and now suddenly you want to be writer," he says. "You can't make up your mind. And it's the same with women, you change your women as often as other people change their socks," he says.

"Egil's right, Trond," Else says quietly. "And it's high time you realized that," she says. "Well, well, don't tell me you agree with Egil," Trond cries. "You and Egil?" he says, with a wry bark of laughter. "Well, there's a turn-up for the books," he says. "Oh, dear," Else sighs. "Don't you see what's going on here?" Egil says. "Don't you see that you're trying to be Dad?" he says. "Don't you see that you're trying to carry on where he left off ... with this pathetic Bohemian lifestyle of yours?" he says. "You miss Dad, Trond," Else says, and a moment passes, and I'm still sitting here, staring at them, being their audience, while they sit around the table, acting out their family drama, their chamber play and I sit there, acting as spectator.

"Know what," Trond growls. "I've never heard such a load of pop-psycho bullshit," he says, shaking his head, then he takes a large swig of his wine, puts his glass down and shakes his head again, kind of smiling to himself. But Else doesn't back down and Egil doesn't back down, and I stare at them and it's almost unreal, I think, how they can behave like this at Sunday dinner, it's almost beyond belief. "You'd do better to carry on from where your strong, healthy father left off," Else says. "If you're going to be like your dad, you should try to be the way he was before he started drinking," Egil says, and he eyes Trond solemnly and Else eyes Trond solemnly and I stare open-mouthed at them, they're like a two-headed troll, lashing out at Trond, laying into him and I just sit here watching. "You know," Else says, "I feel much the same now as I felt that time when we almost lost you," she says. "We see you fading away, slowly but surely, before our eyes and it's so hard to watch," she says. "I can't just sit and watch you go the same way as your father," she says, nodding at Trond's wineglass and smiling sadly. "Look," she says. "We've each had one glass and you've drunk almost a full bottle," she says. "This can't go on, Trond," she says, and then there's silence and Trond is angrier than ever, he lowers his knife and fork, straightens up and looks straight at Else.

"What the hell is all this?" he cries and I flinch slightly as he says it. "We care about you, Trond," Else says softly. "We're worried about you," she says, and I look at Trond and I can see how mad he is and he nods curtly, angrily at Else. "Well, stop it," he cries. "I'm a grown man, for Christ's sake," he says. "I'm still your mother, Trond," Else says. "And it worries me when I can see that you're not all right," she says. "But I am all right," Trond says. "It is possible to lead a different life from you and still be perfectly all right," he says, then there's silence again and a moment passes.

"Well, I can tell how mad it makes you if we suggest that you drink too much, Trond," Egil says, suddenly dropping the sarcastic tone. "What are we supposed to make of that, do you think?" he asks calmly. "I don't give a fuck what you make of it," Trond roars suddenly and I jump in my chair. I stare at Trond and Trond stares at his plate, and he eats quickly, angrily, grinning desperately, and he gives a faint shake of his head, he's losing it now and I simply sit here staring at him, sit as if stunned, and I feel my mouth fall open. I close my mouth and swallow, never taking my eyes off Trond. This is almost unreal, this is almost beyond belief. "What a sorry bunch you are," Trond says, speaking with his mouth full, and his voice quivers as he says it. "Take it easy now, Trond," Egil says calmly. "Don't you tell me to take it easy!" Trond roars, making me jump in my chair again and I stare wide-eyed at Trond, because he's losing it now, I can tell by his face, he can no longer control himself, now there's going to be trouble.

"Know what ..." he says, then he pauses, shakes his head and grins fiercely, grinning with his mouth full, and I gape at him. "Know what," he says again, and his voice is shaking more and more, "Sometimes I find myself thinking that you two are actually miserable," he says. "You're miserable and you simply can't understand why," he says. "You've followed the recipe for happiness and the perfect life to the letter and you can't understand why your solid, respectable middle-class existence doesn't taste better than it does," he says, shaking his head and sneering, getting himself more and more worked up, and I stare wide-eyed at him. "And then," he says. "And then," he says again, "when you see me following another recipe and you see that, unlike you, I'm pleased with the result, it pisses you off, you start attacking me and the life I choose to live, you start making out that I'm sick. It would be too hard for you to admit that there might be something wrong with your recipe, and then you start psychoanalysing me and saying there's something wrong with me," he says. "That's so bloody typical of you two, making out that everything you don't agree with is actually the result of some trauma or problem of mine, that way you don't have to have a sensible discussion about it, that way no one can get at you, you put yourself above reproach," he says, his voice quivering more and more, and he nods curtly at Egil and he nods curtly at Else. "It's you two that are sick," he says. "It's not me, it's you," he says.

There's silence again, and I don't take my eyes off Trond, and a moment passes, and then suddenly Trond starts to laugh and he shakes his head incredulously as he laughs. "Well, that shut you up," he says. "Look at you, picking at your food and looking so bloody serious," he says. "You've put on those bloody oh-so-concerned masks of yours and now it's supposed to dawn on me that I'm running off at the mouth again," he says. "You act all concerned, and I'm supposed to think that there's good reason to be concerned about me, and that ... and that ..." he says. "It makes me so fucking mad!" he roars, spraying spittle, and I jump yet again.

And there's silence. And the moments pass. "You need help, Trond," Egil says softly. "I'm fine!" Trond roars, a roar that comes from deep in his stomach, and his eyes widen as he roars and I feel my mouth fall open again and I simply sit there staring at him. "Can't you get that into your head?" he roars. "I don't need help, I'm fine!" And there's silence again and the moments pass. "We love you, Trond," Else says suddenly. "And we're here for you," she says, and I look at Trond and Trond stares fixedly at his plate and his mouth falls slowly open and he doesn't look up from his plate. I stare at him open-mouthed and suddenly I feel a ripple of fear run through me, because he's about to lose it completely, he's gone so far now that he no longer knows what he's doing, and there's silence, then Trond looks up, and stares straight at Egil, and Else and I just sit there watching. A moment passes, but Trond doesn't lose it, he takes a deep breath and lets it out with a little sigh, then he bows his head, looks down at the table and shakes his head despairingly.

"God Almighty," Trond says, and he puts a hand to his head and runs his fingers through his long, thick hair, then he raises his eyes and regards Egil and Else despairingly, and there's silence, and a moment passes. "It's hard for us to know how you're feeling," Egil says. "But we realize that you're hurting and we want to help you," he says, looking at Trond. And Trond holds his eye as he slides his hand out of his hair and lets it drop down into his lap, then he he looks at Egil and shakes his head and gives a sad little laugh. "Amen," Trond murmurs. "What?" Egil says. "You're dyed-in-the-wool fundamentalists, the pair of you," Trond says, and a moment passes, then Egil sighs helplessly, and he looks at Else and Else looks at Trond and then she sighs.

"What's that supposed to mean?" Else says. "The whole point of life is to turn ten øre into twenty øre and anyone who believes otherwise is a heretic," Trond says, and he laughs that sad little laugh again and shakes his head yet again and Else looks at him and frowns. "Oh, honestly," Else says and she opens her mouth again, about to say more, but she doesn't have the chance. "Don't," Trond sighs, raising his hand then lowering it and resting it on the table again. "This is getting us nowhere anyway," he says, then he carries on eating, and a moment passes, then Else lets out a sigh and Egil shakes his head gently and they too carry on eating. Me, I carry on not eating. I'm still sitting looking at them and there is total silence. It's like being in a cinema just after the end of a very powerful film, and the moments pass, then all at once I seem to wake up and come to my senses, all at once I see what has just happened, what exactly has been going on: they've turned me into a guest in my own house, this is my house and they act like I'm not even here, they've made me a spectator, their audience, and I simply let it happen, I'm sitting here putting up with it. A moment passes, and I feel so humiliated. Another moment passes, then I suddenly place my knife and fork on my plate, looking down at my hands as I do so, and my mouth suddenly widens into a little smile. I feel cold and angry. I look up at Egil and he's already looking at me and frowning.

"What's the matter?" he asks and he looks at me, but I don't reply, I just sit there smiling and looking at him and there's silence. "Silje," he says, but I don't reply this time, either. "For goodness sake, Silje," he says, looking almost scared now, and he never takes his eyes off me. "What's the matter with you?" he says, but I still don't reply. "Silje?" Egil says, a little louder.

Then: "Would you excuse me?" I say. It just comes out. "What?" Egil says, looking as if he can't quite believe his ears and I feel a bubble of laughter breaking free inside me when I say this, and I look at him, still smiling, and Egil just sits there staring at me, and a moment passes, then he shakes his head. "Honestly," Egil says, and a moment passes, then I get up from my chair and I realize how surprised I am that I'm doing this, that I'm leaving the table in the middle of dinner. I pick up my wineglass, place it on my plate, pick up my plate with both hands, look at Egil and smile and he sits there with his mouth hanging open and the laughter rings out inside me, I can scarcely believe that I'm doing what I'm doing right now, it's almost as if someone else were doing it.

"Silje," he says. "Yes," I say. "We're not finished yet," he says. "I can see that," I say and I stand there bolt upright, smiling, and he looks at Else and he looks at Trond, then he looks at me again. "No, really, what's the matter?" he says, and a moment passes and I look at him and I'm on the verge of replying, but I don't, I don't know how to reply, nor do I need to reply. "Silje," he says. "Yes," I say lightly and I feel so airy and indifferent, all of a sudden I feel strangely happy. "What is the matter with you?" Egil asks, looking confused, looking genuinely concerned, and his reaction delights me. I smile at him. "Oh, Egil, pet," I say, and my voice is light and happy. "There's nothing the matter with me."

"This is all our fault," Else bursts out and she gives a little cough. "I'm sorry, Silje," she says. "We shouldn't have brought this up now, it wasn't the right moment," she says. "And just after Oddrun's funeral, too," she says. "But Trond and I will go now," she says, and I look at her and I smile that airy, indifferent smile. "No, don't even think about it, Else," I say, and I look at her and she gives me a funny look and it delights me to be doing this. "You haven't finished dinner yet," I say. "And besides, I'm going out anyway," I say. It just comes out, and I hear what I'm saying and this strange feeling of delight grows and grows inside me. "You're going out?" Egil says, widening his eyes and creasing his brow. "And where, might I ask, are you off to?" he says, and I look at him, and I smile that airy smile. "Oh, just out," I say and my voice is light and happy. I say it as if it were the most natural thing in the world and I give a little shrug as I say it. "Silje," he says. "You're scaring me," he says. "I'm scaring you?" I say and I look at Egil and he eyes me in astonishment and Else gazes solemnly at the table, and a moment passes and then I walk off. I carry my plate and cutlery through to the kitchen, set it all down on the worktop and I come back out of the kitchen again with a smile on my face, step into the living room, then out into the hall. I slip on my shoes, hardly able to believe that I'm doing this, it's almost as if someone else were doing it.

"Silje," I hear Egil shout, but I don't answer. I open the door and walk out onto the front steps, then I walk down the steps and out onto the drive and as I set off down the drive I hear the door opening behind me. "Silje," I hear Egil say, but I just keep walking, I don't look back, I walk past the rubbish bins and out onto the pavement, feeling strangely light and happy, then I hear Egil running after me and I stop, and I look at him and smile.

"What is all this?" Egil says. "Why don't you come with me?" I say. It just comes out and I hear what I'm saying and once again I'm amazed by what I'm saying and I stand there

looking at Egil and I smile. "Come with you?" Egil says.
"We can't just leave," he says. "We have guests," he says.
"Oh, what do we care?" I say and I hear what I'm saying
and I get such a kick out of saying what I'm saying. "Let's
just get in the car and go," I say and I hear what I'm saying,
in my mind I can see Egil and I driving off, and I realize that
I really want to do this, and I realize that if I really do do it
there will be a price to pay, and I look at him and smile and
I raise my hand and pick a stray hair off his suit jacket and
he just stands there looking at me, and I pick off another
hair, and a moment passes and he stammers something
and shakes his head helplessly again. "And where would
we go?" he asks. "We could just drive, and see where we
end up," I say. "Kind of like a road movie," I say and I
hear what I'm saying and I've no idea where the things I'm
saying are coming from, it's as if someone else is talking
through me. "Silje," he says. "What is all this, really?" he
says and I look at him and I laugh again. "Hmm?" he says.
"Are you coming or aren't you?" is all I say. "Silje," he
says, raising his voice a little and eyeing me gravely, and I
give him that airy, indifferent look, wait a second or two,
then simply shrug. "Oh, well," I say, and my voice is airy
and indifferent and I feel airy and indifferent too, and a
moment passes, then I simply turn and walk away. "Silje,"
he says again, but I don't reply and I don't turn round, I just
walk away and Egil must think I'm losing my mind and I
realize it amuses me that he should think that.

The time when we went for a beer down at the Quayside:

The big supermarket chains came to Namsos in the early Eighties, if my memory serves me right, and by the late Eighties they had put most of the small shops in and around the town out of business. I would probably have noted this development, but possibly not thought too much about it if it hadn't been for Mum, who was furious when the butcher in Vika was forced to close and this, the only butcher's shop left in the town, was replaced by the cheaper, but greatly inferior supermarket meat counters where, as Mum remarked to us, you risked being served by people who didn't have the slightest interest in food and could scarcely tell the difference between leg and shoulder. This was a perfect example of the way in which the ruthless forces of capitalism left their stamp on the local community and our daily lives, she said (with an ill-concealed dig at my dad, who had been a businessman and a capitalist), and when she sent us out to pick up the last few things she needed for the party she was having that evening, we were a little put out to find that we only had to buy perfectly ordinary salmon and not something which the untrained – or so we assumed – assistant at the meat and fish counter would never have heard of, something like filet mignon, for example. And not only were we cheated of the pleasure of sighing in exasperation at an incompetent shop assistant and, hence, at the entire alienating capitalist system, we were much abashed and put well and truly in our place when we got to the counter and gave our order, because when the assistant – a plump, kindly woman with a strong North Trøndelag accent – asked if we wanted a cut from the top end or the bottom of the fish, we had no idea which was the better, and once she had explained this to us and advised us to go for the top half it was hard to hold onto the image of ourselves as discerning customers, highly critical of both produce and service.

Afterwards, when we emerged from the delightfully cool supermarket and the sun began to blaze down on our bare shoulders, you suggested that we sit down outside somewhere and have a beer, and although I was all for this I wasn't sure whether we should, seeing that it was almost thirty degrees in the shade and we had two kilos of fresh fish in a carrier bag. You said you were sure it would come to no harm and, although I wasn't convinced, I said okay and we strolled down to the Quayside, ordered two ice-cold beers and found ourselves a table for two over by the harbour railing. Not until my beer was half drunk did I notice that Jon, Eskil and their dad were sitting just a couple of tables away. Jon's dad, a notorious hardman, was serving a lengthy prison sentence for smuggling drugs for a biker gang to which he owed money, but had recently been granted parole. Jon had told us about this, but not that his dad would be coming to see them, and I was so taken aback that I nudged you and some of your beer splashed over the rim of the glass and onto the table, where it lay in a shining, faintly quivering little puddle. Just as you turned to see what had put me in such a flap, a big guy with glistening, beer-sodden eyes and a mean-looking grin on his face got up off his chair and walked over to the table at which the three were sitting. I don't remember his name, but he was a local up-and-coming thug and anyone could see that he was out to provoke Jon's dad and thereby challenge the older generation of hardmen. And, despite the fact that Jon's dad was on parole and had, therefore, a lot to lose by getting into a fight, this turned out to be pretty easy to do. When the young guy planted both hands on the table and started mouthing off about how all cons were sex-starved and how it was a well-known fact that most of them resorted to screwing each other to satisfy their urges, Jon's dad looked him straight in the eye: a look that was clearly no mere attempt to seem tougher than he actually was and thus intimidate the challenger, but a sign that the formidable temper for which he was renowned was already close to erupting. All the other people in the café, particularly those who knew Jon's dad, grasped this and the atmosphere grew suddenly tense. A middle-aged woman with a husky smoker's voice, a plastic rose in her hair and enormous white breasts bulging out of a bra several sizes too small, got up, walked over to the lad and told him to come away with her to another table, there was something she needed to talk to him about. And although he must surely have seen this for the ruse that it was and realized that she was simply trying to drag him away before there was trouble, he went with her. He was still grinning and muttering, "Ooh, you're so scary," at Jon's dad, but everybody could see that he was terrified. He must have realized it too, and the more apparent it became to him that he had made a fool of himself and that he was also in danger of losing his reputation as a ruthless hardman, the more set on revenge he became. After fifteen minutes of plucking up his courage, he was back again, leaning over their table, looking meaner than ever and with an even bigger grin on his face. Jon's dad let him hurl a few obscenities at him without saying or doing anything, but when the young thug asked him whether he preferred to be on the top or the bottom, he could no longer restrain himself. He got to his feet and, after asking the pathetic, but obligatory question as to whether this guy wanted to step outside for a moment, there followed a brief, but very nasty tussle in which the younger man didn't even manage to raise his fists before Jon's dad kicked him in the balls, put his hands around the back of his head, dragged it down and drove his knee up into his nose again and again, grinning wrathfully through clenched teeth all the while and asking the kid whether he still thought he was dealing with a poof or what.

Not only would Jon's dad lose any future right to parole, in addition to the conviction for assault and battery that he would most probably receive for beating up this young man, he would also have to serve the full eight years of his sentence for drug trafficking, and I could see how losing his father like this, when he had only just got him back, would utterly crush such a fragile artistic spirit as Jon's. His face seemed to dissolve as he stood there watching, and a moment before his dad let go of the young man's head and let him slump to the tarmac (when I saw how he dropped I was immediately struck by the aptness of the expression "to fall like a sack of potatoes"), he turned and took to his heels. You didn't notice this right away and although you were a much faster runner than Jon you couldn't catch up with him. You came back looking shaken and dismayed. "It's life or death now," I remember you saying, and although I didn't know as much as you did, and although the situation did prove to be more serious than I then thought, there's little doubt that you were overreacting. The scene with Jon and his dad had roused your longing for your own father and with this coursing through you your sympathy for Jon was all the greater, so you construed the situation as being much more serious than it actually was. I don't think I'd ever seen you as upset as you were when we got back to our place, called Jon's house and received no answer.

Later that evening, after we had got good and plastered on the gin brought by one of Mum's more eccentric guests (he claimed, in all seriousness, to be able to talk to birds), I tried to make light of this episode, to cheer you up. After talking about the fight in general and in particular about what a bad role model Jon's father was for his sons, I remarked with apparent casualness: "Yep, some men should have left and never come back once they'd done their bit and fertilized the egg." Not until some time later did I realize that, while I had meant to make you feel better by saying this, it might in fact have given you the idea that I was belittling how hard it had been for you, to grow up not knowing your father. You were pensive, morose and irritable all evening and when you asked for another shot and the guy who could talk to birds said he thought you'd had enough, you grabbed his goatee and tugged, dragging his head down until for a moment he was as bent as a hunchback. I laughed my head off at that.

The time when I was so mad at you:

We had been over at Jon's house (ate crisps, drank fruit squash, saw *Betty Blue*, loved it all three of us) and were walking home when you found a long colourful lady's scarf by the roadside. And out came the actor in you. You wound the scarf round your neck a couple of times and slung one long-fringed end over your shoulder with an effeminate toss of your head, and as we strolled on through the August night you regaled me with imitations of Berit, who was going through some sort of midlife crisis at the time and endeavouring to keep the fear of death and the feeling of pointlessness at bay by being passionate about things she had heard it was worth being passionate about, more specifically art and culture. I sobbed with laughter as you mimicked the earnest and rather pompous way in which she recited poetry, and when you were finished you gave another little flourish of the scarf, placed a hand over your heart and with fluttering eyelids asked rapturously if that wasn't quite beautiful.

Only half a minute later we came upon the scene of the accident. Åge Viken's car had run straight into the tree, the front end had been shunted back into the middle of the vehicle and the front wings were wrapped like two steel arms around the tree trunk (just as his wife Anita Wiken wrapped her arms round their son Arvid when he brought her the news) and while Knut Borge and Leif 'Smoke Rings' Andersson compèred *Swing and Sweet* on the still-functioning car radio, the engine wept petrol and oil onto the cushiony, pine-needle covered ground (as Anita's tears fell onto her son's brown hair?).

The car was a red Volkswagen Beetle. With its smooth, rounded lines it really did look like a large beetle and just as beetles wriggle out of their old shells, Åge Viken was in the process of wriggling out of his shell: the driver's door was wide open and his hand dangled in mid-air like a shrivelled feeler, and while the headlights resembled enormous bug eyes staring fixedly into the darkness, the broken aerial called to mind a spindly insect leg. On the ground just outside the open driver's door was a pool of blood, with a broad, glistening ribbon running from it into the dark forest, rather like a red carpet along which Viken could walk into death.

That is more or less how I remember it: like a painting, or possibly a sequence from one of those baroque and highly stylized films by Peter Greenaway (which we loved, unlike Jon, who thought them far too pretentious). Softly, slowly we edged towards the car, our eyes wide and intent, and once we reached it, once we were standing over the dead man, you suddenly took off the scarf you had found, unwinding it from your neck much the way you would uncoil a mooring line from a bollard on the dock, and – as if it were the most natural thing in the world – you opened the passenger door and laid the scarf on the seat.

Then we walked away from there, softly and without saying a word. This was before they erected street lamps along the path through the forest to the housing estate; the darkness closed in around us, rather like wood closing around nails in a wall, and when we eventually stopped short and turned to one another we could barely see each other's faces. "We'd better run and tell somebody," I remember you saying, and then we started running – not fast, as one might expect, and not frantically, in a fit of delayed panic, as one might also expect, but quite calmly and with what I remember as a sense of wonder and confusion at what we, or rather you, had just done.

During the hours and days that followed this wonder and confusion turned for me into remorse and guilt. That ladies' scarf might make Anita Viken think that her husband had been on his way home from a date with another woman when he crashed, she might begin to wonder who this woman might be, she might even recognize the scarf and know whose it was (this was not entirely unlikely, since it was quite an unusual scarf and people who wear unusual clothes tend to be noticed in a small town), she might even go so far as to accuse some totally innocent woman of having an affair with Åge Viken. This in turn could have major consequences for this woman's own marriage, if she was married. And then there was Viken's son: his whole view of his father might be altered when he learned about the ladies' scarf, he might start to dislike or even hate his own father. Or perhaps this unexpected image of his father as something of a womanizer would bring out the Casanova in him and lead him to cheat on his own girlfriend.

There was no way of knowing what might go through their heads if their imaginations gained the upper hand, but no matter how many awful scenarios I painted for you, and no matter how mad I got, you would not agree that we had to call Anita Viken and tell her everything. It was a work of art, you said, before launching into your usual rant about how it was an artist's job to jolt ordinary people out of their humdrum existences (if only for a moment), thus enabling them to see themselves and their surroundings from an unwonted angle. You would send Anita Viken an anonymous letter telling her the whole story, you said, but you would wait with this until her imagination had "turned her concept of reality inside out and upside down," as you put it, because the greater the contrast between fantasy and reality, the more powerfully and more clearly she would experience the reality when all was revealed.

So from that point of view you were doing Anita Viken a favour, you said, you were doing the same favour for her as we endeavoured to do for ourselves when we flirted with death and suicide. Writing and reading as much about death as we did, collecting bones, hair, skin and nails, applying for summer jobs at the slaughterhouse simply in order to see animals being killed and attending the funerals of strangers, all of these were attempts to get as close to death as possible, in order thereby to gain a fresh perspective on life, you said – although I was perfectly aware of this, of course: this particular topic had been thrashed out so often that that viewpoint had become something of a cliché to us. This was one of the reasons why, one day, in an attempt to actually do what till then we had done little more than talk about, you suddenly bent down, picked a mushroom at random from the forest floor (we had gone for a walk in the wooded hills around Namsos) and popped it in your mouth. "You have to learn that you're mortal in order to appreciate life," you declared loftily.

Well, you certainly learned you were mortal that time. Of the three of us I was the only one who knew a little bit about fungi – Mum was a keen mushroom picker and I had gone mushroom gathering with her lots of times – and when I asked you to describe to me the one you had eaten (I hadn't managed to get a good look at it before you popped it in your mouth) and it sounded to me as if it might be a Deadly webcap, a very common species in pine forests, you, Jon and I were thrown into a state of shock that would last for about two weeks. My face was white and grave as I told you that just a tiny crumb of Deadly webcap was enough to cause permanent kidney damage and that a whole one, such as you had just eaten, could be enough to kill as many as ten people. At first you played it cool, merely pooh-poohing Jon when, tearfully and more distraught than I had ever seen him, he begged you to see a doctor right away (he even started pulling and tugging at you to make you come with him). But it wasn't long before you turned quiet, pale and thoughtful and by the time we got home and found, on reading Mum's book on mushrooms, that it was too late to do anything once the poison had been absorbed into the bloodstream and that it could take it up to fourteen days for symptoms to appear, to be followed by a swift and agonizing death, there was no doubt that this was a state you were now anxious to escape from. During your worst fits of panic I could actually see the beads of sweat breaking out on your chalk-white face and it was the sight of you lying on Mum's sofa that prompted me to write a song containing the line, "The cigarette lies in the ashtray, curled up in the foetal position"; lyrics to which, by the way, Jon added a lovely tune.

Fourteen days later, however, when you still hadn't taken ill, you couldn't tell us often enough how happy you were that you'd eaten that mushroom. You felt stronger and fitter than ever before, you said, and one evening when we were eating pizza and watching *The Deer Hunter* on video you insisted on playing the Russian roulette scene over and over again and kept pointing to Christopher Walken and saying, "There you are, guys, that's me."

We talked about all of this in the days after you left that ladies' scarf in Åge Viken's car, but although you managed to pacify me, you did not manage to convince me that what you had done was right, and when I said that losing her husband was actually enough in itself to jolt any woman out of her humdrum existence and that "this work of art of yours" (said with a little snort) was, therefore, not only unethical, but also unnecessary, you had no valid argument to offer. "But you have to admit, it was beautiful," was all you said, and then you gave that charming laugh that always softened my heart.

The time when we were entranced by a crane:

My hair had dried after our swim, but the salt had left it stiff and bristling and when we hopped off our bikes and were wheeling them up the steep slope I suggested that we pop by Jon's house to rinse ourselves off with the garden hose before setting out on our photo shoot. That was fine by Jon, but we would have to keep the noise down, he said, because his mother hadn't slept a wink the night before, she'd been in so much pain, and now she was lying sleeping immediately above the tap for the hose. We looked at one another, you and I, and rolled our eyes slightly when he said this, I remember, because it was so typical of Jon to focus on and then blow out of all proportion the problems that might arise if one did this or that. The tap for the hose and Grete's bedroom window were situated, if not on different sides of the house, then certainly far enough away from one another that we would have had to really shout and scream in order to wake her, and I was about to breathe a sulky "Yeah, yeah, Jon", but it died on my lips because we were now so far up the slope that we could see across the flat stretch ahead of us and suddenly I caught sight of Arvid, watching a gang of construction workers tearing down an old house. So I drew your attention to him instead.

"Imagine working in this heat," was the first thing Arvid said to us when we reached him, and he pointed to the four workmen on the site in front of us, their coppery bodies glistening with sweat. Three of them were standing smoking and chatting while the fourth was sitting in the cab of a crane with a gigantic, rust-brown steel ball suspended from it by two steel chains – the sort of thing that I had only ever seen in my old Donald Duck comics. "Yeah," we said and we said no more, so entranced were we by this comic-book machine. We simply stood and stared as the man in the cab began to pull the slender, black-knobbed levers, causing the steel ball to swing back and forth a few times, gradually rising higher and higher in the air and swinging faster and faster until eventually it smashed into the wall of the house, sending chunks of bricks and mortar flying like the bricks of a Lego house and come crashing down, sending up clouds of sand and greyish-white dust. I rested my elbow on my searing-hot bike seat and pointed to the twisted brown rods of reinforcing steel protruding from what was left of the wall: the shreds and fragments of mortar that clung to their tips made them look like bum hair with bits of shit stuck to it, otherwise known as dingleberries. You chuckled when I said this to you, but only minutes later this same comment was to prompt another display of ghastly sentimentality from Jon.

It started with me remarking, after we'd been cycling for a while, that Arvid had been looking a bit glum. You said he was probably feeling a bit glum. He had spent most of his childhood living with the eldest of his aunts, who had given him enough in the way of food, drink and clothing, but far too little in terms of warmth, closeness and love, and with whom he had, therefore, a somewhat strained relationship. But from birth until the age of nine, when the dog tipped over a forgotten candle in their holiday cottage and started a fire in which his father and mother died, he had lived in the red-brick house we had just watched being demolished. "He doesn't talk much about the time when he lived there with his parents, but he gets quite emotional whenever he leafs through the photo album from those years," I remember you saying, and Jon got upset at this and shocked at me for comparing the remains of Arvid's childhood home to pieces of shit, as he said.

At first we thought he was joking, but once we realized that he actually wanted to be taken seriously and that this was merely another attempt to appear sensitive and caring we told him to cut out the bullshit, and shortly afterwards, after we had propped our bikes up against the garage wall at Jon's place and gone to rinse off the salt, I made a point of screaming so loudly that I woke Grete. I laughed and blamed it on the ice-cold water, but it was clear from my grin that I was lying and that made Jon mad, and then of course he refused to come on the photo shoot after all, which would have been absolutely fine, not to say a pleasant relief if we hadn't needed Jon to hold the light. He was well aware of this fact, of course, and milked it for all it was worth. He went all sad and dejected-looking, making it quite clear to us that it would be difficult to persuade him to come along, although not impossible of course, because in that case he knew we'd be on our bikes like a shot, leaving him behind, and this in turn would rob him of the pleasure of having us beg and plead and say that we really wanted him to come with us. I don't know how long we sat in their garden coaxing and cajoling him, maybe half an hour, maybe an hour. We – or rather you, since I detested his play-acting and had to stand back a bit so as not to ruin everything by coming straight out and saying exactly what I thought – tried to soften him up by turning on the charm, being artificially bright and cheerful. It wasn't until he started going on about how hard it was for his mother, though, and about how much pain she was in that you not only took the time to listen to him, but actually managed to look as if you were interested in what he was saying, and then he began to thaw. "Oh, all right, I'll come," he said at last (as if he were doing us a big favour), but by then he had, as so often before, succeeded in killing most of the enthusiasm and creative spark in both you and me, and no matter how hard we tried, we couldn't summon up the energy necessary to take a good picture. Jon, on the other hand, was suddenly in sparkling form and when we got to the point at Merraneset, where we meant to take interior shots of the old German bunkers, he was the real live wire of the group, burning with enthusiasm and bursting with ideas. He was like a parasite, he sucked the energy out of us. The more invigorated he became, the more we withered away and, although our thoughts on this may not have been entirely clear at the time, nonetheless we sensed how all of this hung together and it filled us with a rage that we found harder and harder to contain.

The time when Mum received some good news:

Mum was lying sleeping with her mouth open and you, I and some of her friends were sitting in a semicircle round the hospital bed, rather like teeth around a tongue. She must have eaten just before we arrived because the staff hadn't taken away her plate and although the window was open the faint smell of boiled sausages still hung in the air. In my mind's eye I suddenly saw link upon link of red frankfurters marching into her gaping mouth, like in a cartoon. And just as in cartoons such things tend to segue into something else, so the frankfurter links turned into a string of red railway carriages steaming into a dark tunnel, an image which prompted me, quite out of the blue, to utter loudly and clearly the words "sausage train". In the split second before the others could respond to this I pictured a train whose passengers were all dead bulls, horses, cows and sheep, all crammed into dark, airless compartments, but then, when I became aware that the heads of everyone else in the room, including you, had swivelled (owl-like) towards me, and when the funny looks I was being given alerted me to what I had actually said, this image went straight out of my head (although I did use it later in an advert for vegetarian food) and I burst out laughing.

If anyone else had been there with me they might well have thought that I wasn't quite myself, what with the state Mum was in, and that was why I was behaving as I was, but none of those present was of a sentimental bent. They may have looked a little confused when I said it, but then, like a somewhat sluggish engine, the laughter sputtered into life and suddenly everyone around the sickbed was splitting their sides, and this, of course (and not surprisingly), woke Mum.

As soon as she opened her eyes I could tell that she had good news for us. The person looking out through her eyes now was happy and much less frightened than she had been in the days before her admission to hospital, and after making a crack about what rotten friends we were, laughing and enjoying ourselves around her sickbed, she told us that the doctors had found nothing wrong with her and that in all likelihood a lack of sleep combined with overwork, too little food and far too much alcohol was to blame for the problems with her sight, the nausea and the incident when she had fainted and fallen off her chair.

The worry she had felt until the doctors had given her the good news I would later come to picture as a kind of virus that passes from one host body to another, because it was probably hearing her talk about diseases that could lie dormant in the body for decades all undetected, only then to suddenly wake up and destroy a life in next to no time, that gave you the idea that your biological father might have suffered from just such a serious hereditary disease, and the next thing I knew it was you, and not Mum, who couldn't stop worrying that you were sick.

Such a disease would explain why your mother refused to tell you who your father was, I remember you saying. Because people who knew from an early age that they were suffering from a serious illness often succumbed to other ills. While some might be plagued by depression, anxiety or other forms of mental illness, others got it into their heads that they had to live life to the full while they could and ended up as alcoholics, drug addicts or decadent pleasure-seekers of one sort or another. And that being the case it was not surprising that your mother felt you were better off not knowing, or so you thought.

"So now you're looking for a soldier rapist with a tic who also happens to be suffering from a serious hereditary disease," I said, and as before you laughed out loud when I joked about your fantasies concerning your father's identity.

The time when the Weed pointed at us and laughed:

When Mum and my husband and I were in Namsos a few weeks ago we went for an evening stroll by the river. After several weeks of hot, dry weather the water level was much lower than normal and among all the other rubbish that had accumulated on the river bed over the years, I spotted a rusty old fold-up bike with red and yellow detonating cord wound round the spokes. A greyish-green blanket of sludge had draped itself over the seat and initially I thought that this was what gave the bike the look of a drowned horse, the steed of a medieval knight, lying there with its cape (or cover or whatever it's called) rising and falling with the current. Only half a minute later, though, when we were halfway across the old wooden bridge and I turned and saw the bike and the rest of the scene from another angle, I realized that this notion stemmed from something else entirely, namely from an incident when this guy whom we used to call the Weed pointed at us and laughed.

The Weed was only two or three years younger than us, but if not retarded, he was certainly a bit simple, and happiest therefore in the company of kids a few years younger than himself. One day when you and I were walking over the old bridge that Mum, my husband and I crossed a few weeks ago, we saw him and these younger chums of his in the little car park on the other side. They were playing at being knights at a tournament, riding around on their bikes, each with a stick for a lance, yelling and zooming round and round, knocking imaginary opponents off their mounts and hurling them to the ground, to the ecstatic cheers of the king they served, fair maidens in towers or whatever other witnesses to their deeds they saw and heard in their minds. But when the Weed spotted us he slammed on the brakes, slewing round and gouging a dark-brown streak in the gravel; and there he sat (wobbling on his seat for the first half-second), with his lance in the air, pointing at us and hooting with laughter, his mouth wide open. His eyes were round and avid, they flicked back and forth between us and his chums in a way that made him look like a stoat or a weasel or something of the sort. "Lovebirds, look at the lovebirds!" he yelled and I can still hear the wild, whinnying laugh he let out.

But then something happened which we both found rather sad. Because even though the Weed's chums were three or four years younger than him, they no longer saw anything particularly embarrassing about girls and dating and all that stuff and after a quick glance at us they eyed the Weed blankly, shrugged and said, "So what?" And then they all stood there, the Weed included, thinking the same thing (so it seemed): that yet another batch of kids was about to overtake the Weed in the maturity stakes.

And this was exactly what we were talking about a little later when we walked into your kitchen and found Arvid sitting with his elbows on the table and his head in his hands, his fingers sticking out of his unusually tousled hair like the antlers of a young reindeer. He didn't say anything, but when he got up and came over to you, more gliding than walking with his face red and swollen from weeping and his arms stretched straight out in front of him like a sleepwalker in a cartoon or a zombie in a B-movie, we knew right away that something terrible had happened to your mother; that Berit was dead. Unlike me you didn't start to cry, your face was tight and expressionless and for a little while you appeared to be more concerned with how to avoid putting your arms round Arvid, but that you couldn't do, because he flung his arms around you, buried his face in the hollow of your shoulder, hugged you tight and rocked you from side to side, as if you were two exhausted wrestlers in the ring. Not until you asked what had happened did he release you. You gave a little wriggle, shaking off the hand that still rested on your shoulder. It dropped limply to his side and a disappointed, almost hurt look came over his face as he told you that she had collapsed and died in Ole Bruun Olsen's shoe shop and that it had probably been a heart attack.

I didn't realize it then, but now I see that it was Berit's death and the freedom from obligations and expectations that the death of a father or mother always entails that lay behind the change that took place in you over the weeks that followed, or rather – perhaps it's wrong to say that you changed, perhaps it would be truer to say that you were now able to make choices that you had long wanted to make, but which, out of regard for what Berit might think or believe or feel, you could not bring yourself to make – like moving in with me, for example.

We didn't live together in the attic at our house for that many weeks before you left for Trondheim and I went to Bergen, but I remember how grown-up I felt when we brushed our teeth and went to bed together without shagging, or when we sat, bored out of our skulls, at either end of Mum's russet Chesterfield sofa (a foretaste of settled coupledom), the very sofa that I'm sitting on now, as it happens, with my laptop on my knees and one of Mum's rosé wines on the table next to me – which, by the way, leads me to think that the death of a father or a mother does not make us as free as I just suggested, after all. At any rate, being here in the flat Mum lived in till she died, and being in much the same situation as she was in when she was not much older than I am now, I can't help feeling that I'm taking over her life. I've always described the phase I'm going through at the moment as time to think, a breathing space, but – and without dwelling too much on this when it holds so little relevance for you anyway – I would go so far as to say that I feel as though I'm being sucked into the way of life she began to adopt after Dad died, the life that from the age of ten or eleven I was used to seeing her lead. So maybe Jon was right, after all. Maybe it is harder to break free than I always thought (oh, God).

Trondheim, July 5th 2006. A showdown

I'm lying on the sofa staring at the ceiling, and I hear Egil arriving home, so now I'll have to get up, now I'll have to make it look as though I've been doing something and when he asks why I haven't been at work I'll have to say that I had a headache or something. I get up off the sofa, walk across the living room and into the kitchen. I go over to the fridge, open the fridge, crouch down and take a look inside. There are leftovers from yesterday, maybe we should just heat up the leftovers for dinner.

"Hi," I hear Egil say. "Hi," I say and I hear my own voice, and my voice sounds tired. "Where are you?" I hear Egil ask and I peep over the fridge door and there he is, looking down at me. "Ah, there you are," he says, and he smiles. "Yes," I say. "I thought I'd start making dinner," I say. "But ..." Egil says, and he looks at me in astonishment and raises his eyebrows slightly as he puts down his briefcase. His shoulders are covered in stray blond hairs. "But weren't we going out to eat?" he says, and I remember that we were supposed to be going out to eat, and I look at him and smile. "Oh yes, that's right, so we were," is all I say and I stand up, give the fridge door a little nudge and it closes with a soft thud, then I stand there looking at Egil and Egil stands there looking at me, then he gives a little shake of his head.

"You've been saying for ages that you'd like to go out and eat," Egil says. "Yes, I know," I say. "Christ," he says, and he looks at me and raises his eyebrows, and a moment passes and I look at him and sigh. "There's no need to make a big deal of it?" I say. "I'm not making a big deal of it," he says. "I just wonder what's got into you lately," he says, and he looks at me and raises both eyebrows again and gives his head a little shake. "You're not yourself," he says. "Is it because of your mother?" he asks. "If there's anything the matter with me it's certainly not because of her," I say. "Well, if it's got anything to do with us having to cancel the trip to Brazil, you don't have to worry," he says. "I can take the last week in September off instead," he says and he looks at me and I look at him, and a moment passes and then something seems to break loose inside me, something heavy, and it feels like a landslide sweeping through me.

"Well," I cry, "you've got a bloody nerve!" I say and I can hear the fury in my voice and I've no idea where it comes from, this furious voice, and I jerk my head at him and he draws his head back slightly and gazes at me in astonishment. "Huh?" he says. "You're so unbelievably condescending to me," I say and I hear what I'm saying and I don't know where it comes from, what I'm saying, it's as if someone else is talking through me, and the person who's talking through me is absolutely furious and I realize that I'm becoming absolutely furious as well, and Egil stands there looking baffled. "What on earth do you mean by that?" he says.

"I'm really pissed off with you, Egil," I say. "You! The trip to Brazil has nothing to do with it, and the fact that you dare to bring that up is so condescending," I say. "Do you really think that I'm so ... so easily pleased?" I say. "Just treat her to a little trip or something every now and again and she'll be happy. Is that really how you see me?" I ask. "I'm really pissed off with you, Egil," I say. "With you," and I hear what I'm saying and I've no idea where the things I'm saying are coming from, I've no idea who it is that's talking through me, but I'm seized by, I'm caught up in this fury and I glare at Egil and he looks bewildered and alarmed. "What is it, Silje," he asks, "has something happened?"

"Oh, would you just listen to me," I shout and I hear myself shouting. "I am listening," he says. "No, you're not fucking listening," I cry. "'Has something happened?' you ask! I told you, you're pissing me off," and a moment passes and Egil just stands there eyeing me gravely, then he walks up to me and he puts out his hands and now he's going to put his arms round me and I feel the fury erupt inside me and I brush his hands away. "Stop it!" I yell at him. "Don't go playing the psychologist!" I yell and I feel my eyes widening, the fury making my eyes widen, and I stare at Egil with big, wild eyes, and Egil looks at me in alarm. "I'm not playing the psychologist, I only want ..." he says, then he stops and just stands there looking at me.

"You just want what?" I cry, "you want me to see myself as a hysterical female who needs to be soothed and comforted." I say. "You want to shift the focus away from yourself and the fact that you would try the patience of a saint," I say, and I hear what I'm saying, hear how credible, how genuine it sounds and I've no idea where it comes from, what I'm saying, it just comes out.

"Silje ... you don't even believe this yourself," he says. "Stop telling me what I believe and what I think, dammit!"

I shout. "I'm sorry … but, er," he says, and he glances to one side, flings out a hand, then turns and eyes me helplessly. "Do you really think I'm that calculating?" he asks. "Do you really think that's why I wanted to comfort you?" he asks. "You're always making me feel guilty about something," I say. "Even when I know I'm not really to blame I always end up believing that I am," I say, and I hear what I'm saying, and I hear how true what I'm saying is and I feel my confidence growing. "Oh, honestly, Silje," he says. "You can accuse me of a lot of things, but saying that I'm to blame for you feeling guilty for everything under the sun, that's going too far," he says. "Aren't you the one who's always saying how you women learn from when you're little girls to turn grief and anger and shame inward? Right, so don't go blaming me," he says. "Well, you being the way you are doesn't help, that's for sure," I say. "Me being the way I am?" he says. "Yes," I say. "Okay, now that you'll need to explain," he says. "All your nit-picking, it's all just petty stuff, but when you put it all together it's … it's unbearable," I say. "Like the way you came in and switched off the lamps in here in the middle of the day, or the other day when I was cooking pasta," I say, staring at him, "and you suddenly walked in and moved the pot to another ring that was closer to it in size," I say and I hear what I'm saying and it suddenly occurs to me that what I'm saying is true. Egil really did come in and switch off the lamps in here in the middle of the day and he really did walk in and move the pot while I was cooking pasta the other day, and I look at Egil and Egil looks at the floor and Egil runs his hand through his hair and sighs.

"Yes, well," he says. "If it was just the once I wouldn't have bothered," he says. "But you do it every time you make dinner," he says. "I mean, as far as I'm concerned that's exactly ..." he says and then he stops. "It's like going into the bank and paying money into the electricity board account and not getting anything for it," I say, putting on a whiny voice and screwing up my face as I say it. "I've heard it all a hundred times before, so spare me." "Well, why don't you just stop doing it?" Egil says. "Then you wouldn't have me nagging at you," he says. "Why do you think?" I cry, then I pause with my mouth half open, and my eyes wide open. "I do it to provoke you, obviously," I say. "I'm sick and tired of your nit-picking and I have to make some sort of protest," I say, and a moment passes and he just stands there looking at me and gently shaking his head. "How about talking things through instead?" he asks. "I can't be bothered discussing things with you, Egil, because I know you're right," I say and I almost give a little start when I hear myself say this, because what do I mean by it, what am I saying now, where's this voice taking us now, and another moment passes and again he just stands there staring at me. "I'm sorry, Silje, but now ... now I'm confused," Egil says, giving me a puzzled look, and a moment passes and then my mouth opens. "I'm not stupid, Egil," I say. "I know very well it's a waste of energy to put a little pot on a large ring, but the fact is that you can waste a lot of other, much more precious, energy by constantly fussing about piddling little things like that," I say, and I hear what I'm saying and I hear how true it is, what I'm saying, I hear how well put it is, and my confidence simply grows. "I may overdo it sometimes," Egil says. "But it just so happens that most of the days in life are ordinary days, and if we don't give some thought to the habits we acquire in our ordinary everyday lives we're not going to have very good lives," he says. "Oh, spare me the platitudes," I say and again I make a face. "The problem is that ... well, you're ... you're such a tight-ass," I say. "I think we'd both be much better off if you were a little more easy-going," I say. "Because I can't be bothered ... I can't live up to all of the ridiculous demands you make," I say, "and I can't be bothered feeling bad about all my silly little mistakes," I say, and I hear what I'm saying and I hear how genuine the things I'm saying sound and I've no idea where all this is coming from.

"Ah, now I'm starting to get the picture," Egil says. "Well, it's high fucking time," I say and I hear how triumphant my voice sounds, it rises almost to a falsetto at the end of the sentence, and I look Egil in the eye, seething with anger, and Egil looks straight back at me. "It's your mother you're talking to, right?" Egil says, and he looks at me, and I just gape at him, what does he mean by that, what's he blabbering on about now? "Huh," I say, frowning. "That's who these complaints are actually aimed at, isn't it?" he says. "Your mother." "What are you blabbering on about?" I ask. "You may not see it yourself," he says, "but I see it, because I lost my father and I can clearly remember how it felt, to know that it was too late to say all the things I'd meant to say," he says. "I'm sorry," I say, narrowing my eyes and shaking my head. "Now you've lost me," I say.

"There are times when I hate my father for treating my brother and I so differently," he says. "And I knew I would have to talk to him about that if I was ever to come to terms with what that did to me – the poor self-image, the jealousy and ... yeah, well," he says. "I never dared to, though," he says. "And when he died I was left with all these accusations and grievances and no idea of what to do with them except to offload them on to Trond," he says. "All the anger, all the sludge, all the stuff that had been building up inside me and that I really ought to have taken out on my father, I took out on him," he says. "And now you're doing the same thing to me," he says. "Don't you see that?" he says, and then he pauses and there's silence, and I wait, I wait for the voice inside me to reply, because now I have to reply and I pop my lips. "You know what?" I say, and then I stop. I look at the floor, shake my head and a moment passes, then I look up at Egil again and I open my mouth and I wonder what I'll reply, but I have no chance to reply because Egil jumps in again. "It's a perfectly natural reaction," Egil says. "It's all part of the grieving process and once you're able to distance yourself a little from Oddrun's death you'll see that I'm right," he says and there's silence again and I look at Egil and I raise my eyebrows and shake my head. "Do you think so, Egil?" is all I say. "Well, you paint a pretty harsh picture of Oddrun," he says. "Or, at any rate, of the way she was before your father died and she began to let her hair down," he says. "I've heard more than a few stories about the lengths she would go to in order to make you understand what nice girls did and didn't do," he says. "And as far as I know you never plucked up the courage to confront her about that," he says and then he pauses for a moment and I just stand here looking at him and I shake my head and grin ruefully. "For fuck's sake, Egil," I say. "So if you look at it that way it's good that you lash out at me like this, that you don't give a toss about being a nice girl," he continues. "Because it means you're finally rejecting the rules and regulations she imposed on you and that you've always felt bad for not following," he says. "I felt exactly the same when my father died. I was grief-stricken, heartbroken, but I also felt freer than I had felt in a long time," he says.

"You know what, Egil?" I say, and then I pause and something's got to be said now. "Either," I say, "either you're so stupid that you actually believe all this pseudo-psychological crap you're spouting or you're every bit as dazzled by your own brilliance as I think you are," I say, and I hear what I'm saying and I'm trying to figure out what I actually mean and I look at Egil and realize I can't just leave it there. "Dazzled by my own brilliance?" Egil says. "Yes," I say and then I pause. "You simply cannot believe there could be anything wrong with you," I say. "If anyone criticizes you it has to be for one of two motives: either they're out to get you for some reason or they've got it all wrong," I say. I couldn't agree more with everything I'm saying, what I'm saying is true. "It's not really you I'm getting at, it's my mother … my mother!" I say, my voice rising almost to a falsetto at the end of the sentence. "Have you ever heard anything so downright fucking stupid?" I say.

"You can say what you like, Silje," Egil says. "It looks like I've touched a soft spot, though," he says, and a moment passes and I just stand here staring at him. "For fuck's sake," I say, then I pause "Would you listen to yourself, Egil," I cry, my voice almost cracking with delight and fury and I fling out my hands as I say it. "This is exactly what I'm talking about," I say and as the words leave my mouth I realize that this actually is exactly what I'm talking about. "When I get mad at you like this you automatically dismiss any idea that I might have reason to be mad at you," I say. "You immediately assume that I'm mad at you because you've touched a soft spot," I say, and I hear how true it is, what I'm saying, and I realize how furious I am with him for being the way I say he is. "In your world you're always right, Egil," I say. "Why are you like that, why are you so pathologically afraid of not being perfect?" I say.

"Hey," he says. "Now I think we ought to just calm down a bit, because this isn't serving any purpose." he says. "Listen to yourself," I cry. "You're trying to evade the issue again," I say. "Silje," he says, jutting out his chin as he says it and blinking both eyes slowly as he says it. "Take it easy," he says and he holds one hand up, palm outward and I stare at him and the fury grows inside me, because now he wants me to think that I'm being hysterical again; the calmer and more responsible he appears to be, the more hysterical and out of control I'll seem and he wants me to seem hysterical, and I feel my eyes bulging in their sockets and I stare at him with wild, staring eyes and a moment passes and I have to calm down now, I mustn't fall into this trap, I have to pull myself together now, and I take a deep breath, I have to breathe more slowly now.

"It's no use," I say, and I hear my voice quivering with anger, and a moment passes and I look at him. "I'm not getting through to you," I say, sounding a little calmer now, and there's silence, and I hold his gaze as I shake my head. "Could you not make a little effort to listen to what I'm saying, Egil?" I say, and a moment passes and Egil looks at me, then suddenly he draws breath and sighs and I realize how angry this makes me, him standing there acting as if he despairs of me but is, nonetheless, a big enough man to listen to what I have to say.

"All right," he says, and he looks at the floor. "I'm sick of it, Egil," I say, "and I have been for a long time," I say. "I'm sick of you taking me to task for everything I do that doesn't measure up to your standards for proper behaviour and good manners," I say, and I hear what I'm saying and I hear that I'm saying the same as I said just moments ago and Egil sighs again, then he gives a breathy little grunt and sends me a look that says he's fed up hearing me harp on and on about this. "I'm sick of it, because it makes me feel that I'm never good enough," I say. "I've heard all this before," he says, giving me a studiously jaded look, then he closes his eyes and nods and at that I feel the fury explode inside me. "You've heard my words, yes!" I roar at him, and Egil's whole body flinches and he gazes at me, shocked, and I take a step towards him and I stare at him with my big wild eyes. "But you haven't taken in a single word of what I've been saying," I cry. "Because as soon as it registers with you that I'm actually criticizing you, you go on the offensive, without giving any thought to whether my criticism is reasonable or not," I say, and I hear how true it is, what I'm saying, and for the first time it seems as if he is actually hearing what I'm saying, for the first time it seems as if I've got through to him. His face changes, the calm expression is gone and all at once he looks flushed and angry. And I stare angrily at him.

"Well, let me tell you something, Silje," he says. "If what you say is true, then I'm certainly not the only one in this house who sets impossibly high standards for other people," he says. "Oh, really," I cry. "And what, pray, are these impossibly high standards that I set for you?" I ask. "Well, I'll tell you," he cries. "You set unreasonably high standards for how I'm supposed to respond emotionally, for the feelings I'm supposed to show," he says. "I see," I say, holding his gaze. "Meaning?" I say.

"Meaning it seems it's not enough for us to love one another," he says. "It's not enough that we respect one another and treat each other decently, we also have to live up to all your ideas of the great love affair," he says. "You're supposed to be the only woman in the world who can make me happy and I'm supposed to be the only man who can make you happy," he says. "There's no end to the depth of the feelings you expect us to show to one another," he says. "I feel like an emotional bloody acrobat sometimes and I just can't take it," he says.

"Well, let me tell you something, Egil," I say. "We wouldn't have lasted a week as a couple if it hadn't been for such hopelessly romantic notions, as you call them," I say. "Oh, really?" he says. "Oh, really?" I cry. "What do you think would have happened to us if either of us had started telling the other that they could be replaced at any time by anybody?" "I see, so you're saying you could have swapped me for just anybody," he asks indignantly. "No, it's you who's implying that," I shout. "No," he says. "You've got it all wrong," he says. "If we're to function as a couple maybe we need illusions like that," he says. "But the point is that the role you've given me in this charade feels so implausible that I have real trouble playing it," he says. "The things you've scripted for me to do and say seem so false that I sometimes find myself thinking that everything we have together is false, that our whole relationship is founded on imaginary emotions," he says and then he pauses for a moment and he stares at me and I stare at him. "Do you know what I think? I think you miss your father!" he says.

"What?" I say. "This tremendous need you have to feel that you're the only woman I could ever love, I think this could be traced back to the image you have of you and your father," he says. "Oh, honestly," I say, "I don't know whether to laugh or cry," I say. "How often have I had to listen to stories of how he used to shield you whenever Oddrun threw one of her tantrums?" he went on. "How he looked after you and gave you all the love that you needed, but that Oddrun could never give you," he says. "Daddy's little darling," he says. "Precious little Silje," he says. "That's what you miss now, that's how you want me to make you feel," he says. "I've often thought that that's why you have such huge expectations where love is concerned," he says, and the moments pass and he stares at me and I stare at him.

"What is it with you?" I cry. "Why do you have to link everything I say or do to my parents and things that happened when I was a child?" I ask. "I mean, if I were to psychoanalyse you the way you're always psychoanalysing me, I could say that you are the way you are because you grew up with a father who loved your brother more than he loved you," I say. "I could maintain that the reason why you're so dead fucking set on being perfect is that you're still a love-starved little boy who's doing everything he can to win as much of your dad's attention as he gave to Trond," I say, and I hear what I'm saying and I realize how pleased I am with what I'm saying and I've no idea where the things I'm saying are coming from, they just come. "Perhaps that's what your pernicketiness and your pragmatism is all about. Perhaps this is a technique you've developed in order to be as perfect as you believed your father wanted you to be," I say, then I pause for a moment, not taking my eyes off him.

"The only problem is, though, that it's so bloody easy to say something like that," I say. "But we're not that simple, Egil," I say. "Even you're not that simple," I say. "Perhaps it would be just as true to say, for example, that your nit-picking and your craving for perfection is part and parcel of the job you have," I say. "One might perhaps say that the nit-picking and the pragmatism and everything else is a strategy you've developed in order to do a good job," I say, "a strategy designed to enable the shop to survive in the marketplace," I say, and I hear what I'm saying, and I've no idea where it's coming from, I can't remember any of this ever entering my head before, it just spills out of me, and a moment passes and I don't take my eyes off Egil and I see a resentful look come over his face.

"Don't tell me you've become a socialist along with everything else," he says wryly. "All I'm saying is that I'm sick and tired of the way you reduce me to a victim of my own childhood," I cry. "I'm fed up with all your pseudo-psychological spoutings," I say and I nod sharply at him, never taking my eyes off him. "Oh, well, pardon me for being so stupid," Egil snaps. "Oh, for God's sake," I say, and again I screw up my face and I gaze at Egil and smirk. "So, are you going to start acting all hurt and hard done by now?" I ask.

"No," Egil says. "I'm simply telling it as I see it," he says. "I was stupid enough to believe in those pseudo-psychological spoutings and I still am as a matter of fact," he says. "It may sound facile, but that doesn't mean there's nothing to it," he says, and he pauses, stares at me. "I can't live up to the standards you set, and if your father were alive today I doubt if he'd be able to live up to them, either," he says. "He's never loved little Silje as much as he does now, twenty-five years or more after his death," he says, "and nobody can compete with a man like that," he says.

"D'you know something, Egil?" I say, my voice quivering with anger. "The man you're competing with isn't dead," I blurt and I hear what I'm saying and I realize how surprised I am by what I'm saying. "In fact, he couldn't be less dead," I say and I've no idea where it's all coming from, it just comes. "And what's that supposed to mean?" Egil asks and he looks at me and frowns and now there's nothing for it but to keep going. "It means exactly what you think it does," I say, and I stare at him and I'm struck by how plausible I sound and I can see that Egil believes what I'm saying and I see how his face changes, his face grows pale and still. "Oh, yes," I say and I'm laughing inside, a great peal of laughter rings out inside me and I stare straight at him and nod. "That's precisely what it means," I say, my voice quivering slightly.

"Who?" Egil asks. "I doesn't matter who," I say. "Is it that smarmy bastard you were talking to at the Christmas party last year?" Egil asks. "It doesn't matter who it is," I say again. "The hell it doesn't," Egil says and now he's losing his cool. "But why should it matter?" I ask. "Because I want to be sure I punch the right man," he says. "Oh," I say with a contemptuous sneer. "Don't be so pathetic," I say and I look at Egil and Egil stares at me. "It's him, I know it is," Egil cries. "I saw the way you two were drooling all over one another," he says. "Christ," he says.

Then there's silence again and the moments pass and I hold his gaze. "Well, if I've been doing emotional somersaults and if I've been trying to get you to do them too, it might be because I've been trying for so long to save our marriage," I say and I hear what I'm saying, and again I'm struck by how true it sounds. "The worse things got, the harder I tried," I say. "And feelings may have ..." I say, and I pause for effect and in my mind I see how I look, and I see how natural I look, how genuine I seem and I look at

Egil and I see how pale he is. "I don't know," I continue, "feelings may have run pretty high sometimes," I say, and a moment passes, then Egil takes a deep breath and lets it out again, and he shakes his head, then he walks straight past me without so much as glancing at me, walks over to the wicker chair under the window, sinks down into the chair, bends forward and runs his fingers through his hair. He sits like this for a few moments, then he straightens up, lets both hands flop into his lap and sits like this, gazing blankly into space, laughing mirthlessly and shaking his head, and yet again I'm struck by how true all of this seems, it seems almost more true than what is actually true, more real than what is actually real.

"I feel so stupid," Egil says. "I feel so fucking gullible and so ... ridiculous!" he says. "Here I was, thinking that everything was okay," he says. "Christ, and all the time you've been ..." and he breaks off, looks at me again and pauses with his eyes fixed on mine. "Who is it?" he says and his voice is suddenly deeper than usual, and it strikes me as very apt that his voice should be slightly deeper than usual, and it strikes me that this seems more and more real. "No," I say. "I'm not going to say who it is," I say.

There's silence again and Egil looks at the floor and the moments pass, then he suddenly looks up and gazes at me, his eyes wide and intent. "It's Trond," he whispers and I hear what he says and I realize how surprised I am when he says it. "It's fucking Trond," Egil says, and more moments pass, and we stare at one another, there's total silence and I'm just sitting here staring at him and the longer I sit like this the more convinced he'll become that it's Trond. And I picture to myself that it's Trond I've been having an affair with and it strikes me as very apt, assigning this role to

Trond, and the moments pass, and I feel my heart pounding and I feel my pulse pounding and I just sit here.

"For fuck's sake, Silje," Egil says, staring at me in shock. "Have you been cheating on me with my own brother?" he cries. He stares at me, looking more and more shocked, and now he's utterly convinced that I've been cheating on him with Trond, and I just sit here, I make no effort to deny what he's saying, it could have been Trond I'd been unfaithful with and it's so appallingly apt that he should believe Trond's the one I'm having an affair with. "For fuck's sake," Egil says, then he looks at the floor again, runs his fingers through his hair again and I just sit there staring at him, and I realize how powerful this is, it feels as though we've hurled ourselves into some sort of force field, and I feel the power coursing through me, life courses through me.

"Now I see why you're always so nice to him," Egil says, "and why you're always so keen to stand up for him," he says, and I hear what he's saying and yet again I'm struck by how true this seems, how all the pieces seem to fit and how much more real this is than what is actually real. "So that's why we never get to meet his new lady friend," Egil says. "It's you he's ... All that about the waitress is just a pack of lies," he says, and he looks me in the eye and he pauses. "How long has it been going on?" he asks. "Not very long, a few months." It just slips out. "And how many people know about it?" he asks. "Not very many," I say. "Not very many?" he says, raging now. "In other words, more than just the two of you," he says, glaring at me, and I hold his gaze and a moment passes, then he lowers his eyes. "It's so ... it's so humiliating," he says, sounding distraught now. "Okay, so who else knows about it?" he asks. "Do any of my friends know about it?" he asks. "Don't ask me that,

Egil," I say, and I picture myself as I say it, picture how my face takes on a slightly agonized look and I can almost feel the pain which this agonized face reflects. "It doesn't really matter," I say. "It fucking well does matter," Egil cries. "It matters to me because I'd like to know which of my friends I can trust," he says. "None of your friends know about it," I say. "Oh, don't give me that, dammit," he says. "If none of them knew anything about it you would have said so as soon as I asked," he says, staring at me, and he waits and I look at him, saying nothing, then I look at the floor.

"They know, they all know," he says softly, then he pauses. "I can tell by your face," he says, raising his voice slightly, then he pauses again and I just stand there saying nothing, and the longer I stand like this, the more convinced he'll become that he's right, and I just stand there. "Fuck's sake, Silje, I'm all alone now because of you, do you realize that?" he says and I look up at him and he looks at me and then he turns away and the moments pass and then all of a sudden he starts to laugh. "Oh, this is so funny," he says and he laughs in a way I've never heard him laugh before. "This is so bloody funny," he says. "So that's why Trond has been drinking so much lately. God, I've been so blind," he says, and I hear what he's saying and yet again I'm struck by how well he gets the pieces to fit, how true it all seems, truer than the actual truth.

"And what do you intend to do now?" he says. He's sitting with his elbows on his knees, looking at the floor, and he gives a faint shake of his head and a moment passes. "What do I intend to do?" I say. "Well, it was you who fucking started this," he cries. "Well, I can't be the only one to blame for our marriage going so badly wrong that it's come to this, can I?" I say. "You've got some fucking nerve," Egil yells and I flinch when he yells and he straightens up and glares at me. "Not only do you cheat on me with my own brother," he cries. "And not only am I just about the last one to know about it," he says, "but now you're blaming me for it." "No, I'm not," I cry. "I'm saying that it happened because of the way our marriage has turned out, and I think we're both equally to blame for that," I say, and I hear what I'm saying and I'm struck by how well I'm arguing my case. "Bullshit!" Egil snarls at me. "This is your fault and yours alone, this has all come about simply because I couldn't live up to the ridiculous standards you set for how a man's supposed to behave when it comes to love and romance," he says. "You're living in a bloody romcom and since I haven't been able to comply with your demands you've gone and thrown yourself at that idiot brother of mine," he says. "There," he says, "in that hopeless dreamer you've found someone who can satisfy your ludicrous romantic yearnings," he says, then he pauses, gives a bitter laugh. "But when it starts to become routine it'll start all over again," he says. "And you'll go looking for somebody new," he says, grinning fiercely at me. "Just you wait," he says triumphantly, "just you wait, you'll see I'm right," he says.

"There you go again," I cry, "putting yourself above reproach," I cry. "Stop saying that, dammit," he yells at me. "It makes me sick to hear you quoting that moron brother of mine." "Well, you do it," I yell back and the fury erupts inside me. "If I'm having an affair with another man it can't possibly be because of what's happened to us, can it?" I roar. "Oh no, it's because I'm not living in the real world." I pause and I glare at him and my eyes feel as though they're growing too big for their sockets. "How far are you actually prepared to go to maintain the illusion that you're perfect?" I roar. "The real world is too dull for me, so I have to take a lover who can bolster my faith in a romantic fantasy world." I hear what I'm saying and I hear how true it is, what I'm saying, how right I am. "What a load of bloody rubbish!" I roar. "You're the one who's living in a fantasy world, Egil. You! You're living in a fantasy world in which you're perfect – and anyway, it's not true!"

There is total silence. "What's not true?" Egil asks, and he looks straight at me. "I'm not having an affair with Trond or anyone else," I say and I hear what I'm saying and I realize how surprised I am by what I'm saying, by the fact that I'm giving the show away just like that. "And I never have, either," I say. "It's not true," I say, and I look at him and I try to smile an airy indifferent smile. "Huh?" Egil says, and he stands there with his mouth half open, staring at me, his eyes round and intent. "It's not true," I say. "I lied," I say, then I let out a high, rippling laugh and the moments pass and Egil just stands there gazing at me in astonishment. "Oh, come on," he says. "Do you think you can get out of it that easily?" he says, but I can tell by his face that he doesn't quite know what to make of me. "It's true," I say. "I lied," I say and I smile that airy, indifferent smile.

"But," he says, then he pauses. Then: "Why did you lie to me?" he asks. "I don't know," I say and I give a little shrug and I give that high laugh again, but my laughter is too bright, my laughter is too shrill and something suddenly breaks loose inside me, something large and heavy breaks loose and I can't stop it, and Egil is eyeing me gravely and I look a little to one side of Egil and try to keep smiling that airy, indifferent smile.

"Silje, what is it? What's the matter?" Egil asks, and I hear the creak as he gets up from the wicker chair. "You've got me really worried now," he says, and I hear him walking towards me and I look to the side and try to keep smiling that airy, indifferent smile, but I can't, this big, heavy thing breaks loose inside me and it falls through me, it falls and falls and I feel my head start to spin. "Is it true; were you lying?" he asks. "Yes," I say briskly, trying to sound bright and cheerful, but it's no use, it comes out as nothing but a forlorn little gasp, and now Egil walks up to me and now I feel his hand on my shoulder and I can tell that he means to draw me to him and comfort me, and a moment passes, then I brush his hand off my shoulder.

"Silje," he says gravely. "I really hate ending up like this," I say, and everything slides and falls inside me and my head is spinning faster and faster and my eyes flick back and forth. "I really hate it," I say. "Ending up like what?" he says. "All overemotional and unhinged," I say. "A hysterical female, or the standard image of a hysterical female," I say, and a moment passes. "But I'm not," I scream. "I'm not a hysterical female," I scream. "And yet I always end up seeming like one," I say, and a moment passes, and now I feel the tears welling up. "And now I'm going to start crying, too," I say and the sobs roll through me and this great heavy weight falls through me. "Oh, shit!" I gasp and then there's silence and I feel Egil's hand on my shoulder again.

"Silje," he says. "No," I scream at him, and he jumps when I scream, and I brush his hand off my shoulder again. "Don't touch me!" I scream. "Silje," he says. "Just don't touch me," I say. "I don't understand ... I feel so confused," he says. "You make me feel so confused, Silje. I want to help you, because I know you're having a hard time of it," he says, and he looks at me, his eyes wide and intent. "But

I don't want your help," I cry. "I don't want to be this hysterical female who goes to pieces and has to be helped and comforted by you," I say. "I hate that, I hate you and I hate myself and I ..." I say, and then I collapse in floods of tears, I double up, put my hands on my knees and gaze at the floor, I shake my head and the tears roll down my cheeks. "I don't know what to do," I sob. "I'm so tired, I hardly sleep at all at night now, I just wander around in a permanent daze," I say.

"Come here," Egil says, and he takes a step towards me, puts his arms round me. "No," I scream, and I raise my fists and pound his chest, and I see the look of bewilderment on his face as he staggers back a pace or two. "Would you just listen to me for once?" I scream. "Back off!" I scream, but he doesn't back off, he comes up to me again and he raises his arms and he puts his arms round me again and I try to push them away and I try to shove him back, but it's no use, he's too strong and he holds me tight. "Let me go!" I scream, and I wriggle and squirm. "Let me go!" I scream again, but he won't let me go. "Silje," he says. "Calm down! Silje!" he says and he holds me tighter still and I feel his warm breath on my neck and I feel his fingertips digging into my back. "There, there," he says, and there's a moment's silence and then I feel the strength start to drain out of me, this strength I've been filled with, this life I've been filled with, it seems to seep out of me and I feel myself snuffing out, feel myself withering and dying and I don't have the strength to keep going and I bury my face in the hollow of Egil's shoulder and I cry and he strokes my back and I cry and cry and he rocks me gently from side to side.

"I'm sorry, Egil," I say, and I hear what I'm saying, whatever was talking through me is gone and I can hear myself giving in. "I'm sorry," I say. "It's okay, Silje," he says softly. "I don't mean to be like this," I say. "I don't know why I'm like this," I say. "Why I say things like that to you when they're not true," I say. "It's okay, Silje," he says, and then there's silence and I straighten up and I look to the side, I can't look at Egil right now, so I stare at the cooker. "But I'm hardly ever happy any more," I say. "And it hurts so much," I say. "I have everything I could possibly want, but I'm never happy, and I don't know why," I say. "Sometimes I think I've figured it out," I say, "suddenly I feel I understand, and then … the next minute it's gone and I'm still none the wiser," I say and there's silence again and then all of a sudden I start to cry again, all the fury and strength is gone and I feel that heaviness inside me again. "I'm hardly ever happy any more, Egil," I sob. "And that's hard on you and the kids," I say. "They're suffering because of me," I say. "I can tell … and that makes it even harder," I say, and I cry and cry, and Egil's hand strokes and strokes my back. "Oh, Silje," Egil says, and he hugs me tight. "You mean the world to me and the girls," he says. "Oh," I say, wiping the tears from my cheeks, "don't say things like that, Egil," I say. "It took me just days to get over Mum's death, and I don't think my kids would need much more than that to get over me," I say and I hear what I'm saying and I realize how much it hurts to hear what I'm saying, and I realize how empty and heavy and tired I am. "Nor would you, come to that," I say, it just slips out. "What are you saying?" he asks, and a moment passes, and I give a big sigh and wipe away the tears. "I don't know," I say. "I just don't know any more," I say, and the moments pass and there is total silence. "I love you," Egil says, and the moments pass and I sigh. "I love you, too," I say.

Trondheim, July 20th 2006

The time when Jon silenced the birds:

It was early in the morning and the birds were chirping and twittering in the hedge, but you and I and Jon were still sitting drinking at the kitchen table with our host – a guy from Molde who had just moved in (he had a pigeon chest and upper arms too skinny to accommodate normal-sized tattoos – "Is that a baby eagle on your bicep?" I asked, and of course he was offended). We were reluctant to call it a day, but all the bottles were empty and none of us was willing or able to cycle over to our place to fetch more booze so we just sat there on our kitchen chairs, trying to prolong the party by eking out the last drops in our glasses. Our host told us that he actually had a jerrycan of illicit liquor in the basement, but because one of his suppliers had just been charged with selling methanol he wasn't a hundred per cent certain it was safe to drink (only ninety-six per cent certain as he said in an attempt at humour), so it was probably best not to touch it until he'd had it checked out, but you weren't having any of that, of course, because you had suddenly spied a chance to do a Christopher Walken and play Russian roulette again. So, on the pretext of going to the loo, you snuck down to the basement, filled a half-empty cola bottle with what was either ethanol or methanol, and then there you were, back in the kitchen, all set to risk your life. "I'll test your hooch for you," you announced to our host with a grin and, thinking that you had mixed the cola with water and that this was all a big joke, he laughed when you put the bottle to your lips and started to knock back the pale-brown liquid. But when he saw the looks on Jon's face and mine he realized that this was no joke. The smile on his face froze and after opening and closing his mouth a few times he got halfway to his feet and shouted out a stammered "It's true, it's true, it could be methanol, really," but that didn't stop you. of course. You went on drinking until the bottle was half-empty, then you lowered it and held it out in front of you. You burped, wiped your glistening lips with the back of your hand and then you grinned and asked if anybody else wanted to try it. You ran your bleary vodka-soaked eyes round the room and, knowing full well that Jon was as shocked now as he had been when you picked and ate an unidentified mushroom, you stopped at him. Then, in a gratingly jaunty voice, with all of his pathetic suicide attempts in mind, you said: "Hey, Jon, you wouldn't mind tasting it, I'm sure, seeing as you're planning to hang yourself anyway." At these words Jon exploded. With a rage I would never have thought possible of such a weak and pathetic character he leaped out of his chair and knocked the bottle out of your hand, sending it spinning across the kitchen, out of the open window and into the hedge, abruptly silencing the twittering birds, then he brought his face right up to yours and yelled that you were the biggest coward he'd ever met. You tried to convince yourself and everybody else that you were brave, that this was a way of living more intensely, when in actual fact it was a way of running away, he roared, and after a long, furious tirade about how selfish and self-centred you were, he asked if you really thought he was so stupid that he didn't know why you behaved the way you did. "You don't dare say straight out that you don't want anything to do with me any more, so you try to push me away by acting like an arsehole, don't you think I know that?" he screamed, and I clearly remember the other people from the party, a bunch from Molde who had helped our host move in and were now crashed out, fast asleep on the living room floor, being woken by his screaming. Some of them lay where they were, only shifting a little like logs rolling in the surf, but a few sat up and stared at the two of you in alarm. You were still grinning and trying to look as if you weren't in the least bit bothered by any of this, but when Jon, quite beside himself with rage and despair, turned to the guys from Molde and yelled, "We're gay, you know; him there, he doesn't dare admit it to himself or anybody else, but we're gay and we've been lovers for almost two years," the grin faded and I'm not sure whether the look on your face was one of hurt or sadness as you shook your head and told Jon that you were afraid there must be some misunderstanding. You weren't gay, you mumbled and you had tried to tell him this many a time. Unlike him you tried to take the things you believed in and talked about seriously, you said. For you, it wasn't just empty talk when you referred to Schopenhauer's grand theory on mankind's collective suicide or when you quoted Zapffe, saying, "be infertile, and let the earth be silent after ye". You actually meant what you said, and since no child would ever result from two men having sex, gay sex was not only acceptable, it was the safest and best way for two people to have sex. "It's just a pity that it doesn't come as naturally to all of us," you added.

Only later did I realize that you had actually been telling the truth. At the time I thought, as did the others I assume, that this was all nothing but a ridiculous excuse. Since we were sleeping together and I knew what you liked and didn't like to do in bed, and since I knew how willing you were to experiment and try new things, sexually as well as in other ways, naturally the thought that you might be a closet gay never occurred to me, as it probably had to the other people present. I simply assumed that you were embarrassed by the fact that everybody now knew you had had sex with another man and had therefore seized on the first excuse you could think of. But the more I thought about it and the more I saw how unbelievably uncompromising you could actually be and how willing you were to stand up for what you truly believed in, the more certain I became that you really had "made a serious attempt to live as a homosexual", as you later put it. Whether this fanaticism and refusal to compromise came to be seen as an aspect of the mental illness you were eventually diagnosed as suffering from, I don't know, but I wouldn't rule out that possibility.

That Jon, the only one who knew you as well as I did, doggedly maintained that you were homosexual was naturally just wishful thinking on his part. Although I was surprised when he confessed to being gay, once he had said it it seemed so obvious and apparent, not only because of his slight, girlish figure and rather effeminate manner, but also because certain things he had said or done that had puzzled me suddenly made sense. Suddenly I understood that it was the muscular half-naked guys that had been the real attraction when he insisted on watching even the crappiest music videos on MTV (although he had always laughed, of course, and said it was the fact that they were so crappy that made them funny) and suddenly I understood why he (and you) had been so shocked when his dad beat up that young guy outside the Quayside: not, first and foremost, because his dad would end up back inside, but because his dad clearly believed there was nothing in the world worse than being gay and because, as Jon (drama queen that he was) remarked to you later, "every time he hit that guy it was like he was hitting me". Looking back on it, it was also clear to me that Jon, typically, had played on the role of fragile victim that being gay in a small town had accorded him, as you could confirm. You were the only person who had known that he was gay and you told me how sick and tired you had been of having to listen to his constant moaning, of always having to be sympathetic, having to console him and cheer him up, and of having to rush to his side at all hours of the day or night because he was threatening, yet again, to kill himself. He tried to convince himself and you that being gay in a small town was a nightmare, but in fact he loved it, you said, and what I had construed as sentimentality, self-pity and melodramatics on Jon's part was nothing compared to what you had had to put up with.

When I think of all the stories you told me about this, about the extremes he would go to, and when I think of how Jon has not only never come out of the closet – even though that should be no big deal in 2006 – but has also had a long-term girlfriend, I'm almost inclined to believe that he isn't gay at all, but was simply playing the part of the poor, oppressed homosexual to gain sympathy and closeness and to make himself seem interesting.

And naturally it was this side of him that eventually became too much for you. Instead of trying to alienate him by acting like real arseholes, as we had in fact been doing all that summer and autumn, we should of course have told him how fed up we were of constantly being dragged down into his black hole, how sick and tired we were of him killing all our enthusiasm and creativity by indirectly forcing us to feel sorry for him or to take a bleak view of things. But such things are easier said than done. We had kind of grown together, like an old married couple (if you can say that of three people), and right up until that morning after – the last time I would see Jon for many, many years (he did call a few days later, it's true, but when, as usual, he said that he couldn't remember a thing about the party, we let him know that enough was enough and that he needn't bother calling again) – we had chosen to nag and snipe at each other rather than simply go our separate ways.

During the weeks that followed we flourished, you and I, both creatively and as a couple. Had it not been for the fact that we moved to different cities to study and hence, despite a few valiant attempts to maintain our relationship, gradually drifted further and further apart and eventually lost touch completely, I can't help thinking that the whole of my adult life could have been very, very different.

The time when we shut ourselves away in a cottage in the mountains:

A stoat had got stuck in the chimney at the cottage and there it had stayed, rather like a tumour in a throat, until it froze or starved to death. After shovelling away some of the old, coarse snow, you climbed up onto the roof, and while I alternated between being inside, hunched down with my head half inside the chimney and my face upturned, and outside, peering up at you and shading my eyes with my hand so I could see you properly, you tried to shove the stoat down the chimney with the aid of a long fishing rod we had found in the cottage. And eventually you managed it. The emaciated, frosted body was stiff and rock-hard, I remember, and it hit the soot-blackened, though originally red, bricks below with a little clunk.

Afterwards I picked the animal up with both hands and carried it across the creaky cottage floor and out onto the front step. I was about to toss it into the dense thicket of gnarled dwarf birch, but you asked me not to and minutes later I was sitting on the step, nodding and applauding with wry formality while you presented what you called the first artwork of our stay. (Inspired by The Band, who shut themselves away in a cottage in the mountains to write what was to become *Music from Big Pink* we had decided to spend a week at the cottage up in the mountains at Dovre, being creative in all sorts of ways.) You nailed the stoat's little back paws to the tree stump just outside the cottage door so it stood on its hindlegs like a tiny stuffed polar bear. That done, you took a step back in order to admire your handiwork along with me and talked about how great it would look when the sun came up and its warmth caused the creature to slowly cave in on itself like a whey-faced old man collapsing and expiring.

Later, once we'd lit a fire, eaten our cheese sandwiches and opened the first bottle of red wine, I presented what we recorded as the second artwork of our stay. While we were eating we had discussed how long we might be able to survive in this place without any outside help, and inspired by this conversation I wrote a story which – although, like the earlier piece I mentioned, I don't remember it word for word – told how, hundreds of years after a nuclear disaster brought about by our own generation, our descendants crawled up out of the dark subterranean caverns in which they had been hiding and how, when their children – who had never seen the starry night sky before – asked what they were, those yellow things twinkling way up there, they were told that they were droplets of pee from a god who was shaking his cock.

Only now do I see that this piece was probably inspired as much by you and what you were going through at that time as by our entertaining discussion of how long we would survive in the wild on our own. Because, just as those descendants of ours in my story were in the process of inventing a mystical universe in which to believe and to steer by, so you were in the process of inventing a past in which to believe and to steer by. We had always made a big joke of it when you presented your countless theories as to who your real father might be, but even though I knew you didn't say what you said just for fun, I didn't realize how seriously you actually took it. You were already well on the way to developing the mental problems that would later lead to you being hospitalized and undergoing therapy, but I didn't see that. Not even when the aforementioned fear that your father might have suffered from a serious hereditary disease turned into hypochondria did I realize that there was a problem. I shook my head despairingly when you began to read up on all sorts of different diseases and it disturbed and exasperated me the way you would detect symptoms of MS one day and some obscure syndrome the next, but it never occurred to me that this was one of several signs that you were gradually being swallowed up by your own imaginings and speculations. Looking back on it, it's easy to say that I ought to have seen what was happening, but a lot of things that I would construe as symptoms today, now that I know you were actually ill, I merely interpreted then as interesting and intriguing aspects of your personality, and since we didn't only endeavour to be open-minded and tolerant, but tended almost to cultivate the weird and the unusual, I couldn't see that something was wrong. You were just different and the way we saw it, true children of individualism that we were, being different was almost always a good thing.

The time when we took a picture of the light with a capital L:

The sun was out, but it had just been raining and with every little puff of wind the leaf-heavy birch branches lifted slightly and sent a beautiful, shimmering shower of raindrops falling onto our driveway. I wanted to take a picture of it, but you felt it was way too kitschy. To some extent I agreed with you, but the trees looked so droopy and dejected, like a crowd of people mourning and weeping for someone they had lost, and I thought that if we could just capture that it could still make a good picture. So we stepped over the huge, shining puddle in the middle of the gravel path and made our way over to the postbox on its stand. We positioned ourselves with the sun behind us and you raised your new Nikon SLR only to promptly lower it again because, hanging from the beam in our empty garage, just a few yards away, was a narrow black cable with a solitary light bulb suspended from it. I totally agreed with you when you said that that light bulb made one think of a gallows, and that the image of a gallows would go well with the drooping, weeping trees in the foreground.

We took a few shots and if we had left it at that this incident would probably have been forgotten by now, but we didn't leave it at that because, in an attempt to expand upon the narrative contained within the image, we fetched a thick length of rope from the basement (an old fire rope, as far as I remember) and used this to make a real hangman's noose. We fixed this to the beam a little in front of the light bulb so that when we stood on the spot from which we had taken the first shot, we had the weeping crowd in the foreground, then the gallows and finally – as if framed within the noose – the light bulb, which was of course supposed to call to mind the Light itself.

As always when working on our art projects we were pretty hyped up and in our excitement we forgot to take the noose down again when we were finished. It wasn't until late that same evening, some time after Mum and I had left for the hospital to see Gran, who was failing fast by then, that you went out to the garage to remove it. It was dark outside, and when Arvid came to drop off a bedside table, some board games and a box of books that you'd left behind when you moved out, his car headlights looked to you like the eyes of a wild beast at night, or so you told me later. He had turned slowly into the drive and kind of coasted straight towards the garage. Then he spotted you, standing on a stool, fiddling with a noose – a sight which caused him to slam on the brakes, fling open the car door and dash over to you, sure that you were about to kill yourself.

Nothing would convince him that this had not been the case – well, it wasn't that long since Berit had died and he thought you were still devastated by her loss. I cycled down to the vestry and told him all about our photography experiment, thus confirming your version of events (or so I thought). But Arvid was convinced I was lying out of a misplaced sense of loyalty to you and he subjected me to a veritable tirade of platitudes on the nature of brotherly love. Not until I got home did it occur to me that the photograph would prove I'd been telling the truth, but when I mentioned this to you, feeling a little flustered and sure that you would be pleased, you told me that you had already destroyed both the photo and the negative.

You had never destroyed a negative before, nor would you ever have dreamed of doing so, it was a matter of principle with you so I knew you were lying, and since I could only see one reason for you to lie, namely, that you didn't want Arvid to see the photo, I realized that at some point you had made up your mind to let him think that you actually had been about to do away with yourself, and this you did eventually admit, claiming that it was a part of the work.

Since this act constituted a realization, so to speak, of the narrative contained within the image, I could see the logic in what you said, but just as I had hated lying about what we had seen and heard during the Holseth Landslide, and just as I had hated leaving that ladies' scarf in poor, dead Åge Viken's car, I hated you doing this to Arvid. You would send him the noose picture later and tell him the whole story, you said, just as you had sent an anonymous letter to Anita Viken to explain how that scarf had come to be in her husband's car, but it made me feel sick to think how worried Arvid would be about you until he received the photograph, and how let down he would feel afterwards. I got really mad, I remember, yelling at you and telling you how selfish and cold and cynical you were, but at the same time I couldn't help admiring you for being so uncompromising in the pursuit of your ideals, and if I am right in suspecting that you have not in fact lost your memory at all, but that all of this is simply another art project that you've embarked on (you crafty devil), then I can only say that I admire you for still being as uncompromising as ever.

I have to say that I had a suspicion, right from the start, that your memory loss was a piece of performance art. I'm only mentioning this now, though, before closing this letter, partly because I've enjoyed fooling you into thinking that I had been totally taken in and partly because I've never been, and I'm still not, altogether sure that I'm right in my suspicion. Maybe it's the liar in me that I see when I'm so suspicious of you? Maybe I'm exaggerating and placing too much emphasis on that side of you? Maybe the person whom I think may be pulling the wool over the eyes of everyone he knows is actually a reflection of myself? On the other hand, the fact that you liked to play Russian roulette, and had such an urge to risk life and limb every now and again, makes it all the more likely that you would put yourself in a situation in which you could end up suffering from shock, brain damage or some other trauma that would result in amnesia. I really don't know what to believe. I hold both scenarios to be equally possible.